Black Heart

Josef Peeters

Edited by:

Sarah Farrugia
HEARTT Writing & Editing
cosmo12@bigpond.com / + 61 417 527 123

ISBN-13: 978-0-6484561-2-4
ISBN-10: 0-6484561-2-9

DEDICATION

To Marlies, for being there.

CONTENTS

ACKNOWLEDGMENTS

I would like to add my support for all the victims out there who identify with the sentiments in this story. Don't let the bastards win. Fight back and stay strong at all costs.

THE CATALYST

There comes a time in everyone's life when a decision must be made. A defining point where a person acknowledges a limit to their tolerance threshold. A time to reverse the trend. For Melco Malkovich, that time came quite unexpectedly. Without so much as a second's pause to ponder the possible ramifications of his actions, Melco allowed pure adrenaline to release a rage buried so deep in his psyche that no one, least of all Melco, knew of its existence. The roiling, white-hot fury blew the lid off all logic when it finally erupted in the mind of the gentle, unassuming soul.

While out walking along a seaside esplanade in the suburb of Sandgate one afternoon, Melco heard the sounds of a scuffle coming from an adjoining park. Keeping mostly out of view, he neared a group of young schoolboys surrounding a smaller boy on the ground.

"Whatsa matter poofy-boy? Cat got ya tongue? I asked ya where ya goin'? Weren't thinkin-o-gettin' past me and the boys without payin' ya way, were ya? Hand it over," said the obvious leader of the pack.

"Yeah, whatsa matter poofy-boy... "

"Shut the fuck up Nobby! I already said that! No need for ya ta repeat it, dickhead. Now, pay up fuckwit, or I'll make ya eat one-o-me turds after me and the boys have taught ya a lesson."

"I, I don't have any more money, Lonny, you took the last of it yesterday. *Maman* won't give me any more till next Monday before school," complained the boy on the ground, bleeding and dirty from being thrown around and onto the dirt.

"Listen to that '*Maman*' shit would ya? Speak fuckin' English ya girly prick. Me-n-the boys are gonna have ta teach ya a lesson about not havin' enough money ta get through the neighbourhood, poofy-boy."

"I don think dat's going to happen, boys," said Melco stepping from behind the bushes, surprising all but Lonny.

"Yeah? Sez fuckin' who, arsehole?" Lonny demanded.

"Says me, now go on, off with the lot of you."

"Stay where ya are fellas, he can't do shit ta stop us. Ya betta fuck off mate 'fore I call me dad on yiz for perveratin' us minors. Go ta the slammer for a real long time for that sort-o-shit."

"Been 'perverated' a few times yourself have you, Lonny? Is dat how you know about dat sort of stuff at your age? What are you, eight, nine years old? Been touched up a bit by a friend of the family or an uncle have you?"

"Fuck that! I wouldn't let no one touch me like that. Kill 'em first, and I wouldn't get in no trouble neiver. Kids don't go ta jail, so's I can do whateva I want and get away wiv it."

"Not today Lonny. Now I'm only going to ask you nicely one more time, to leave de boy alone and go home, or wherever your kind crawls to," said Melco.

"Fuck y... "

Lonny never had time to finish the curse before he found himself on the ground with a ringing ear. As Lonny rose he was greeted with a flurry of punches from a man demented with rage, almost foaming at the mouth, with a seething hatred burning in his eyes. Melco was transformed in the blink of an eye from his usual demeanour of patient tolerance to one of insane aggression. Then, as abruptly as it began, it ceased, with Melco standing over the unconscious boy, panting, confused, yet secretly hungry for more. Caution stayed his hand but the seed had been planted. The incident warranted a new direction for Melco, requiring a drastic review of his way of life. His heritage. His accent. His persona. Possibly even his name.

"Now de rest of you need to go before I start with you. Drag that lump of shit with you and never touch this boy or any other boy again. Let this be lesson to you dat you will not *always* get away with it. There are repercussions for this thing you do. I... "

The four other boys wasted no time hanging around to hear any more from the stranger, hastily grabbing the unconscious Lonny by the arms and dragging him from the park. One or two of them crying with fear.

"You alright boy? Are you hurt badly?"

"I will be come Monday. I wish you hadn't done that Mister."

"I'm going to give you my business card and I want you to call me, anytime, if any of them so much as look at you bad. Anytime, night or day. Now, let's get you up and home, eh?"

"You have no idea what you just done Mister. Lonny's father is a policeman. He gets away with everything because his dad always backs him up. Got a teacher fired from his job once when he sent Lonny to the headmaster."

"I can look after myself boy. What's your name?"

"Kim Giraud, Sir."

"French?"

Kim nodded solemnly. "I don't think Australian kids like my name much. They think it's a bit of a girl's name."

"If it wasn't your name they'd find something else. They run around in packs led by a Lonny, just looking for ways to make someone's life miserable. You should tell your father what's happening to you. Doesn't pay to keep it in, trust me."

"My *papa*... died, last year, in a car accident. I went to private school before that, and this stuff never really happened there. *Maman* can't afford it now, so I go to public school where they call me all sorts of names and take my lunch money from me."

"Listen to me, Kim Giraud. I meant what I said. Call me if they ever touch you or call you names again. You have my word that you can rely on me to make it right. *D'accord*?"

"*Oui Monsieur.*"

Lonny's father succumbed to a swimming accident before his son regained consciousness. The timely coincidence ensured that neither Kim nor Melco were bothered by the family again. Nobody could understand why the policeman went swimming while his son lay in a hospital bed with serious injuries. Melco heard nothing more of the incident, while the remainder of the boys involved never spoke about that afternoon in the park.

***

It would probably be fair to say that Melco was no different from any other individual trying to live life without attracting unwanted attention - for whatever reason. He had stopped attending therapy years ago, fooling both the therapist and himself that his problems had been expunged. He lived quietly, attended to his duties as a car salesman where he earned good pay and got on well with everyone, albeit superficially, allowing him, over time, to become a substantial property owner.

Nobody had ever been able to get close to Melco Malkovich, the immigrant from Serbia, who first arrived with his parents on Australian soil in the early sixties. At the tender age of two, Melco spoke little enough of his native tongue, let alone the strange language of a new country. Not that he remembered back that far.

As with all young minds, he soon learned the new language readily enough, though his native accent persisted well into his adult life. He had good, basic intelligence. He was a well-behaved boy, never causing his loving parents the slightest difficulty in his early years. Polite to a fault, respectful of his elders and only ever spoke when spoken to as he was taught. He was brought up with the values of an older generation. Melco knew and understood his place at the dinner table. Never interrupting his parents or their guests while a conversation was underway, knowing which fork to use with which course.

He knew the appropriate etiquette of a middle-high class family with no real entitlement to that elevated prominence. Nevertheless, his parents wanted to make sure that their boy had the best chance at making something of himself in a new land. Never mind that his mother cleaned and ironed laundry for their neighbours and his father worked as a builder's labourer for minimum wage. Or that their rented house was merely a run-down shack on the outskirts of town was of no consequence, or that the food on the table resembled more the fare from the war-torn country they had fled rather than from the abundant new world promised by his father.

Mr Malkovich was typical of his Slavic origins with a body built like a tank and a face that resembled meatloaf. His acne-pocked visage and flattened nose could deter the most inquisitive from curiosity about his background. While it would appear to an outsider that the parents, especially the father, ignored their only child, nothing could be further from the truth. Mrs Malkovich, perpetually in black, said little, but devoted all her love and attention to her beloved son, while her husband slaved away in the tenuous building trade to provide the best he could and always made time for Melco.

A smile from his father and a loving hug from his mother was all that a boy like Melco could ever want. He had very little reason to complain and seldom did during his pre-school years.

With the building industry in Australia run by overly zealous unions, employment was irregular at best, but Mr Malkovich managed to keep them housed and fed, while his wife kept the house immaculately clean and her son schooled in manners and matters that would see him, she hoped, rise above their lowly station. Neither parent ever felt shame or embarrassment for their economic circumstances. Both knew that they would have to sink to the very bottom in the new land before reaching the level of conditions in their home country. They knew they were blessed.

After having spent the requisite time in a hostel for migrants, the Malkovich family ended up in a small town in northern Queensland, in the northeast of Australia. The area was predominantly a sugarcane growing district and the family settled quickly into their new life. Ingham was a mere dot on the map in those early years. Not that it changed all that much in the years to follow. It was a hodgepodge of nationalities and personalities with a distinct small-town flavour where everyone knew everyone else and all that happened in their lives. Life progressed comfortably for the Malkovich family with no discernible disruptions. Only one small concern affected the family - the onset of their child's bed-wetting, at an age when it was assumed that most children would have grown out of the problem.

Melco showed no outward signs of stress or problems with his schooling. His report cards identified no learning difficulties. When questioned by his parents and family doctor, no reasons for the continuing problem came to light. Mr and Mrs Malkovich had no choice but to wait it out and hope that Melco would grow out of it, albeit later than most children. No amount of halting his fluid intake before bedtime, nor wise council by a doctor, or therapist, could either find the cause or stop the condition. It was eventually accepted without too much fuss and minimisation of any embarrassment for Melco. Mrs Malkovich simply washed his bedclothes and pyjamas every day, keeping a plastic protector over the expensive mattress to ensure it was not ruined entirely. Despite her meticulous attentions, Melco's room and Melco himself still smelt like a piss trough.

Nightmares and sweats, followed by somnambulism, added to the litany of difficulties affecting the young boy as he progressed through the grades. Neither parent was aware of the blood, bruising, or other complaints hidden beneath his clothes until they were too numerous and obvious to be hidden any longer. On questioning, Melco merely shrugged and expressed surprise, explaining that he was accident-prone. The boy always delivered his reply with a smile. His grades continued to impress while his silences grew longer. No amount of cajoling would entice the boy to reveal anything by way of a reasonable alternative explanation.

Everything eventually came to a head many years later after the boy had entered high school. Melco showed an interest in joining the army cadet programme, a joint initiative funded by the Australian Defence Force and government schools. The diminutive lad, showing no signs of following his father in stature or nature, revelled in the discipline of the programme, excelling at precision marching and marksmanship. A bivouac to Townsville, an hour away from Ingham, planned by the programme, had Melco excitedly packing his kitbag, and polishing his boots and brass to a flawless sheen.

An unexplained accident, resulting in his hospitalisation following the camp, saw Melco quit school to begin work as a junior cane-cutter. The reasons for the 'accident' and evidence of anyone's involvement were denied the parents initially. Despite their best efforts, and heartfelt threats, Melco refused to give away any details and never gave any indication of reversing his decision about leaving school. Mr Malkovich's threats to evict him from their home had no effect on the boy, while Mrs Malkovich's passionate entreaties held no sway. Melco would leave home if they forced it - that much was made abundantly clear.

After Melco had been working at the back-breaking, thankless job for a year, always dressed in overalls despite the sweltering heat, showing no sign of regret, shrugging off all signs of his youthful 'difficulties', his parents were forced to concede that their boy would not be persuaded to return to his studies.

Over time, he eventually grew to an acceptable height and weight in the eyes of all who knew him, continuing to dress from neck to toe whether working or not. Once he had saved enough money from his labours, he relocated to the 'big smoke'. It was as big a town as Melco had ever seen. There were structures taller than the three-story Canegrowers building in Ingham. What a stir that had caused during construction. Melco had only been a child then, but he still remembered the local drama surrounding the building's height. He could not believe how magnificent it was, how thrilling it had been to experience riding an elevator for the first time. Three stories up, three stories down, three stories up...

Melco vividly recalled the playground rocket erected in the centrally located park. Endless hours spent climbing the structure to sit at the top level overlooking the park, imagining himself as an astronaut taking off from Earth, leaving all his woes behind, then descending on the slippery slide when he returned from space and back to ground level.

Everything about Melco seemed perfectly normal as he went about living his life in Brisbane while he worked his way steadily to a sales position in a new car dealership at the northern end of town. Always wearing a stylish suit and well-oiled, thick, black hair swept back severely. At the age of thirty, it was clear that he was a man of means, earning over $100k most years, owning several homes and cars outright.

All that changed on that fateful afternoon when he finally allowed his inner rage to surface.

THE BOARDER

Detective Arnold Ryan opened his front door on hearing the timid knock. Steeling himself for the confrontation if it was another hawker or religious nut, he squared his formidable shoulders and frowned in readiness as he swung the door open. What he saw gave him no reason to release the tension in his bunched muscles. The indeterminately-aged, oddly-appearing man with a decidedly distorted face, standing almost as tall and as thick as himself, looked for all the world like another bible-bashing idiot set to give Ryan the spiel.

"Yeah? Whadda ya want?"

"Detective Ryan? I'm Michael Miller, we spoke on de phone, about de... the... room for rent?"

"Oh, right. C'mon in, sorry about that. Get fuckin' Jehovah's Witnesses out here all the bloody time."

Ryan led Michael down the hallway to the living room at the rear of the house where he invited his guest to have a seat on the settee opposite his recliner. Ryan took his time, using his professional skills to take in all the features of his prospective housemate. Medium height and heavy build with some visible scarring around the face. Cosmetic surgery Ryan assumed. Otherwise, a fairly unremarkable face that could have blended into any crowd. A good crown of thick, wavy black hair had Ryan touching his thinning scalp in subconscious envy.

"You're not a religious nut, are you? I'd have to tell you to leave if you were," asked Ryan.

"No Detective Ryan. I am an atheist."

"You'd better just call me Ryan, okay? You have an accent?"

"Trying hard to lose it, but yes."

"Hmm. As I was saying. My name is Arnold Ryan but most just call me Ryan. Can't have you being all formal if we are going to be living under the same roof." Ryan reclined in his chair, taking a slug from the beer next to him. "Get you one?"

"I'm good. Don't normally imbibe before nightfall."

"Imbibe! Are you trying to be clever? Making a judgement? It's my day off and I'll start..."

"None of my business Ryan. I don't care what you drink or where and when you do it. Sorry if I sounded uppity. I'm a bit nervous and trying to make a good impression."

"Nervous? What are you nervous about?"

"I've answered a few house-share advertisements today and have found de... the... advertisers to be less than genuine about the accommodations and themselves. I think one lady was a prostitute, and one fellow was a drug dealer. You are last... the last one on my list and I was hoping it would turn out. It's a nice house in a nice neighbourhood with plenty of trees, a walking track, and a pool nearby."

"Yeah, it is a great neighbourhood. People here like having a copper next door as well. You got any problems living with one?"

"What you do is essential to a way of life, why would I have a problem with that?"

"Not everyone sees it that way. People sometimes see us as the lowest of the low for what we do. I've been called every name under the sun, and then some. Did some searches on you by the way."

"I'd have been disappointed if you hadn't."

"Disappointed?"

"Well, you wouldn't be much of a detective if you didn't do a background check on a stranger looking to share your home? If you hadn't put my name through every database at your station I would have been very surprised. Find anything nasty that I'm not aware of, any unpaid parking tickets?"

"Not a thing. You've had a few tickets in the past couple of years but always paid in full before they were due. Impeccable references and good work record in Brisbane up to six years ago. You aren't employed at the moment as far as I can tell, and I don't want any dole-bludgers living here."

"I buy and sell homes in the area after I do some basic renovations. I sold my last one very quickly before I had a chance to purchase another suitable property. I need somewhere to stay until I do, and while I am renovating. If it all works out between us, I will stay on. If you get sick of me, I'll move into my house when it's habitable. I would be willing to pay a month in advance with a substantial bond if I feel right about it."

"Up to me to feel right about it."

"Not *just* you, Ryan. I have to feel good about living here as well. We might not get on. I understand completely about a probationary period for both parties to appraise the compatibility or otherwise of the other."

"Yeah, okay, I'll buy that. I couldn't find much about you prior to ten years ago. Care to explain that?"

"I spent some time overseas before I finally decided to return to Australia. I love this country dearly but it took living elsewhere for me to realise that. I've seen some horrible truths about the world we live in. Seen terrible poverty and war-torn devastation in many places, Africa in particular."

"Explains the accent. How did you live while you were over there?"

"Inheritance. My parents passed away and left me sufficient funds to live frugally overseas for a time. When the money dwindled and I had seen all I needed to, I came back. Never regretted going. I was extremely lucky to run into someone from this town while I was overseas. He gave me a recommendation for employment upon my return.

"That person's relative offered me a good job as a rent-collector and handyman in Brisbane. It was during that time, coupled with night classes, that I learned all the skills I needed to go out on my own after I saved enough money for a deposit on my first run-down project. Been doing that for a few years here now, due mainly to the recommendations from the person I met overseas. I love it. It gives me certain freedoms and allows me enough spare time to pursue other hobbies and recreations."

"Such as?"

"I like to keep physically fit. I walk, run, swim or hit the gym at least once every twenty-four hours, early morning or night. I enjoy reading and watching movies on my computer with my headphones on. I keep mainly to myself and don't mind my own company. Some would say I am quiet to a fault. I don't engage in endless conversations and I never enter into any talk about religion or politics. That's me in a nutshell."

"Well, Mike... "

"Michael, please? I don't like nicknames or abbreviations. I call people what they like to be called, and I ask the same courtesy. If that is a problem for you, feel free to say so and I'll be on my way."

"Bit touchy about that, huh? Nah, it's okay, I hate when people call me Arnie as well. I won't hold that against you. Look, you check out okay and I think everything I've heard so far pans out. I'm willing to try you out for a probationary period of say, three months and we'll go from there?"

Michael moved his meagre belongings into the house the following day after the detective had finished work. They agreed to a roster of shared chores and cooking duties, out of bounds areas, and general conditions of co-habitation. Michael would use the main bathroom as his own while Ryan would use the bathroom attached to his main bedroom. Favourite TV shows did not come into play, as Michael would not watch any TV in the living room, preferring to retire to his room early to watch DVDs on his laptop.

Both men left the house early most days to go to work. In Michael's case, to scour the district for a potential project – a 'Renovators Dream'. Ryan worked long hours, so Michael had a meal prepared for him most evenings. If Ryan had to work extra late, he would find his meal in the oven keeping warm. Michael had an occasional beer with his meal, or a glass of wine, while Ryan drank heavily most nights and on his days off. They lived an amicable arrangement that suited their individual lifestyles. Ryan needed the rent money to manage his mortgage payments after a recent interest rate hike, while Michael found the location amenable to his needs. Neither men were overly friendly, nor did they seek confrontation. It was viewed purely as a business arrangement.

Ryan did not bring home any female friends, only the squad room boys. They visited regularly for drinks and snacks for Sunday footy sessions on Ryan's big-screen-TV. No objections were ever raised on account of the raucous laughter and shouting belching out of the living room on those occasions. Business and occupations were generally discussed when the pair were seated for dinner. A cordial atmosphere ensured an equitable existence for both. A year passed before either realised how comfortable they were with their living arrangement.

"I found a suitable project to work on. I purchased the property this afternoon. Not too far from here, in Forest Beach on the waterfront. Bit of a hovel really. I may think about knocking it down completely and starting again," said Michael.

"Oh, sounds great... I suppose."

"Something wrong?"

"Um, no, just... wondering if that meant you were thinking of leaving?"

"Only if you want me to. Like I said originally, I still need a place to stay while I'm making the new place liveable. I don't have to move at *all* unless I find it inconvenient or I don't like where I am. I have no complaints about living here. I didn't think you did either. At least, you haven't said anything?"

"No, no. All's good mate. No worries. It's been great having you here. Got used to your company and I sure would miss your cooking, that's all. Sorry, I, I got a big case I'm working at the moment and I'm not good company at all."

"Anything you can talk about?"

"Not in detail, ongoing investigation. A real bad one. Papers don't even know the half of it. You probably read something about it?"

"Don't read the papers, don't watch the TV."

"What, you don't catch the news at all?"

"No."

"How do you stay informed? Aren't you interested in knowing what's going on around you?"

"I have read enough and experienced enough violence overseas and in the newspapers to last me a lifetime, thank-you. I really do like to live my own life without all the bad news spoiling my day."

"Don't know how the fuck anyone can live like that, without knowing what is going on around them."

"What good would it do for me to know about your homicide?"

"Who said anything about a homicide?" Ryan asked with an edge in his voice.

"Ryan, you told me you were a homicide detective. I know you probably don't get much of that in a small town like Ingham, but you just said it was a bad one. People don't usually associate that description with a burglary or speeding infringement, and I know you don't routinely attend traffic accidents."

"Thinking of taking my job someday? Nice detecting. You got a good ear and probably a good memory too, all the things you need for my line of work. Yeah, it was a homicide, a nasty one. The body wasn't discovered until long after he was dead. Okay, so the newspapers already know about the most unique factor in the case. They even gave the killer a moniker for it - *The Minstrel Killer.*"

"I don't understand, what does that mean?"

"The victim's face had been blackened."

"Minstrel?"

"Yeah, like, Al Jolson? We had a popular show on TV here years ago called the 'The Black and White Minstrel Show', where all the white singers had blackened faces and white lips, to loosely imitate Negroes, I suppose. Not very PC these days that's for sure."

"So, do all your cases end up affecting you like this? Kind of messes with your efficiency doesn't it?"

"Nah, you grow a tough skin when you've been in this game long enough. I knew the vic... er, victim, in this case, that's all."

"Sorry. You knew him well did you?"

"Went to school with him more years ago than I care to remember. Met in passing a few times since then, never really got together or anything. He worked in the council after school and I never really mixed with that crowd. No, didn't know him well anymore, but still, he was my age and now he's gone in pretty ghastly circumstances. No one deserves to go the way he went. Can't say much more about that. I'll get the bastard, mark my words. I'm good at what I do. Not as quick as the younger ones these days, but still know my way around a murder scene better than most."

"I'm sure you'll do well. I'll be pretty busy for the next few months, and I may be back fairly late, or even not at all some nights. Don't send out de... the... search party okay? I just like to finish certain daily goals when I'm 'in de zone' if you know what I mean? I always take a swag with me in the back of the ute in case it gets too late, or if I have a drink after work."

"Thanks for telling me. Try not to be too noisy if you come back late okay?"

"I doubt you would hear me over your snoring Ryan. I sometimes wonder if you aren't inhaling part of your ceiling and that you don't get ill from it."

"You must be dreaming or something, I don't snore," Ryan challenged.

"Could have fooled me."

"Listen, bud... "

"Michael."

"Sorry?"

"My name, it's Michael. Not bud, mate, pal, or anything other than, Michael, no middle name, Miller. Anyway, I'm off to bed for an early start. Lots of demo work ahead," said Michael as he left Ryan to brood over his reactions.

REPERCUSSIONS

Victor Kugelweis was tidying up his paperwork for the day. It had been a semi-profitable week for his ailing Real Estate office. He had finally managed to offload the old Peterson house at Forest Beach after a protracted negotiation with a relentless solicitor acting on behalf of his client. It was difficult to sell the seaside lots despite their beach frontages. The daily tides retreated so far out that only muddy stretches of the beach could be seen for hours. The tidal banks sent unpleasant aromas across the seaside community whenever the water receded.

After Victor shut his computer down, he gave some thought to the night ahead. Friday night with no plans seemed to be the norm for him these days. A messy divorce had seen him alone more often than he enjoyed and with insufficient funds to afford the lifestyle he preferred. Once considered to be a prime catch within the small community, Victor had allowed himself to go to seed. A sagging paunch now replaced the washboard abs of old. His fine, blonde, Scandinavian locks now thinning to baldness and his ice-blue eyes lacking the lustre for which he was once a local legend.

He had attained his adult stature at the age of fourteen, making him a giant among his classmates. Unfortunately, he grew no taller as the years passed, making him less than average height in his maturity. His sporting days had been superseded by his drinking days. His 'friends' were more his ex-wife's friends, or so it seemed, as few of them remained in contact after the divorce. Much of his business and many new contacts had been introduced by his charismatic wife while they were together. These days, he was lucky if he managed to sell a house every six months. He couldn't afford to advertise the few listings he maintained. Lately, it was the rental properties, where he acted as a landlord, which provided the only real income.

The Peterson place had gone for a song, way below list price. His commission on the sale would total only a few hundred dollars after tax; half of which should have been paid to the secretary whom he had recently made redundant. Victor sighed as he walked around the empty office turning off the lights. As he stood outside locking the glass door, he briefly heard a static buzz before he fell to the footpath in a jerking heap.

When Victor regained his senses, he found himself restrained and gagged, in the dark, lying on a rough surface. Metal bands secured his wrists and ankles, restricting the slightest movement. The restraints bit painfully into his flabby flesh. His head was secured by some rubber material. There was a familiar smell hanging in the dark, reminiscent of his youth, but he couldn't quite place it. He could not lift his head more than a few millimetres against the semi-pliant bond stretched tightly against his forehead.

He was unable to make out anything of his surrounds, barely able to hear a few distant sounds above the thudding of his heart. Familiar, distinctive bird sounds he vaguely recognised, but that was all. Something else, like a repetitive, pulsing sound he could not quite distinguish. Too distant. The only thing he could pinpoint for sure was a mouldy staleness around him. Cobwebs and dust. Victor panicked the longer he remained alone, in the darkness. He was clueless. He could feel the blood pulsing in his veins. *Was that what he could hear?*

Then, from the darkness beside him, a click, followed by a whispering fizz. A beer being opened! He knew that sound and the accompanying aroma better than any other on earth. A stubby of beer having the top removed by an opener. Not the screw type, so common these days. His mouth salivated at the sound, his body yearning for the cool frothy liquid sliding down his throat. Victor drank at least a dozen or more stubbies of Fourex each day. He could almost taste the golden liquid through his gag. Tears formed at the corners of his eyes, so desperately did he need the cool, refreshing, hit of malt and hops.

He felt momentarily relieved, realising it must be a trick being played on him by his friends. *Yes, an early birthday prank by...* Confusion returned to him when he knew of no friends likely to do *anything* for him. He gradually realised he was in deep trouble. He had no friends, no work companions, and no relatives left alive to play pranks on him. *His bitch of a wife? Ex-wife!* No, his ex-wife would not be clever enough to organise it, or stupid enough to interfere with her income stream. Victor paid her excessive sums in alimony after their messy divorce, after she had accused him of screwing the secretary. The bitch would not endanger her bank account. His mind drew a blank. He had no money to speak of, no assets of his own and no one who cared enough to pay anything for him in ransom. There was no logical reason for anyone to be doing this.

"Figured anything out yet, Herr Kugelweis?" an accented voice cut through his thoughts.

Victor smelled the beer clearly. The distinctive smell of fermented barley, seasoned by hops, wafting over him, causing him to salivate into the cloth rag stuffed into his mouth, making him retch. Victor's bladder let loose with his increasing fear, causing the acrid stench of urine to obliterate the happy aroma of the beer.

"Oh dear, you seemed to have pissed yourself, Victor. Nothing has really happened to scare you...yet. Have you really come down so far to be terrified over every minuscule thing, that you piss yourself and cry like a little girl? No, I mustn't say that. Very derogatory to girls that. Like a, like a cry-baby then. Dat's better, eh? Must be politically correct these days, mustn't we?"

Victor continued to whimper and retch into his gag while the tears flowed freely down his cheeks. His eyes had adjusted a little to the darkness in the time he had been awake. He could make out dark shapes around him, but they made little sense. Nothing distinctive enough to recognise, for him to place in an ordinary setting. He could tell he was inside a room. A smallish room without an echo. Therefore, he assumed, he was not in a garage or warehouse. Sounds were muted like there was something hanging on the walls to muffle sound from the outside. No. He corrected himself. *To muffle any sounds from the inside.* To muffle sounds Victor would make when his captor decided that the 'yet' time had arrived.

He could stand the silence no longer. Despite fearing every syllable uttered by the stranger, the voice was preferable to the excruciating silence. Victor's sphincter muscles were threatening to betray him. He had already achieved shame by pissing his pants, he did not want to increase that by shitting himself as well. The silence stretched on for an eternity until another beer was opened in the dark. A brief ignition as a flame erupted in the night. *A lighter?* Lighting a cigarette. In that fleeting moment of illumination, Victor saw a mouldy ceiling, sagging with water damage. He saw a room with a window, boarded up by plywood. Garishly painted walls of a bygone era, peeling with age in between the insulation batts stapled to the old timber, tongue-and-groove, panelling. *Shit!* Victor inhaled sharply. He knew instantly where he was. It was only a month ago he had shown the potential client's solicitor through the old Peterson place.

"Yes, yes, yes, good, I believe you recognise de... the... place. I believe you advertised it as *'Down the end of a street, backing onto native bushland, with the ocean as your only neighbour'.* Bloody good spin you put on all the negatives of this place to make it shine like a prime beachfront property in that crappy blurb you had next to the blurry photo. Typical real estate hyperbole. Do you people actually read the shit you write? Vomit-worthy! It suited my purposes though. I couldn't believe my good fortune when I found out you were a realtor, Victor. It gave me the perfect cover to study you and learn your routines."

Victor felt a chill pierce his body right through to the marrow. The voice he heard dripped with malice. Whatever it was that Victor had done to piss the person off, the outcome was not looking positive. He tried to recall anything about the client, tried to discern a reason the person may have had to feel animosity. The deal had been transacted entirely through the solicitor. He had only ever heard the client's voice over the phone one time. He recognised nothing in his memory that gave a reason for his capture.

"In a moment my dear Victor, you will feel a little pinprick in your arm, followed by a rather warm sensation flowing through your body making you feel much like your piss made you feel, only on de inside. While I was overseas, I stumbled across a marvellous experiment involving autistic children. Seems that some have a condition called Neural Hyper-excitability which causes hyper-sensory sensitivity. After exhaustive studies to examine the cause, they eventually discovered an infinitesimal amount of clear liquid secreted by the brain of a person with ASD, autism spectrum disorder. A hypophysiotropic secretion of the hypothalamus. Once recognised and harvested, it was able to be synthesised, then improved, causing the injected subject to develop neurophysiological hyper-responsivity that was off the scale. How's that for a mouthful, Victor? Had to practice those terms many times to get them right. What all this means is that you will feel every little sound, sight and touch like a devastating blow. The touch of a feather to your skin will make you feel like you are being sliced by a razor blade. However, I will be using *real* instruments of torture until you tell me what I want to hear."

In the dark, he could feel the client, *what was his name*, cut away his clothing. Victor felt the cold steel of the cutter against his cheek as his captor made sure that Victor understood the consequences if he resisted. When all his clothing was removed, he felt the slight pinprick in his left arm, then the immediate sensation of welcoming warmth infusing his body. Victor sighed.

"Now Victor, I am going to remove the gag. No one will be able to hear you scream but I would still much prefer if you refrained from doing so. You will not want to even whisper in a few moments anyway, as the repercussions of the oratory overload will make you wish you were dead. I will be whispering my questions to you and it will feel like I am screaming at you."

Victor felt the dirty rag being removed from his mouth. He tested his jaw to ascertain its condition. His body continued to experience the warmth infusing his torso and limbs, like a gentle immersion in a warm bath, soothing, comforting, all while being lulled into a false sense of comfort. As he lay completely naked, Victor discovered the first feeling of heightened sensation, while experiencing the breath of his captor blowing against his bare flesh. It did not feel painful... yet.

A coldness, a stark, biting, coldness being applied to his face. *The smell, oh, the smell*, starting to tingle unpleasantly in the nose. He knew the smell yet couldn't place it. The coldness against his face felt like ice. Like dry ice beginning to burn his skin. His muttering felt like a growing cacophony, intensifying, building to a terrible crescendo. It took everything Victor had to calm himself, not to call out. Knowing that any loud noise would be like a lance going into the eardrum.

Then, then, *oh God, more ice-cold burning,* on his genitals. Then pure, white-hot agony as the coldness escalated into fire, as if his crotch was being eaten away by acid. His scream pierced his ears. A knife, twisting into the eardrums with every decibel until he managed to shut his mouth. Tight. Even the sound of his lips meeting made an unbearable racket. His crotch was on fire. Petrol was thrown on and set alight, for sure. Victor saw no flames, yet the intense pain meant it had to be true. Nothing else he knew could produce such acute pain.

"Toothpaste," whispered the person. "Hurts like a bitch *without* the serum in your system. I know! Yeah, intensified like that, I bet that's just the worst, huh? Stuff on your face doesn't sting though. No, that's just decoration. That's just a bit of black boot polish. Does this ring any bells, Victor?"

"Nnnnnnnyahhhhh!"

"Shush Victor, You mustn't be too loud. Whispers only or you will be very, very sorry. Now, I'll ask again. Does the treatment of the boot polish and the toothpaste ring any bells for you, Victor?"

Victor's eyes nearly leapt from their sockets trying to indicate a 'no'. "I can't quite see in the dark Victor. I'm going to guess that the answer is no. Perhaps some more toothpaste then? I could rub it directly onto your knob for you? You haven't enjoyed that particular sensation yet."

"P, p, please, no. I, I don't know what you want."

"Really? You have no idea what boot polish on the face and toothpaste on the groin means?"

The touch alone of the man's fingertips on his penis sent spasms of anguished throbbing through Victor's body. When more of the cold toothpaste was applied to the exposed glans of the penis after the foreskin had been pulled down, Victor screamed until he fainted. When he regained consciousness, the man was speaking.

"... keep on working until I give you another injection. Victor, you need to open your eyes very, very slowly. I have a dim light on which will hurt."

The blinding, searing light threatened to scorch his retinas; smouldering eyeballs that would leave nothing behind but burnt out sockets. Victor squinted in the candlelight wishing for a return to the darkness. The person stood above him with a sadistic grin, made comical and more twisted by the clown face. No, not a clown exactly. A black face with exaggerated white lips. A parody. Like that old crooner, he had seen a movie of just recently. The Al Jolson Story. That was it. His befuddled brain refused to retain much useful information. The intensity of the pain had eased to tolerable levels. He knew nothing about the boot polish or the bloody toothpaste. *What could this maniac possibly want from him?*

"Does the name, Melco, mean anything to you? Ah, I see by your reaction that it does. Maybe I should have asked this question earlier."

Victor remembered the name from another time and place so distant that he barely recalled any details. His brain was too far gone to remember much more. "I think I remember a boy by that name," gasped Victor.

"Excellent. Finally, we are getting somewhere. Do you remember the boot polish and the toothpaste now?"

"No, sorry, Mister..."

"I want to know who came back that night. Tell me and I will be merciful. I will kill you quickly and end your miserable existence without prolonging the terrible pain. Who was it?"

"I, I'm sorry. I don't know what you are talking about."

Rock music exploded into the night shattering Victor's hearing, bouncing around inside his skull like a ricocheting bullet. ACDC, the legendary heavy-metal rock band of his youth tortured his addled brain with wave after wave of vomit-inducing intensity. In reality, the volume was set at only a moderate level, but to Victor, he was at their live concert plastered to the enormous stage speakers belting out the tune and the lyrics at decibels higher than human tolerance. The light. The sounds. The smells. The terrible sensations on his skin were propelling Victor to breaking point. Unbearable. Then, blessedly, the sound was muted, the candle moved away from his eyes.

"Any closer to remembering, Victor?"

"M. Mel. Melco. M-Malko... Malkovich?"

"Yes, Victor. Melco Malkovich. What do you remember?"

"Did... , didn't like him. Played around with him a bit."

"PLAYED AROUND? PLAYED AROUND WITH HIM?" screeched Al Jolson. Victor groaned with the pain. His own voice adding to the torture. "Is that what you call the perpetual, brutal, physical and psychological abuse you inflicted on a little boy, Victor? The daily torture of a young boy by a gang of thugs too cowardly to face up to him alone? No, no, no, no, Victor. That will never do. You need to admit to far more than 'playing around'."

Victor watched on in dread as the person showed him the retractable utility knife he had earlier felt against his cheek. Sweating profusely, shaking with terror, Victor forced himself not to make a sound as his abductor lowered the blade to his abdomen. A nanosecond later horrific pain seared into Victor's psyche.

Holding his mouth closed tightly against screaming out, gnashing his teeth together until they chipped, the exquisite agony continued. From beneath the epidermis that transmitted the gruelling torture through his nervous system, his entrails were slowly emerging into the light. Like a male giving birth to a monster, his insides bulged out of his grotesque paunch, relieved to be free of its restrictive prison.

Victor blacked out several times during other procedures slicing him shallowly from neck to knee. Never enough to cause the finality he desired. A saline drip sustaining his bodily fluids. More and more sadistic measures were visited upon the hapless, quaking form. Salt and lemon juice in the open cuts, cigarette burns, the Taser used on him at the outset. Hour after hour. Victor was never again allowed the opportunity to admit that he remembered. Remembered the boy Melco Malkovich. The pretty little boy all the girls liked when he first came to their attention in primary school. How Victor and his friends systematically shoved, punched, ridiculed and embarrassed the boy for more years than he could recall.

Returning mentally to the scenes involving Melco Malkovich allowed Victor to block out a few of the milder tortures assailing him. 'Smelly Melly' he thought they ended up calling him at one stage because he stunk of piss most mornings. It began around grade three or thereabouts. The kid had some kind of weird accent... *Holy crap, this person has an accent!*

Victor was already quite stocky at that age, with long blonde hair and the chiselled Scandinavian features forming in his face. He was popular back then, especially with the girls, and he liked them back. Couldn't help himself around them. Always wanting to see more of them than their checked school dresses allowed. He sat beneath the outdoor stairs to catch a glimpse of panties, or in the case of one of the young teachers back then, bare flesh and a hairy bush. Miss Anderson never wore underwear as far as he was aware.

After informing his friends of his discovery, they congregated under the stairs regularly, just to wait for Miss Anderson to happen by. Each of them lusting after that briefest of seconds between only one set of steps where they would gain a clear view of that delectable patch of curly red hair. Sometimes, they imagined they saw the gash clearly through the dense foliage. Other times, they were wholly content with a perv of the bare, well-rounded bum as the bush moved past. They cursed the day she began wearing slacks.

With Melco, in the beginning, it was just a bit of pushing around and name-calling to get a rise out of him, but they were sorely disappointed. He never said a word, never showed any fear and continued attracting girls no matter how much he and his buddies tried to embarrass and ridicule the boy. They learned early on never to approach him individually, as the boy fought back ferociously, effectively, even against the might of Victor who had grown into a big, strong boy, by the fifth grade. Their strength was in numbers, and they used the strategy to great effect. They enjoyed the daily routine, planned their days around it at times, ensuring teachers were never present.

When they all entered high school it evolved into an all-out offensive. They smashed his bike whenever he rode to school. They stole his school bag with his lunch and books. They beat him senseless whenever they were pissed off with him over some imaginary slight. Stole his tuck-shop money. Stole his clothes while he was showering after sports or physical education class. He would have to go to the headmaster's office to get punished for walking around the school grounds in a towel that Victor and his friends made sure was ripped off at least a dozen times or more, leaving the boy naked in front of a crowd, always on hand when a show was on.

Unfortunately, those sort of tactics more or less back-fired on the boys, as girls liked what they saw of the naked boy. His hairless chest and sinewy, toned, muscles, developed from the physical necessities of running and fighting every day, multiplied his admirers. Some of the girls in their school were actually ignoring advances made by Victor and his buddies. The thugs were starting to find it difficult to scare up a bit of nooky. Sex was the only thing on a young man's mind in those days. Victor especially, as he matured early into a solid, hairy-chested Adonis with golden locks and sapphire-blue eyes.

However, that was the extent of Victor's memory. He remembered nothing more of the boy past high school. In fact, he did not recall the boy at all during his final year. He did not remember much of anything past that when alcohol and drugs figured prominently in his daily life. He no longer cared about what he remembered. He believed, correctly, that he was a dead man either way. This man, he supposed it was Melco, looking like an old entertainer, was obviously out for revenge. Victor's battered senses continued to cling to the last vestiges of life, despite an abandonment of hope, and the loss of any fully-functioning future.

Victor suffered another injection, soothing most of the mind-numbing pain. Lights and sound no longer pierced him like a white-hot knife. He could make out the greyish-purple sausages of his guts trimmed with blood and other bodily fluids oozing from his stomach. The rest of his body was awash with blood from a thousand cuts.

"Back with us again are we, Victor? Good. I can see you have had enough for one night, but not to worry, we can pick up where we left off tomorrow and the next day and the next, until you tell me what I want to know or you die. Oh no, you shouldn't look at me like that Victor. I don't want you to die. No, no, not at all. If you make it past a week, I will let you live, like I did your friend Clayton. Clayton McCormack, remember him? Yes, yes, he lived long enough for me to let him go. Not that help arrived in time to save him, mind you. Tragically, he passed away not more than a couple of months ago."

"Clay?" Victor offered feebly.

"Yes, of course, Clay. Your good friend from back in the days of good old torture and mayhem. He couldn't or wouldn't tell me what I wanted to know either. I consider my methods pretty persuasive, so I would have to admit that he probably didn't know.

You probably don't either, so we will just have to have a bit of fun together, won't we? Lots of things I can think up to make our time together as enjoyable as it was for you and your friends back then."

"Mel, Melco?"

"Yes, that's right. You invented many new and exciting ways to have fun back then, didn't you? All at the expense of one innocent young boy who never did a single thing to warrant the punishment he received. Well, we'll remedy that oversight in the next few days, won't we? I intend to inflict on you all the misery, shame and heartache you caused during those years. I'll have no end of interesting things to show you. Did you ever zap ants with a magnifying glass when you were young? Hmm? I'm going to open the skylight up there to do the same with your eyeballs tomorrow, while you are under the influence of the serum of course. Wouldn't want you to miss out on the *full* experience."

Victor passed out again as the person known to him as Melco snickered softly at his own humour.

INDICATIONS

"What's your best guess, Doc?"

Doctor White, chief medical examiner for the Herbert district, feeling every bit of his sixty years, looked at Detective Ryan with an arched brow. It was always the same with any homicide investigator, but especially true of Detective Ryan. They always wanted a TOD (time of death), before his autopsy even began. He sighed wearily, knowing how important it was to have an estimate as early as possible. He was close to retirement age and he had seen enough death and destruction of the human body to last several lifetimes. He was worn out, burned out, shelled and thrown out, but never, never in all his years as a doctor and medical examiner had he witnessed anything like the wholesale butchery meted out to the last two corpses to show up in the morgue. He shook his head in despondent wonder at how many others may appear at the hands of the Minstrel Killer.

"At least a month ago, possibly as long as two. We'll have a clearer picture once the entomologists have had time to study the larvae. The post-mortem devastation of the victim is so extensive that I doubt I could give you a more accurate guess even after the autopsy. Ryan? I have never seen such an act of unadulterated, sadistic, torture in all my time in the city or here. You need to promise me that you will catch this monster. If anyone can do it, you can. I am an old man, I want to get out of here to begin enjoying my retirement. I will not achieve that enjoyment if I leave here with this... this atrocity unsolved."

The putrefaction permeating the sterile theatre was causing Ryan's eyes to burn. He had long ago learned to contain his stomach contents while viewing a cadaver, but today he was being tested to the limits. He would feel and smell the putrid stench clinging to his clothes and skin for an age. Nothing would touch the foul miasma coating him in this filth. He could shower under steaming hot water with the most powerfully scented soaps and disinfectants money could buy and not get anywhere close to removing the cloying stench of death invading his pores.

"I'm thinking of calling it quits myself Doc. I've had enough too. Firstly, though, I will not rest until I have this evil bastard, dead or alive. He's got two of my friends now and I'll get him if my life depends on it."

"Do you believe it does?"

"What?"

"Depend on it. Do you believe your life depends on it? You said yourself that they were two of your friends."

"You saying I might be a target?"

"I'm asking if you think you are. Any enemies out there?"

"Doc, I got them coming out the wazoo. You don't get to be a detective as long as I have without making a list of enemies that would fill a dunny roll, especially with my local agenda. My mates, though, particularly Clay, Clayton McCormack, I haven't associated with for a bloody long time. A bit hard to keep up a friendship when you're a cop and your mates are doing drugs and shit. Nah, nobody I've put away would connect me with those two. Wouldn't make sense to target such old mates if they had a beef with *me*."

"Do you have anyone else close to you whom they could target?"

"Not really, but it just doesn't wash Doc. Can't see the perp trying to get at me through these blokes. They don't mean that much to me anymore. Our friendships go way back to high school days and before. I grew up with them, but we all lost touch after high school and I became a cop. Cops don't have many civvy friends. All that, 'Us and Them'."

"Be that as it may, it might pay to look into it, unless you believe in coincidences."

"Kill any two people in this town and I am likely to know them or went to school with them. Shit, you know that. Did you know them, or of them? You're a bit older than I am but you probably know *them* and most other folks here don't you?"

"You're right. I'm... just, just... "

"Yeah, I know exactly how you feel. I'm *just*, as well. Just tired, just fed-up and just plain angry at the bastard, mongrel piece of shit in our town capable of this. Make any guesses on what was used?"

"Are you kidding me? What wasn't used? Take your pick, Ryan, and a pick may well be among the items! Look at his eyeballs, scorched by a laser or something similar after having his eyelids sewn open. All of his digits have been removed by different methods as far as I can tell at first glance. That's twenty different instruments of torture just there. I can't tell conclusively at this point, but I would say his genitals have been chewed away pre-mortem. They don't appear to be normal post-mortem predation by scavenging animals on a corpse. I reckon this, this demon, placed hungry animals, possibly rats, in a container over the victim's crotch while he was still alive."

"Fuck! How can anyone do that to another human being?"

"*Another*, human being? You're attributing *human* qualities to *this* perpetrator? Spare me, please Ryan. I have no sympathy for this *thing*, whatever his reasons. If he ends up on my table here at the morgue, I will resign that very second. I could not in all good conscience permit myself to treat his cadaver with the respect I afford the rest. Now go, let me do my work, and you go catch this animal. Will I put your name down as the person to officially identify the body?"

"Yeah, Victor had no one else, poor bugger. His parents died a long time ago. His ex-wife refused to come down and even his secretary was too angry with him at being owed wages to help out. Fuck, I idolised this bloke as a kid. He was... a superb figure of a man. Could have had any woman he wanted and done anything he liked. How could a man like that let himself go?"

"I'm sure our tox-screens will point to his particular pleasures."

"I already know what you will find. He loved his beer and his dope when he could afford it. He got busted once for growing the stuff at one of his rental properties. Claimed it was a tenant but that didn't stick seeing as he had no proof of renting the bloody place. Sad. That just about summed up his life after the drink got hold of him. Sad. Ruined everything for him, his marriage, his business, himself. Tell me something? He was found by a fisherman washed up in one of the mangrove swamps near Dungeness. Were his similar injuries the only reason you connected it to the Minstrel Killer immediately?"

"No. You guessed right that it had all been washed off, but there were still traces of boot polish in his ears when he came in. He was found face-down in the mud wasn't he?"

"Yeah. That would have taken care of the rest on his face. Hard to tell the difference between the mud and boot polish by that time. So, pretty much the same MO as Clay?"

"Superficially," the doctor nodded his affirmation. "Different methods to reach the same conclusion, though."

"Spontaneous?"

"Some, yes. Most, I would say, were calculated in great detail. The perpetrator knew what he was doing, how to inflict the maximum amount of pain while keeping the body functioning. There is also some troubling evidence of massive muscle trauma not essentially attributable to the specific injuries I see. I will let you know more about that."

"Thanks, Doc, send me the full report when you're done. I appreciate your time."

"Catch him, Detective. Preferably alive so I don't have to deal with him.

"Try my best Doc."

"You always do Ryan, you always do," muttered the doctor to an empty room as he prepared to perform the Y-section.

TENSIONS

Ryan flopped down on his sagging recliner with a heavy sigh as he popped a ring-pull on a can of VB. He knew he should not be such a traitor to his home state by drinking southern, Victoria Bitter, but he didn't like Fourex, the Queensland brand, never did. He seldom drank beer if truth be told; only when he was extremely thirsty or hot. He drank beer to quench a thirst and spirits to get sozzled. He would open a bottle of cheap Scotch later in the evening.

His housemate was not home again so he would have to get off his fat butt to cook dinner if he wanted to eat. Damn, but he missed the bloke's cooking. Ryan would probably just order another pizza so he could relax in the recliner. He couldn't be bothered with the hassle of cooking for himself. He rarely did when he lived alone. Life had been pretty sweet since he took in the tenant. He still found it difficult to afford his *favourite* tipple, but all in all, things were on the better side of glum with the extra money coming in.

He had only had the one small run-in with the bloke a few months ago, other than that, it had been an amenable arrangement between them. Couldn't blame the bloke for not wanting to just leave without having his bond money returned. Ryan still hadn't organised that little detail. Ah well, he'd get around to it, eventually. Fact is, that money went quickly on a poker game and lots of booze. An expensive night out with the boys that one. Somehow, he had to find another twelve hundred dollars to place in a trust account he had yet to set up.

Ryan couldn't believe his good luck getting a guy to pay him $150 per week for a room in his house and a twelve hundred dollar bond. Eighteen hundred upfront, all in cash, and the bloke signed the agreement covering Ryan's arse all the way to the bank if the bloke defaulted in any way. Ryan would ensure that a default occurred so that he would not have to return the fellow's bond. Trouble was, the bloke knew enough to keep making his landlord inspect his room every three months, and always demanded a receipt upon payment. If Ryan tried to use an excuse like needing to purchase another receipt book, the bloke would withhold payment until such time as he could immediately provide a receipt.

The bastard kept everything above board so well that Ryan had to dig deeper to find a loophole somewhere, make the bloke default in a way he hadn't thought of. He might consult a buddy who knew a bit about finding ways around a contract. Couldn't ask Amos who drew up the iron-clad document - too much of a goody-two-shoes by far. The prick wouldn't risk so much as jaywalking. Ingham actually had a few traffic lights now, which Amos always used. Took a while for civilisation like that to catch up to the small rural township.

Reminiscing about Ingham, prompted Ryan to think about Victor Kugelweis and Clayton McCormack. He had grown up with them almost from kindergarten. Never really connected with them until the last two years of primary school. Inseparable during high school, then drifted apart as they each went their different paths after their final exams and graduation. Doc White had asked whether the murders were connected in that regard. Ryan insisted that it would be damned uncommon for any two individuals, murdered within the town, not to be related in one way or another. Two locals at any rate.

He smiled wistfully at several good memories they shared, the girls they enjoyed. Except... that line of thought conjured up a sour note or two that Ryan found hard to identify. High school and girls, a boy reaching puberty and the height of his sexual awareness. He recalled the small gap they had found in the blockwork to the female showers. That was the problem, though. If his memory was correct, they were relegated to perving for much of the time instead of the more tactile pleasures associated with girlfriends.

He and his friends seemed unlucky when it came to love back then. Girls generally rebuked their individual advances for some peculiar reason that Ryan could not recall. Victor was adored by the girls as they were going through primary school. Clay was known to befriend the opposite sex readily enough. Even Ryan, in his awkward youth, remembered a girl or two hanging around him... until high school. *What the hell was it in high school that dried up the attention?* As Ryan puzzled over that conundrum, Michael Miller's dual-cab ute pulled into the driveway, stopping short of the garage door to which only Ryan had a remote control.

Ryan heard the front door being unlocked as his tenant returned home early that evening. Michael went straight to the kitchen where he began to unload.

"Came to a little over a hundred, so you owe me fifty unless you want to go back to your processed stuff, like cardboard pizza?"

"Does that mean you're going to come back earlier to cook from now on?" asked Ryan.

"More often than not now that I'm well into it. Got most of the weather prevention stuff sorted and not looking like I need to remove any more walls or roofing, so there won't be so much pressure for me to complete projects on the day any more. Most of the outside stuff is done. Now I can relax a bit with the insides. We can keep our shopping separate if you prefer?"

"Nope. Missed you're cooking I have to admit. Fifty bucks is fine. You want the cash now, or you want me to deduct it from your rent?"

"Either way. Deduct it if you like. How about a spaghetti bolognese? I can do a short version that doesn't require a long slow cook."

"Yeah, whatever," said Ryan dismissively.

"Something wrong?"

"No, why?"

"You just seem a bit preoccupied, that's all."

"Another Minstrel Killer victim showed up. Christ! Why the fuck would you not read the papers or watch the news?"

"Already told you why. Not interested."

"Well, don't you think you should be interested in your community, the people who live here?"

"Just because I lived here a long time ago doesn't mean it is my community any longer. Never was... "

"Hold up! What? You used to live here? When? You never told me that."

"You never asked. It was an awfully long time ago."

"No, that's not possible. Your name would have come up in my searches."

"I went by a different name back then. A foreign name. It seemed prudent to change it to a more Anglicised name when I got older."

Rising out of his chair to confront him in the kitchen, Ryan glared at him over the counter while Michael nonchalantly prepared the evening meal.

"So, what the fuck was your name before you changed it?"

"Why on earth would you want to know that?"

"What makes you think I *wouldn't* want to know the prior name of my tenant who misled me?"

"Misled you? How exactly did I do that?"

"By not divulging the truth, that's how?"

"Care to elucidate?"

"Oh, again with smarmy shit. Elucidate this, arsehole, you lied on your rental application, which means you forfeit your bond."

"I really resent the name-calling, Detective Ryan. Without actually going to get my copy of the contract, I can fairly-well guarantee you that no question of former names is indicated. I'm not sure what's gotten into your craw all of a sudden but I do not like the inference that I have been anything other than totally honest with you in my application."

"I don't give a fuck about what you think. You lied to me by omission."

"If the question is never asked then omission is not possible. Regardless of that fact, I don't see that it has any bearing on the matter or makes the slightest difference. Have I shown any indication of being less than a perfect tenant? Found any sign of theft or vandalism to your property? If I were a suspicious person, it would almost seem to me that you are deliberately searching for reasons to withhold my bond money."

"I can bloody-well throw you out any time I want... "

"Not without evidence of wrong-doing on my part. If you wish to inform me that you no longer require my tenancy to continue for other reasons, a minimum of two weeks' notice is required by you, in writing, with my full bond to be returned on the day of departure pending a room inspection. I have kept a copy of all your satisfactory room inspections which indicate no damages, no reasons for you to withhold my bond. This is the second or third time you have confronted me with some bogus infraction of your contract in order to keep my money. Either give me written notice or stop badgering me."

"Do you realise that you are talking to an official law-enforcement officer? Do you really want to get on the wrong side of the law?"

"Your threats are wasted on me, Detective Ryan. As with all previous conversations, I am recording this one on my phone; a habit I have had to form once you began making false assertions. Copies of all typed transcripts of those conversations are being held by my lawyer in his office safe."

Ryan's jaw clenched, seething at his tenant's calm and infuriating manner. It galled him no end that he was unable to intimidate the man the same way he managed to do with felons he arrested. His formidable bulk was normally enough to coerce the worst of them into submission and cooperation. If that ominous presence failed, his facial features, revealing unmistakable brutality, usually sufficed thereafter. Ryan was not a person to be trifled with. He succeeded where others failed. His solve-rate was far higher than departmental averages.

Michael continued his exasperating indifference by ignoring the smouldering looks coming from the detective. He threw the sliced onions into a pot with a generous dollop of butter and a squirt of quality olive oil. Once the onions had caramelised nicely, he added the premium beef, pork and veal mince, fresh herbs, crushed garlic and seasoning. He allowed the meats to brown well before adding the final ingredients. He then adjusted the heat to a simmer, allowing the flavours to infuse gently into the meat in the covered pot. He then acknowledged the detective by staring back at him, challenging him.

"Well, Detective Ryan?"

"I want to know your name, your real name."

"My real name, my legitimate name in the eyes of the law, is, Michael Miller. I have already told you that."

"What was your name before you changed it, arsehole?"

"You're the fucking detective, find out yourself if you're that interested."

"Why don't you just tell me yourself? Got something to hide?"

"I would gladly have told you my former name had you simply asked nicely. The moment you started threatening me and calling me names, you lost that opportunity. Now, are we going to dance around with legal arguments all night about our rental agreement, or are you going to finally pony up the bond money with a written notice? Twelve hundred dollars and you forego keeping any of my advance rental payment if the room is in good order and I have not, legally, defaulted. Are we going to continue this animosity for falsely conceived indiscretions, or can we work past it?"

"I'm warning you... "

"No! I'm warning you, Detective. I will sue you for harassment if you continue with these absurd allegations and your pathetic attempts to intimidate me and keep my money. The law, your law, is there to protect both sides in a dispute. If you think you have a legitimate case against me, I suggest you have your lawyer put it in writing, then have your man contact my man and they can do lunch or something. Otherwise, keep your fucking warnings to yourself. Here is a business card from my lawyer's firm. Just call the secretary and she will put you in touch with one of the partners. They all know me well, and have all represented me at various times in my real estate dealings."

After leaving the business card on the kitchen counter, Michael exited the kitchen to walk to his room, leaving Ryan to brood over their conversation.

SUSPICIONS

"Lorenzo. Hey, Lorenzo. Wake up. Christ. You stink!"

Ryan was shaking the derelict slumped within his filthy space under a bridge just outside of town, his usual digs. Trying desperately to breathe through his mouth to avoid the stench assaulting his nostrils, Ryan half dragged the man away from his grimy cardboard shelter. Unable to rouse him from his drunken stupor, Ryan threw the lightweight man into the Herbert River. After several moments, fearing he may have drowned the man, Ryan walked toward the edge of the water. Lorenzo Catani rose to the surface spluttering in a hazy panic.

"What? What the... fuck? Who? Cunt! Who the fuck threw me in the drink? Which one-o-you cunts... "

"Calm down Loz. It's me, Ryan."

Lorenzo squinted at the man on the bank, trying to recognise him, failing. He struggled to the bank where he hoisted himself unsteadily to a crawling position. He began to cough and splutter as the last of the water was expelled from his lungs. His chest hurt, his head felt like it was ready to blow apart. He struggled to his feet, attempted to glare at Ryan, before charging him. Ryan simply side-stepped the charging Lorenzo, to see him fall face-first into the dirt. Another charge once Loz had regained his feet, saw him ending up in the river once more.

"Getting sober by any chance?" asked Ryan as Lorenzo once again dragged his aching body from the water, where he collapsed in a heap at Ryan's feet. "Jesus Loz. Take it easy will you? I just want to talk to you. C'mon over into the sun here so you can dry out a bit and I can ask you some questions.

Lorenzo reluctantly crawled over to a sunny patch beside one of the bridge's concrete pylons. He laid back against the warm concrete, squinting at the detective squatting before him. He patted his soaked shirt and pockets, coming up empty.

"Gotta smoke, Cunt... stable?"

"Don't start that shit with me Loz. I was promoted to detective a long time ago, and you know it. You also know I quit smoking about the same time. Christ, the fags nearly killed me when I got too slow on the job. I couldn't run some scumbag down and he nearly got the drop on me. I've got a thermos of coffee with me. You need it to talk straight?"

"Think the swim did the trick, *Defective*."

"Aww, cut out the bullshit, will you? Not my fault you're a lousy drunk. You and bloody Victor, Jesus! Both of you stinking, rotten drunks. Victor could have been anything he wanted, now he's lying in the morgue, a slab of meat. And that's where you'll be real soon if you don't wake up to yourself."

"Fuck off! I don't drink coz I have to, I drink coz I want to."

"That's the biggest load of crap I ever heard Loz, and I've heard 'em all. Listen, I'm not here about your drinking. I couldn't really give a rat's arse if you want to kill yourself like this. Did you hear what I said? Victor Kugelweis is dead, lying on a table at the morgue, murdered, in a really, really unfriendly manner."

Loz's laughter turned to a painful, racking cough.

"Oh, so you think that's funny?"

"Well, yeah. Is there a *friendly* way to murder someone?"

"If you saw what I saw you wouldn't be asking that dumb question. Clay's gone too."

"Gone where? Where's ole Clayton fucked off to?"

"Depends on your beliefs. He's dead dickhead!"

"Clayton?"

"Yeah. And Victor. Both murdered by the same person or persons. Brutally tortured for days or weeks, maybe months, then dumped in the channel."

"Fuck!"

"Yeah, fuck, is right. Look, Doc White said something and even though it sounds bloody ridiculous, I need to ask you some questions."

"Don't I have to be completely sober before it's legal to ask me questions that are admish... admiss... able in a court-o-law?"

"I'm not arresting you for anything... yet. Are you going to stop being an arsehole for a minute? Your life, such as it is, might depend on it."

"Ryan, what are you talkin' about?"

"I'm talking about maybe you or me being next, dipshit."

"Why the fuck would you think that?"

"I don't *really* think it at all. Just following up on something the Doc said. Two of our friends from back in the day got murdered by a serial killer, Ingham's first. The papers are calling him the Minstrel Killer because he blackens their faces with boot polish."

"Ha-ha. That's funny."

"It is not bloody funny."

"You used to think it was bloody hilarious."

"Loz, I have never found murder to be in the slightest bit funny. I don't know what... "

"Not, not murder, mate. The other, the... "

"Loz?"

Lorenzo Catani had passed out. Ryan slapped him hard. Rousing him only slightly before the man lapsed into his alcohol-stupor once more. Although Ryan was contemplating leaving his childhood mate to suffer the consequences of his excesses, he succumbed to a distant feeling of guilt. He dragged the unconscious man to his unmarked police sedan. He placed the appropriate amount of plastic sheeting over the back seat, a precaution he always employed when dealing with drunks, before placing the body of his emaciated friend in the car. Ryan drove the man home after taking care of some shopping. Then, after struggling to remove the filthy rags Lorenzo wore, Ryan dumped him in a hot bath.

Ryan laboured for nearly an hour to clean the built-up grime and filth from his friend. The stench was unparalleled. Stale urine and faeces clung to the insides of his trousers. *By all accounts,*

Lorenzo Catani should not be alive, thought Ryan. He had to shave off the prodigious hair growth, from groin to head to save himself the onslaught of nits, lice, crabs and all other greeblies hiding therein. Once dry, he doused the body in a delousing powder. He was struggling to carry Loz to the spare bedroom when Michael entered by the front door.

"Whew! What is that smell?"

"Yeah, sorry about that. I have to clean up the bathroom and burn his clothes; so don't go in there. I, I, got something I wanted to ask you. Let me put this guy into the spare bedroom first. Okay?"

"Yeah, just let me close the bathroom door. Not sure I can stand that smell. You better use a lot of disinfectants when you clean up in there, and I hope you haven't used any of my stuff on him?" Michael asked as Ryan ignored his question to unburden himself of the limp figure in his arms.

"No, Michael, I wouldn't do that," said Ryan after exiting the spare room. "I bought some stuff at the chemist to use." He led the way to the kitchen where he offered Michael a VB. Michael accepted the proffered can with trepidation. They both stood in silence as they swigged from their beers. "I need to ask you something... "

"I'm listening."

"Yeah, right. That used to be a good mate of mine and he's in a bit of trouble. I want to help him and I need him to be here for me to do that properly."

"Here? In this house? Is this about kicking me out again?"

"Whoa, no, no, nothing like that, okay? In fact, I'm offering you a job, if you're interested?"

"What sort of a job? I'm pretty busy down at the beach house... "

"Yeah, well it's sort of like that work that I need doing. I can't have me mate in the house. That... that would spell disaster for everyone. He won't stay in official detox, and I can't get him into one without his permission. He hasn't broken the law so I can't get him signed in by the courts either. My only option, if I want to help him, is to have him here. I reckon there's enough room in the garage to build a soundproof room where I can keep him till he gets better."

"You want to keep him here against his will? Not exactly within the tenets of the law is it?"

"I think I have that angle covered. It's a bloody stretch, but I think I can make it legal if I place him in witness protection."

"Wouldn't make much of a witness."

"No, he didn't witness anything. I might be able to swing it with the chief if I tell him the bloke needs protection against a possible murder."

"Is there someone that wants to murder him?"

"It's a stretch, as I say, but there may be a connection between him and what is happening at the moment. At least, it's the only way I have of keeping him here. It's for his own good. He's a goner if he stays out there on his own. He weighs nothing and drinks like there's no tomorrow. I doubt he's had a decent feed in a year, just scraps from the bins."

"And you want me to build you a sound-proof room in the garage to house him? How do you intend to pay me, you can't even come up with my bond money? And why would I help you when you obviously don't like me and just keep inventing ways to be rid of me?"

"You going to hold that against me, are you?"

"Nothing has ever been resolved, Detective Ryan. I assume you want me to bill you my hours in lieu of rent payments? That might stretch out to quite a few months in advance without accounting for the materials? Why would you be asking me to stay that long if you didn't want me here, and what protection do I have if you give me written notice before I have acquitted the funds?"

"I'm sorry if it sounded like I was trying to get rid of you Michael. I admit that I have been less than cordial with you of late. I don't mind having you here as long as you don't lie to me ag... sorry, as long as you don't lie to me. If you draw up a list of materials you need and give me a quote for your labour, I will sign whatever you want to cover you and we'll go from there, eh? Just one thing, though, it has to be done pretty quickly. We don't want him going ape-shit on us when he wakes up and he isn't in a locked room. He's is going to be very pissed off when I tell him."

"What makes you think he will be able to tolerate it?"

"I've had some experience and I have a... friend, who used to be a full-time nurse who'll be persuaded to help me. We'll put Loz on a drip and a catheter for the first month. Keep him fairly sedated while we build up his body a bit and feed him some antibiotics. After that, we'll slowly decrease the drug dosage until he gets clean. He won't be happy. That I know for sure. He'll probably hate my guts forever. If I manage to get him clean, it will be worth it."

"*Keeping,* him clean is the hard bit. How long do you reckon you can make it stick? As soon as you let him out of the room, he'll go straight back on the bottle."

"Well, I'm going to give it my best shot. He was a good mate back in the day. I'm trying to make up for not keeping in touch with him over the years. What do you say? Can you help me out? I won't forget it?"

"Will you get off my back and stop trying to invent new ways of getting rid of me?"

"Yeah, got my word on that. Sorry, Michael, I'm a very suspicious person by nature and occupation. You have actually been a very good tenant. I'm lucky to have you."

"I'm not feeding him. You can cook for him and pay for it out of your own pocket?"

"No problem."

"I'll take some measurements, get a quote and a list of materials to you in the morning, okay?"

"Yeah, yeah, that'd be great. And you can do the work pretty quickly?"

"I should be able to knock it up in two or three days once you accept the quote and conditions."

"Great, great. He'll be totally comatose for at least a week or more anyway, but the sooner I get him in there, the better for everyone concerned."

"Do you want a normal lockable door, or just a padlock and bolt? I have a heavy-duty padlock you can have, never been used?"

"Yeah, that'd be good enough. Do you think you can make it sort of permanent so I can use it as a storeroom afterwards?"

"No problem. If you don't want it to be temporary, it will be a bit cheaper actually."

"Thanks, Michael, I really appreciate it."

"Don't thank me too quickly, you haven't seen my bill yet."

"You won't try to rip me off, I trust you. Too bloody squeaky clean to do anything dishonest."

SHARING

When Craig Ball woke, he found himself cable-tied to a chair facing an image of his naked body on a television screen. The live feed coming from a compact camera which stood on a tripod to one side of the old TV set. Craig had a large piece of duct tape across his mouth, preventing him from sounding out his surprise and indignation at being bound and gagged. He looked about him in an effort to identify his surroundings. A deep and foreboding fear enveloped the retired schoolteacher, disabling his normal thought processes.

The room he was in smelled musty. He shivered with a cold dread. His wrinkled eyes shed a tear as he envisaged a dire outcome resulting from his excesses. Retirement had not been easy for Craig Ball. With very little to occupy his mind, he had taken to the gee-gees rather heavily. His short-priced bookie had obviously had enough of Craig's excuses, deciding to scare the living shit out of him. He would finally have to sell his house and car to make good on what he owed. If he got enough for the house in the currently depressed market, that was.

Craig's wife had deserted him, and his children disowned him long ago when the gambling became too much for them to handle. His constant abuse and threats while listening to the Saturday morning tips and the pursuant races in the afternoon on the radio had ensured he remained alone. He no longer had friends who would miss him and his neighbours didn't know him. He could be gone for months without anyone noticing. He wondered how badly he would be beaten. They wouldn't kill him, or else they would have no way of recouping their money. He stared at his skinny, pale, body with his veins clearly evident all over him. His shrivelled penis resting in its nest of grey pubic hair looked pathetic on the TV screen, like some puny little helmeted worm.

He looked away from the screen, disgusted to see the way he had let himself go. He'd had no end of young admirers back in the day. He could have had so many of his young female students if he'd had the courage to accept their numerous offers of sex. He'd been the envy of the teaching staff at Ingham High for many, many years. His once long, wavy, sandy-blonde locks had been replaced by a bald pate that made him look like an egg on legs. The old-style black glasses he wore, reinforced the aging image.

His life no longer engaged him once he lost the power to attract the opposite sex. His young students laughed at him and made open jokes about him as the years passed. Depressed, despondent, and utterly without appeal, he drifted into a world where he could lose himself in the rush, the thrill of the win. The terrible sadness of the loss. The bitterness and rage at the injustice and unfairness of a horse, his horse, losing its rider, faltering at the starting gate or any other damn thing affecting a horse to ensure it came stone, motherless, last, causing the never-ending spiral to continue.

So absorbed was Craig in his self-loathing and admonishment, that he did not recognise the slight movement behind him in the live video feed. Unable to avoid it, Craig continued to stare at his miserable, naked form occupying the chair, so lost in self-immolation that he failed to perceive the shadowy figure approach from the rear. He stared so long and hard at the disgraceful sham of a man he had become, that the image on the screen became pixelated, blurry and undefined. Craig's tears shamed and depressed him further until he felt the jarring blow against the side of his head that caused a klaxon to go off within his skull.

Stunned by the force of the blow, he watched as the shapes on the screen coalesced into a recognisable image. He saw the person standing behind him with an oddly shaped weapon, too far out of the frame and focus to distinguish. Craig felt sure he was incapable of detecting sound from his damaged ear, felt sure it would be permanent. His brain felt as though it had been smashed from side to side within his skull. His good ear picked up the alien sound of his own muffled keening as if it came from a woman. He did not recognise the feminine-high tone as his own.

He did not feel the trickle of warm fluid oozing from his paralysed ear. His senses were too overwhelmed by the sheer impact of the stunning blow to register anything beyond his own agony. His eyeballs felt bruised, as though they had been slammed against their sockets. How his head remained attached to his body, he could not guess. Slowly, painfully, sight regained its lucidity, and Craig squinted to focus on the screen in front of him, to see his assailant... *naked, a black face...* standing rigidly behind him, holding... *what?* He couldn't make it out.

"Ping-pong Mr Ball, remember? You used to love holding classes. Thought you were a Master at the sport. God's gift to female students and the sport of table-tennis, or Ping-pong as you still called it back then, huh?" The person behind him held a ping-pong bat, a paddle. The *racket*, he corrected himself, was the official term used in professional sports circles.

Craig had been slammed with a table tennis racket that felt more like a baseball bat. He would not have been surprised to learn that he had indeed been belted with a baseball or cricket bat. The ringing in his ear so loud that he could barely hear the accented voice of the person. The sound muffled and indistinct, like he was underwater.

"A teacher, Mr Ball, is charged wiz de care of der... *their...* students in all aspects. Teaching in a public school is not just about enriching the intellect Mr Ball. It is about the complete persona of a student, their well-being, to formulate within them good cognitive skills with which to face the outside world, to enrich the body and mind with purpose and knowledge. A teacher, Mr Ball, must encapsulate many areas of expertise to assist the mind of the student. All that they require to graduate as a full and complete person. Above all, Mr Ball, a teacher should ensure the *safety* of their wards at all times, to guarantee that their school years are happy and productive, free from the anxieties yet to face them on the outside. A 'good' teacher, that is. Were you a good teacher?" asked the person, ripping free the tape covering Craig's mouth and replacing the thick spectacles that had been forced askew by the blow.

Craig felt that any way he answered the question, barely audible in his ruined ear and only just managing to register in the good one, would be the wrong answer. He thought about the question for a time, pondering the truth. If he were honest with himself, he would have to answer in the affirmative. However, he did not think it was the answer his captor was hoping to hear. Craig tried to study his surroundings while he mulled over the answer. His captor was clearly deranged.

Bare, grey walls gave the impression of concrete, although, the sound was not quite reverberant enough to make a positive conclusion. No windows. One door that he could see, bare of paint, revealing its solidity. This was not one of those cheap hardboard doors with honeycomb cardboard infill. It had three-inch brass butt hinges holding it to the sturdy timber frame. Hung to perfection, without a sound as it swung inward with a slight breeze. Joins in the walls indicated sheets of some description, without jointing paper or plaster fill. Cement sheet more than likely. Fresh, unpainted. A basement or garage perhaps. Tool benches on two sides gave the impression of a well-organised workshop.

Craig squinted in the glare of the overhead fluorescent bulb, looking back to the screen in the hope of examining his captor. A tallish person... *a man...* he supposed if the image on the screen could be trusted. Then he realised that his chair was shorter than a normal chair, which might make his jailor seem taller. He did not recognise the features, or the cold dark eyes that were hidden behind a blackened face, made ridiculous with exaggerated white lips. Could not guess at a reason for his inhumane treatment by the thug, naked as far as he could tell, with unusual markings. Craig twitched when he peered down at the concrete floor, discovering plastic sheeting beneath his chair.

"Yes, plastic. Can't have you getting my clean floor filthy with your guts and blood now, can we? You didn't answer my question,

Mr Ball. Are you a good teacher?"

"Who, who are you?"

"Don't you recognise me? I'm not surprised. I've had major facial reconstruction since you last saw me. Not from vanity mind. No, I would never voluntarily undergo such horrendous procedures in the name of beauty. I was never a 'hunk', I realise, but neither was I the deformed person that I became after... after school. And of course, there is the... makeup? Answer my question before I give you another taste of my encouragement."

"I, I won awards and commendations. I... Yes, I believe I am a very good teacher."

"Because you are a good educator? I have no doubt you are perfectly capable of giving lessons that might be remembered long enough for someone to recall the facts in an exam. That is about education of the intellect, the very *least* a teacher should impart. I am talking holistically. The whole student experience while attending an educational facility. The joys and pleasures of learning in a friendly, cordial, atmosphere administered by caring teachers. To provide a student with a happy experience that will stay with them for the rest of their lives, building them into a person of prominence, capable of anything they set their mind to. Nurture of the mind and body to become complete in maturity. Now, do you possess *those* attributes, Mr Ball? Do you have what it takes to produce a completely educated and wholesome graduate with well-adjusted emotions?"

"I, like to think that is true," stammered Craig, knowing and fearing the result of an incorrect answer.

"Based on the number of students that sing your praises no doubt? Hmm? What about the rest, though? The ones that find you less than capable, remarkably short on talent and ability? What of them, Mr-bloody-Ball? What of the ones you allowed to fall through the cracks of your observations, the ones you felt were undeserving of your vast experience?"

"I don't think; I don't under... "

"Oh, come now, Mr-fucking-Ball! You are supposed to be an educator, you cannot possibly misunderstand my words. Did you ever once think about the poor buggers who did not fit into your visions of student perfection? Did you give a thought to the ones who were denied the full, 'Ball' experience?"

"I treated... "

"NO!" screamed the person into Craig's good ear. Rounding on him, leaning so close to his face that Craig could taste the waves of pure hatred emanating from the person. "Oh, no you don't. Don't you dare try to tell me you treated all your students the same. That is an objectionable lie Mr Ball, one punishable by all manner of diabolic treatments. However, you need to truly appreciate *your* whole experience, holistically. Pain is so much more than what you know. I am able to enhance your terror a hundred-fold, a pain so exquisite and enduring that you will believe you have passed through the gates of hell. Just a little prick now, and a little time. Time to reflect on your answers."

The person backed away after jabbing Craig with a needle. Craig was astounded to see the bare torso of his captor for the first time, displaying no discernible genitalia! As a wondrous warmth permeated his limbs, Craig noticed the scarring in the shape of a hand on the groin area where the genitals were missing. On closer inspection, as the person stood still before him, Craig began to observe the many individual puncture wounds adorning the entire body. It was then that he came to an obvious conclusion, "So, so, this isn't about... Bernie?"

"Is Bernie still at it? Still a short-priced bookie? Would've thought all that went out the window with legal betting on the internet. Oh, but you can't put it 'on tick', there, can you? Bernie can extend some credit to idiots like you who think you can actually *make* money by gambling. How much are you into him for? Must be substantial for you to think this is about him. Hmm?"

The sound of his captor's last 'Hmm', thrummed along Craig's nerves like an extended bass note, reverberating, increasing to a painful crescendo. Craig's bonds were feeling like they were slowly slicing through his flesh. His bare backside rasped against the wood of the chair like he was absorbing a million splinters. The more he struggled, the worse it felt, the louder he gasped. Each and every tiny sound amplified to unbearable intensity. Craig heard everything now, with such unbelievable clarity and such volume that he felt his eardrums might burst. It was only when he realised it was his own screams punishing him, that he was able to quell his oral protestations.

Argh, the stench! Fuck, what is that? Oh, no, please don't. Whatever it is, it hurts, cold, so cold, help me, someone. What is that? I can't stand the smell, it's burning my nostrils, my throat. STOP! Please stop, no... Black. I know that smell... boot polish, I remember... why? At least it only hurt for a little while. My face, my face is black. Shit! Heard about, heard, no, yes, read about this. What the fuck? The Minstrel Killer! Faces and, oh no, no, no. Please don't kill me. "Please, please... "

"Please, please, what? You have to speak up Mr Ball. I haven't taken as much as you, I can't hear what you hear. Am I speaking too loud? How about a bit of soft music to soothe you?"

Craig's pitiful screams competed with the trembling tones of Deep Purple's, *'Smoke on the Water'*, instantly intensifying his abject misery by a magnitude of ten. The famous opening riff pounded through the air and Craig's nerves like a sledgehammer. He could not stop screaming, though he desperately attempted to jam his mouth shut. Everything hurt as his body strained against the bonds, stiffened and quivered with the onslaught to his senses. Breathing hurt, holding his mouth closed hurt, feeling one eyelid mashing against the other caused spasms, which in turn hurt more. Light, sound, feeling, even his brain machinations were an agony. Craig did not last until the end of the song. Blissfully, he fainted.

***

Fuck! Oh Jesus, make it, make it... stop! I, I can't... terrible, can't, no, can't take anymore. What? What now? Where? Oh shit, the pain, the fucking pain... can't open eyes, no, too, too bad.

"Come on Mr Ball, I know you're awake," whispered the person. "I'm going to turn off the fluorescent lights so that you can open your eyes. Just a couple of candles so that you can still see, okay?"

Craig opened his eyes cautiously, expecting the light to stab him with its intensity. He was relieved to find the harsh glare gone, replaced by a barely acceptable flicker of flame. He... *What the fuck? Oh, oh no, what, what have I done to deserve... Bernie? No, no, not the bookie is it? Some other perverted fuck, torture, oh, oh it hurts so badly.* Craig forced his mind back to the present, to view his tortured body hanging by barbed-wire to a wooden cross. His blackened face and his head wrapped with a barbed-wire crown to imitate the laurel of thorns worn by his saviour. His entire blood-soaked body entwined within the barbs. *Why, why, why? At least, at lea... yes, not hurting like before. Sick fucking cunt... I'm gonna, I'm fuck...*

"Do you like your cross, Mr Ball? Made that especially for you seeing as you're right into that religion shit. Thought you might like to suffer for humanity like your saviour. I've saved you the nails, though, and I've administered the antidote to my serum for the time being. You're hurting, but not overwhelmed like before. Hurts like fuck doesn't it - when that shit kicks in? Don't worry, you will get more of that... much more."

"Wh, wh, why?"

"Hasn't the memory stolen through yet? Surely there can't have been anything more memorable than that one episode? Or was there worse, with others? I asked if you were a good teacher, Mr Ball. You said you believed you were. A good teacher protects their students from harm Mr Ball. All harm. When you ignore the helpless pleas of one of your charges, day after day, month after month, year after year, you fail in your duties. Remember a name from that time? An unusual name with foreign, Slavic implications? Remember a particular boy who asked you to help him? *Begged* you to help him with all his little heart?"

"I don't... Many of my students asked for help over the years. What, who, are you referring to?"

"Ever had any problems with bullies in your school, Mr Ball? Ever had one of your students ask you to intercede on his behalf because he just couldn't take the abuse any longer?"

"School is, is a... testing ground. Kids all finding the natural pecking order, trying... "

"Listen to me, you stinking bag of shit. School is not a predatory *testing* ground for thugs to hone their skills or get their rocks off by intimidating others. It is supposed to be a place of learning, a safe and secure environment in which to expand the knowledge base. Sure, there are societal lessons to be learned but not at the hands of brutality, Mr Ball.

"You were charged with the wholesome care and education of the young boys and girls placed in your care. To deny one in favour of others who meet your definition of fine, strapping young lads *testing* their mettle against one another, is an appalling attitude. When those favourites get completely out of hand to cause grievous harm to mind and flesh, that failing attitude becomes criminal neglect.

"The crime was not reported. The boy suffered for life as a result. You are about to pay for your neglect of that boy Mr Ball, a hundred times over, as the boy had to suffer under your tutelage."

"Who?"

"Can you really be that ignorant of your own failings not to remember the little boy strung up in the barbed-wire as you are now? I know you don't know the answer to the question I asked the others, so I will not bother to ask you. I just want you to remember the gross negligence you displayed by sweeping the crime under the carpet. Do you recall the boy? You found him strung up in barbed-wire that morning with a blackened face. You passed it off as a prank gone 'a little awry'. Washed him up and that was that. Didn't inspect his wounds thoroughly. Didn't see to his hospitalisation. No investigation, no punishments or even reprimands for a vile act of savagery upon one of *your* charges."

"Cadet Malkovich?"

"Ah, so you do remember. Yes, you were in charge of the squad of *cadets* on bivouac that weekend when the... incident occurred. You pretty much knew who was responsible but did nothing. What was worse, is that you did not send the boy to the hospital immediately after you found him. Did not bother to investigate his condition further to determine other possible injuries. Did you?

"What you didn't care to find out was that the prank had gone way beyond anything as playful as a blackened face of boot polish or toothpaste on the cock and balls to make them sting a bit. Even wrapping his arms carefully within the strands of the barbed-wire fence, although way beyond the parameters of a joke, was not the worst of it.

"Oh, no, the 'joke' didn't end there. No, one of the *pranksters* came back afterwards, after the group had left. Came back to... complete the task, to ensure that the boy would never forget, cause him such torment and pain that the boy would suffer all his days. *You* are about to suffer for that boy's pain and anguish.

"You betrayed a boy's trust in you to ensure his safety and well-being, Ball! You fucked up big time and will suffer as you have never imagined suffering before. With my serum, your pain will know no bounds, and I will ensure you stay barely alive to *share* that same pain as that boy."

"Melco, Melco? Please... I'm, I'm... sorr... "

HARD TIMES

"How's the patient?" asked Michael.

"Not good. I don't know what's going on with him. Every time it seems as though he may be coming good, he suddenly regresses at a rate of knots. I've had a doctor and nurse in here at different times and no one can really tell me what's happening with him. Six months! His screaming just guts me. He, I don't know, seems to hate being in his own skin or something. Never seen a case of the DTs like it. Only have to touch the guy and he goes berserk. Can't talk too loud, no bright lights, can't do anything with him. If I'd known it was going to be this hard I would never have done it," admitted Ryan.

"Give yourself a break, Detective. You need a rest every now and then. Let someone else take over for a while."

"I have to hand it to you, Michael, you did one helluva job with that room. As loud as old Lorenzo screams, I can't hear a peep from him out here. I know you didn't charge me as much as you should have. Far as I'm concerned, you're rent-free for the next six months, okay?"

"Nup, not okay by a long shot. Costing you a pretty penny to keep it up with your mate. You need the dough, so I am back to paying rent as of this week. Don't get me wrong, I liked having the extra cash in my pocket each week, but enough is enough. Maybe I can help out a bit with your friend? Not looking after him, just lessening your financial burdens a bit, eh?"

"You're alright, Michael. Good on ya."

"Think nothing of it. Least I can do. You changed nurses?"

"Yeah. I don't know if I'm right or not but something felt off. Lorenzo should be coming out of it by now. He gets a little better, starts making some conversation and eating a bit, then, POW! Back to square one with all the yelling and screaming, but not like anything I've ever seen. Way, way over the top. No proof or anything but I just thought maybe the nurse is making it so her job lasts a bit longer. She is an ex-con, so my detective antennae are twitching like mad. If he starts to get better now with no recurrences of his back-sliding, I'll know she was the problem. Then she'll be fucking sorry, I tell you. I'll come down on her like there's no fucking tomorrow. She'll rue the day she messed with me and my mate, Loz."

"I see you're giving me my padlock back?" Michael asked pointing to the padlock on the dining table between them.

"Yeah, wanted to make sure she couldn't get back in if she had a key cut or something. Had a locksmith come in and put a new deadbolt on the door. I want to guarantee that no one gets in that room without my authority."

"I hope you don't think I have entered the room?"

"What? No, why would I? Course not. No reason why *you* would want to go in there. Is there?"

"None at all. I hope it solves the problem and he gets better. No one should suffer like that."

Detective Ryan dove into his plate of wiener-schnitzel, mashed potatoes, and steamed broccoli with gusto. He reached across the table to grasp the tomato sauce with his fist, squirting an obscene amount of the liquid onto his meat. Michael watched with dismay as his meal was desecrated with the abominable, sickly-sweet flavouring. He stared in horror as the Detective continued on to spray his vegetables with a liberal, red coating as well. Michael had to endure the same performance for almost every meal he cooked, even those with which he served a rich meat gravy!

Michael prided himself on his culinary expertise in many cuisines. Most of his skills were picked up from reading books and experimenting with various recipes. He had slowly but surely been dumbing down the dishes he cooked of late to resemble nothing more than meat and three vegs, his landlord's favourite kind of food. Anything more culturally refined was wasted on the detective who knew nothing about good food despite his bragging to the contrary.

"Teaching your food to swim?"

"Huh? What was that?"

Michael pointed to the meal bathing in a pool of tomato sauce.

"Oh, I see. Ha-ha. Good one. I, um, sort of got into a habit of doing that from early on. My old man was a lousy cook. Actually, no, not lousy, lazy. He was a lazy cook. He and mum split up eventually when... Then it was just him and me as I got into high school. Dad could really cook well when he put his mind to it and made the effort. During the week he said he worked hard and was just too buggered to be bothered. Boiled fucking potatoes! I swear every meal we had... boiled fucking potatoes. Not mashed, not fried, and not baked occasionally, no. Fucking boiled, ordinary, bland old potatoes and a bit of steak. No seasoning, no gravy, no herbs, nothing! Then every couple of days he would make the most boring meal of mince and rice imaginable. If I didn't have tomato sauce on hand to drown that shit, I couldn't have stomached it. Been doing it ever since. Force of habit I probably won't ever break. Sorry if you are a bit... sensitive about it."

"I just thought you said you liked my cooking when I first came here."

"I did, and still do. If I didn't, I would really lash out and cover the meal with sauce."

Michael cringed when he thought about how much sauce that implied. The detective had poured nearly half a bottle onto the dish before him! With all that sugar and those artificial preservatives in him, no wonder the detective was looking a lot older than his years. "How's your investigation going?"

"What, the Minstrel thing? Nah, big knobs from Townsville have taken over that one. I get to chauffer the bastards all over the place while they pretend they are better than us."

"So, no new leads, no closer to catching Ingham's first real serial killer?"

"Thought you weren't interested?"

"Only because it is causing you some grief. I couldn't help but overhear some conversations in the cafe and read some of the headlines in the newspapers on the counters. Bit overblown for only two bodies if you ask me."

"For two, it probably would be a bit over the top but a third victim was found the other day. Turned out to be my old headmaster from back in the day. Shit really hit the fan then. Even some boys from Brisbane coming up to add their two bob's worth. Mr Thornton disappeared over three years ago and just turns up now. Seems like our killer has been around much longer than we thought."

"With all the modern technology we see on the TV cop shows you should have some idea of who the bloke is by now? Assuming it's a bloke."

"Bastard is too bloody clever to leave a fingerprint or a sample of DNA for us. None of the samples of dirt from the fingernails of the victims, water from the lungs or stomach contents reveal anything specific. Two bodies dumped in the channel and the headmaster was found in an empty house lot being dug up for foundations. All with traces of boot polish on their faces. Then, get this; two of them had toothpaste on their genitals, like some prank that kids pull on each other. Couldn't identify that with one of the victims though, because the genitalia was missing. All victims have been tortured so badly, for so long, it makes my blood boil. Doc figures the principal was held and tortured over the course of at least a year according to some of the older wounds. Shit! Shouldn't be telling you this. Not public knowledge yet."

"Don't worry, I won't say anything. You must have some sort of mental picture of the killer. One of those profile things?"

"Schools out, pardon the pun, on that. The psychs are conflicted over it, dishing out all sorts of bullshit. Everyone wants to get their name on a paper about this one, fighting over each other to get it right and have the opportunity to write a book about it. First, they reckon he has to be youngish, then they think he's older, real hatred, but totally calculated. A lot of planning went into these murders, so we have a typical clever bastard, probably with a high IQ. The lady shrinks reckon he's impotent, the blokes think he's latent homo maybe. How the fuck they get that I don't know. No one really knows anything that's of any use!"

"I would have thought you'd be glad to be off the case, at least, not the one responsible for solving it?"

Detective Ryan finished eating his meal as he ruminated on the question. "Yes and no. I'm torn between wanting to nail the fucker that's done this to people I know, and wanting out of the investigation because there is too much pressure from everyone to solve the bloody thing. Another man went missing more than a month ago now. An old teacher of mine as well. He may end up being victim number four the way things are going. It might be for the best that I am not responsible for the investigation anymore. If I was the first one to catch up with this psycho, I may not want to bring him in alive."

"Who's missing?"

"Can't tell you that. No offence, but I've told you too much already."

"So, why the black faces? Any explanations for that so far?"

"I don't get it. Why so many questions? Thought you didn't give a shit about the news?"

"I'm only curious because it's so close to home. You being involved, I mean. And you can't go two feet in this town without someone mentioning the damn thing. I was just making conversation. Don't want to tell me, that's your prerogative. You're right though, it makes no difference to me either way."

"It means nothing to you that people are dying at the hands of a psychotic serial killer? That either makes you a cold-hearted bastard or an idiot. Which way are you leaning?"

"That is not a very nice thing to say, Detective. I like to think I am somewhat... indifferent. I have a lot on my mind with the restoration at the moment and I simply do not have the energy to spare for all the hypotheses floating about at present. One thing I know for sure, though. There are always two sides to any story."

"What's that supposed to mean?"

"Has to be a reason for what the killer is doing and especially for the way he is doing it, don't you think? I mean... black faces? That is a pretty specific calling card. Must be a whole lot of inferences to be made from that. Seems to me that everyone is concentrating on all the wrong things. If I were investigating these murders I would be placing a lot more emphasis on finding a motive for the black faces. That seems to be the key I reckon. Find an answer to that and I think you will get closer to finding him... or her."

"What do you think it could mean?"

"My opinion is irrelevant."

"Be that as it may, you must have an opinion if you bring it up and make such a point about it?"

"Still irrelevant. Doesn't matter what I think. I'm not a cop."

"You'd be surprised at how many crimes are solved by outsiders helping the cops. Be it a hunch or a sighting of the perp caught on a home CCTV or a phone camera. An anonymous tip to the Crime Stoppers hotline accounts for a fair percentage of solved crimes hereabouts and nationally. So if you have something to say about it, spit it out. Tell me what you think the black faces of the victims could mean."

"Could be as simple as the prior persecution of a black man for all I know. I didn't say I had a theory, just that the black faces were intrinsic to the murders. Find the angle on that and you will be right on the trail to finding him or her in my humble opinion. The cruelty of the crimes indicate a certain amount of animosity? Would that be a fair assumption? You said there is hatred involved for someone to do that to another human being? That leads me to deduce a connection somewhere between the victims and the killer. Retribution for perceived wrongdoings? Revenge? Something like that."

"We've looked at all the angles, don't you worry. Every possible theory has been examined from all directions with nothing conclusive surfacing. We can come up with all sorts of theories on our own, but they remain conjecture until some piece of evidence corroborates the theory. We have no evidence connecting the victims to a single person of *any* colour at this point. We have scoured their school records and employment histories and come up with nothing. We're drawing a big fat blank on this bastard, so if you have anything at all to offer I would definitely like to hear it."

"My only thoughts were that such anger, as displayed by the killer, would seem to stem from a deep-seated base. Something going back many years to possibly a childhood matter. Something so traumatic in the killer's past that has caused the need for a reckoning of some sort. There was obviously a catalyst that sent him there, but more importantly, the black faces stand out as a blatant clue left by the killer to draw attention to his plight. It has a certain significance that the killer needs to have recognised, identified. The killer is pointing you in the right direction but no one seems to want to go there."

"All well and good, but you give nothing substantive to pursue."

"I told you that anything I said would be irrelevant. The man who doesn't even listen to the news! I'm not surprised that I have nothing to add to the investigation." said Michael rising from his chair. "Sorry I brought it up actually."

Ryan watched Michael disappearing into his room. Michael said something that flicked a switch in the detective's mind. Nothing that he was able to consciously grasp and identify, just the wafting of a ghost-like image before his mind. Ryan knew that it would not come if he forced it. In the past, anything like that required him to leave it alone. Eventually, the elusive thought or connection would make itself known. He reflected on his boarder for a moment. The man was helpful and kind to a fault, yet there seemed to be a darkness about him. Undefined though it was, there was a glimmer of uncertainty about the man, and this irked Ryan.

Ryan was nothing if not intuitive. He had relied on his inherent intuition his entire career. It had helped him out on many occasions when tying up a case had seemed all but lost to him. While the Minstrel case was no longer within his purview, it did not mean that he no longer thought about it. It was close to him because his former friends, possibly a former teacher, and his old principal were involved. Ingham was his town, his community and he would be damned if he could be told to have nothing to do with its worst serial killer. His mind was caught up in the case twenty-four-seven and not likely to stop until it was solved. He had nothing pressing to keep his mind away from the case at any rate, and ferrying around the big knobs like some lackey just fuelled the fire within.

He knew the black faces of the victims counted for something. Any fool could deduce that. It had to be significant for the killer to repeat the act so often. What it could mean? Well, there was any number of possible explanations, none of which had been proven. Sooner or later, there would be a slip-up by the killer. A clue, a fingerprint, DNA, something to give him a lead, a conclusive element to follow up on. He would show the big knobs a thing or two about local detectives. The longer the pressure was off him to solve the crime, the more scope it gave Ryan to investigate from the periphery.

He pushed away his empty plate, then rose from his chair. He removed a gold key from around his neck, which fitted the newly-installed lock on Lorenzo's room in the garage. Ryan walked to the connecting door between the kitchen and the garage, opened it and stepped through. To his left was the roll-up garage door. A metre to his right was the front wall of the room Michael had built within the garage, with its own dead-bolted door. Ryan inserted the gold key, kept on a lanyard, under his shirt. He needed to be sure that he was the only person with access to his friend's room.

Lorenzo lay on the single bed, soaked in his own sweat, sheets twisted and disarranged from his continual tossing and turning. His emaciated body looking like something out of deepest Africa where malnourished children beg for scraps of food. Ryan had to keep

Lorenzo sedated for so long that he wondered whether he might not be replacing one addiction for another. His mate's regressions seemed to cause him untold agony, the worst Ryan had ever witnessed. Mopping Loz's brow, Ryan hoped he had found a solution to the problem. He really did believe that something was amiss with the nurse he hired. Ryan couldn't fathom how his mate could simply regress so badly without some sort of interference.

CHANGES

"Detective, a word?" asked Senior Detective Sergeant Trent Barron.

Ryan eyed the burly detective from Townsville with a disdainful glare, affording the man the faintest of nods to acquiesce. He was getting close to loathing the pair of detectives he had been ferrying around for what seemed like years. Neither of them so much as glanced his way amiably, let alone included him in their investigations.

"We'll duck in here for some privacy if that's okay?"

"The interview room?" Ryan asked.

"Bit crowded in the meeting room at the moment. Not a problem is it?"

"I guess not. Just a bit unusual, that's all," said Ryan as he passed through to the room, reserved for interviewing persons of interest in a crime.

Before he could take the chair usually occupied by the interviewing officer, the Townsville detective quickly slipped into it, leaving Ryan with no choice but the other side of the table. The second Townsville detective, Brian Chalmers, slipped inside surreptitiously, to stand at the door after closing it. Ryan looked about him uncertainly before taking his seat.

"So, what can I do for you fellows? How's the case coming along?" asked Ryan shrugging off his ill-feeling toward the pair as best he could.

"Oh, you know, one small step at a time. Following leads, addressing inconsistencies, that sort of thing. Brian and I wanted to ask you a few questions about the latest victim, to get a local perspective, from someone who knew the victim. Background and town opinion of the man, social circles and that sort of thing, Detective Ryan." said Trent.

"Well, that's strange."

"Strange, Detective Ryan?"

"What, not, Arnold now?"

"If that is what you prefer, I can call you Arnold."

"That's all you have been calling me since you got here. No hint of recognition for my rank or standing within the force at all until now. But that is not what is strange, *Trent*. I've been here all along willing to exchange information and give you both the local flavour and all I have received so far is indifference, at best, from both of you. Why ask for my help of a sudden?"

"How well did you know the third victim, Edward Thornton?"

"Not well enough to know his first name was Edward, actually. I only ever knew him as Headmaster or Mister Thornton. Why?"

"We'll get to that. Ever been to his house or meet with him socially?"

"No."

"Ever meet him in your capacity as a law enforcement officer?"

"No. Why are you asking me these questions and why are we in the interview room? I'm not liking the way you are, *having a word*. What gives?"

"Just an informal chat, Arnold, no need for concern," said Trent smiling broadly, showing a perfect set of glowing white teeth. The fake smile made Ryan even more uncomfortable.

"Informal, my arse. I have every reason to be concerned... Trent, because you are acting entirely out of character and have placed me in an interview room where you are sounding like an interrogator. Now if you will excuse me... "

"Sit down please, Detective Ryan. I have a few more questions to ask you, which... Gary... has agreed to."

Hearing the name of his boss made Ryan do a double-take. Observing the seriousness of the two detectives forced Ryan to gradually resume his seat. Gazza, as he was affectionately known to his small cadre of policemen and women, always let it be known that his staff came first. For Gazza to have thrown Ryan to the wolves had him swallowing hard on the bitter taste of betrayal. Ryan was well used to the tactics being employed by the Townsville detectives. He had been taught all the same interview techniques himself over the course of his career. Make friendly and informal, get to know the interviewee on a personal level, make them believe you are a friend, on their side and so on. What purpose the detectives had for using the techniques on him was puzzling in the extreme.

"Okaaaay. You have my full and undivided attention, Trenty-boy. Fire away."

"You will address me by my given name or rank, Detective Ryan."

"Oh, Christ! Another one who gets all sensitive about his name being shortened... or lengthened in this case."

"Meaning?"

"I have a boarder who is a real stickler for that as well. Gives me the shits. Since when is it not okay to call someone, Mike or, Mickey when their name is Michael? For fuck sake."

"Be that as it may, my request stands."

"Come on, Trent. Fair go mate. One cop to another... what's up?"

"Detective Chalmers and I appreciate all the groundwork you did before we arrived on the scene and apologise for the jurisdictional conflict. We know it sucks big time to have a case taken away from you. Not our fault, though. And, we are just following orders like you. Can I just ask you a couple of questions regarding your movements and any involvement you may have had with the case after we relieved you?"

"I don't understand."

"Come on, Detective Ryan, we know you have been investigating the case on your own time. Unobrusively," admitted Trent holding up his palms to waylay the certain objections that were forthcoming from Ryan. "I make no accusations of interference. You are conducting interviews and such with friends and acquaintances on the sidelines, discreetly, making sure you never step on our toes."

"Oh, you know about that, huh?"

"Of course. We may be from the city, Detective Ryan, but we have our own sources of information here. There isn't much we don't know."

"Except the important stuff, like the identity of our worst serial killer?"

"Oh, we have a few leads to follow. We haven't yet exhausted our avenues of enquiry. Far from it. Now, if we can return to our previous question? Would you mind telling us if you have accessed any of the evidence involved in the current investigation, or examined the body of the latest victim, Edward Thornton?"

"No, I haven't. I have followed my instructions on that matter as directed by my superior."

"So, apart from your private interviews of which we are aware, you have not handled any evidence pertaining to the last victim, or participated in any post-mortem procedures?"

"Again, no. My answer hasn't changed in the last five seconds."

"Are you absolutely sure of your answer, Detective Ryan? You are one hundred per cent certain that you have not examined any evidence involved with the latest victim?"

"Jesus! What the fuck is this about? I've already told you twice now that I have not touched anything, nor been present at the morgue for the post-mortem. You are really starting to piss me off with this."

"In light of this information, Detective Ryan I must now inform you of your rights... "

Ryan sat there stunned by the revelation that he was now being treated as a person of interest in a major crime. His mind slowly absorbing the information being cited as if he were relating it to one of his prisoners, not having it directed at him. Cascading thoughts and images pummelled his brain, all vying for supremacy. None of them making much sense. Like stepping into a muted void, Ryan saw the lips moving on the detective from Townsville but heard only muffled, unintelligible whispers. Time slowed and everything took on a surreal aspect like he was locked into a Dali painting of melting clocks.

Attempting to bring order to the chaos of conflicting emotions and thoughts battling within him, Ryan gradually began the process of methodical sorting and compartmentalisation. He began to retrace his steps since the announcement of the third victim, his old high school principal, Mr Thornton. He ran through the memories of his actions and movements, attempting to confirm or deny his answers to the accusations. Then he remembered that there hadn't been any direct accusations as such, just hints of something bordering on an accusation.

"Are you telling me that I am under arrest? I am being charged with a crime? Murder? Me, a serial murderer? You're off your bloody scones!"

"At this stage, you are a person of interest in our investigations, Detective Ryan. If you submit to answering some of our questions we may not press charges immediately."

"Okay then, what have you got on me? Has to be something pretty substantial for you to go through with this charade."

"We'll get to that. Detective Ryan, why have you built a secret room in your garage?"

"Why the fuck would you be asking me about that, and how did you even know about it? If you have been to my private residence and searched it without informing me or presenting me with a signed search warrant I will nail your nuts to the wall and use 'em for target practice."

"No one has been *inside* your home, Detective Ryan."

"Then how do you know about the room I had built?"

"We have our sources. So, you admit to building a secret room in your garage?"

"Nothing secret about it."

"Did you apply for a permit to build a permanent structure within your garage?"

"Look, no, alright? I didn't get a building permit for it, but no, it is not a secret."

"What was the purpose of the room?"

"To house a sick friend of mine for a short time."

"You have a three-bedroom residence, Detective Ryan, with only two of those rooms being occupied at present. Is that correct, or do we have the wrong information there?"

"What I have or do not have in my house or how I choose to utilise the interior of my home is none of your fucking business."

"It most certainly is our business if something of an illegal nature is occurring at your residence, Detective Ryan."

"Well, then. You are just plum out of luck on that score, Detective Barron, because there is absolutely nothing of an illegal nature occurring now or at any time in the past, within the walls of my home. So go fuck yourself, you pompous arse-wipe."

Ignoring the insult, "I would say that the detainment of a fellow human being, a friend as a matter of fact, in a locked room you had specifically built for the purpose, against his will, falls heavily into the category of illegal activities, wouldn't you?"

"I don't know how you are getting a hold of this information, but you have it all arse-backwards that's for sure. I am helping my friend, Loz, Lorenzo Catani get off the grog. I had to build a room, especially for the purpose so that he wouldn't injure himself while coming down, or harm my property. All perfectly innocent and entirely explainable."

"Except there is no evidence of any doctor having prescribed any such treatment for the man you mentioned? It is a small town, Detective Ryan, and we have canvassed every doctor within the district? Unless you tell us you received an order by a doctor from out of town perhaps?"

Ryan grimaced. He had hoped to keep Doc White's name out of his scheme. "Look, since when is it wrong for a bloke to do a solid for his mate, eh? Loz was in a bad way. I've been around drunks long enough to recognise the signs that he was on the way out."

"Were you succeeding?"

"Come again?"

"Succeeding, Detective Ryan. Were you succeeding with the extremely dangerous task of helping a friend to detox without a single medical qualification or experience?"

"Weeeell... "

"Well? Were you succeeding with your amateurish attempt at helping a friend through a very dangerous treatment? What were you using to assist him in that regard? Where did you come by the medications we know you were administering?"

"How...? How could you possibly...? The nurse! That bloody bitch! She's told you a whole lot of bullshit because I had to let her go. I couldn't trust her. Just when Loz was coming good he... "

"Deteriorated, rapidly, every time the nurse was *away* apparently," said Trent.

"She accused *me* of interfering with him? I let her go because I couldn't trust *her*. Are you going to take that... woman's word, an ex-con, over mine?"

"Where is your friend now, Detective Ryan?"

"What are you talking about? You know where he is. He's in the room I had built especially for him, to help him before he died from alcohol-related causes."

"Under a false agenda?"

"Pardon?"

"Witness protection?"

"That was just... that was... "

"Covering your arse? Just in case someone like me started asking questions?"

Detective Barron let the questions sink in for a while. Allowed his interviewee to percolate the questions in his mind for a time, make him realise how foolish his answers sounded once he had the time to look their conversation from a different perspective.

"Care to tell us the exact whereabouts of your friend, Detective Ryan?"

"What, are you fucking deaf? I already told you... "

"Yes, yes. You told us he is in the purpose-built, soundproof room within your garage. Only, that isn't true, is it? We know for a fact that no one matching the description of your friend is in that room. In fact, the room is entirely empty, Detective Ryan. We know this because Ms Carlisle grew concerned enough to check on her former patient after you dismissed her abruptly, only to find the room empty."

"Now I know you are talking bullshit because there is no way that bitch could get back into the room. So, whatever she has told you is one hundred per cent fabrication. She couldn't get into the room because I changed the lock and I have the only key here... around my neck," stated Ryan as he unbuttoned his shirt to reveal the hidden key on its lanyard, realising too late how deeply he was incriminating himself.

"She didn't have to enter the room, Detective Ryan. In fact, she didn't even have to enter the garage. The garage door was open and one wall of the purpose-built room was lying flat on the garage floor when she arrived, allowing her to see into the room without entering. We did a drive-by and observed the same conditions as described by Ms Carlisle. Where is your friend, Detective Ryan?"

"I have absolutely no idea. This is all news to me."

"Own any other property, Detective Ryan?"

"Can only just afford this one mate."

"Come now, Detective Ryan. It took us only moments to discover the existence of another property in your name, located in Dungeness?"

"I haven't been there since me old man died. It was his fishing shack. I inherited it a long time ago and have never been there since I inherited. I detest fishing and I hate that swamp house."

"So the recent renovations to the garage were performed by whom?"

"Dunno what you're talking about. What renovations?"

"Is that where you moved him because the nurse twigged to your Modus Operandi?"

"My fucking what? Are you on drugs? My Modus-fucking-Operandi? I was helping him detox. I was... "

"Torturing him according to our witness."

"Come on you son-of-a-bitch, tell us what you did with him?" spat Detective Chalmers, tearing himself off the wall violently, whipping Ryan around in his chair, gripping the front of Ryan's shirt in his ham-like fist, and shouting directly into his face.

"Take it easy, Detective Chalmers, mustn't give the man an excuse to call our methods into question."

"Are you kidding me? Good cop, bad cop? Really? Oh, you two are a fucking joke. Get in my face again like that Chalmers and I'll plant my forehead on your ugly nose so hard you'll have it sticking out the back of your head. If you two are being straight up with me, that Loz is gone from my house, then I have no idea where he could be. If you reckon I had something done to my father's old fishing shack, then prove it. I don't have two spare cents to rub together to spend on any sort of renovations on a dump out in the mangroves.

"The fact that I'm even talking to you without a lawyer present should indicate my transparency. I have nothing to hide and I have done nothing wrong. I admit that taking on Loz's detox on my own was probably a stupid thing to do in hindsight, but no way was I doing anything to deliberately *harm* my friend. The reason I opted for witness protection was, yeah, to cover my arse in case, *Loz* went troppo on me, that's all. It was mentioned that the first victims were known to me and that maybe my friends and possibly myself may have been targets. While I didn't go for that at all, I did take the time to visit Loz. When I saw how far gone he was I thought I might be able to use that info and help him at the same time.

"And, as a matter of fact, I do have experience with that kind of thing. Me old man was a full-on drunk. Used to belt me and my mother around every Saturday night and then some. Had to dry him out more times than I can remember after mum finally left him, always at that old fishing shack where there were no neighbours to hear him. That's why I don't go there, too many shit memories. With,

Loz, everything would go great for a while, then it all turned to shit in the blink of an eye. I suspected the nurse of having something to do with that. That's why I sacked her."

An uneasy silence ensued while the testosterone levels cooled to a mere simmer. Chalmers returned to his silent place by the door while Trent regarded Ryan carefully.

"Care to explain how the coroner managed to find *your* hair in one of the many wounds suffered by, Mr Thornton?"

"What? That's impossible!"

"Are you doubting the veracity of forensic science?"

"I don't care what you think you found, I had nothing to do with the murders. I have not been near, nor spoken to Mr Thornton since I left High School, over twenty fucking years ago."

"We also found his DNA at your shack, confirming that Mr Thornton had been kept there while being systematically tortured for over a year!"

"Well, that explains the first bit, don't it? Course some of my hairs got mixed up with that, I was nearly living there with the old man while he was drying out. Someone had to look after him. If someone used the old man's shack to carry out the crime then some of *my* blood, sweat, tears and skin, and probably the old man's, were bound to contaminate the evidence. So while you are here busting my chops over some bullshit that rotten nurse cooked up, the real killer is running around using old places around here to torture people, and now it would appear that he has Loz."

"That is one possible way of looking at it. Another may be that we have a suspect with connections to all three victims, who abducted one, Lorenzo Catani and kept him locked in a purpose-built, sound-proofed room against his will, while allegedly inflicting tortures of unknown methods upon his person. Then we have evidence from the suspect show up on the third victim, the only forensic evidence to have been found during the entire investigation, I might add, and traces of the third victim's blood found in the remodelled garage of a beach-side shack, close to where all the victims were found, owned by the suspect. Now you tell me, what we are supposed to infer by those facts, Detective Ryan?" remarked Trent, reclining in his chair with a satisfied smirk.

Ryan knew that look. It was the confident smirk of a detective who believed he had solved a crime, who was looking forward to wrapping up the case file in a pretty silk bow before handing it all off to the public prosecutor. After everything had been duly noted with crossed 'T's and dotted 'I's, all that was left for the detective, was to appear in court to testify as to his part in the arrest and subsequent interview of the defendant. The two fools from Townsville thought they had the Minstrel Killer pegged, tagged and bagged. His boss believed it as well, which was why Ryan was being hung out to dry.

Ryan admitted that the evidence against him, while wholly circumstantial, would be enough to sway *him* if he were the lead detective. He knew the whole witness protection angle to protect himself against any backlash from Loz once he regained his senses, was tenuous at best. That his ploy might completely backfire to implicate him in some plot to abduct and torture his friend was, while laughable in reality, unsettling in hindsight. Ryan could see how some of his actions of late may have been misconstrued. If he was wrong about the nurse, he could understand how that might play against him in a very damaging way. It then begged the question of how his friend had deteriorated during his treatments if the nurse was not responsible. No one else had a key to the room. He was foolish enough to have admitted that earlier. *Was it even true, though? His boarder had given him the lock with two keys originally. What if Michael possessed a third key? There was no reason for Michael to want to harm Loz if he did have a key.*

Ryan's conditioned instincts were going into overdrive in order to sort through all the information to arrive at possible conclusions. Trouble was, while he knew none of the allegations against him were true, other than detaining a friend against his will, it looked to all intents and purposes like he was guilty. He was going to need some extraordinary luck or clever thinking to work his way out of the mess he was in.

Trent Barron reclined further on his metal chair, risking overbalancing as he rocked back on its two rear legs. His smug countenance did not fully reveal just how confident he felt that he had solved the crime of the century. His name would be synonymous with the best of the best in law enforcement history. His name would appear in every paper and tabloid for years to come as the person to solve the North's first true serial killer crime. With one person known to be missing, they were looking at probably four victims so far. Who knew how many others there were. Trent was basking in the glow of triumph. His wife and children would be bursting with pride when he picked up his haul of medals and accolades for this one. He may land a book deal and maybe even retire to a lecture circuit. He would finally have the money to take his wife on a real honeymoon. Magnetic Island was great, but it wasn't Paris or Rome.

Brian Chalmers, Trent's long-time partner sensed the victory in his bones and could see his partner lining up the suspect for the *coup de grâce*. Trent was practically salivating. Brian always deferred to his partner, never minding in the least that Trent got to deliver the final nail in the coffin nine times out of ten. He knew his role in the interview process and that suited him just fine.

Brian accepted that his partner could present better in the role of chief interviewer. He was not made of the same stuff. While both men were of similar height and build, their personalities were light-years apart. Brian harboured latent tendencies that he had not shared with another living soul and Trent was married with three burly boys set to take after their handsome father. Brian sighed inwardly.

Ryan became agitated in the ensuing silence, feeling the menacing noose tightening inexorably around his flabby neck. He was not used to being on the receiving end. He did not like it one little bit. In fact, he couldn't stand the thought that anyone saw him as a criminal. Being a copper was more than a job to him, it was his life. Every time his old man belted the crap out of him over fanciful issues on Saturday nights after he staggered home from the pub, he swore he would get him one day. Battered, bruised and bleeding, he would then have to cop more of the same when he tried to come to his precious mum's rescue. Ryan knew he was going to become a cop before he entered high school. It was around the first time he laid into his pop with all his might and came out on top one fateful Saturday night.

The following week Ryan warned his old man before he sauntered off down the road for his usual binge that if he came home drunk and raised one finger or uttered one word in anger, that he would be stone-cold-dead the following morning. Peter Ryan did not return home that evening, nor any other Saturday evening for the rest of his life. Instead, he staggered to his car and somehow managed to drive himself to his fishing shack in Dungeness. Sunday afternoon he would come back to the house with a hangover as always, but with nothing unkind to utter. He never again spoke a word to his son. That was okay by Ryan. He lived in semi-peaceful conditions thereafter. Arnold Ryan lived in the same house until his father was over seventy and so thin as to be almost transparent.

Although Ryan was loathed to do so, wishing him dead the entire time, he took on the responsibility of drying his father out on several occasions. He would stay on the wagon for six to eight weeks at a stretch, then go on a bender for weeks at a time. The last time Ryan cared for him, staying on in the dilapidated, rusting, iron shack, with his father remaining as silent as a corpse, he watched as the old bastard finally expired. It was one of Ryan's happiest memories. He hated his father more than he could say, blaming him for the cancer that finally killed his mum. Blaming him for his lousy life. When Ryan saw his father's chest rise ever so slightly for the last time, he walked to his bedside where he looked down upon the emaciated frame occupying the single bed with the horsehair mattress. He bent over to him to make sure the old fuck had carked it and spat squarely in his face with a thick glob of phlegm. *'Good riddance. You really were an evil cunt.'* Ryan remembered whispering above the corpse.

Ryan did not attend the funeral. Never gave his father's burial or graveside a single thought. The cheapest service available was purchased with not a single word to be spoken for the deceased. Ryan would not allow one word of consolation to enter his vicinity, nor brook any false platitudes. He told anyone that had a mind to ask that he was pleased as punch that the old bastard had finally had the sense to do the right thing by dying.

Ryan became a cop because he wanted to make sure other little boys didn't suffer the same abuse as he did. He dedicated his life to the cause, working untold hours to advance himself. Unfortunately for Ryan, his superiors recognised the investigative talent in him, promoting him to detective in short order. Ryan wanted nothing more than to plod the streets as a uniform cop keeping an eye out for arseholes like his old man. His reputation grew and every man in Ingham knew what he risked if he raised a hand to strike a woman or child while Arnold Ryan wore a badge. Many a wasted mongrel had tried and failed taking on Ryan when he was called to a domestic dispute. Ryan actively sought those calls while the rest of the force avoided them like the plague.

A deep sadness enveloped Ryan at the thought of his career ending in such shame. He would not, of course, accept things lying down. He would fight the allegations with all his might. He would probably have to sell the house to pay for his defence. *What the fuck, it was only money.* The most pressing question. *Where the fuck was Loz?*

JUDGMENT

His head throbbed so badly that his thoughts were obliterated. He was unable to focus, unable to move, incapable of cognitive processes. He was in the dark somewhere and all his energies were centred on the one overriding, completely dominant factor, an inexorable urge to drink. His body and mind coveted the oblivion of alcohol so desperately that nothing else mattered to him. His movements of the past few days or weeks were unimportant and totally incomprehensible to him anyway. He had been living some sort of horrific nightmare where all he wanted was to curl up inside a bottle to drown out the pain and the visions.

He could not recall the events leading up to his present condition, could not recall his last moment of clarity and had no recollection of anything beyond the alcoholic haze of many years. He knew he had lived in town at some time, then moved a few times to... *everywhere* it seemed. Always on the move, next stop, next hovel, park bench, wherever, until even those memories were lost to him. He vaguely recalled a bridge somewhere. Did it mean anything? He didn't really care. Didn't want to know. Couldn't remember and had no need to. In the end, it all came back to where he could get his next bottle? How he would manage to pay for it and where he would have to go to drink it without being hassled by cops or Abos.

Bloody Abos would always know if you had some fags or booze on you. Come bumming around, making you feel guilty about not sharing, and fair enough too. They were not averse to sharing when they had some grog or ciggies. He was known to bounce around on top of a black woman or two in his day as well. Before the booze and bad living had put an end to such proclivities. At least he would not catch a dose again. *That sucked big time! Fucking dirty bitches running around giving a fellow a dose of the clap while he was too drunk to refuse a roll in the grass! Jesus, but his head hurt! Where the fuck am I? Why can't I move? Everything hurts like a...*

"Good morning, Lorenzo," said the voice once a light had been turned on. "Glad to see you could join us. Touch and go there for a while. Not feeling too well, huh? Not surprised. You've been on a cocktail of different drugs over the last few months that were bound to leave you with good old-fashioned withdrawal symptoms that might cause some pretty nasty headaches, to say the least."

Lorenzo watched through slitted eyelids as the stranger circled him, making him dizzy and nauseous. The bonds securing him to the platform beneath him were some kind of rubber with a familiar smell taking him back to his childhood. *Inner tubes!* He could never forget that particular smell. He worked for a time with the old lady who owned and ran the bike shop next to the hairdressing salon when he was young. It paid enough to keep him in ciggies and mull all through high school. He wriggled against the taut rubber tubing across his forehead, chest, hips, knees and ankles. The half-hearted effort left him weak and wheezing.

"No use struggling, Loz. In your condition, you would be hard-pressed to stretch your bonds even minutely, let alone escape them. You present rather a dilemma for me, Lorenzo. I find myself having to care for you first in order to entertain myself later. At the moment, there is nothing I could do to you to inflict more pain and misery than you are experiencing as a result of your own bad habits and lifestyle. So your first round of torture will be of your own making, with me rendering medical assistance to ensure you last long enough to endure the second round where things will become really interesting."

"Who…who…are...?"

"Who am I? Your worst fucking nightmare, that's who. You have been my guest for a while now and there were times I really didn't think you were going to survive long enough to appreciate my skills. You are a useless old drunk, Lorenzo. Seems like most of the inhabitants of this berg are these days. Your body has wasted away to mere skin and bones while your mind is barely functioning. I have had to keep you on a strict regimen of high-performance drugs and protein infusions to prevent you from leaving my company too soon. That would be like a premature evacuation, haha, which would never do. Over the next few weeks, you will start to feel the withdrawal hit you all over again as I gradually decrease the drugs that are masking it at present. You will suffer like every other two-bit alcoholic who enters rehab. I am going to enjoy watching you suffer, but I will not be able to... enhance that suffering again. Not just yet. It will be a lesson in patience for me.

"If your brain ever recovers some of its higher functions, you may be able to work out who I am. I will then ask you some questions, which I will want answered. Failure to satisfy my curiosity will result in pain on an unheard-of scale. You are usually too inebriated to actually feel anything. I have the perfect solution for that in my little bag of tricks. A certain serum I helped to develop while I was overseas. Virtually untraceable even with modern-day science. Mostly natural, so it doesn't show up in the usual toxicology screens. A doctor would really have to know what he was looking for to find it. My little concoction, tried and tested on simpleton volunteers from impoverished families promised a meal or two, will attune your senses to unimaginable heights."

"But... why?"

"Penance. You must be repaid in full for the treatment meted out by you on innocents."

"Off ya fucking rocker. I never... "

"I hardly expect you to remember anything at all in your present condition you mangy mongrel. It will take more time than initially intended. I had to change tactics drastically because your mate abducted you. That put a real spanner in the works that did. Bloody do-gooder! His turn is coming don't you worry. Clay, Kugelweis, Mr Ball, and old Thornton have already had the pleasure of my company. Mr Ball has decided to stay awhile longer. Not *much* longer though. Sewed him up good as new, pushed his guts back in and started all over again. He has withstood the harshest of my treatments so far. Really quite surprising. I thought he would die of fright before I even began to administer my loving attention upon him."

"Don't under... understand. What could I have... what di... "

"What did you do to deserve this? You and your friends were responsible for ruining many lives as you laughed your way through school. Your verbal and physical torment spiralled in intensity as you aged and grew more confident. You thought it was all just a hoot, didn't you? Well, there was one boy in particular who gained your malevolent attention. One you singled out for daily abuse for many years. Your crimes against him are just too many to list and that is the reason you find yourself here at my mercy."

"Oh, oh shit! Smelly-Melly? No... "

Before Lorenzo could say one word more, his captor had retrieved a tomahawk from somewhere nearby, severing Lorenzo's left hand from the wrist with one almighty, THWACK! Lorenzo screamed more from the startling impact and sound than from any pain he had yet to feel. He watched in utter horror as his captor brandished a butane torch, aiming the flame at the stump of his arm spewing a fountain of blood. *That* pain was something Lorenzo *could* feel. Nothing would mask the effect of the flame searing and sealing the flesh like a sirloin steak on the barbeque. Lorenzo was restrained from thrashing around too violently in order to keep him 'safe' from further injury. His captor wanted no competition from accidental injuries causing more harm than he. He wanted to savour the fruits of his malevolent skills.

ATTRACTION

Cindy Naylor did not check herself in the cafe's bathroom mirror before returning to her table for the breakfast she had ordered. She knew she would see the tell-tale wrinkles forming at the corners of her eyes and mouth revealing the age and the life she lived. Too many parties with far too many nights ending up in a stranger's bed, hungover and regretting her excesses. Alcohol, drugs if she could get them, and lots of sex with all the wrong kinds of blokes. Fellows whom she remembered for only the briefest period after their romp in the sheets.

Not for the first time did Cindy take stock of her situation with a frankness that she and others found disturbing at times. Facing up to reality was a complete downer, but she had to force herself to look closely at what had become of her life. Born and raised by loving parents in a shithole named Ingham, in Northern Queensland. A town of wogs, nips, chinks, micks, and abos mainly, with a smattering of other nationalities in the mix, Cindy had laid and tested them all, she felt. Not once did anyone strike her as the kind of man she would like to move in with, have a relationship with lasting longer than a week. God forbid *marrying* any of the losers!

Her good sense implored her to take it easy for a change. Rest the kidneys and the liver while it was still possible. Maybe even start to recover from all the addictions that assailed her? Nah, she knew she was getting too old to simply stop, and she saw little point in doing so. She had no one to stop for. Nothing to rescue herself from. Loneliness was everything it was cracked up to be.

Lately, though, she began to suspect that she might not be able to rustle up a bit of company as easily as she once had. Slim pickings and too many men knew of her reputation about town. Menfolk, in general, seemed a lot younger than they used to be. It was hard to find someone around her age to talk to these days. They were all either young pups or old farts.

God, her throat was dry! Felt like the bottom of the proverbial birdcage. If she hadn't known better, she would have sworn that whatshisname had taken a dump in her mouth last night. Cindy thought she may have to get rid of that thought very quickly before having a bite to eat. No, Cindy Naylor did not require the mirror to see that the once crystalline green eyes had turned a little milky, that her perky little breasts had definitely sagged of late. The lipstick and mascara she wore no longer successfully hid the ravages of time and intemperance on her once beautiful face. Cindy managed to hold down an urge to vomit as she passed the mirror, mulling over her entire life with profound sadness. She smoothed down her lightly wrinkled blouse and denim skirt before heading back out to the cafeteria on Herbert Street.

Back in the day, the old Wintergarden Theatre next to the cafe had old canvas seats. As uncomfortable as those seats were, she longed to go back there just one more time, sitting in the back row with Victor Kugelweis, the most beautiful boy she had ever seen.

Oh, how she had swooned for that boy. Losing her virginity in that theatre on that particular night with the most handsome boy in Ingham, possibly all of Australia. Only to be rebuffed a few days later when she confronted him about having another girl on his arm.

Damn, but she chose wrong every single time back then! She went around with Victor's mates just to get a rise out of him. Nothing! Didn't lift an eyebrow, even when she let Clay fondle her breasts openly, right there in the same cafe where she now found herself.

Clayton McCormack and Arnold Ryan, what arseholes. How Vic could possibly have hung around with such losers was beyond her understanding. Add that pathetic piece of crap, Loz, to the mix and they were just awful together. Constantly trying to outdo one another. See who could get the loudest laugh or the most admiration from the girls. They couldn't see how negatively they impacted on the females. How pathetic Cindy and her friends thought they had become over time, especially after what they did to that poor boy. Cindy couldn't recall his name anymore but she saw the kid clearly in her mind as if it were yesterday. Often bleeding from one wound or another, or wheeling his broken bicycle home after having it destroyed by the thugs. Running naked through the schoolyard after having his clothes hidden or torn to shreds.

She had silently admired the boy for holding his own against the gang of four pitted against him. He never showed fear, never showed pain, or humiliation, no matter how hard they beat him or taunted him. No matter what they did, that boy showed more guts than all the other boys put together. Cindy and her friends soon shifted their allegiances, leaving the gang of four much to themselves for the rest of high school.

Cindy recalled only a little of what happened to them after that. She knew that Ryan had ended up on the police force. She had been picked up by him more than once for drunk and disorderly behaviour. She also knew that Lorenzo Catani had really done a number on himself, living in a cardboard box under a bridge, from what she could gather of the local gossip. If she wasn't careful, that might be her a few years. Of the other two, especially Vic, she had deliberately wiped the memories.

Cindy made her way down the stained linoleum floor to her booth, only to find a man seated there. Cindy fumed inwardly at the invasion of her reserved booth. Had she not placed her light cardigan and overnight bag on the seat in plain sight for anyone to see? Could the arsehole not see that the booth was taken? Cindy was in no mood for this kind of trespass. Everyone knew it was her booth, where she sat every morning to have the same bacon, eggs, and hash browns without fail for more years than she could remember. Just as she was about to let loose with a volatile rant...

"I'm sorry. I didn't see your gear there until after I had ordered. There was nowhere else to sit. I have been here for a time now and I am nearly finished, so if you don't mind, I'll just rush through this and be on my way?"

Completely deflated after winding herself up, Cindy found herself shrugging off the infamy perpetrated by the handsome stranger, to sit opposite him with a smile. "That's okay, take your time, no need to rush on my account. I was a while in the bathroom. Bit of a rough night. I'm surprised *my* brekky hasn't arrived yet," declared Cindy casting about for the waitress who knew her order off by heart. "I'll have to have a go at Marla for that."

"My fault again, I'm afraid. When you didn't appear after your breakfast arrived earlier, I had them take it back to keep warm for you. Sorry again... Miss."

"Cindy, Cindy Naylor. Thank-you... "

"Michael Miller. Pleased to meet you," he said shaking hands with Cindy over the table just as the waitress sauntered over to the table with Cindy's plate of food.

"Thanks, Marla. I thought you may have forgotten me this morning," said Cindy shyly.

"Goodness, how could I ever do that to our best customer? Just as well the gentleman here asked me to put it in the oven for you. Wouldn't do to be eating cold bacon and eggs, love."

"Thanks, Marla, you're a peach," Cindy said with an affectionate smile.

"Oh, don't thank me, love, thank your gentleman friend there."

"He's not... " Cindy let the statement trail off as Marla quickly slipped away to serve another customer waving at her. She turned to find Michael Miller disregarding the conversation and Marla's last remark as he ploughed into his breakfast with gusto. "Not from around here then, Michael?"

"Not lately, no."

"Meaning...?"

"Just that I used to live here a while ago."

"How long ago?"

"Why do you ask?"

"Oh, it's, it's just that I've lived here all my life and don't recall having seen you here. Not likely to forget a face like yours."

"Oh? You mean because of the scars?"

"What? No, no, of course not. Oh shit, I've put my foot in it again, haven't I? Please forgive me. I'm not quite with it this morning. I meant that I would not have forgotten a good-looking man like yourself had I seen in him in the past. I didn't even realise you had... scars. Sorry."

"Apology accepted then. Now if you don't mind, I'm just going to finish my breakfast and leave you alone if that's alright?"

"Wow, that's quite the brush-off. I just gave you a compliment."

"And...?"

"Oh, you're probably gay then. My bad... "

"You automatically think that because I didn't acknowledge your compliment and haven't engaged in small talk with you that I am gay? Perhaps I am uncomfortable with forward women who say inappropriate things at the breakfast table? If the roles were reversed and I had tried to hit on you this soon after our meeting I am sure you would have been quite offended and possibly even called for the manager to have me removed."

"Look, buddy... "

"I am not, nor ever will be, anybody's 'buddy'. Kindly stop insulting me and please, just allow me to finish. Ah, I see a spot has just opened up."

Michael moved himself and his plate of breakfast to the empty booth quickly before Cindy was able to think of anything snappy to say. Cindy sat there wondering what on earth she had done or said to make the man so angry with her. Despite her brain being sluggish because of last night's excesses, she could not quite recall anyone having ever treated her so dismissively. She was used to snaring her men without much effort. Not that she was actually... Well, she guessed she may have been trying to sweet-talk the man a little. Outright rejection just did not sit well with Cindy Naylor, head cheerleader, high school captain and everybody's idea of a good time.

The man, Michael somebody-or-rather, *Miller*, she thought, sat in a booth against the opposite wall of the diner a few rows down from her. The food before him gradually disappearing into his mouth. It galled her that the man had paid scant attention to her and had the temerity to take her compliment for granted as if she gave them out willy-nilly to just anyone. Of course, she absolutely did give them out to just about anyone to get what she wanted. Flattery was her most effective tool in apprehending her next victim... er... lover. It was a game that Cindy played extremely well, a competition of sorts, with herself, to triumphantly proclaim success over the opposite sex at will.

They, men, had only themselves to blame. If they had not used her so shamelessly in her youth only to cast her aside like yesterday's leftovers, she might not be the person she was today. Bloody Vic Kugelweis and cohorts, *and those others*. Cindy had made a vow to herself after that painful episode when she had fallen madly in love with the demi-God-like Scandinavian bombshell. He had taken that precious commodity reserved only for someone very special, her virginity. After that he then moved on to his next conquest without so much as a second glance at the distraught girl he had left in his wake. The girl who had nearly ended it that night, slashing at her wrists with the bent blade she had extracted from the disposable razor.

The scars still showed even now, right there on her wrists for all the world to see if they had a mind to. Well, they were hardly visible to an outsider anymore, if truth be told. To her, they stood out clearer than blood on a crisp white sheet, her blood as it had pumped out in pulsating jets that night. If she hadn't yelped involuntarily at the sight, her parents may never have found her in time. Her stint in the hospital after that, in group therapy and one-on-one consultations with the shrinks, was a nightmare she would never relive no matter how bad things became. She would never again fall into that bottomless pit of despair. And definitely not over... men!

She almost spat on the floor as she had often seen men do. As filthy and disgusting as the habit was, it aptly described her feelings toward men. She made it through all the mumbo-jumbo dished out by the shrinks. Listened to all the weeping drivel spewed out by the other girls in her group; simpering, fractured, boring females. All slaves to the opposite sex. Like life couldn't continue without them. Well, she had felt that way once, and once was the only time she would give the world the satisfaction of that little show of weakness.

Cindy Naylor did not allow her one mistake to go unheeded in her mind like all the other girls she had seen returning again and again to the clinics with the same problems. She had learned her lesson particularly well. She fed off that lesson, ensuring that no man ever attained a fraction of her affections, ensuring she used every man she could, then tossed them as quickly aside as she had been. Especially after... Well, she was not about to visit that memory any time soon.

The town, the world, was full of Vic Kugelweisses, thinking they were gods, lording it over helpless women. Some men beating their wives and children, some cheating on their spouses, some just being jerks. She, Cindy Naylor, would see to it that they paid for their indiscretions or unseemly behaviour. Many an Ingham wife received an anonymous tip that their husband had cheated on them with her, never revealing whom that might be. She gave them information only a wife would know about intimate details of their husband's anatomy. If the foolish woman did not believe her, then she would soon receive a photo or two in the mail. Cindy always took snapshots of every lover she had seduced, while they slept off the effects of sex.

They were pathetic. Couldn't even last more than a few moments after sex before they were snoring their heads off. Not that Cindy really minded. It saved the ridiculous small talk and inane confessions of love or guilt assailing their little minds. It was then a simple matter of taking a photograph of their most noticeable feature in an area not normally visible. It could be a birthmark on an inner thigh or bum cheek, a tattoo, a piercing, or simply a photo of his member that his little woman would recognise instantly, flaccid or not. Of course, nothing worked quite as well as just taking a picture of the sleeping man as he lay in the nude upon a strange bed. That was quite sufficient nine times out of ten.

There was not the slightest spark of remorse for the affected women in that scenario. Cindy felt it her duty, a sworn obligation, to show these woman what worms they had for partners. How incredibly fragile was their hold over them? How unbelievably weak they were when it came to the wiles of another woman. That Cindy was assisting in sending half of the female population of Ingham into therapy did not register in her mind. That she was personally responsible for an increased rate of suicide among young females in Ingham did not enter her thinking. She could not allow facts like those to dissuade her from her calling. She would continue with her purpose as long as she had breath in her lungs.

The bastard across the aisle from her represented a serious blemish in that record of achievement. A worrying pre-cursor to a possible future in which she may no longer be able to attract members of the opposite sex with her alluring looks and seductive personality. A time when age, gravity and nature placed at risk all she had worked so hard to attain. Of course, Cindy never thought that her cruelty and self-disgust had been the sole cause of her destructive behaviour.

She did not recognise that her mission was causing her self-immolation. Her subconscious was clearly alerting her to the fact that she was erring in life by inflicting such pain and suffering on members of her gender, yet she ignored those warnings to her own detriment.

Without understanding the cause, Cindy Naylor continued to abuse her body with a steady intake of alcohol and drugs, a diet of nothing more than take-away food, and a lifestyle that almost certainly would attract another bout or two of a venereal disease or worse.

Seething inside at the insulting rebuke from the stranger, her senses were quivering with the imminent challenge. It may be the last hoorah for Cindy Naylor before she hung up her metaphorical spurs. The challenge of conquest was upon her and she would brook no interference from friend or foe. The foe being herself more often than not, warning her to cease and desist before her mind finally gave out. Cindy had been a powder keg ready to explode the moment she set her mind on her course of action all those years ago. The mind was both delicate and almost indestructible at the same time. With resolve, it was possible for it to withstand the rigours of pressure and mental strain for long periods, however, not indefinitely. There had to be a reprise in the symphony of hardship assailing the fragile mind. The melody would fracture it eventually. Cindy's mind was nearing ground zero.

Knowing that an eventual end to her mission was inevitable, was not the same as admitting defeat. Cindy was not yet ready to concede. She accepted this one, final challenge. She would make it her swan song. She understood that time had been against her of late, but she sensed that she still had a role to play one more time.

He obviously saw what Cindy had known she would see in the bathroom mirror had she taken the time to look. She would have to clean up her act to seduce the stranger. She would have to apply the necessary creams and make-up to bring back the vitality of her once beautiful features. She would have to tone up again to make sure there was some bounce left in the breasts, and that her skin regained that healthy glow. It would all help to give her back some self-esteem and some assurance of longevity if her mind and body were clear of substances and returned to a healthy state. A win-win situation.

MISSING

Ingham rocked one summer's evening, but not from any concert. The explosion was heard near and far, sending the townsfolk into a panic not seen in Australia since the time Darwin, in Australia's far north, had been targeted by Japan in February of 1942. The foundations of Ingham trembled as the devastating blast tore through a well-known landmark, Ingham High School. Debris was scattered over a wide area, landing within the township and surrounds. Like the black devils experienced during the cane burn-offs of the past, before cutting the cane green became possible and preferable, the town of Ingham was visited with a black rain once more.

Of course, in the modern-day climate of terrorism, thoughts of a car bombing or something even more sinister, was on everyone's mind, including the police. Sirens heralded the arrival of a squad of emergency vehicles converging on the disaster area. While most did not immediately recognise the school as having been the target, they were aware of the general location of the catastrophic blast. The citizens of Ingham scattered in all directions, panicked with thoughts of further explosions. Pandemonium reigned as many motor accidents added to the confusion.

People rushed to get home, ignoring road rules, to protect their loved ones or to check on their whereabouts. The streets were flooded with frantic folks unsure of what to do, having never experienced such a calamity. One would have thought that with the ever-present danger of cyclones menacing the northern regions of Australia that the citizens of Ingham might be better prepared for emergencies. Alas, such was not the case, as many more were injured and killed through blind panic, than from the initial blast. Gunfire could be heard as some folks had armed themselves for a possible invasion, shooting innocent folk who were coming to check on their safety.

Older people in the retirement villages and nursing homes were suffering seizures and heart attacks as their carers headed home. Panic bordering on mania gripped the town in its repercussive clutches. Authorities, stretched to their absolute limits, were unable to restore peace and order. Human error was eventually blamed for accidentally triggering the Cyclone Warning System whereby the local news radio and television stations were automatically broadcasting the repetitive and annoying sirens of impending doom from the skies. Anyone with a moment to reflect would have known that the stillness in the air, albeit littered with ash and floating embers, did not presage the onset of cyclonic conditions.

The floating embers, namely the air-borne conflagration of thousands of textbooks and notebooks stored at the public high school, sparked innumerable spot fires throughout the district, touching on the desiccated cane fields in readiness for harvest, with drying leaves eagerly accommodating the embers' lust for propagation. Parched backyards and fields alike attracted more fires, exhausting the dwindling resources of the besieged township. Ambulances, the hospital, and all the clinics in town were at capacity dealing with the injured and ailing flooding their premises.

For over twenty-four hours after the blast, authorities still struggled to restore order or contain the fires threatening Ingham. Looting had subsided marginally as all police personnel, retired, on leave, active or otherwise had been recalled to maintain an authoritative presence on the streets. Units from neighbouring towns and cities were seconded to assist with the action.

"Well, hello stranger. Care to tell me what's going on and where you've been?" asked Michael in irritation.

"For once, I'm glad you're not keeping up with the news, 'cause it's all bullshit. We are not in danger of a cyclone and there don't appear to be terrorists responsible for the explosion that wiped Ingham High off the map. I was detained for a while," Ryan explained in an uncomfortable manner.

"Detained? Your 'fellow officers' went through this joint like rabid dogs, including my bloody room! You were nowhere to be found and unreachable by phone or otherwise. Care to elucidate?"

"Care to tell me how Loz managed to get out of a locked room for which I had the one and only key?"

"What has that got to do with anything, and why should I be able to supply you with an answer?"

"I assume that Loz had some help seeing as he was incapacitated at the time. I was told that an entire wall had been disassembled and was lying on the garage floor when the police arrived?"

"I don't know what you are implying, and I am more than pissed off at having had to deal with all your crap over the last few days, including cleaning everything up after the raid, and having to go into town to pay your electricity before it was cut off! So don't you dare come the highbrow detective with me. I don't know what happened to your mate or who helped him out of the room where you detained him against his will. Something I will make sure to remind the authorities if ever the question arises, Detective Ryan. I would be very careful about your tone with me and what you imply."

"Why is the room back in one piece?" asked Ryan, ignoring the implied threat in Michael's response.

"Can we get out of the hallway to discuss this like civilised human beings? I don't like you attempting to cower me with your bulk in this confined space."

Without waiting for a reply, Michael turned abruptly to enter the living room where he sat on a single lounge chair with a cup of cooling coffee resting on an occasional table beside it. Michael made himself comfortable as he watched Ryan reluctantly follow him to a lounge chair opposite.

"I fixed the wall in the process of cleaning this place up. As for your friend, I have no idea where he might have gone other than back to his usual digs to get pissed again. No way are you going to keep *him*, off the grog. Too far gone."

"How could Loz manage to remove the wall from the inside?

You said you made it a permanent structure as per our agreement."

"Loz did not get himself out, he had help from the outside. The stud walls I put up were sheeted on the inside, first with plasterboard and then acoustic cladding. I made the walls up in frames which I then bolted together and secured with masonry anchors to the concrete floor. How much more permanent did you want it?"

"Why wouldn't you have nailed the frames together as a normal carpenter would?"

"I really don't like your tone, Ryan. My nail gun happened to be at the shop for repairs at the time, and I didn't fancy a stint on the hammer again. I did use batten screws as well as bolts to secure the frames to each other. More than sufficient for permanency in anyone's books. I assumed it was your pals that removed the wall when they raided the joint. I also assumed you had been 'detained' for what you were doing to your friend. I knew that the coppers' buddy system would eventually see you released, though."

"Loz is missing, and they thought I had something to do with that as well... "

"As well as what?"

"As well as the Minstrel murders."

"And yet here you are."

"They called on everyone available to help restore order after the school was blown up."

"Convenient."

"I'm not off the hook yet. They found things which place me in an awkward position. Unexplainable things."

"Doesn't explain your sudden attitude toward me once again."

"The jury is still out on you, Mr Miller. I admit that I have never fully warmed to you. Something about you gets under my skin. I may have overreacted about some things, but I don't trust you, and I guess I never will. I would prefer if you found alternative accommodation. I will have your notice in writing to you by this afternoon, and your bond money in full upon your vacation of the premises, including the fortnight's advance payment made by you if you vacate by this afternoon. If you give me a forwarding address, I will get your mail to you?"

"Just as well I am not dependent on this house for a place to lay my head. The reno is coming along nicely. No need to forward mail as I never indicated to anyone that I live at this address. All my mail, I'm surprised you failed to notice, arrives at a mailbox I rent at the post office. I will be gone by no later than four this afternoon. Be sure to have my letter and my bond money in full by then. I warn you... "

"Your money will be here. I haven't touched a bank account that I inherited from the old man. Even though he was a lousy rotten drunk, he still managed to put away quite a sum for a rainy day. I never wanted anything to do with it, but I couldn't think of a better person to have it than you."

"You really have it in for me, don't you? I have never once... "

"I've been a detective for a long time, Miller, a long time. I have a sense about people. I understand more about them than they do most times. I sense a darkness about you. There is an undercurrent that flows beneath the facade you display. There are ripples that I detect when I am speaking to you and observing you that have me on edge, that have my nerves quivering like a well-plucked guitar string. I detect a falseness in you that you don't quite succeed in disguising. You and I will cross paths in a professional capacity one day, Mr Miller, and on that day I will be happier than most to see *you* squirm for a change." seethed Ryan as he vacated his chair.

He walked to the kitchen where he reached inside the fridge to retrieve a can of VB. He popped the ring pull, all the while watching Michael's face with intense interest. Michael merely smiled with feigned amusement at the detective's words. He was unconcerned with the detective's threats.

Michael Miller repaired to his room where he would see to packing his few personal possessions before vacating the premises. He smiled to himself as he ruminated on the words from the detective. "I sense a darkness about you." It was an odd thing to say about a relative stranger. It was also very vague and disturbing for Michael, as he had witnessed that darkness in others. He had been around the block a few times and seen things, experienced things he would rather forget. He had seen people who exhibited that very darkness that the detective mentioned. He did not think that Ryan knew just how dark people could become.

Michael had experienced more than his share of cruelty at the hands of people suffering discontent with themselves and the world. He had seen the worst of human nature in war-torn countries across the globe, particularly in Africa. He had seen suffering and torture on a scale that made Hitler seem a pussy in contrast. He had seen the living heart torn from a human's chest, still beating, black as coal. The sadistic mongrel who had finally been captured by the African tribe with whom Michael had been staying, was brought to the centre of the village of round huts, rondavels, made from local soil mixed with sacred cow dung.

The white man they brought into the village had been caught poaching on their tribal lands. He had also been taking liberties with small children he found wandering along the well-used paths, ensuring their silence afterwards by stringing them from the nearest tree - by their scrotums if a boy or with a meat hook piercing the vagina if a girl. He had disembowelled a few tribesmen when cornered against a kopje where his escape route was compromised. Michael remembered clearly the dead, soulless eyes of the man they brought in, bloodied and half-dead. They tied him to a post in the centre of the village where he was kept barely alive for days in the blistering hot sun. In the man's position at the base of the pole, too exhausted to remain standing, every villager took their time to urinate, or expectorate on him, or throw their faeces at him.

He was offered only cow's piss to drink and shit to eat. One morning, after the tribe had held a meeting of the elders the previous evening, where much was inhaled and consumed that could alter a man's perception of the world, the Shaman, in full regalia, pranced noisily around the pole shaking rattles of human bones and shrieking maniacally. The villagers formed a mute circle around the scene, Michael included. He watched in fascination and dread as the Shaman finally made an end to the ceremony. Breathless, eyes turning up in the sockets to reveal only the whites in a demonic display, the Shaman produced a knife of carved shale from his coat of lion's hide. He squatted before the victim in the familiar way of the native African, able to squat at rest for many hours at a time, as comfortable as any European sitting in a leather armchair.

Eyes boring deep into the soul of his victim, the Shaman breathed his foul breath over the hapless man recoiling with distaste. Without preamble or further ceremony, in the blink of an eye, or so it had seemed to Michael, the Shaman had made an incision under the man's ribcage, reached inside, whereupon he produced the beating organ after ripping it free. The crowd then went into a frenzy of shrieks and laughter combined with that unique ululation that only African woman can attain and sustain for long periods of time. A sound that permeates and stabs the air surrounding them, that penetrates to the bones. It is a sound of anguish and exultation all at once.

Michael watched in horror as the man's organ continued to beat for a short time; black blood dribbling from the obsidian vessel. Michael was unsure about the origin of the heart's colour, whether the Shaman had magically done something to produce the effect, or whether the explanation he was given was true, that a truly evil person is possessed of a black heart. Michael was willing to believe the explanation for he had witnessed the deeds of a truly evil man. He had cried for the children they found along with the rest of the village. He had attended the funerals of the menfolk found mutilated beyond recognition. He had heard the keening cry of the mothers and siblings in mourning for their loved ones and seen the results of the man's poaching on the local elephants and rhino.

He wholly believed in true evil from that point onwards. His landlord, Ryan, knew nothing of darkness in a human, was wrong to accuse Michael of bearing such infamy. It disturbed him deeply to be 'tarred by the same brush' as the evil man he had witnessed dying in Africa, then fed to, and rejected by, the hyenas that night. Not a single animal or insect neared the man's remains during the days that followed. Michael did not like to be associated with such evil as he had seen, but he knew that Ryan did not know of what he spoke, had no knowledge of what Michael had witnessed. He shook his head with sadness, tremors of horror assailing him as the memories persisted.

Ryan sat down again in the living room with his beer. He did not know why he had said anything to Michael about what he felt. He hadn't planned it. He was not usually given to spontaneous or impulsive revelations of his feelings. He wasn't even sure of its accuracy he had to admit. He went with his gut, which usually served him well, though, on this occasion he may have been premature, or possibly even wrong. His tenant had given him no indication of anything other than cordiality and bonhomie. He was in fact, a perfect tenant. Always paid on time, meticulously clean, and generous with cooking and other chores.

So why had he suddenly evicted the man? Why did he feel so... so what? Worried? Concerned? Could it be? Could Ryan possibly feel fear, was that it? Did he feel fear in his gut? Did that fear make him say those things that he wasn't really thinking? What was there to fear about the man? No, Ryan was making too much of it. His tongue had not been in sync with his brain for once. There was nothing to fear about the man and Ryan was more than capable of handling most men in most situations. He was mistaken and regretted his decision instantly. He would have difficulties with his mortgage as a result of his impulsive gesture.

He mentally kicked himself for failing to recognise his reckless actions for what they were. He knew better than to act without thought. His normal decisions were based on sound reasoning and investigation, never *feelings*. And yet, gut feelings are exactly what he utilised during his career, and to great effect. His boss, Inspector Gary Sanderson, would not be pleased if he knew.

Thoughts of Gazza brought up the pain of betrayal he felt. Gazza had been more of a father to Ryan than his old man ever was, taking him under his wing from the moment he entered the force. He could understand how it may have looked to his boss, could empathise with the man for having felt let down by his protégé, but that didn't excuse him for not giving Ryan the benefit of doubt. Gazza didn't have to throw him under the bus like that no matter what the circumstances. He should have taken Ryan aside and questioned him personally.

Ryan then started to work through that silly notion, recognising it for its stupidity immediately. Gary could not allow his personal feelings to be brought into question.

It was up to Ryan to sink or swim his way out of the deep end into which he had been thrown. It was Gazza's job to stand back from the allegations against him, for Ryan to prove his innocence without the 'old boy' network seemingly in play. He would not allow himself to influence an investigation he knew to be totally bogus. Gary was actually speaking very clearly to Ryan by his stance. He was saying; go ahead throw whatever you want at my best officer, nothing will stick. Ryan will know from my absence that I believe him one hundred per cent.

Ryan felt so relieved that he was on the verge of tears. It had been tearing him up inside to think he had been abandoned by his boss and best friend. Of course, he'd hardly had the time to think it through clearly. While he was cooling his heels in the lock-up, all he could think about was the worrying evidence found by the detectives and Loz's disappearance. Then the shit really hit the fan when the school blew up. Everything happened so quickly that he had given little thought to the problem of his mentor. His release to help out on the streets came as quite a surprise. He doubted very much that it would have happened had the Townsville boys really believed he was the Minstrel killer. Still, it was a concern to know that the only real evidence against someone in the case led to him.

Who would have known that I never went to my dad's shack?

Who would take the chance to make repairs or alterations to the shack in which to house a victim, always believing I would never show up? That my hair would show up on the victim is a no-brainer anyone could work out. A fucking year or more! Some arsehole had kept his old headmaster in that shack for all that time, torturing him? That takes some king-sized balls to carry that off. So some fucking handym...

Ryan had a thought that wasn't worth his time. He had given the fellow enough grief without any kind of decent excuse. He wouldn't allow himself to go down that particular road. Ryan had to get himself showered and fed before he hit the streets again. Everyone was putting in double and even triple shifts to stem the flow of panic and looting happening in his little town. The numerous fires were all under control, but the townspeople were still in shock and the undesirables were taking advantage of that.

The initial investigations had produced ambiguous results, at best, about the cause of the explosion. That it had started in the science lab had not come as a surprise. That it had been blamed on an unattended Bunsen burner had Ryan disbelieving the report. He rejected out-of-hand that the science teacher, a meticulous man about safety, could have left a burner alight after his last class. That his lab-assistant had also managed to miss it, stretched the theory beyond acceptability. That the errant flame then somehow blew up the attached underground gas cylinder and all the lines, was simply not worth contemplation. So far, no one had come up with anything conclusively signifying sabotage. Authorities were no longer considering a terrorist angle as there was simply no evidence to back it up.

As Ryan set about showering, while a ready-to-eat meal was being nuked in the microwave, he pondered all the alternatives to an accidental explosion. Motivation seemed the key element lacking in such a scenario. There was no possible motive for blowing up an empty school. If there was a saboteur, he had waited until the school was empty of children before igniting the fuse, and no communication of any kind had been received by phone or otherwise from terrorists claiming responsibility. Of course, even if they knew something about a terrorist, the police were not about to broadcast any such thing.

An amazing coincidence to have a major catastrophe and a serial killer hit a small town like Ingham simultaneously. Ryan entered a new arena of thought about a possible connection. *Disgruntled student? Someone from Ingham High School with an agenda over perceived indiscretions? Against former students and the school in general? The Minstrel Killer's victims all had a connection to the school. Had to be a student from the past if that were the case because Mr Thornton had been retired for quite a few years.*

Ryan tried to punch holes in his new theory, arguing all the points for and against. The arguments against came up very short. In fact, he could think of none immediately. The serial killings bore the traditional hallmarks of being personal. There was pure hatred fuelling these sadistic crimes perpetrated on his friends. Mutilation and torture on an unprecedented scale, surpassing all the known textbook cases. This nut-job was in a category all on his own. The pundits would be rewriting the textbooks with this whacko.

What could possibly have pissed off a person so badly at school to warrant such cruelty? Ryan had enjoyed the whole school experience so much that he was at a loss for an answer to that question. The worst incident he could recall concerning the school, or rather a student from the school was an alleged gang rape many years ago. Nobody was ever charged over the incident because the football team all vouched for each other. It was one girl's testimony against fifteen upstanding citizens of Ingham in the townsfolk's favour for having won the inter-school trophy that year.

Nailed Her! Cindy 'Nailed Her' Naylor! She was pretty much known as the town bike, with everyone having ridden her. Ryan had managed it once. She was plenty pissed-off when she wasn't believed. Haunted the cop shop for a year or two bothering anyone who would listen. Nobody did. Wrote her off because of her bad rep around town, long before the incident. Footy team swore it was a consensual gang-bang, claiming that Nailed Her hung around the locker room begging for it the entire year up to the finals. Most of them were pissed and stoned off their scones though, as Ryan recalled from having read the report upon entering the force years later. He wouldn't have put it past them to have covered for one another if they got carried away with something that night. It all smacked a little of too many guys saying almost the same thing bar a few different words.

Could Cindy Nailed... he had to stop using that awful term, Naylor, have had the balls to blow up the school because of that? Could she have something to do with the Minstrel Murders? Mr Thornton would definitely have been an obvious target for her if she carried such a grudge. Clay had been on the footy team and she had gone out with Kugelweis at some point, thought Ryan. He didn't truly buy it, though. There was no reason for the long hiatus between the... incident and what was happening at present. Cindy had moved on with her life, still hunting anything with legs, and causing untold grief for the married men of Ingham, but hardly anything of an evil nature. He made a mental note to have a talk with Cindy despite his reservations.

Ingham was his town, he knew it inside out, and all its citizens intimately. He could not convince himself that any local had a big enough beef with his friends or the school to commit acts of barbarism and terrorism. Yet, the more he thought about the possibility, the more convinced he became that there was a connection, that someone with a grudge was on the rampage, and that grudge may have had something to do with Ingham High. It stood out to Ryan as a common denominator.

Opening his sixth can of beer had Ryan making an introspective examination. Six cans in the space of an hour was a little fast, even for Ryan. He began to see a pattern, the same type of pattern he had witnessed in his old man.

"Shit! I'm turning into a fucking drunk just like you. I may not be beating up on a wife and kid but I am drinking myself into an early fucking grave like you, and Loz, and Vic, and... shit, like just about everyone I actually know. Clay knew how to throw them back as well. All a bunch of fucking pisspots. FUCK!"

Ryan hurled the full can of beer at the living room wall where it exploded in a cloud of froth, dribbling slowly down the wall.

Maybe I'm not as good at my job as I once was because of my drinking? Do the boys in the squad know? Is that why I've been on the outs? The looks?! In the eyes, those looks. I've known that look. I used to have that look for my old man. A mixture of pity and disgust, but something else as well. Something we didn't want to recognise, something we couldn't face, I couldn't face... empathy. Somewhere in the back of my brain, I recognised myself following in his footsteps. I empathised because I knew I was probably facing the same road to self-destruction. That's why I helped the cunt

TIRED

"Come on sleepy heads, time to wake up. If I have to be up in the middle of the night then so do you arseholes."

Lorenzo Catani slowly became aware of his surroundings. The first thing he understood, was that he remained a captive, secured to a plywood sheet that he imagined was set upon saw horses, much like the fellow beside him. *INNER TUBES!* He knew he was right about that smell. Rubber bicycle inner tubes secured the man's head to the plywood sheet, the same as he. Some sort of U clamp or saddle type thing held wrists and ankles securely. He did not recognise the man, though, it was difficult to turn his head around enough to have a good look.

Lorenzo shook with dread and fear as he watched the comical, evil, blackened face of his captor hovering over him with a desperately tired manner, yawning compulsively. The man looked for all the world like he could sleep for a year. Lorenzo guessed that if the man rubbed away the blackening agent, he would still be left with huge dark circles under his eyes. He didn't appear to be wearing anything.

Then he noticed something that truly shocked him. *What? It can't be? Nothing between the... legs? Woman?*

The other man secured to the plywood sheet beside him did not stir, but Lorenzo saw a slight rise and fall of the chest to indicate that life persisted despite the ghastly injuries suffered by him.

When Loz allowed his eyes to wander to the ceiling for the first time, he was startled to see his own image and that of his neighbours' in a large mirror. They were naked. While he, Loz, had a severed hand to show for his ordeal and aching horribly, his neighbour, whom he somehow recognised as Mr Ball, despite the fug in his mind and the massive injuries, had a huge cross carved into his chest and abdomen, stitched together with a crude fishing line or similar.

His body was black and blue with evidence of brutal treatment by his tormentor, pockmarked with innumerable small puncture wounds. His scrotum was the size of a rockmelon. Loz never really liked any of his old teachers but they didn't deserve what this lunatic was doing.

"I see you recognise your old teacher, Mr Catani. Good. I put the mirror up there for you to take it all in, give you a ringside seat at your own show. I think you have dried out sufficiently. I expect you are desperately yearning for some liquid encouragement, Mr Catani, and that will be bothering you some. I assure you, it will be the least of your concerns in the very near future."

Loz watched as the maniac strolled casually over to a workbench beneath a well-organised wall of tools arranged on a pegboard. The ubiquitous outlines of the respective tools indicating a perfect position for each implement ostensibly employed in the act of torture. Loz had given up on life so many years ago that he couldn't remember a time when he felt deserving of it, entitled to a 'normal' life like the other citizens of Ingham and the world. He had loathed himself and his pathetic circumstances from about the time he left high school, left his friends, his sense of belonging.

He had been metaphorically conjoined with his mates in high school from before kindergarten. It had always been a family away from his own upon whom he relied. It was the security of deeply ingrained friendships that transcended his extended Italian hierarchy. It was joy beyond joy on a daily basis to be with his friends through thick and thin, always sticking together and supporting one another no matter the odds or circumstances. He wrongly believed it would continue after school. When everyone went their separate ways without so much as a decent goodbye, Loz began to feel the terrible weight of loneliness bearing down upon him. The unbearable pain of being separated from his lifeline had crushed him beyond despair.

In the beginning, the drinking was to fill in the hours he was alone after work, while his best mates were off doing their own thing, to the police academy, or in the case of Clay, a job on the city council which kept him away for months at a time. He was incapable of maintaining a permanent job when his drinking and drug intake escalated. He was eventually thrown out of his rented unit when he failed to pay his rent two months running. His myopic life dwindled down to one overriding obsession - booze. Torn away from his sole purpose for living, nothing else mattered in his lonely existence.

Some people were like that, needing the constant companionship of fellow human beings in order to survive. A type of animal pack mentality where the group only survives when they are all working together as a cohesive unit, as a single organism made of individual components. Lorenzo Giuseppe Catani yearned for that community cohesion as much as he needed oxygen to survive. Without it, he was a ghost drifting aimlessly in search of release to the ether, the cosmos, whatever. He grieved over the loss of his best mates once they left high school. The times he ran into them accidentally on the street, were not occasions of joy. There was no welcome in their voices and no happiness in their eyes to see or speak to their old school buddy, Loz.

"Won't be a moment fellas, just getting your little cocktails ready to help you with the experience. Hmm, had another syringe here somewhere. I'll be back."

Loz saw Mr Ball's entire body quake, almost like a seizure. His eyes, now open were wild and terrified. He seemed like he was about to expire from pure fright.

"Mr Ball? It, it's alright, Mr Ball, he's gone. It's me, Lorenzo Catani. Remember me, from your class, way back when?"

Craig Ball regained focus momentarily, peering at the image on the mirror above him. He no longer recognised his body as his own. He saw the other person strapped down next to him. A very anaemic-pale, rake-thin person in the bright lights. He found it difficult to focus his thoughts, could not quite assemble the information his eyes presented. The name of the person registered somewhere deep in his subconscious, but he couldn't be bothered with it. He knew what was coming when the Minstrel returned with the syringe. He knew about the cocktails soon to be administered. Knew the pure hell he and his companion were about to undergo.

"Hey, Mr Ball, stay with me okay? Concentrate, calm down and concentrate. Who the fuck is this bitch and what is going on? The voice sounds a bit familiar. Do you know who it is?"

"M, M, Mel, Melco... "

Loz wasn't sure he heard right. *Did the old fella say, Melco? He couldn't possibly mean, Smelly Melly from the old days surely? Wait, that's what happened to my hand? I called the lunatic that name and he...* Loz's brain couldn't cope at the best of times with names, but he would never forget that particular name from his past. Melco Malkovich. Boy that brought back some fond memories of him and his mates in their prime. The mischief they got up to would impress old Satan himself. But it didn't seem possible that the black-face person was Smelly Melly from the past. Even with the disguise, it didn't seem possible. "Mr Ball? You can't mean, Smelly Melly, surely? It's a she. Hasn't got anything downstairs, you know?"

"Re, remem, remember the barbed-wire? Mel, Melco... found him... barbed... "

"Oh, yeah, I remember that. On bivouac in Townsville. We had some fun with old, Smelly that night, that's for sure. You mean he told you something about that?"

"Wrapped, wrapped me, oh, Jesus! He, he wrapped me in barbed-wire after... ahhhhhh, the pain. Make it stop pleeeeease?"

"Jeez, calm down will ya. Nobody here but us at the moment. This prick wrapped ya in barbed-wire ya said? What the fuck for?"

"Said, I, wasn't... good... teacher. Said I have to be... pun, punished for not... for not reporting barbed-wire... "

"You mean this nut-job is actually Smelly Melly come back for revenge or some shit? No way! Why now for fuck sake? Why would he wait all these years to come back? And where is his tackle? No fucking cock and balls! I think I saw a tattoo or something down there. Like a hand... black. Doesn't make any... Oh, shit!"

Although the momentary revelation caused him to shiver, he immediately lost the connection. Confusion reigned where thought processes once existed in Loz. He couldn't quite latch onto the details of their exploits with old Smelly Melly. His addled brain could only conjure up the euphoric feelings of power, the hedonistic supremacy that overcame him when they were all together against that dweeby nerd with the foreign accent and the pissy smell. He recalled with startling acuity, the exact *feelings* connected with Melco, but not the deeds themselves. The fuzziness in his brain did not clear away to allow those facts to surface. He watched as Mr Ball's tremors gradually decreased. Whatever the sick fuck had done to his old teacher had him piss-scared. If what the old bloke said was true, that the sadist had wrapped him in barbed-wire? It explained all the puncture wounds covering the old boy's body.

The stitched-up cross on his chest and abdomen looked to be from very deep cuts. Loz's eyes strayed to the wall of tools, to the outline of a Stanley knife, which he recognised clearly. It was missing. Looking in the mirror, he could see the knife resting on the bench. It had a dark blade, not the normal stainless steel colour he associated with it. Loz gulped as he realised the blade had been coloured by dried blood from his neighbour. Loz then noticed his teacher's fingers, or lack thereof, for the first time. Broken, twisted, shortened or blackened remnants of what were once the digits of the religious man who taught him at Ingham High. The fingers that grasped the chalk that wrote on the blackboards endlessly, class after class, day after boring day and year after fucking year.

Loz noticed that his toes were in the same shape. He winced at the obvious pain his teacher had suffered at the hands of the black-faced lunatic. That he might suffer the same treatment, *while sober*, did not bear thinking about. Loz saw nothing around him identifying a possible means of escape. He was secured to the plywood board beneath him so firmly that he could barely move. His head and neck were bound by the inner tubes. There was a modicum of play in those bonds, but insufficient to use to his advantage. He was surprised at how lucid he felt for perhaps the first time in many, many years. He could not guess with any accuracy how long he had been held captive but knew it had been long enough for him to go through the worst of the withdrawals.

He could not remember going through it, not really. Very fuzzy. It hurt. *That*, he could remember. It felt like his insides wanted to come out, like they needed to escape his skin. He felt an army of biting ants crawling all over him, eating him alive. He had horror visions floating through his head that he thought would be the end of him. Thankfully, he could not remember details of those visions. There was an inner calmness to him that he had not expected. Panic is what he believed he might exhibit under the circumstances. Calmness and clarity were strangers to him.

"Who...? Who came... back?"

"What are you talking about, Mr Ball?"

"Someone... needs to... I mean, he, needs... to know. Who came, who, who went back?"

"Came back to what, from where?"

"That, that... night... wire."

"You're not making any sense there, Mr Ball. I dunno what you're talking about."

"Biv... bivouac, Townsville. Who... went back?"

"Went back to Townsville?"

"That... that... night. He, he said, he... ahhhhh, no, I don't know anything. Ahhhh, stop, no... "

"Stop, stop screaming would ya. That shit is really getting on my nerves old man. No one is doing anything okay? He's not here at the moment. What's with this needle anyway? What's he got in that? What's it for?"

"The worst possible pain imaginable," said Mr Ball in a chillingly clear voice.

"Suddenly got your voice, huh? Had to make that bit real clear did ya? Are you in pain now? You really look like he's gone to town on ya." asked Loz innocently.

Craig Ball laughed hysterically for a few moments, subsiding into wracking sobs that threatened to cause him some sort of respiratory failure. Finally, the sobs ended, the steady breathing returned. "The pain now is nothing. What, what comes, is like nothing on earth. I want to die. Can you kill me?"

"What the fuck? Did I hear you right? Can I kill you? Even if I could, I wouldn't. Stop that shit, alright? We gotta get outta here and tell the world about this fucking psycho. You gotta suck it up,"

"Fuuuuuuuuuck youuuuuu! Kill me. KILL ME. I want to die. So will you once, once... oh, oh fuck, no? Not the stuff, no not... please, not again. Anything, anything. I'll do... HELP!"

"Will you stop that bloody screaming? Far as I can tell, no one can hear you except me, and him."

"Tell, tell him, please? Who, who came back. Tell him, tell him who, tell him. Who came? Tell... came, tell."

"I dunno what you're talking about. Can't tell the crazy fuck nothing if I don't know."

Loz's words were lost on his neighbour while he rambled on incoherently. At least he wasn't screaming. Small mercy that it was. *How the fuck am I supposed to tell anyone anything?* He didn't know what day it was most of the time. He couldn't recall where he'd been a week ago, let alone what happened back in school. At least, he supposed it had something to with back then. *Barbed-wire? Where did that come from? What do I have to do with it? Melco Malkovich?* Loz strained his mind to think back to the time period when he had been the happiest of his life. Him and his buddies all together. Doing the shit that made them laugh and all was good with the world.

Townsville. It had something to do with the bivouac to Townsville. There *was* something about that. Like a feather touching the back of his brain, a tickle disturbing the cobwebs in the deep recesses of his memory, a recollection slowly emerged.

He was in the cadets with his buddies and there was a trip to Townsville planned. They were going to be trained in the latest firearms replacing the old .303s. They would go on hikes, orienteering courses, raft-making and survival-skill classes. They would be camped for several days by a river somewhere in the bush near the barracks in Townsville. Mr Ball was there as an officer overseeing his squad from Ingham.

With a jolt, Loz suddenly remembered something significant that caused a sharp intake of breath. His body stiffened. His eyes swivelled left to right as images flashed across his mind like an old slideshow. In with a slide and on to the next while the first was being replaced in the carriage. With one final push to the last slide in the pack, all the memories of that time, that one particular incident came flooding back, overwhelming Loz with its intensity.

"Mr Ball! Mr Ball, did you, you know, ever tell anyone?"

"Tell... tell anyone?"

"C'mon, Mr Ball, stay with me now. Did you tell anyone about him, about Melco? When you found him?"

"Did... not... couldn't," Craig whispered. "Who... who... came back?"

"Stop with that already. Whadda ya mean who came back?"

"To the scene Lorenzo, to the scene of the crime. I asked old Craigy-boy here but he didn't know. I didn't think he would but I had to ask just the same. So glad *you* remembered, Lorenzo. I see my treatments have worked sufficiently on you to bring back some clarity to your otherwise dull and cloudy perspective. I was not going to start on that particular question for a few days with you. I wanted to tenderise you a little first, get you in the right frame of mind to answer truthfully."

"If that is really you, Melco, you are one sick fuck to do that to your old teacher, to my friends. You're getting nothing from me. I don't care about dying. I've been dying for years and welcoming it."

"Foolish man. Dying is not the worst thing that can befall a person. It's the living you will fear more than anything else in your miserable existence. You haven't feared anything because you were too far gone. Now that you are sober for perhaps the first time since leaving school, you will know fear such as you never believed existed. I have de... umm... I haff... shit! Not now. I haff... can't... umm. What zis...? Okay, I don't know, dat... okay. I... umm, am going to... "

The man walked away abruptly, leaving Lorenzo with an eerie impression of déjá vu. Lorenzo had seen more than his fair share of minds affected like that. He saw them every day in his world. Minds addled by drink or drugs or both. Minds so far gone that the incoherent ramblings were comforting to someone likewise affected. Wouldn't be Kosher to have a lucid mind amid the drunks. It was embarrassing if someone came along while a drunk was incoherent, espousing logic or common-sense. That was anathema to drunks. Couldn't abide that shit when a drunk's mind was awash with garbage, drifting in and out of coherence.

He had roomed with a bunch of guys once in a boarding house, a real dump. A cockroach-infested, overrun by rats and mice, dump. It was in his early days as a career drunk, so he was not quite as wasted as he would have liked to be. He had older men returning from their night out, who would casually piss in the hall outside his door. He made the mistake one night of opening the door only to find a man pissing on his legs. Lorenzo paid the man back one night by waiting until his neighbour had collapsed onto his bed with his front door left open. Lorenzo stood on the end of his single bed, where he unzipped his fly and pissed all over the sleeping man and his bed.

Another man who lived down the hall was a dope-head. Lorenzo was not sure what his particular poison was but knew it to be fairly potent shit because that guy was totally off with the fucking fairies. He was forever running around with a little piece of wood into which were driven twelve brads in two parallel lines of six. Woven between the brads was a matrix of copper wire. The lunatic ran around the house most days yelling about the juxtaposition. Somehow he got it into his head that the particular positioning of his wires on that little board allowed him to communicate with aliens. It was all in the juxtaposition of the wires according to him. He loved that word - juxtaposition.

That was not what this fellow sounded like. This fellow displayed a sure sign of a brain malfunctioning, in meltdown. It was very clear to Loz that the person, of unclear gender, not convinced that it was Melco, was fatigued, which could be causing the memory lapse, or it could be something more. It definitely reminded Loz of his drunken buddies who never seemed to be able to finish a sentence or hold on to thought once they were over the edge. That clearly defined line between sober and not. That delicious moment when the world stepped away from the drinker, to leave them with a pleasant fug in which the real world dissolved. The moment every drunk savoured, the attainment of which was paramount and all-consuming, the desperate need for oblivion, the escape from all things real, the release that required more and more substance to attain.

This, this weirdo with the black face and the white lips looking like some circus freak, was definitely not the full quid. Some synapses were faulty upstairs, not connecting, that was for sure. It came on suddenly, though. Loz identified no lead up to the episode. One minute he or she was talking better than Loz could ever hope to, yet in the next minute, was imbecilic. The person could not remember what he was going to say. Loz was not sure if that boded well for him and his cohort. The loss of faculties could presage an irrational episode in the freak, or it could afford them a time of amnesty. The cretin was obviously volatile enough when he was firing on all cylinders to torture and mutilate fellow human beings. Who knew what it was capable of when things went awry?

Loz did not like the fact that he could think rationally, that he could reason out different scenarios or that he was capable of analysis. It scared him that he ought to be frightened, yet he wasn't. *Well, that was actually an oxymoron, wasn't it? And how the fuck do I even know what an oxymoron is anyway? Or, perhaps he had just had the cleverest thought of his life? No, now he was thinking like Mr Juxtaposition.* When that weirdo started explaining in highly technical terms how his alien antenna worked, it all sounded rather feasible at the time. Now, it just sounded like the baloney it was. Psychobabble and bullshit. Paranoia in the extreme, coupled with an intellectually trained brain operating on reflex. Muscle memory attributed to the brain, working on pure automation.

Loz tried hard not to allow himself to sink back into the intolerable state where he yearned for something so intensely that it obliterated all other thoughts and emotions. Life in that boarding house had altered his personality to such a degree that he no longer trusted himself to have normal conversations or thoughts. He had accepted the ramblings in the house to become a state of normality with which he was comfortable. Any derivation from that perception was a dangerous road to travel. He would not embark on a journey to reality if he could reasonably avoid it and yet, here he was, sober after many long years. Sober and thoughtful, mindful of the present and aware of the past with far too much clarity. Like a person subjected to brilliant light after being in the dark for a very long time. The light would be totally overwhelming, just as his thoughts were so daunting, that they made him ill.

He went back in his mind to Townsville, the bivouac that he and his friends attended. They had been on an orienteering exercise, having to follow some damn compass headings to arrive at flagged destinations. It was a blisteringly hot day in the scrubland, in their BDUs with full kit. Loz and his mates were lagging behind, not caring to follow their platoon leader, not interested in learning anything on such a hot day. Their only interest lay in making mischief and lollygagging. They had confiscated a fellow cadet's stash of tailor-made cigarettes, which they were steadily puffing down to ashes. Loz had smuggled a bottle of overproof in his kit to help them survive the extended, meaningless hike.

They didn't need a compass to find their way back to the camp. They had only to find the river and follow that back downstream to find their base. The flags and booby-traps along the way were for the nerds and bum-crawlers, the ones who wanted to advance in the cadets to officer status. Loz and his crew knew that the cadets were to be disbanded the following year due to insufficient funding and lack of enthusiasm by schools and members. Numbers had been dwindling every year since inception, with the current year standing at an all-time low. Loz, Vic, Clay, and Ryan settled themselves by the river to get well and truly wasted. With some primo weed and overproof rum, they were truly marinated before lunch.

Their revelry did not abate as the afternoon wore down. In fact, they were so drunk and stoned, they began to sober up. As night fell and they made their way back to camp, they progressed to a state of weary delirium, laughing hysterically at everything and nothing. Far from wanting to crash for the night though, Loz convinced his compatriots to engage in one more prank before the camp ended. He explained his childish plan with as much detail and enthusiasm as he could muster while feeling weary after the day's excesses.

"Nah, c'mon enough already, Loz. I'm fucked," managed Clay as he sunk wearily to the ground.

"What's the matter with ya, ya pussy? Can't take a bit of weed or a drink then?" asked Loz.

"I'm in. I'm game. It's our last night here fellas, time to make a statement before all this ends for good and we all go our separate ways after school this year." Victor Kugelweis egged on.

Ryan added, "I'm bloody tired, but yeah, time to show him, once and for all."

"He needs to be taught a lesson not to fuck with any of us. He got me a good one in Abergowrie when you fellas weren't there," said Loz.

"Shame! How the fuck could you let him beat you, man? Fucking shamed us," said Clay.

"That little twerp can fucking fight I'm telling ya. One-on-one anyway. No match for all of us. He's got it coming. Whadda ya say, fellas? I'll grab the gear. You guys go haul him out of his tent. I'll join you and we can take him to that spot near the river we scoped out earlier, near the fence line, and make sure he stays quiet. If we're going to do this we better be quick and fucking quiet about it," said Loz.

Donning grease paint camouflage and armed with cable ties, the boys stole into the night, creeping up to the last tent in the row. Clay stood to keep watch as the others entered the tent, silent as cockroaches. They returned soon after with their victim wrapped in his hutchie, bound and gagged. With three big boys carrying him, they made good time through the moonlit bush to a clearing near the boundary fence next to the river. Lavarack Barracks in Townsville was home to the 3rd and 11th brigades, an enormous complex housing the Australian defence force's largest contingent of armed personnel, 4,500 soldiers and nearly 300 civilian workers, encompassing all their necessities like groceries, banks, doctors clothing stores and entertainment.

It took the boys over an hour to reach their destination, having to stop and rest periodically with their struggling captive. They were quickly losing their patience with the boy who would not stop fighting back. They were forced to lay into him with boots and fists several times in order to gain a smidgeon of control. They were exhausted by the time they threw him to the ground for the last time.

"No way are we going to able to hold that cunt down while you do your shit, Loz. He's fucking strong for such a short-arse prick," said Clayton McCormack.

"Yeah, whew. What a fucking trek! That little bastard has worn me out. How about we have another toke and a snort before we proceed fellas?" encouraged Loz.

Vic agreed, "Good idea. Open that second bottle Loz. I need a hit."

"We better not take too long fellas, they'll be blowing reveille pretty soon and we better be coming out of our tents at that time," said Ryan.

"We got ages yet, Ryan. What's a matter, eh?" asked Loz.

"C'mon open the fucking bottle ya dumb wop." Ryan retorted.

"Who you calling dumb? Fucking got no brains neiver ya dumb

cunt," sniggered Loz.

"Yeah? I'm off to the Academy after school, where are you going?" asked Ryan

"Shit, I'm really gonna miss you bastards after we finish school this year."

"Yeah, it's been cool. What a fucking blast. Dad lined me up a job with the council after I leave. Straight from school to work and helping out with the family mortgage; shit! Thought I'd be able to bum around for a couple-o-years at least," said Clay.

"I'm going to help out my old man in his real estate office. Now that's something I never thought I would do," admitted Vic.

"Yeah, I always thought you was gonna go to Hollywood or be in the soaps you know?" said Loz.

"Fuck that! The soaps? The Days of our Drearies? Nah, movies are okay, but not that shit. Nah, I don't want to go to college with a bunch of poofs learning about acting and shit. I'd rather be earning some money when I leave. Dad makes some pretty good coin in his business."

"Yeah, you're family's flush that's for sure. Good house, a flashy car and ya always have some coin on ya, Vic. Glad to know you'll be sticking around the old neighbourhood." said Loz sadly.

"Enough with reminiscing already. We going to do this or what?" asked Clay.

"Course we are, just slow down there buddy. Have a hit first then we get down to it. Have a slug-o-this and light up that joint." pushed Loz.

For the next twenty minutes, the four amigos drank the bottle empty and smoked several joints. Each time the bundle moved too much for their tastes, they took turns to sink a boot or a fist into the squirming mass. During a lull in the conversation, Loz had an epiphany. He suddenly knew how they would be able to restrain their captive long enough to accommodate their prank. The perimeter fencing consisted of a very high chain-link fence, but there were fence lines within the large compound to keep soldiers out of live-ammo practice areas. Those areas were cordoned off with barbed-wire fences with signs on every segment warning off potential trespassers.

"We'll string him up in the wire. That'll keep him still enough for us," suggested Loz.

"Hey dude, that's like, barbed-wire. That's probably going a bit far, eh?" said Ryan.

"After we strip him, we'll use his gear to wrap around the bits that are touched by barbed-wire, that way he won't get hurt too much? C'mon ya bunch-o-pussies," said Loz

Loz led the others to the bundle that continued to squirm with renewed energy upon hearing their plans. The foursome struggled with the boy, stripping him naked until they finally managed to wrap him in the strands of barbed-wire. There were four separate strands, which had sagged at one point where the post holding them had come free from the ground. Melco's arms, wrapped in his clothing, were intertwined and cable-tied between the top two strands while his ankles, similarly clad in his torn clothing, were secured in a spread-eagle pose in the bottom two strands. His struggles gradually ceased as it became evident that the more he struggled, the worse he made it. His clothes protected him to a certain degree only. He could feel the barbs whenever he strained against his bonds. Cable ties prevented the strands from releasing him.

"First, we give you a bit of camouflage there, Smelly. Not gonna waste expensive grease paint on ya, though. Bit-o-boot polish should do the trick eh?" explained Loz as he undid the lid of the Kiwi boot polish that every cadet owned to keep their boots shining enough to satisfy their officers.

The boys mistook their victim's tears for fear instead of a natural response to the sting inflicted by the boot polish in his eyes. The misread tears inflamed their lust for predatory power over their hapless captive.

"So, who's got the toothpaste?" asked Loz.

"I have. What're we going to do with that?" asked Vic.

"You're going to rub it into his nuts and his knob, stupid."

"What the fuck for? And call me stupid again and you'll be joining him."

"Sorry, Vic. I thought you would know. It stings like buggery when you wipe toothpaste on someone's nuts, but especially on their knob."

"Fuck that! I'm not going to touch his cock."

"Well, Clay can do it then. Give the tube to Clay."

"Aww, I dunno about that Loz. He'll squirm a lot if we do that."

"So?"

"We could really get in trouble if we hurt him too badly, mate."

"He's protected by the clothes, Clay. He won't be able to hurt himself. You gutless? I thought we all agreed?"

"Jeez, will ya give me the bloody tube for fuck's sake. Let's get this over and done with and get the fuck back to camp," snarled Ryan.

"Don't forget to peel back his foreskin. Gotta get it directly on his knob for it to have a real effect."

Ryan stumbled in front of the boy, extending his left arm for balance. His hand brushed against the boy's face, then rested on his chest before Ryan finally regained his stability. A breeze whispered through the tree branches overhead. The full moon shone brightly enough for them to forsake their torches. Ryan squeezed the toothpaste onto his right hand, then peeled back the skin from the boy's penis with his left after wiping the boot polish off. Strangely, the boy ceased all his struggles, seemingly accepting his punishment for unknown sins. Ryan spread the toothpaste onto his victim with relish, massaging the paste generously, covering the entire groin.

"What the fuck? How come he doesn't feel anything, Loz?" asked Clay.

"I dunno. Is the toothpaste out of date or something? He should be squealing like a piglet."

Ryan looked into the defiant, bloodshot eyes of the boy as he remained stock-still. His stare bore into Ryan's retina like a lance, causing him to back away. The boy raised his head to look at each of his captors in turn, piercing them with stares they would not soon forget. There was no movement from anyone as time ticked by. Frogs croaked amongst some river reeds. Overhead, the wings of flying foxes could be heard as they went about their night's aerial acrobatics in search of fruit. Red eyes glaring out from the blackened face glinting in the moonlight threw the boys somewhat off guard.

"Fuck me, is he getting a stiffy? Did you manage to turn him on, Ryan? Oh boy, you must have the magic touch there, eh? Wanna do me next?" teased Clay.

"Maybe that's why he isn't screaming. You got him all horny," said Vic.

"What the fuck are you guys talking about, he hasn't got a stiffy. That's just how the white paste looks in the moonlight you fuckwits."

"Tell ya what, he isn't small down there, though eh?" admitted Loz. "Dunno why he isn't screaming but. Old toothpaste I reckon."

"C'mon, let's fuck off. This is boring. I'm knackered and it'll be morning soon," said Vic.

"Yeah, orright, let's scarper, eh boys?" suggested Loz.

"Hey, we can't just leave him here, like this. We have to get him out of the wire fellas," said Clay.

"Nah, it's loose enough for him to get out I reckon. Let's go before we get into trouble," said Loz.

The boys took one last disturbing look at the boy in the wire glaring back at them with bloodshot eyes spewing pure hatred and venom through the black face, Ryan's smudged black handprint on his chest standing out against the white flesh. The posse headed off into the night. Loz had never seen the boy again after that night. Loz finished school that year and his real troubles began from that point in time.

"So what is he after, Mr Ball? We all went back to our tents afterwards. How can anyone give him the answer when there is no answer to give that he will accept, and what gives with his loss of memory. I know that scene. People like me, on the booze, lose their memory like that, or guys on drugs. This bloke must be on something."

"Not so, Mr Catani. There are many other reasons for the behaviour you witnessed. In my case, a form of dementia. F.F.I., fatal familial insomnia. I have a rare disorder inherited from my mother, bless her heart, from which I will eventually perish. There are a few variations in symptoms, severity and longevity, but in all cases, fatal. In my case, I have developed insomnia to such a degree that I have not managed one night's sleep in a long, long time. You just witnessed another symptom gradually making its presence known. I have dementia. The onset, at least. I may still have a few months before I am a vegetable.

"Dementia, the very disorder that led to the discovery of this little cocktail I am about to give you. I travelled to the far reaches of the globe after reading a letter I inherited from my mother when she passed away, informing me of the condition bequeathed to me. I had no idea she had it or from whom she received it. I never did get to meet my grandparents after moving to Australia. It is a prion disease that mainly affects the thalamus, the part of the brain that controls the sleep-wake cycle.

"My researches into studies and experiments on the thalamus led me to discover the experiments on the hypothalamus being conducted on autistic children around Zimbabwe. I found dear Mr Mugabe was responsible for a host of interesting deeds. Hated, though he and his kind have been throughout history, like the infamous Doctor Mengele, they too have benefitted mankind. At least, to the type of mankind that would take advantage of such an opportunity."

"So, you're back to get revenge on us huh, Melco?"

"I have never truly left this disgusting little town and its putrid population. I have it up here in my head wherever I go. I will remedy that little problem soon enough. First, though, I must have answers. Who came back?"

"To Brylcream? Yeah, I came back to Brylcream just like the ad said."

"You are a very funny man when you are sober, Mr Catani. It will be interesting to see how funny you are after I have given you an injection. As Mr Ball will testify, the results are quite spectacular. You will know pain on a scale that you could not believe was possible. Poor, poor, Mr Ball has had to suffer intolerably, yet he clings to life so tenaciously. Mr Thornton, though, now there was a challenge. He withstood all my treatments for ages. Alas, only physically. Mentally, he perished relatively soon."

"You always were a twisted little cunt, Smelly. What happened to that big cock of yours? You had one-o-them operations? You a transgender freak now, Smelly?"

Lorenzo felt the jab of the needle into his thigh as the Minstrel lunged forward with a fierce growl. A moment later he felt the liquid infusing his system, enveloping him in its warmth and comfort. Loz watched as he stepped away with a sinister grin on his white lips, a grotesque parody on the minstrels of old that he remembered his parents watching. Of course, the contrast of white lips on a black face was not as pronounced on the old black and white TV set as it was in the flesh.

Loz began to feel an uncomfortable prickling sensation on his back and buttocks, from the rough surface of the plywood sheet against his bare skin. Sounds of his neighbours breathing were becoming louder and clearer, and the aromas permeating the workshop, sawdust, oil, and other unidentifiable products, stung his nostrils sharply. His own heartbeat sounded like the thundering waves during a tropical storm, pounding relentlessly, wave upon wave on the sandy shore.

Fuck, what is that bloody smell? Ugh, it really stinks. What? What's he doing to my... shit! My face! Don't put that shit on... my... fuck! Boot polish. It really is that fucking little cunt, Melco. Getting... even. Oh, shit that hurts so fucking... God, my God, help me. The smell, can't breathe. So... bad. What, what now? Oh no. No, no, please don't put that shit on my balls please, oh God.

Lorenzo's screams could be heard above the stereo in the corner blasting out a Pink Floyd number - *Another Brick in the Wall*. In truth, Lorenzo's screams did not have to be loud to drown out the stereo. To Lorenzo, that low volume would sound a hundred times more powerful. His own screams would inflict more pain than was possible from the stereo with the volume set so low. To the man, that scenario did not play into his sense of order as the controller. He needed to be responsible for inflicting the most amount of pain. He saw himself as the sole purveyor of punishment, to be held in awe for his methodology. He twisted the knob on the stereo to full volume.

"We don't need no, education. We don't need no, thought control... Hey, teacher, leave us kids alone."

"All in all, Lorenzo, you're just another brick in the wall," said the man once the volume had been turned down. You had better learn to keep your screams down, Mr Catani, or else you will be subject to some real heavy metal coming out of those speakers. Pink Floyd is loud, but not deafening. I have a surprise for you, something I've been saving up just for you. It was your idea after all, wasn't it? That much I have found out.

"It was all your idea to have some fun that night. You came up with the idea of the boot polish and the toothpaste, didn't you? Great prank, Lorenzo, but it all went too far. Happens to quite a few rookies doesn't it, the boot polish and the toothpaste? Wrapping arms and legs in the barbed-wire, though, that was over the top, even for your vindictive little brain. How you managed to convince your cohorts to go along with that one is a great mystery.

"Somehow you managed to convince yourself that *you* were the victim after being beaten fair and square in school when your thug mates weren't around to protect you, huh? No sense of fairness in that, Mr Catani? Being bested in a one-on-one situation, where the better man wins? No sense of honour declaring that the better man won and have done with the conflict? No, of course not, your kind has no honour. You just come back to the fight with a bigger gun or more soldiers. It is your kind that makes the human race the one big fucked up mess that it is.

"But even as far as you all went that night, it wasn't satisfying enough was it? No, one of you had to come back. One of you insipid cowards had to come back to inflict the final, fatal insult to injury. Yes, I said, 'fatal' Mr Catani. Fatal because the boy you all knew died that night. Inflicted with a life-altering injury, the boy he once was disappeared, never to return. The once, happy little boy who suffered at the hands of relentless school bullies for so many years, had finally been hurled over the edge to fall into an emotional abyss from which there was no return.

"Those responsible, this town, the gang, will suffer like no other person has suffered in history for its neglect of that boy who died. Mr Ball, who knew about the tragedy, never said a word, never sought to assist the boy, never punished those responsible. Mr Thornton, the Head Master learned of the incident and neglected to investigate. Seems everyone in town, including the police, knew what happened eventually, but did nothing. Not that you lot were worth protecting mind you, not for that reason. It was just that no one wanted anything to do with investigating a tragedy befalling some peasant migrant's son. Some fucking foreigner. Not worth the effort! Then, then it really began, and that is the second question I need to have answered. I need to know who masterminded the rest.

"Well, Mr Catani, you will know pain like no other. I have here another needle with a dulled point. Yes, I don't want to inflict pain with the needle, you see? I want it to slip into the urethra without puncturing the walls. It's what's inside the syringe that will provide the amusement I desire. I can see you keeping your eyes shut. Fair enough, I would be too. Hurts like a bitch. The lights? I will just explain then, that I have battery acid in the syringe, which I am about to inject up the eye of your pathetic little, shrivelled up worm. Don't worry, I'm sure the worm doesn't work anymore anyway."

EXPLOSION

Ryan was sitting at his desk when the two Townsville detectives walked into the station. He saw them go into Gazza's office with a large trunk. Through the Venetian blinds of his boss's office, he witnessed much gesticulation and arm-waving concerning the large item, which ended in the two detectives presumably being told what they needed to do with it. Judging by the way they were heading his way, he could further assume they were about to pass that particular buck on to their local stooge; namely, himself.

"Hey, Ryan, seeing as you're back on the force, you can make yourself useful and haul this over to evidence. The print boys have to go over all the tools in it when they get through with the school. All stops have been pulled to get a lead on that before we get some techies coming back to our case."

"What tools?"

"We believe it contains all the tools used to mutilate victim number three, which turned out to be victim number one, actually. Found it at your fishing shack. Tell us it's yours and we'll wrap up the case in no time?"

"Dream on, mate. As I said, I haven't been to the shack since..."

"Since your old man died. Yeah, yeah, yeah, so you say."

"Proved me wrong yet?"

"Working on it." Trent paused as he was about to walk away with his partner in tow, removing his latex gloves. "There is something about you that rubs me the wrong way, Detective Ryan. Don't think for one second that you are in the clear. Brian and I will be keeping close tabs on you every step of the way. Every step of the way."

"Sure, waste your time with surveillance on me, morons, while the real killer gets away on your shift. Great detect... " Ryan's last words hung in the air as the detectives strode off, purposely throwing their gloves on the floor.

Ryan watched the smug bastards strike off for the meeting room where they had set up their base of operations. The fishbowl, as it was named, was in the centre of the floor. Used most commonly as a briefing room for their daily schedules, it was conveniently located in a central position for all staff. Even when not present inside the room, officers sitting outside the fishbowl could usually listen in while they were attending to incoming calls at their desks.

Ryan eyed the large trunk on the floor. Making sure the detectives were unable to see him, he opened the lid after donning his own latex gloves. Inside, was an assortment of domestic and professional tools for use in carpentry or home maintenance. Wood saw, hacksaw, pliers, tin snips, nail punches, vice grips, and G-clamps, just to name a few, all with angry blotches of dried blood on them. Something struck him as odd. Nothing definitive that he could identify immediately. Possibly nothing at all. It was a minute mental twinge in the back of his mind that tickled his detective antennae. He saw nothing else that gave him any direction to pursue in a matter from which he was, unfortunately, excluded anyway.

With a heavy sigh, Ryan hefted the heavy trunk from the floor. He marched the burden down the corridor to the evidence room at the back of the station. He gave the necessary paperwork to the custodial officer in charge of evidence and lost property before heading out of the station to track down Cindy Nailed Her. *Shit! He had to stop that.* He had known her by that moniker for so long that he found it difficult to call her by her right name. It was very wrong of him he knew. Getting the name out of his head, though, was a whole different story. Besides, he had a completely different reason for not wanting to use the name, a reason he had yet to come to terms with.

Outside the station on Palm Terrace, he turned left to head uptown toward the cafe where he had once seen her. If she wasn't there he would have to try the one downtown on Herbert Street, which was where he eventually found her. The cafe looked fairly deserted. A couple of waitresses and two customers by the look of it. The owner, a burly, old Italian in greasy whites, was tending the grill.

"Hey, Luigi, throw some of that slop you call bolognese on a plate for me, will you? I'll be sitting over there with Miss Naylor." Ryan walked over to Cindy's booth where he sat opposite her uninvited. "Looking good there, Cindy. Been down to the beach huh?"

"Cryin' Ryan, how the fuck are you?"

"Now, now, Cindy. Be nice. I didn't use your usual name, so let's lose the name-calling, shall we? I don't even remember how you came up with that one for me anyway. Care to... elucidate?"

"Elucidate? Fancy-schmancy word there for a fucking D?"

"Yeah. Had a smart-arse bloke living with me for a bit. Kinda picked up on a few different words."

"Boyfriend?"

"Watch it. I seem to recall *me* being one of the many who 'nailed her'?"

"So you're latent, so what? Late with everything else, why not that? Never been with a woman in all the time I've known you after we got it on. Your name? Cryin' Ryan? Don't you remember blubbing when I turned you down the second time?"

"I came off an all-nighter. I was yawning so bad I could hardly keep my eyes open. Now stop your shit before I run you in again."

"On what charge?"

"I'll think of something. Not too hard with you. Got complaints about you coming out the wazoo, Naylor. Enough to keep you tied up in the station for months, so cut the crap. I want to talk about something different, an old matter."

"Not doing drugs anymore. I cut out that shit after you picked me up a while ago. It was only a couple of times I popped a tab or two. Jeez, get off my back will you?"

Ryan quieted as Luigi came down the aisle with his order. The grubby store owner placed the burgeoning plate of pasta before the detective with a scowl.

"You wanna anything else?"

"I'll grab a coke after I'm finished. Shit, Luigi, can you get any more on this plate, or what?"

"Your mamma, she notta cook for you, eh? You need-a some-a food, make-a you big anna strong."

"You leave my mum out of this you big fat wop. And get a clean apron for fuck sake. That one is evolving into something that's going to take over your cafe soon. Probably more intelligent too."

Luigi guffawed as he strode back down the aisle to the kitchen. Ryan waved away the waitress who was ready to descend on him to take his drink order. He turned his attention back to Cindy who was sipping her coffee, probably some fancy skinny-cino or some such shit with soy milk instead of good, wholesome dairy.

"I want to talk to you about your case, from back in school." Ryan watched as Cindy drew a sharp breath. The coffee cup rattled on the saucer as she placed it down in a hurry. Ryan watched her carefully for any signs of ingrained intent. He knew it would be difficult to distinguish hatred for her rapists from murderous intentions, but he hoped he might get lucky. Something in her demeanour might give him the impression that she harboured more than just passive aggression.

"Thought you and your cronies had given up on that. Didn't believe me if I remember correctly. Had it coming because of the way I was flaunting myself around town."

"Not everyone felt that way or thought that, Cindy. They were just stuck for an avenue of investigation when every one of those boys and their parents vouched for them and corroborated each other's stories that night. Some prominent citizens in that... "

"Fuck them, and fuck you lot! Made up your minds before you even got to the parents. Fucking prominent citizens, my arse. Bunch of fucking white-collar criminals sticking up for a bunch of rapists, and you cops bought it all. Every rotten lie. Left me looking like the perpetrator of a crime against them! Good on you. Get out of here. I have nothing to say to you."

"*I,* wasn't on the force then, Cindy. Been directing that anger of yours in a different direction lately?"

"What do you mean?"

"I mean have you expanded your base of operations to more than just screwing and blackmailing every man in Ingham?"

"Never asked for money from anyone, so how could it be blackmail? Prove it."

"Emotional blackmail can be just as potent as monetary blackmail. Harder to prove, though, I'll grant you that. Doesn't mean we don't know what you're doing."

"Go ahead and run me in again in that case, otherwise fu... "

"Swear at me one more time and I *will* run you in. Promise. Now, can you dial it back a few notches, please? I am going to eat some of this here pile of spaghetti Luigi heaped on my plate while you talk about what you've been doing lately. Include some times and dates alright?"

"Not sure what you want me to say. For the past few weeks I've been at the gym most mornings, then at the beach most afternoons. Trying to get clean and fit again... from booze! Don't go getting on your high horse. I told you I never really did drugs. You just happened to catch me with a few tabs of ecstasy that one time, that's all. I wanted to quit booze because it was getting a bit out of hand and, someone I was trying to hook up with... "

"Knocked you back? Finally found out you weren't all that hot anymore, huh? Bet that was a shock to the system. Eye-opener and all that? So who was the *un*lucky target?"

"You're a pig."

"Yeah, yeah, I'm a pig, so what? You're a slut and I'm a pig. Gee, what news! Who was it?"

"New guy in town. Michael something."

"Miller? You're shitting me? Michael Miller?"

"You know him?"

"Mister-E-lucidate-himself? Yeah, I know him. He was boarding with me."

"So, that's why I've never seen you with a woman all this time? Bloody faggot."

A vice-like grip circled Cindy's wrist, slammed her hand on the Formica tabletop with such a volume that eyes swivelled their way. Ryan increased the pressure as he pierced her with his blue-grey eyes. Cindy felt the heat and the pain ascending her arm as the vibrations travelled upward. Ryan released her only when he realised they had an audience. He returned to his pasta.

"If you don't watch that filthy mouth of yours I will haul you in and lock you up. Got me? I'm not fucking around. Now answer my fucking questions without any more stupid references to something that isn't true. Have you been anywhere near the school lately?"

"What school? It isn't there anymore."

"I know that you dumb broad. I'm talking about *before* it blew up and rained all over the town."

"I wouldn't go back there if you paid me. After what happened to me there? Are you insane?"

"I'll take that as a 'no' then?"

"I left school the day after it happened and never went back. Am I glad the school blew up? You bet! Am I sorry I didn't think of it? You bet! Did I do it? Get real. What do I know about explosives?"

"Who said anything about explosives?"

"Oh, wow, you got me then Detective. It must have been me seeing as you so cleverly trapped me into that little confession. Jeez, you wouldn't be asking me about it if it was a gas leak like they claimed on the news."

"Got your smarts back now that you're off the booze, huh? So you haven't tried to get even with any of the blokes involved that night? Other than your one-woman crusade to defame every married man in town? Own any guns or property around town?"

"Only the one house my parents left me and no, no gun. Why, did someone get shot? Please tell me it was one of those bastards?"

"You heard about, Clay and, Vic?"

"Who hasn't? It's all anyone talks about in town anymore. That and the school. People around here are shit-scared to go out at night with that creep running around free, while you mongrels do nothing."

"You're on your last chance with me. One more smart-arse comment or insult and I will drag you out of here by the hair all the way up the street to the station where I will keep you for days. Capish?" asked Ryan, deliberately mispronouncing the Italian word for the more Anglicised version

"*Si Signore,*" retorted Cindy with a smirk.

"Now, answer my question."

"I forgot, what was it?"

"Been thinking of getting your own back against any of those blokes, like, Clay and, Vic?"

"I never said they were involved that night. Arseholes that they were and I wouldn't have put it past them, but they weren't there, so why would I have anything against them?"

"So, you haven't spoken to them since when?"

"I haven't even *seen* Clay since he left school. Heard about him and his promotions in the council, but never spoke to him again. Vic was always hanging around town, so I saw him plenty of times, never spoke to him, and I certainly wouldn't have done something like that, to him."

"Like what?"

"What the papers said, torture and stuff, jeez. That's just gross, lopping off his fingers and that. How could you possibly think I had anything to do with that?"

"Have to follow up on all possibilities, that's the job. You had a very good reason in your mind, to blow up the school and torture the headmaster... "

"What? The headmaster? Mr Murphy?"

"No, Thornton. The headmaster from our time. Papers haven't got a hold of that one yet, so shut up about it."

"But, he's been missing for ages, hasn't he? What happened to the old bastard?"

"Same as the others. Butchered, for the better part of a year or more, most likely. What am I going to find if I do a search of your place, Cindy? Any hidden rooms where you have one or two football players stashed?"

"No, but I hear you're no innocent when it comes to hidden rooms. Seen your mate, Loz lately, Detective Ryan?"

The colour drained from Ryan's face. Before he could react to her words, Cindy quickly removed herself from his reach and raced out the door. Faced with the mound of remaining pasta on his plate, Ryan slowly shovelled the food into his mouth, taking his time, mulling over the responses to his questions. When he finally finished, he strode the few paces to the front counter where he slapped down a ten-dollar note, grabbed a bottle of Coke from the fridge and headed out the door.

On Herbert Street, he thought about crossing over and cutting through the park, set neatly between the two highways inbound and outbound through town. He needed some time to think about where Loz might be. Cindy had shaken him with her comment. He did feel responsible for Loz and his subsequent disappearance. If not for taking him into his custody, Loz may well be drinking himself into another stupor under the bridge at that moment.

Mid-stride, mid-thought, with one foot, raised slightly off the green grass of the park, the elusive feeling he had before leaving the station suddenly surfaced with perfect clarity - *hidden room- hidden compartment!* Before Ryan could plant his raised foot on the grass, an ear-shattering blast and a thundering shockwave caused him to reel backwards. Struggling backward to keep balance, arms flailing either side like he was teetering on a tightrope, Ryan allowed himself to fall to the footpath while he gawked helplessly at the police station on Palm Terrace. Only a few hundred metres away, it had been levelled by the blast, a mushroom cloud of dust, debris, and smoke, rising from the remains.

Flames leapt high into the cloudless sky, while a couple of the buildings close to the station suddenly erupted into flames. Nothing but a smouldering ruin and a couple of sandstone walls marked where the police station had stood only seconds before. Toward the rear of the station, where Ryan had been only a short time ago, was a gaping hole, with a ruptured water main gushing a fountain of water metres into the air, dousing the fire around it. Ryan sat on the concrete path, a profound sense of dismay and loss etched on his features. He wasn't able to rouse himself, wasn't able to rush to assistance, crippled by the grief of losing his real home and the only true family he had ever known.

Unabashed tears flowed freely from his eyes locked on to the devastation of the most important aspect of his life. His friends, his... boss. *Oh, shit no! Gazza! Fuck, why? What is going on in this town... but... this? This means... it has to...* Ryan fumbled in his trouser pocket to find a handkerchief to mop away the tears as he clumsily stood up. His hand found something foreign among the loose change. A piece of paper that shouldn't be there. Puzzled, Ryan read the neatly folded note. He froze. YOU'RE NEXT.

CINDY

"She had to have been the one to somehow slip it into my pocket," said Ryan.

"So, without your knowledge, in the middle of a cafe, she somehow manages to get a note into a detective's trousers without him or anyone else noticing? That's your story, Ryan? You really expect Detective Chalmers and me to accept this bullshit from you? You say the explosives had to be in the bottom of a false compartment in the trunk, which *you* handled last. Then you miraculously connect the Minstrel Killer and the explosions together in some cockamamie theory of yours because you find a mysterious note in your pants? That about it?"

Seething inside with grief and anger channelled toward the two Townsville detectives who had been grilling Ryan for the past five hours, saw Ryan reaching a boiling point.

"Look you pair of fuckwits. I loved these guys I worked with, love the force, and wanted nothing else but to join the police since I can remember. My boss... G, Gary, was almost a father to me. More of a father than my own could ever have hoped to be, and you pair of dim-witted arseholes really believe I would have blown it all up, including the best person to ever come into my rotten life? I'm telling you, you are the ones indirectly responsible for this and when I prove it, I am going to bury you both. The trunk didn't look right for some reason, which I didn't pick up on until I was reminded about the hidden room in my garage."

"Yeah, we got that. You had a sudden bright, shiny moment when you figured it all out. A hidden compartment in the trunk, filled with explosives because the weight of the trunk for the number of tools in it didn't gel and the size of the interior was off-key? Convenient that you figured all that out too late to save your 'father-figure and friends'?"

Ryan reached for Trent Barron's jacket lapels, only to be brought down again with a thump by Detective Chalmers standing behind him with his massive paws on Ryan's shoulders. In the darkness, outside the temporary demountable building hastily erected in the large carpark at the rear of the devastated police station, strobing lights indicated the continuation of the investigation into the bombing. The search for body parts continued. Ryan was disconsolate at losing his mentor and good friend, Gary.

He could not be more disappointed that his friend was gone and the two detectives from Townsville had somehow been spared. They had left the building moments before him in their cruiser and were miles away when the blast detonated. Ryan had been across the street at the park, in full view of the devastation wrought upon his mates, some of whom he saw staggering from the remains of the building, alight from head to toe. He could not un-hear their terrible cries of anguish as they realised they were dying. He could not un-see the horrible vision that planted itself deeply into his subconscious, taking root for eternity in his troubled mind. The enormous cloud of dust and debris that erupted from the blast rained down its corrupted legacy upon the town of Ingham for hours afterwards.

Residents living in the small section of suburbia behind the station reported charred body parts turning up on their roofs and in their backyards. One elderly Italian lady turned up at the ruins with a bloody eyeball she had located in a pocket of her husband's shirt that had been hanging on her washing line. It was yet to be determined who the eyeball belonged to but Ryan recognised it for that of one, Constable Audrey Temple who manned the front desk most often. She always had a good word to say and knew everyone by name. A kind, considerate person who had been a newly-wed the previous year and had only recently admitted to being pregnant after being pushed about her sudden illnesses most mornings.

All of them! All of the people he loved most in the world had expired in the blast while being handed out their daily assignments in the fishbowl no doubt. His boss would have called them all together after the two detectives had left, to discuss the school and what still needed to be covered by way of following leads and questioning potential witnesses. The school was being given top priority despite the Minstrel Killer remaining at large. There being very little to go on in that case other than background checks, the grunt-work that all detectives shied from mostly.

Ryan still could not understand the reluctance from the Townsville boys to accept that it was deliberate on the part of the Minstrel Killer to leave behind his weapons of torture for them to find. The killer had been extremely careful not to leave behind any clues before that, so it came as quite a surprise to Ryan when the evidence was brought in from his shack.

Ryan had no way of knowing whether the tools were part of his inheritance or not. He couldn't remember entering the usually closed garage of his old man's shack. He had not witnessed any 'renovations', ostensibly to soundproof the walls. His father never parked his car in there and Ryan had no need to look into the garage while detoxing the bastard. He had no wish to know anything more about the old prick by poking around. No need to look through the shack, grounds, or garage after his old man died. He made a mental note to amend that by having a look at the shack the moment the clowns from Townsville were finished with him. He needed to see what had changed.

The killer had to know the trunk would end up in the station's evidence locker for testing. That the station was the target seemed obvious to Ryan, if no one else. The explosives were deliberately planted in the trunk, which was set to explode. *How was it set to explode? Automatic timer? Remote detonation? That would infer that the killer was nearby with knowledge of where and when the evidence was stored.* Ryan was so far the only person who believed the crimes were connected. If he could not convince others of his theory the carnage in his town would continue. He had to talk to

Cindy again. She had left the cafe before him, and may well have seen something he hadn't.

The Minstrel Killer was out there making a mockery and a sham of his town, a disaster area in which its citizens were in grave danger. No one seemed to be spared the wrath of the demented Minstrel. Luckily, no children were attending the school when it was attacked. Only a groundsman and a janitor on duty, both injured but in a stable condition. The death toll from the attack on the police station stood at twenty-two with another four seriously injured in the hospital sure to be counted in the death toll. Six passers-by had been injured but were expected to recover. Twenty-two plus another four likely, and the three victims they knew of made a total of twenty-nine victims of the Minstrel Killer so far, shaping up to be Australia's worst serial killer. Officially, though, only three victims had been attributed to the crazed murderer. Loz was missing and presumed to be held captive by the killer, as well as a missing school teacher from his time, Mr Craig Ball.

It took three years before Thornton's corpse showed up in the vacant lot. Who knew how many others were out there being held against their will by the madman, who had finally shown himself in a note, only to be disbelieved by anyone *but* Ryan. There were no further reports of missing persons at least. Ryan hoped that would continue. He was despairing for his friend, Lorenzo. Given how fragile Loz was when last he saw him, Ryan feared his swift demise under brutal torture, the likes of which he had seen on his cohorts, Clayton and Victor.

"I can only emphasise what I have been telling you, Detective Barron, that I know the crimes are connected. The Minstrel Killer has not left behind anything prior to the tools in the trunk. Don't you think it strange that a serial killer leaves behind his weapons like that? You can't have seen that before, surely?"

"It doesn't matter what we have or haven't seen before. We only have your word for the possibility that the trunk's secret compartment contained the explosives that destroyed the station.

There is nothing left of the trunk to verify your dubious claim. I'm sure that Detective Chalmers and I would have detected such an anomaly had it been true."

"Oh, so that's it is it? You didn't find the bloody compartment so it wasn't there? Fine bloody detective you are. Rather hang something on another detective than think you could have been mistaken. What about the bloody note? Did I give that to *myself*?"

"Totally clear of anything bar your fingerprints yet again, and no other way to trace it back. Ordinary copying paper and printed on any one of hundreds of Canon printers sold in Ingham over the last few years. Totally untraceable even if we were to upend every household in Ingham with one of those printers. You think you're very clever, don't you? Give yourself a get-out-of-jail-free card and we will immediately suspend suspicions of you? Get real. Because of that note, you are our number one suspect for the murders. Not the school or the police station. We don't think you're insane enough to blow up your friends."

"You cannot seriously believe that I am a serial killer after all my years of service on the force?"

"Weirder things have happened. Many an officer has gone off the rails given sufficient cause in their minds."

"Are you arresting me?"

"Not at this point in time, no."

"So, I am free to leave then?"

"Leave here, yes. Leave town, no. I expect you to surrender your badge and your passport immediately. You are officially on suspension awaiting an official inquiry into your actions and your movements once the relief squad arrives from Brisbane to help out. They'll be here in the morning. Until then you are free to return to your home and nothing more. If you are found to be anywhere other than your home between now and when we summon you tomorrow, we will place you under arrest and throw you in jail. Wherever we find a cell, that is."

"Brian, follow him. Make certain he doesn't see you. I want to know everything he does including how many sheets of toilet paper he uses. Got me?" ordered Trent the moment Ryan exited the demountable. Brian nodded solemnly before following his surveillance target. "Oh, and Brian? If he so much as suspects you are following him I'll see you end up back on the streets issuing tickets on Mornington Island in the Gulf."

Brian gave him a baleful stare as he stepped from the building into the red and blue lights of multiple emergency vehicles. Rescue workers continuing their gruesome task in the hollow where the station once stood. For the first time in their long partnership, Brian felt as though his partner was erring. Brian no longer believed that the detective he was following had anything to do with the Minstrel Killer murders. He would not voice his opinion, nor would he balk at following orders, but he secretly admitted that for once, he and his partner were opposed.

Brian heard, on his earpiece, every sound made by Detective Ryan through the miniature bug on the detective's collar, planted at the very moment he forced Ryan back into his chair. Their plan worked like a dream, engaging Ryan just enough to ruffle his feathers without turning him psychotic. He and Trent had cooked up the whole plan to enable them to hide the device and track the detective's conversations and movements. Trent believed Ryan would lead them to the missing Lorenzo Catani. The bug doubled as a tracking device, so they could not lose their suspect as long as Brian remained within a one-kilometre radius of Ryan's position. A printed transcript of everything the detective uttered would be immediately available to Trent in real-time.

Brian picked through all the information they had as he drove a reasonable distance behind Ryan's Holden Commodore, down the main street of Ingham, presumably en route to his home. When Ryan's vehicle slowed to make a left turn towards the water tower on Haig Street, which led onto Atkinson Street, Brian became alert. Ryan did not live in this part of town. He was going against Trent's orders. He followed Ryan as he made a right turn into Neame Street, stopping outside a red brick house with a cream-coloured, stucco, art-deco facade. A rose-covered garden arch stood sentinel over the small gate in the fence, through which Ryan entered. A porch light triggered automatically as Ryan approached the door.

"Christ, not you again," Cindy said after she opened the door to the insistent knocking.

"Sorry to call on you late, Cindy but I really need to talk to you."

"Well, this is a new approach for you - civility?"

"Yeah, I guess I deserve that. Look, can we go inside? I do really need to talk to you about something very important. You heard about the police station?"

"Heard it, and heard about it."

"Heard?"

"Naturally. Everyone in town heard the bloody thing. I don't live that far from it you know? Pretty hard for me to not hear it. I was walking home when it went off. Nearly gave me a bloody heart attack. My ears are still ringing. Pity you weren't there at the time." Cindy waited for her barb to strike blood.

"Sorry to disappoint you. Now, can we go inside please?"

Cindy sighed, then led the way down the long hall to the kitchen where she was half-way through her evening meal of salad and paper-thin slices of tuna. She sat down heavily onto the vinyl-covered chair in front of her plate, resuming her dinner. Ryan sat opposite her, taking in his surroundings with a practised eye.

"Nice place you have here, Cindy."

"Mum and Dad's. Left to me in their will and no siblings to share it with. Tidy savings account and a life insurance policy to make sure I didn't go without. I am really very grateful to them for their foresight. So, spit it out. What do you want that you couldn't have asked me this morning?"

"The station blew up *after* we talked, and what I have to ask is related to that."

"Don't know anything about it so you wasted your time coming here."

"Not saying you had anything to do with it, so no need to be on the defensive," Ryan said mimicking her tone and intonation perfectly. "I want you to remember when you left the cafe. Picture it in your mind and talk me through it, everything you can recall no matter how insignificant."

"You gotta be shitting me? My memory is pretty much fried since the booze, Ryan. I can hardly remember what I did five minutes ago these days, let alone this morning, and certainly not about what I may or may not have seen after I left Luigi's. And why would you think I would want to help you out with that anyway?"

"Lot of innocent folks died today, Cindy."

"Cops!"

"And civilians, in front of the station, minding their own business."

"Just like I am doing, minding my own business. Not really concerned about the 'good' folks of this town, and really don't give a shit about cops getting what they deserve."

Shutting down the immediate impulse to explode, Ryan utilised his training to conceal his hostility while interviewing people. "Cindy, I realise you feel you got a bad deal with your case, and you have a legitimate reason to be hostile toward a few officers who may have been able to do more, but that was a long time ago and a lot of the folks that died today had nothing or little to do with it. Constable Temple was about the nicest person you could ever meet, newly married, expecting her first child, and was never around during that time. Cindy, her husband collapsed when we told him and he is still in the hospital. Probably never get over it, losing the two people he loved most in the world in one hit. He'll never get to hold his son or daughter, never get to share with his parents the joy of announcing the birth after the long labour, or sharing those golden moments of a child's progression."

Cindy had stopped eating as Ryan related the heartfelt monologue. She felt ashamed of her inability to compartmentalise the hostility she harboured. It had been in her for so long that she seldom allowed any other emotions to enter. A tear escaped her eye, for the lives lost today, for her life lost so long ago. For the story of a child dying before it had the chance to live a little. For her own destiny as a childless woman, unable to conceive due to the physical trauma she had experienced. Never to fulfil her dead mother's last wishes for a grandchild, or her own desires to hold a baby she may have carried to birth. The bitterness she retained ate away at her every single day and she could no longer circumvent it.

"You cannot even begin to imagine what it was like for me back then. To lose everything and everyone, all my hopes and dreams smashed because those fifteen monsters decided to do as they wished with me, so violently and in every way imaginable. How everyone avoided me after that, my friends, my relatives, everyone. Even when I literally crawled to the hospital with blood and semen coursing down my naked legs, the staff looked down upon me like it was all somehow my fault. Pitying me and avoiding me became everyone's favourite pastime in this town. I never again enjoyed the life I deserved, the life I desperately wanted."

"I wasn't in the force back then, Cindy. I was still thinking about it and working on my entrance scores to the academy when it happened. I looked into the file, though, and I can tell you that I would have handled it differently. Yes, you had a mighty reputation after Vic dumped you like a sack of potatoes, but you didn't deserve the treatment you got from the cops back then, or from anyone else. I apologise for their behaviour. I know it won't change anything for you, but I'm sorry just the same."

"Why?"

"Don't you know? I thought it was bloody obvious. Oh, I knew you were using us to get back at Vic. I didn't care as long as I could be with you."

"What?"

"I fell in love with you, Cindy. I've always been in love with you. It's the reason I never married or went out with anyone else all this time. God, it feels good to finally get that off my chest."

"You can't be serious. Is this another ploy, an angle, a method they trained you in, to get me to open up?"

"No. No, Cindy. I have always loved you from the first time we kissed. I was so jealous when you went with the other boys after Vic dumped you. I could see what you were doing and I understood why. I knew you didn't have any feelings for me but I enjoyed being with you just the same. Treasured every last second of being near you, with you, and inside you. I was mad as hell at what happened to you, Cindy.

"I was equally furious when I finally managed to get a hold of your case file. There was nothing I could do about it. As much as I wanted to, there was simply nothing to be done unless I forced one or two of the parents and the players to recant their stories and alibis. I hit a wall when I hinted at it with some of them. I started to get a bit of a reputation at the station and my boss convinced me about how dangerous it was to pursue the matter, so I eventually had to drop it."

Cindy raised herself slowly from the chair, unsure of her emotional state, or whether to believe the detective. Sure, her motives had always been to ensnare her prey with seduction to the point where she could almost taste the affection and love pouring from them, but this was not what she had expected. This was so far out of left-field that it left her reeling. She staggered over to the refrigerator where she grabbed a bottle of unopened white wine. It would be her first drink in weeks and she shook as she released the cork. She had kept the bottle to tempt her out of sobriety. Tonight she would succumb.

"By the way, I didn't tell you how terrific you look. I couldn't get over the change in you this morning. I hadn't seen you for a while and it really hit me when I saw you looking so healthy, strong and tanned It's probably the wrong time to tell you, Cindy, and I'm sorry for that too. Fucked if I know why. It's probably that I realised today how short life can really be. If I didn't say something now, I'd probably never have another opportunity."

Cindy raised the glass to her lips, eyeing Ryan over the rim until she finally placed the still full glass on the kitchen benchtop. She had made such enormous strides in the fight to stay clean that she couldn't bring herself to erode that effort. For the first time in many years, Cindy Naylor did not feel as guilty and dirty as she used to, even feeling the elusive warmth of pride encroaching on her iron shield. Though far from believing herself to be a teetotaller just yet, she felt she was on the way. She had stuck to her guns and turned herself around. For all the wrong reasons admittedly, but a step in the right direction nonetheless. What started out as a ploy to ensnare another victim changed into a fight to reclaim her esteem.

Ryan didn't dare say another word for fear he was making a whopping great fool of himself. He wasn't sure where the confession had come from but saw how ridiculous it must have seemed to Cindy, who had been mishandled by him more times than he cared to remember. In his romantically inept manner, Ryan had found numerous nit-picky reasons to arrest or question Cindy Naylor over the years, all to remain in close contact with her. He never again had the courage to make a move, to let her know how he felt, going along with the jokes and comments about her in the station.

What he told the detectives about her possibly slipping the note into his pocket was yet another fabrication, a way for him to see her on a professional level. He figured that if he couldn't have her on a personal level, then he may as well find a professional reason to be in her proximity.

Cindy had no words for the moment. She was too stunned to be confident about speaking a coherent sentence. She had gone to bed with Ryan once only after Victor had unceremoniously dumped her for another tart. He was part of a line of men that stretched to hundreds over the years. It wasn't until after the gang-rape that the self-loathing and self-immolation had begun by way of indiscriminate sex with anyone. Ryan had been before that, but she still could not recall if there was any sign of real affection from him back then. She understood why she didn't remember. It was the booze. Her brain had been pickled for a long, long time.

"I don't know if I can process this at the moment. I have thought about you in one particular way all this time governed by the way you treated me. Doing a one-eighty degrees on me has really thrown me for a loop. Is that what you came here for, just to tell me that?"

"No, I told you the truth about that. I didn't come here to tell you that at all, actually. It slipped out before I could stop myself. I only wanted to ask you about what you may have seen on your way out of the cafe this morning. Can you have a go at that for me, Cindy? I know what you said about not being able to remember things anymore, but if you tried, you might be able to picture something? You are clean now. Maybe you can remember something?"

Cindy came back to the table, where she slowly lowered herself in the chair opposite Ryan. "What do you want to know?"

"You left the cafe, which way did you go?"

"I, I went through the park on my way home."

"Okay. The police station is on your left on Palm Terrace, did you happen to look that way at all, see anyone near the building or walking away from it?"

"Oh, come on, you can't be serious?"

"You never know what you may have seen if you don't try, Cindy. You might surprise yourself. Give it a go, please? Just picture it in your mind. As you're leaving Luigi's, kinda smug after having a shot at me and getting away with it. Forget it... history," said Ryan as Cindy was about to protest, or apologise. "Just concentrate on this morning. You've had a go at me and walked out of the cafe and...?"

"I was thinking, thinking about going uptown for a bit of window shopping because some of my clothes were loose on me."

"Did you look uptown? Did you observe anyone around at the time?"

"I did look uptown for a moment, before I decided to ditch the idea of window shopping, knowing that I had more weight I wanted to lose. I had to get to the gym to work on that goal. I stopped at the park, sat on one of the benches for a while, just organising my day in my head. I don't remember seeing anyone in particular until... "

"Until what?"

"Until I saw *him*, actually."

"Him? Him who?"

"Wow, I do remember. I saw Michael passing by the station. Even at a distance, I recognised him."

"Michael? Michael Miller? Are you sure? It is a fair distance from the park to the station? I was thinking more along the lines of people in and around the park at the time. Anyone loitering around who seemed out of place maybe?"

"How come?"

"Just thinking of anyone with a remote detonating device. The bomber may have had to be within a certain range unless it was triggered via a cell phone. That makes the park an advantageous position. The ideal line of sight to the station, no need to look conspicuous just sitting on a park bench, maybe an uneaten sandwich next to you. Are you sure it was Michael you saw?"

"I don't forget faces. It was him, in a bit of a hurry, which was probably why I noticed him. You know, standing out because he is moving faster than anyone else."

"When you say hurrying, do you mean running or... ?"

"Not running. No. More of a quick walk like one of those walkers in the Olympics. I always thought they looked funny. Sort of like that."

"Which way was he heading?"

"Uptown, I suppose. At first, I thought he was heading for the park, then I saw him change direction. It was almost like... "

"What, Cindy?"

"Paranoid I guess, but it almost seemed like he had seen me and changed direction intentionally."

"Why would he have been avoiding you? Oh, that's right. Okay, anything else that looked out of place, or struck a nerve as looking out of the ordinary?"

"No. I didn't notice anyone else in the park, though I couldn't say that someone wasn't lying on the grass somewhere, behind a tree or something. It looked deserted like it normally is at that time of day. I started to walk home and on the way - BOOM!"

"Think, Cindy this is really important. Anything at all whether it was suspicious or not?"

"It was just an ordinary morning, a few folks roaming around the streets like normal, no one specific that I recognised. I wasn't really looking. I happened to notice Michael only because of the way he was moving in relation to others. Don't ask me to tell you who else was on the streets. I couldn't say."

"Alright, Cindy. Thanks for your help. I really am sorry for what happened to you, you know? If I can do anything for you, just call okay? Here's one of my business cards."

***

"You getting this, Trent?"

"Loud and clear. I'll check on this Michael Miller guy. You stay on Ryan's tail if he looks like leaving. We may have to bring the bird in as well for some further questioning of our own."

"You think he's going to try and cover for her?"

"Not sure what to make of the whole romance angle. *I* actually thought he was gay," remarked Trent Barron into Chalmers' earpiece. "Can't figure that he is trying to protect her when he practically accused her of planting the note in the first place. I know what he said to her and all that crap. It's all sentimental bullshit as far as I'm concerned."

"You still think he has something to do with it?"

"Bet my pension on it. He is involved somehow, my gut instincts are never wrong. You keep on him without letting him see you, got me?"

"Sure, like it's so easy to follow someone unnoticed in this small town for fuck sake. He knows everyone, Trent, he's sure to make me if he spots the same car a couple of times."

"Then you make sure he doesn't see the same car a couple of times. If you know he is going to stay put for an hour or two, come change cars, or notify me to have one sent to a specific location if you know where he is headed."

"Copy that. Out."

INTOLERABLE

When Lorenzo woke from his nightmare, he immediately felt the intolerable pain engaging his whole body. He was gagged. Unable to scream. That did not prevent him from letting loose a muffled cry. In the dim light of the flickering candle, his subdued and unintelligible words fell on deaf ears. While Loz had been thrashing about uncontrollably from the effects of the acid injected into his penis, the monster had injected the remainder into both ears of his old teacher. Mr Ball passed out almost instantly, while Loz was not so fortunate. He remained conscious for an eternity suffering the torments of hell. Despite his rough living, Lorenzo had never before experienced such excruciating pain.

The treatment would have been bad enough without any sort of enhancement. With the enhancement, Loz felt that setting light to his crotch after dousing it in petrol could not have caused as much pain as he had already experienced. The continuation of the effects long after the injection ensured that Loz remained in a state of unadulterated distress. Moaning and muttering incoherently into the rag stuffed in his mouth. Loz wished for Death to ride quickly to his aid, to come forth in whatever manifestation Death chose, to end his abject misery. He could not believe that such pain was possible, did not believe there could be worse, wanting nothing more than the sweet relief of oblivion.

"Come on now, Mr Catani, I have given you the second shot, so it can't be that bad anymore? Then again, it probably is? Shit, I wouldn't want that to happen to me. Oh, stupid me, I did suffer didn't I? Maybe not as much as you. I don't know, what is worse? Physical or mental anguish, do you think? I copped a lot of both. I think the mental was probably worst for me. The physical was fixed up with a bit of corrective surgery eventually, but not the mental torment. That still continues today. No amount of consolation or therapy could diminish that pain, Mr Catani, none!"

The man removed the gag from Lorenzo's mouth. Loz's screams released at a full pitch into the soundproofed room.

"You cunt! You fucking, stinking, rotten low-life, fucking cunt! Ahh, I'm going to... ahh, shit! Fuck!"

"Stop being such a drama queen. You are not going to do anything to anyone anymore. You will not survive what I dish out. That is a promise. If you tell me what I want to know I will give you a painkiller. It won't fix the problem of course, but it will give you some welcome relief. I can't imagine how much that might be hurting. Every time you pee, you will get a repeat of that I suppose. Sucks to be you. Tell me. Who was it? Who came back that night?"

"Fuuuuuuck! Fuck off you cunt."

"Really? You want me and my painkiller here, my free journey into relief, to walk out while you continue to experience the effects of my treatments? How about if I give you another shot of the enhancer? Want another session of THAT!"

"No, no, please don't. Not, not that, I'm begging you. Hurts, soooo bad. Please, can't... help?"

"Who was it? Even if you are not one hundred per cent sure, just tell me what you think you know, and relief is at hand."

"RYAN, okay? It, was, I... think. It... I saw, Ryan sneaking out of... thought I was dreaming. So late... shit, pain. Can't think... ahhhh."

"Ryan returned to the camp with you? Then left the tent afterwards?"

"Don't... please... hurts, pain... "

"Answer my question. Was it, Ryan that slipped out of your tent that night? While the rest of you slept?"

"Yes, yes... saw, saw, Ryan leaving the tent. Please... ? Can't... oh... "

"Oh very well. Here, that should make it better. A little pin-prick, then everything should... oh dear. Did I mix up the bottles? I think I did. I might have... yes, judging by your eyes, I'd say I gave you the enhancer rather than the pain-killer. Silly me. I really should be more care... "

Lorenzo's screams drowned out the man's accented voice. Mr Ball continued to wriggle uncomfortably while muttering softly into the gag. Mr Ball found some small comfort in that he was no longer able to hear anything, which meant one level less of torture to his system. He was becoming inured to the pain he thought. Unfortunately, he knew the Minstrel had other methods and far worse instruments of torture to deliver upon his captives. He had been forced to watch endless video footage of his friend Edward Thornton, undergoing innumerable days of utter agony at the hands of the Minstrel.

He had witnessed his own destiny in that footage. Saw how he would suffer. Knew he would die far too late into the process. Every time it seemed that poor old Edward had breathed his last, he was somehow revived, kept alive just enough to survive the next round of punishments, surpassing in intensity and perversity all previous episodes. Eyeballs touched by the rays of the sun through a magnifying glass, larger and larger implements inserted into the nostrils, ears torn from the head with pliers, hair ripped from the roots while entangled in a rotary tool of some sort. Screws of varying lengths up to ten inches forced through flesh and bone, electrical charges applied to the genitalia, and all manner of paraphernalia and matter inserted into the anus.

He recognised a few of the implements used to sever or crush fingers and toes on himself; tin snips, garden shears, a bench vice or hammer. The list went on and on until the events and the pain blurred into one long nightmare where he could no longer distinguish between his pain and that of others on video or in reality. When Loz joined him he thought it might let up for a while. It simply got worse. The serum that the Minstrel injected made every one of the human senses go into a sadistic over-drive. Causing him an apoplectic heightening of everything he saw, heard or felt. He also longed desperately for the oblivion Lorenzo sought. Prayed with all his heart and might for surcease, an end to the appalling pain.

He watched as the Minstrel replaced the gag in Lorenzo's mouth. Saw Lorenzo thrashing about in frenzied convulsions like an epileptic in the throes of a grand mal seizure, but thankfully unable to hear his screams any longer. He was incapable of tears for his former student or himself, any longer. He had come to accept his fate with as much dignity as possible. Though he whimpered in misery, he no longer cared. He knew he had done something very terrible. His neglect had been identified by the Minstrel. His shame had been uncovered. He deserved to die.

"I will be merciful to you, Lorenzo. You've confirmed my suspicions. I will not allow you to suffer for years or even months. I will give you the relief you desire in death for finally giving me confirmation. Ryan! I knew it had to be him. I told him he was next. He will tell me the name of the mastermind. It has to stop, everything. No more. I will be extremely generous with my treatments to him when he comes to join us. I have some truly special surprises in store for him. Thank you, Lorenzo. Mr Ball has to be found first, though. He time has to end and he must be found in a spectacular fashion, according to his beliefs. Poor, stupid, fool. He shall have his own cross to bear.

FOUND

"**Who called it in**?"

"Chap over there, says he came back from an all-night fishing trip, saw it sticking out of the ground next to the boat ramp. Puked to the side there."

"Jesus!"

"Close," suggested Detective Brian Chalmers.

"That's blasphemous, Bri," said Trent.

"Yep, going down for sure when it comes time."

"Is it, is it my imagination or does that post run... through him?"

"Through him, or him around the post, take your pick. Either way, it's pretty sick stuff."

"What the fuck are you talking about, 'him around the post'?"

"Just my impression, for what it's worth. The victim, one Craig Ball, an ex-school teacher at Ingham High according to the Doc, was sawn in half vertically, then laterally through the chest and arms. His innards and a lot of the skeletal structure were removed, then the cadaver was wrapped around the crucifix, and fixed to it with the barbed-wire. Railway spikes through the wrists and feet complete the image of the cross-*in*-Christ garnished with a crown of barbed-wire."

"You gotta be shitting me?"

"Look for yourself. We need some heavy-duty manpower, or a crane to get it out of the ground, so you have plenty of time before it shows up."

"Why aren't you at, Ryan's?"

"I was on-call tonight for emergencies. Not many of us troops on the ground at the moment and they are getting tired quickly doing all the double-shifts. Didn't think it paid to make enemies of the boys and girls here on secondment. Besides, Ryan was snoring like a coal-miner when I left. No way he did this, which pretty much exonerates him don't you think? First one we've seen with the fully-blacked-out face, Trent, so obviously the work of the Minstrel Killer. I followed Ryan to his home where he drank himself steadily into a comatose state on his lounge-room recliner. I even entered the house just to make sure it was him I was hearing through the bug after I got the call. We go knock on his door now, he'll be there, with a hangover, I guarantee."

"Hey, Doc, I need... "

"Forget it, detective. I'm not your man anymore. I quit. This is, is... the worst kind of evil I have ever witnessed and I can't take seeing it anymore. I refuse to retire with these atrocities plaguing my thoughts. I'm off to play golf or tiddly-winks or whatever. Good luck. Catch this perverted prick and make sure he never sees the inside of a prison now that I am no longer about to face him on my table. I have sent for someone else to take over, she should be here soon. Her name is Doctor Amanda Sale. Goodbye." Trent and Brian watched as the doctor stepped into his Toyota Prius and whizzed away, the hybrid electric-petrol engine as silent as death itself.

Dawn was approaching fast, with the requisite tropical humidity set to make the vicinity uncomfortably hot and muggy very quickly. Neither detective wanted to be stuck there waiting for the crane and a new doctor to arrive, with a cadaver about to give off aromas rivalling that of the mangroves surrounding them. Trent turned to view the victim once more.

The face of the victim established a solid pattern indicating a direct link to the serial murders attributable to the Minstrel. Trent was not ruling out a copycat, or an accomplice to Ryan at this stage. If what Brian had told him was accurate, he could not connect the victim directly to Ryan, turning his case on end, and back to square one with no suspects. The Commissioner was going to have kittens when he reported that his only suspect was a dead end. Trent had been pressured to bring the investigation to a conclusion before the people of Ingham and surrounds demanded a scapegoat. The Super in Townsville was being pressed by the Deputy Commissioner who was getting his arse reamed by the Commissioner who got his licking by the Cabinet Minister.

Shit ran downhill and it was all piling up on Trent and Brian at the bottom of the heap. The stink would suffocate them soon if they could not show some progress. Going backwards, from having a suspect to having none, did not warrant speculation. The case may be taken away from them, maybe even by members of the Federal Police. The Feds had been hovering about at the behest of the Minister. Their careers could end up in the toilet instead of with the accolades and awards Trent had envisioned.

"Accomplice. Ryan has an accomplice in this. We need to shake that tree harder to see what falls."

"Trent, I think you're flogging a dead horse there. It doesn't feel right for, Ryan. This is simply not in his retinue if you ask me."

"Not in his fucking retinue? Where'd you pick that shit up, Brian? Off a cornflakes packet or something? About the extent of your reading capacity."

"Insulting me isn't going to get us anywhere. If you don't want to listen to my opinion, then fine, find yourself another partner. I have never gone against your lead, Trent, never, but you aren't right about this. Ryan is not our man. Everything screams it, but you won't listen. If you want to pursue this with him as our only suspect, I will ask to transfer out. I'm not going to sink with you on this one. You're on your own unless you start looking in another direction."

"What fucking direction, Brian? Can you answer me that? What fucking direction? We got nothing else here. Nothing! Tell me where to go instead of putting obstacles in my path damn it. Give me the benefit of your wisdom to provide me with a lead instead of telling me that what I'm doing is wrong. I... "

"Yeah, I feel the pressure too, Trent. It's getting to me just as much. Going off at me won't help. I'm sorry I don't have anything else and I always allow you to lead on every case, but I won't hang around if you insist on going with Ryan. He's probably telling the truth about wanting to help his old mate to detox, as misguided as that notion is. You saw his face when we mentioned the empty room, he didn't know. It wasn't him. Why would he do this to his friends and teachers? It just doesn't add up."

"It's him."

"No way. Look at his record. Brilliant solve rate and he actively seeks out the domestics. He's some kind of hero around here among abused women and children. They practically worship the man, Trent. He may not be perfect, but I don't think he is capable of this, and I don't believe he would be in cahoots with anyone that did. We have to find another direction, maybe even listen to his theory that the bombings and the murders are connected. Can't hurt to try a different approach can it?"

"Someone with a vendetta?"

"Yeah, but not the girl. No way was this a female crime. Look at the strength you'd need to heft this thing into place. That broad looked like she couldn't lift more than about forty-fifty kilos tops. It's a lightweight timber, probably Oregon I'd say. A one hundred by one hundred millimetre post, about three metres long, with a one hundred by fifty-millimetre cross-member, about two metres long, coupled with what was left of the victim, adds up to maybe eighty to a hundred kilos? Not possible for her to do this. Besides, she was with Ryan for a long time last night. Too long for either of them to have gone and done this."

"FUCK! You're right! You're right, Brian. I had him pegged as the perp and haven't looked farther. Haven't considered anyone or anything else. The Super has been leaning on me hard and I figured I had it all wrapped up. Sorry, Bri. I've had my head up my arse with this one. I respect you too much to not listen to you. How about... how about taking the lead on this? Fresh angle, different approach, huh?"

"No, Trent, not the lead. I don't need that. I'm happy to make a few suggestions, which we can both explore together, as a team. We were always a good team when we bounced ideas off one another, Trent. Talked them through, no matter how weird they seemed. Haven't done that lately, and I miss it. I miss my old partner."

"Have I really sunk that low, Bri? I wasn't seeing it."

"You fell a bit hard for the lure of the limelight, Trent. Lately, though, it seemed like the lure outweighed the job. Like the motivation got turned around."

"Sorry again, Bri. Will you be my touchstone again, mate? Keep me grounded while we solve this fucking thing? We are Johnny-on-the-spot here, so it's up to us I reckon. Take someone else too long to get up to speed."

"I got your back, mate, like always. *Team Barron and Chalmers* like the old days."

"Yeah, yeah, *Team Barron and Chalmers*, on the fucking case. Okay, Detective Chalmers, what do you suggest?"

"I think we need to consider the line, Ryan was taking, and I think we should include him."

"Really? Kinda chews me up a bit."

"Yeah, I realise we might be eating a bit of crow there, Trent, especially you. You up for it? I sorta think we need his local input, and we need to at least explore the possibility of the connection to a vendetta and the link to the bombings. Too much happening at once in a small town for it to be separate and coincidence."

"Right, I agree with you on that front. Small fucking pimple on the landscape like this shithole should not be a scene for numerous unconnected calamities. So, we work on the premise that someone with a need for revenge on a grand scale is stalking the community and getting even for indiscretions of the past?"

"That's his take, and I am inclined to agree at the moment. I think we need to go wake Ryan as soon as we're done here. We need to apprise him of the new information and ask for his cooperation?"

"First, though, we have to scour the area now that the light is better, to see if there is anything here to help us. We need to talk to the fisherman as well."

Brian and Trent set about their separate tasks while waiting for a new doctor to show up to supervise the removal of the corpse before the citizens of Dungeness and surrounds took an interest. The fact that the body was in close proximity to Ryan's shack did not go unnoticed by the pair. In all probability, the timber used in the construction of the crucifix came from the stockpile found near the property. They would have to investigate the shack once more.

"Ghastly bloody thing! Worst I ever seen. Bin out fishin' for mosta the night, didn't see nothing or no one when I got in, just that..." said Moe Barnes, a professional fisherman for most of his forty-three years.

"I assume it wasn't here when you went out? What time was that exactly?" asked Trent.

"Pretty near spot-on midnight."

"Now, Moe, I don't want to sound like a smart-arse, but was it nearly, or spot-on midnight?"

"Near enough as makes no diff. Wasn't exactly staring at me watch the whole time, ya know? Better things to do and wastin' time is wastin' money. High tide was only an hour away and had to be in position with me nets when that happened. Answered all these questions already to the other fella. Can't ya ask him what I told him, so's I can git and put me catch in a freezer 'fore it turns?"

"See that corpse up there, you dumb fuck? You think maybe that is a little more important than your stinking fish?"

Moe lazily followed the direction of Trent's finger and yawned. "Not ta me. Lose me night's haul and I can maybe make the rent, or not, depending on the rest of the week. Bad weather on the horizon, so... no, not as important by a long shot. I called it in and I answered ya bloody questions already. Seems a bloke has a right to ensure his kids don't go without a roof over their heads."

"That could be you next hanging up there like that, then how are your kids going to stay under the roof, eh?" pushed Brian.

"Keep a real good insurance policy, I do. Wife and kids should be so lucky if that was me instead-o-that poor son-of-a-bitch up there. Any more stupid questions... mate?"

"My fellow detective will be by your place to get a signature on your statement once it is typed up. You're free to go in the meantime," said Trent.

"Not till after two. Don't want nobody wakin' me before then. Gotta go out again 'fore midnight and doesn't help me to be all tired and shit, goin out ta sea like that."

"Why not, didn't you just say your wife and kids would be better off without you?"

"Reckon I'd be missed a whole lot more-n-you, that's for fuckin' sure. Great bedside manner ya got there, Detective. Reckon ya missed ya callin as a doctor maybe." Moe Barnes grinned wickedly as he passed the detective with a slight bump of the shoulder.

RYAN

Ryan opened one eye when the sound of persistent knocking finally penetrated his dreamless state. He groaned as he lowered the footrest of the leather recliner in which he had slept, yet again. Not for the first time did the detective rue his behaviour. He vaguely recalled that he had promised himself to quit. He believed he had muttered those words to himself sometime in the last few days. His messed up confession to Cindy had him feeling surly with himself. Her flippancy over the confession had left him feeling rejected and more than a little humiliated.

He chastised himself for tying one over when he had clearly decided to abstain. Not that he could remember doing so. He thought he might start with the present day instead of wasting time berating himself. The knocking on the door became loud enough to break his reveries.

"Yeah, yeah, yeah, keep your knickers on. You better not be a fucking Jehovah, I warn you," he muttered as he made his way along the corridor to the front door.

Pictures of him in the various stages of his career adorned the walls of the hallway. No other pictures of himself or his family were displayed anywhere else in the house. He burned the pictures of his father when the old bastard finally kicked it. He found it difficult to find any photos of his mother that did not show evidence of the years of abuse dished out by his old man. Albeit touched up with make-up, her face always showed the remnants of old bruises or a misshapen jawline, a souvenir from the early days when he really let loose. Ryan was always so ashamed that he could not do more to prevent the abuse, but as a child, he simply wasn't strong enough.

"Fuck, not you two again! What now, coming to arrest me for Harold Holt's disappearance, or maybe it was me who took Azaria Chamberlain? Maybe pull me in for the Hoddle Street massacre and the Tasmanian one as well eh? Maybe, Martin John Bryant wasn't responsible for the Port Arthur murders after all?"

"God, you smell like a brewery, Ryan. Do you think it's any wonder we don't respect you or take you seriously? No, we aren't here to arrest you. My partner, Brian here, seems to think that you might have something... something of interest to add to our investigation. I disagree with him. I know that Gary's glistening, wonder-boy's shine is so tarnished that he is almost unrecognisable. But Brian won't listen to me about that, no. He says we have to come here to ask for your... cooperation. Go clean yourself up you disgrace, before I change my mind and leave."

Ryan stood in the hallway swaying slightly as he absorbed the detective's cold words. Undecided whether to allow the unwanted guests to enter, or simply puke on their shoes, he decided to lead them down the hall, waving them to the kitchen while he made for the bathroom. Half an hour later he was back in the kitchen, clean-shaven and looking a sight better than before. Brian handed him a steaming hot mug of coffee. The men left the kitchen to sit at the dining room table.

"Better?" asked Trent.

"A bit."

"You had better straighten yourself out if you want to remain on the force, Ryan. As of this moment, you are on an official warning. Turn up to work smelling like a brewery or staggering around like an old sot once more and it's the end of the line, no more chances. The new crowd coming into man the restored station will not put up with you the way your old boss did. Everybody, from the Prime Minister downwards, is looking at Ingham and its temporary police force. All of Australia is honed into the broadcasts coming out of here about our worst ever serial killer and a mad bomber. There are more and more news crews converging on us every day as well as an army of gawkers, so we all need to look and act our sharpest from here on in. Got me?"

"Not deaf."

"I need you to verbalise it, Ryan. Show me that I am not wasting my time here."

"No more booze, you have my word. I understand."

"What you do and how much you drink on your own time doesn't interest me or anyone else. If it affects your work, it's everyone's business, which comes back to me as acting chief. I don't like the pressure if one of my people fucks up. I especially don't like fuck-ups caused by avoidable behaviour on my watch. I didn't like you to begin with. You reeked of booze at all hours. Couldn't say anything when Gary foisted a useless piece of shit like you on us when we first came here. I can, and will, say a lot now, though. You will look and dress according to your status as a member of the Australian Police Force. You will honour the uniform of that proud institution and the fallen comrades who wore it. Do I make myself perfectly clear, Detective Ryan?"

"Crystal, Sir."

"Right then. Tell me what you think about these murders and your reasons. I want to know everything you know or think you know. You can thank Detective Chalmers for the opportunity to continue your employment. If he hadn't come in here in the early hours to check that it was actually you passed out on your recliner, you would still be my number one suspect for the murders."

"Why, what happened while I was... dozing?"

"Found your old teacher, Craig Ball with a crucifix shoved up his arse. Your alibi, thanks to, Brian, clears you of any involvement... to a point. I am not ruling out copycats or accomplices yet."

"Where did you find him?"

"Show him the pics, Brian. Right next to the boat ramp at Dungeness, near your shack, with timber used from the left-over stockpile, we found there. Did you go and have a look at your old man's shack after we hauled you in?"

"I knew it was off-limits to me."

"Actually obeyed that directive?"

"I have been obeying all your directives, even though it doesn't seem that way."

"Really? Then how do you explain being at Ms Naylor's residence for close to an hour yesterday evening when you were specifically told to return to your house without deviation or pause, where you were to remain?"

"That was you in the blue Commodore, across the street?" Ryan asked Detective Chalmers, who nodded. "It was more or less personal."

"Yeah, yeah, we know all about the unrequited love angle, Ryan. Care to explain the rest of the questioning? And what of Michael Miller?"

"You bugged me!"

"Stop with the indignation, Ryan. You are still not in the clear entirely. Brian slipped a bug under your collar when he man-handled you back into your seat yesterday. Now answer our questions rather than asking your own."

"Okay. Then you know I was with Cindy yesterday in the cafe down on Herbert Street. I went to her place to ask if she had seen or heard anything after she left, which was prior to the station bombing. She would have been at a perfect tactical observation point at the time. Michael Miller was my boarder for a while. You know about that already."

"Right, your boarder. So, why was he seen rushing from the scene of the crime?"

"Don't know that yet. I was going to talk to him today when I came in, if you allowed it."

"Tell me again what you think about these murders and why you believe they're connected."

"Well, seems to me that someone is holding a huge grudge against the high school from around the time I went there, as well as my mates, and the police. I started to think it may have been, Cindy Naylor. She had a bad history with the school and definitely held a grudge with the police for a long time. She claimed to have been gang-raped by the football team and no one believed her when the footy players all vouched for one another."

"If it is her, she has help. No way can a female do some of the heavy work involved, unless she's a shot-putter from Russia."

"Pretty much gave up on the idea the moment I thought of it, actually. Not because of my feelings for her, just that it didn't fit with her. She has had her own version of revenge happening since then anyway. I'm surprised no one has messed with her over it yet. Or perhaps they have and I just don't know about it."

"Anything else you thought of that *didn't* end in nothing?"

"I think we have to go back to the basics on this one. The first body to show up was that of an old friend of mine who worked pretty high up for the council, Clayton McCormack. The first one to show evidence of boot polish on the face and horrific injuries both before and after death. The type of injuries that indicate acute psychosis, but intelligent preparation and planning. Victor Kugelweis shows up next, also a friend of mine, and displaying similar atrocities. The Doc mentioned that they were my friends and perhaps it was an enemy of mine trying to send me a message, or getting to me through my friends. That made me think of, Loz. Lorenzo Catani."

"Alright, I can accept that maybe you had some warped sense of duty to your mate, so you locked him up in a purpose-built room to detoxify him. Why the ruse of witness protection?"

"I wanted to have a legitimate reason to keep him against his will if he ended up getting pissed off at me. I gave Gary a vague purpose of protecting my friend against a possible abduction and torture like my other mates. I... shit!"

"What?"

"I just made a connection between us all and the boot polish... I think. Fuck! Why didn't I remember that before?"

"Care to enlighten us?"

"They were my friends. We were pretty tight as teenagers. Ran around together more often than not, creating nuisances of ourselves most times. There was one time when, as army cadets, we got a bit pissed and played a prank on this student from our school. It got a bit out of hand in the end, but still just a harmless prank. We bundled him up from his tent one night while on bivouac in Townsville. We gave him the old boot polish on the face trick and toothpaste on the balls, a pretty popular prank back then. We sort of had him entwined in a fence at the time, to restrict his movements."

"Would that have been a barbed-wire fence by any chance?"

"Dunno, can't remember. We were pretty shit-faced at the time. That's why I didn't remember it until just now."

"Why now?"

"The photos. The body was wrapped around the cross with wire. It sparked the memory of that kid we wrapped in the wire that night. He looked a bit like Christ on the cross just dangling there with a black face and mostly naked. Tough little shit. Never uttered a sound no matter what."

"Vicious bastards, weren't you?"

"Just kids. Bored. Pissed. Nothing overtly vicious about it, just a prank. Didn't think much of it then, and promptly forgot all about it."

"His name?"

"God, I... that's right. We used to call him... Smelly Melly 'cause he stunk of piss back then. Pissed his bed all through high school we reckoned. Melly... Melco. Melco... same, last... Malko... Malkovich. That's it, Melco Malkovich. Left school before matriculating with us that year. We got our junior certificates and mostly went our separate ways. He... I think, started working in the cane fields after that, then left town altogether about four or five years later and that was the last I heard of him."

"Even though it was a bloody nasty prank which I think went way beyond the bounds of mere mischief, it hardly sounds like grounds for a full-on vendetta?"

"Well, I agree. Only... "

"Only what? Spit it out, Ryan." Trent shot Brian a glance indicating he should be paying special attention. Brian retrieved his notebook from his jacket to take notes.

"Well, we laid it on pretty thick with him at school. He was an easy target smelling the way he did, and it became sort of a competition to find out who could make him scream first."

"So, you systematically and brutally bullied the boy? How long did this go on?"

"I wouldn't say it was brutal. Just kids mucking around. He got up our noses that's all. Pun intended. Bit of push and shove. A bit of name-calling 'cause of his accent. Shit like that."

"Zero tolerance for that sort of thing these days, Ryan. It's called intolerance. Sure, plenty of kids got away with it back then, maybe even considered it a rite of passage among teenagers, but bullying none-the-less. Are you trying to tell me you never ganged up on him? Beat him up a little? Taught him a lesson or two?"

"Might have come to fisticuffs occasionally. Might have fiddled with his bike once or twice, and yeah, I guess we wouldn't have got away with it these days, but it was hardly reason enough to warrant murder, or bombings."

"Maybe not in your eyes, Ryan, but you weren't on the receiving end, were you? I happened to have been bullied in high school before I developed my adult frame, and I can tell you, I would have loved a chance to get even. I can tell you that I hated those mongrels who ran around in a pack. I still bear the internal scars of that period in my life, so don't expect any sympathy from me while you downplay your role in the story."

"It wasn't like that, really. Yeah, alright, we maybe bullied him a bit, nothing like you're thinking."

"You know, the more I find out about you, the less I like you, Ryan, and I didn't much like you from the beginning. Do you think that what you did back then didn't have an effect? You think people are just going to forgive and forget being bullied in school. It can really fuck a person up for the rest of their lives. Teenagers have been known to take their lives rather than face another day in school as the target of abuse and discrimination. These days it's more about cyber-bullying than physical, but just as brutal and just as effective.

What you did to him while on bivouac could have caused untold humiliation, depression, or aggression. Christ, *I* feel like taking revenge on you, why wouldn't he?"

"You're blowing it all out of proportion. It was... "

"Drop it. Where did he live? Are his parents still around?"

"Parents died a while back I think. About ten years ago. They lived in a rented house on the edge of town. I don't think it was ever occupied after them. Something about the owners of the house. I think they went overseas and never returned or something like that. Anyway, the house has remained empty."

"What about the parents' furniture and effects?"

"Not sure. Could be still there for all I know."

"I suggest we start by paying the house a visit. Brian, I want you to start researching the current whereabouts of this, Melco Malkovich. Dig up what you can on him from the time he left here. Ryan, I will make you a promise. If it turns out you ruined this boy, whether or not he has anything to do with the Minstrel killings, I *will* find something to nail you with. That is my solemn promise to you, as God is my witness. I have always hated bullies in all their evil disguises. I hate their pitiful justifications for the crimes they commit, and I especially hate them for the cowards they are."

MELCO

At the northern end of Ingham, on Venables Street, stood the former Malkovich residence, remaining unoccupied and in a state of disrepair, at least, on the outside. In the long, untended front lawn, lived a veritable plague of cane toads, the menace of the north once they were introduced to reduce cane beetle numbers. The house, sitting on a raised concrete foundation, with a front patio of painted concrete, showed serious signs of damp rot invading the eaves and where gutters had come away from the wooden fascia. Mould presented on the soffits and under the patio roof, giving evidence of the extreme humidity and moisture of the north.

The three detectives made their way carefully through the front yard to the short steps leading to the front porch. Noting a few partially decomposed, squashed toads in the driveway leading to the rear of the property, Trent considered the possibility that it may have been used recently. Brian grimaced with distaste as toads hopped about and onto his expensive leather shoes. Ryan merely kicked them out of the way, seemingly amused by the activity.

"I suppose you shoved fire-crackers in their gobs when you were a kid huh?" asked Trent.

"Yep, bungers. Watched them blow up and splatter across the street every cracker night," said Ryan with glee.

"Figures. Only a cruel bastard could get his rocks off blowing up innocent animals with fireworks. That's another strike against your name, Ryan. Keep 'em coming you sadistic prick. Still wonder why I counted you as a suspect?"

"Trent!" Brian warned. Trent gave Ryan a withering look of disdain, before catching Brian's eye with a wink. Brian smiled at the short interplay.

They were such a good partnership that they knew each other inside-out. Trent allowed Brian to take the lead for the time being.

He owed much to his partner, even having had his life saved by the man once. Trent gave him the respect he deserved by playing second fiddle. He would follow Brian's suggestions unless they proved incorrect. In the absence of any other plausible leads, he had little choice. They were unable to come up with much information on Melco Malkovich, other than his stint as a car salesperson in Brisbane up to about ten years ago. Plenty of normal credit card charges, utility bills and property purchases from around the time he left Ingham after working in the cane fields, then nothing for the last ten years.

He amassed a handsome portfolio of properties in and around Brisbane and Ingham while earning good money as a top salesperson, winning several dealership awards. As far as they were aware, Melco never married or lived with a partner, female or male. Modern circumstances decreed that they should consider all possibilities where sexual preferences were concerned.

Melco never acquired so much as a speeding ticket, much less any criminal convictions. Trent did not hold out much hope that Mr squeaky-clean Melco Malkovich was their perpetrator. There was no sign of the man, not even a current car registration. It was unlikely that he suddenly turned into a homicidal psychopath. Just the same, he would not belittle Brian for the direction they were taking.

"Door's not locked," announced Trent as he reached the door.

With a gentle prod of his shoe, the door opened immediately upon silent, well-oiled hinges, making the detective draw his weapon instinctively. The door swung all the way open to reveal a spit-polished timber floor, with spotless gilded picture frames adorning the hallway walls. The air was redolent of cleaning solvents and wood polish.

"Ryan, go cover the rear, while Trent and I go through here," ordered Brian.

"Why are we worried?"

"Jeez, what happened to you? Thought you were some hot-shot

in your day? See the footprints we just made in the dust on the veranda? How do you reckon a door stays silent after a house is supposedly abandoned for so long? How do you reckon the insides clean and polish themselves? Get going. We'll give you a count of ten to get there before we proceed. "Ready, Trent?" Brian asked after a count of ten.

"Sure partner. Trust him to have our backs, though?"

"We're going to push anyone in there *his* way, don't you think? Not worried. After you, partner."

Trent grinned as he stepped carefully over the threshold. Weapon drawn, aimed in the direction his eyes were focused, pausing at open doorways in the hall, all according to standard training. Clearing each room of occupancy before proceeding along the hall. The main bedroom at the front left, unoccupied, cleaned to within an inch of its life, clothes meticulously laundered and hanging dead straight in the robes. Bed made formally with older linen like a picture from a Home Beautiful magazine but not sporting a hundred pillows and cushions as was the current trend.

Brian noted the many framed photos of the Malkovich family in various staid poses, typical of their country of birth. As was acceptable attire of the era and their ethnicity, Mrs Malkovich wore all black, in every photo, smiling demurely and respectfully, while Mr Malkovich's looks are stern and imposing. Melco is dressed to the nines in every shot, with his proud mum and dad appearing as poor cousins in work clothes or well-worn streetwear. Brian also noted several patches where the faded paintwork revealed the removal of a few pictures. Slowly they worked their way forward eliminating every room as they proceeded until they were at the back door.

"Okay, Ryan. All clear," called Trent as he edged open the equally silent back door.

All three men proceeded along the concrete pathway leading to the single garage where they repeated the procedure for investigating the house. This time, when Trent opened the silent side door, what confronted the detectives left them speechless. A dull humming accompanied their advance. Careful not to contaminate the crime scene, oblivious to the stench, they walked in each other's footsteps to the centre of the garage where a single chair occupied the space. In front of the chair, several paces away, sat an old TV monitor, next to it sat a camcorder on a tripod. Playing on the monitor, probably on a loop, were images of Craig Ball tied naked to a chair with a blackened face, while being systematically tortured by an unseen perpetrator, standing behind the camera throwing playing darts at the helpless recipient.

The horrific scene captured their attention in spite of their abhorrence of the images. Despite the macabre setting and the obviously horrendous treatments to his old teacher, Ryan found it difficult to understand the amplified reactions to the almost innocuous torture. Painful as it may be to have darts thrown at you, it didn't seem to warrant the extreme anguish shown on the silent movie. With each dart thrown, the reaction was more like someone had been harpooned by a burly whaler set to embed the barb deep into the blubber. The wild and frantic writhing of the victim, sure to cause more pain, seemed out of proportion.

A few digits were missing from the victim's hand, who had no doubt suffered many more days of abuse after the scene, which played on a loop. The segment lasted about two to three minutes with approximately ten or more darts thrown in that period. Other than the missing digits on hands and feet, the other parts of the body seemed unaffected. The chaotic thrashing of the victim indicated other methods of torture were at play. Mercifully, the recording played silently. During the intervals when darts were not thrown, the body persisted to react to further trials of punishment.

For the first time in many moments, mesmerised by the horrific images, Ryan began to take in the rest of the garage. Blood spatters stained the concrete floor like a Rorschach inkblot, begging him to make sense of the shape. He saw only agony and torment there. Around the walls and on the workbenches of the garage, more blood and gore-covered body organs, innards, fingers, and toes, dried and maggot-ridden, crawling with the new life. Then the stench made itself known. Then the swarms of flies, disturbed by the retching of one of the other detectives, bathed them in a swirling mass that moved almost as one entity, forcing them all to back out of the garage.

Ryan bent over, dry-reaching, unable to produce substance from his empty stomach, shook his head in dismay. Trent, the only person not afflicted by queasiness, was none-the-less appalled at what he had witnessed, unable to voice his concerns, shocked at the brutality. Brian heaved what remained of his stomach's contents into the long grass at the side of the driveway. No one spoke for some time, as each sought a space in their own minds to come to terms with what they saw, allowing their training to compartmentalise the different elements, to remove personality and emotion from the equation.

Finally, Trent said, "Brian, call it in as soon as you're capable. Take your time, buddy. Get out an all-points on one, Melco Malkovich. Give them a description and advise extreme caution and not to engage. Ryan, go call in whoever we have from forensics, all of them, tell them to get here ASAP. Going to take us a bloody month to trawl through all that shit. Brian, we need the techies here to go over that equipment in there. We need analysis of that footage. Search backgrounds. Find an image of the perpetrator. Find any other footage or images we can use. I want the entire block cordoned off. No one in or out. I want roadblocks in and out of town. Car searches for all. Find that son-of-a-bitch!"

"You make it too big and the Feds will take over, Trent. I don't know about you, but I want this sick fuck. I want him bad," grimaced Brian as he rose to his full height, wiping his mouth with a handkerchief.

"Right. Don't broadcast the roadblocks. Organise it all in person back at headquarters. Get going Brian and take Ryan with you. I'll stay to supervise everything here. When you get back, I want you to start the house-to-house with, Ryan. Use his home-town advantage to get in good with the neighbours. Someone must have seen or heard something for crying out loud. I can see that the garage was sound-proofed to a certain extent, but someone must have heard that poor bastard screaming his head off in there for days. By the way, good call. Both of you, well done. We'll get this piece of shit if it's the last thing we do. We'll get him."

Brian and Ryan moved away to the front of the house via the driveway. As they were preparing to enter the vehicle to return to the makeshift station, a gigantic blast from the rear of the house sent them staggering. Ears ringing, bewildered and confused, they managed to gather their wits about them in time to see Detective Barron racing along the driveway, alight, screaming in panic. Brian raced to his aid, removing his jacket as he ran, covering his friend and partner with it upon reaching him and forcing him to the ground. Fortunately, only parts of his clothing had ignited, leaving his hair and face unmarked.

"Ryan, call the ambulance."

"I'm alright. I'm alright, Bri. Just a bit singed. I was bending over to look at something in the grass, my back to the garage when it blew. I think I have a bit of shrapnel in me arse, though. Here, it... FUCK!"

Brian took the piece of bone that he dislodged from the detective's backside, then deposited it into an evidence bag, a supply of which he always kept on hand in his jacket. The bone fragment, obviously belonging to one of the victim's missing digits may be the only shred of real evidence left at the scene once the fire receded. Once Trent had been hauled from the ground, the detectives decided to put some distance between themselves and the house. The bomb squad from Townsville would have to be called in to search the house before anyone else entered. Any crime scene connected to the murders would have to be declared safe by the bomb squad before lab techs and officers were allowed on site.

"It would appear that your hypothesis of a connection between the murders and the bombings has been vindicated, Detective Ryan. I apologise for not having given sufficient credence to the suggestion earlier, it may have prevented... "

"Not sure that it would have prevented anything, but thank-you, Trent. Apology accepted. Sorry if I didn't give you my full support at the start, and even more sorry that I allowed my private life to interfere with my career and your investigation. You have my solemn promise that it will not happen again."

"We are going to need you to bring us up to speed on everything you know about this, Malkovich fellow, including anything you may have held back during our previous discussion? Brian? I want to know everything about this piece of crap including the colour of his favourite underwear. I want nothing left undiscovered, no stone unturned, question everyone from as far back as his birth. Do we know who he worked for here? Who else had knowledge of him from his cadet days, maybe someone at the barracks? We need to know what made this guy tick, especially what *ticked* him off. Ryan, still think it was nothing but a harmless prank?"

Ryan didn't answer. The accusation making him feel uncomfortable. He hadn't revealed *everything* of that night to the detectives, though his memory of the rest was hazy at best. He didn't know if he *could* recall everything. He knew he was fairly wasted and that may be the reason, yet there seemed to be a scratchy irritation in the back of his mind like he knew he was concealing something, even from himself. He kept that notion to himself for the time being. It wouldn't do to give the detective any more ammunition to use against him.

Trent regarded Ryan with a cautious glance, not wanting to provoke further animosity between them. He did, however, note a slight hesitation on the man's part when he mentioned the possibility of undisclosed information pertaining to the night in question or the alleged suspect. He stored that momentary hesitation in the back of his mind for future prognostication. He patted down his body to ascertain the extent of any more injuries he may have incurred as a result of the explosion. Apart from a possible case of tinnitus, and a definite puncture wound in his bum, he seemed to have come away fairly unscathed. Remarkable considering his proximity to the blast.

If Trent had not squatted to the ground to inspect what he thought maybe a footprint in the soil, the outcome may have been very different indeed. Thankfully, the main blast seemed to have had a vertical trajectory rather than blowing out horizontally. Perhaps indicating that the explosive had been concealed in a strong container, a drum that did not immediately explode outward, causing the blast to be directed upward and out. The garage had been obliterated and it appeared that part of the house at the rear had not escaped. They were extremely lucky. Trent's next troubling thoughts centred on the question of why they were so lucky. *Had the madman known when to detonate the bomb? Was he in the area, observing them? Or was it on a timer and they just happened to be out of the danger zone?*

All good questions, none of which had answers immediately apparent, all of which would be investigated. Trent looked about him with a discerning eye, tapping his head in an attempt to knock the ringing out of his ears. Brian was on his mobile firing off instructions. Ryan was also on his mobile, presumably finding some more information about Melco Malkovich from his local sources or friends. There were no obvious places of concealment for a bomber to hide with a line of sight if that was required to detonate the bomb unless he had taken up residence in one of the surrounding houses.

The area would soon be cordoned off, with every house searched thoroughly under the new terrorism laws, giving them a far wider scope than ever before. That the town was in the grip of terror was a no-brainer, using the modern term. That it fell strictly within the guidelines governing the definition of terrorism, was a grey area he was willing to exploit. After all, it was possibly the worst bombing episode in Australia's history, and the town was not out of danger by a long shot. Trent knew he would be battling the AFP, The Australian Federal Police, for jurisdiction in this case. He knew he had to convince the hierarchy that this was about a serial killer first and foremost, who happened to be bombing a few buildings as well.

The only way to achieve his goal of maintaining control of the case was to *take* control from the outset, to make the necessary arrangements before anyone else. To lead. Thus no one could deny that he had asserted the relevant authority required of the circumstances. Proactive steps were being taken and a name had been procured as a possible suspect, the most likely suspect. He sorely regretted the loss of all the evidence in the garage. It would have given the techies and forensics a shit-load to work with. Now, they were back to the grunt-work again. Slogging away at the basics. By the manual, straight out of the academy. House to house searches, questioning anyone who lived within a ten-block radius. Not that there were actually ten blocks around them on this edge of town. The search would continue into the cane fields abutting the edge of the urban landscape.

Trent spared a thought for his wife and kids, how close they came to losing him today. He would have to call Helen in the evening and talk to Mike and Billy. He would remind Brian to call his mum and dad to let them know he was okay. Trent tried to recall if Brian had a current girlfriend. Trent had difficulty remembering any of Brian's girlfriends. *There had to be, right? I've heard Bri talking about them, haven't I?* Try as he might, Trent could not recall a single time that Brian had ever spoken of a girlfriend, serious or not. *Strange.* Trent knew that Margaret and Ben Chalmers would be very worried if their son did not call them after they heard about the latest bombing. Trent made a mental note to keep the reporters out of the area. There was so much to do, so much to organise and sift through. His head spun.

Trent knew from the autopsies that most of the major organs had been missing from the Ball corpse and the others. How much of what they witnessed in the garage had belonged to Ball, he could not say. He could not say whether there had been more than one victim's innards in the garage or not. Hell, there could be many more bodies they had not yet discovered. How many more addresses did the psychopath use? How many more victims? How many more buildings were destined to be blown to smithereens? Their job was to protect and serve. He and his partner had done little protecting and bugger-all serving so far in this case. If they weren't careful they would lose the case altogether and be posted out to Birdsville or somewhere else around there. Possibly the worst posting to receive, anywhere, ever!

His head hurt and his ears would not stop ringing. Trent motioned to Brian that a patrol car was approaching.

"Brian, make sure they put a barrier up to stop all reporters from getting anywhere near this site, and place a moratorium on air traffic over the area as well. We don't want the parasites floating over the top of us, messing up the site any worse than what it is. Ryan, know any of these people around here?"

Finishing his mobile conversation, "Yeah, sure. Lorenzo's mum is just two doors down. She ought to be home and worth talking to I reckon. She usually has the nose for what is happening in the neighbourhood. Hard to understand, though, doesn't speak-a-de English too good and pretends not to *hear* too good if she doesn't like the conversation."

"Could your friend be there?"

"You kidding? He wouldn't risk going to his mama's in his condition. Never come out alive. She is a cantankerous old cow to be around when she gets riled. He'd be too ashamed to show up there. You still don't think the Minstrel has him? You think I took him somewhere?"

"How about you and I go visit the broad?"

"You want me along?"

"You know her. That will go a long way to getting some cooperation. Brian and I are finding it difficult to get that from the locals," offered Trent, as he began walking north along the street.

Ryan was leading the way to a house, which was technically

listed as being a Garbutt Street residence. The Catani house was a typical Queenslander built purposely to take advantage of the sub-tropical conditions, raised on stilts with 360-degree verandas. The open design allowed for fresh air flow under the house to keep the temperatures cooler during the hot, humid months of December through March. While the seasons were hardly noticeable except by the rainfall, summer was always that bit hotter than the rest of the year.

In Mama Catani's backyard was the ubiquitous vegetable garden, known to be present in every Italian backyard. Outside the fenced backyard was a small grove of fruit trees that Ryan and his mates used to raid every season. Five corner fruit sometimes referred to as starfruit or their more formal classification, carambola, were highly prized by the youngsters.

Strolling up the road brought back fond memories for Ryan. As was expected, Mama Catani was in her backyard near the fence appearing to look busy with some insignificant weeds. Anybody could see it was simply an excuse to sticky-beak. She pretended to ignore the approaching detectives, one of whom was well-known to her.

"*Bon journo, Mama.*" Greeted Ryan as they neared the fence.

"Ahh, Bambino. You no pay your Mama no visit, eh? Why you take-a so long to visit your Mama?" she enquired straightening her long-suffering back. Mama Catani was so stereotypically the Italian migrant as to be almost comical. The black dress, the black scarf, the locks of grey hair escaping from beneath the headscarf and the generous moustache on the upper lip.

"Sorry, Mama. I come for spaghetti some time, eh?" Ryan suggested, falling into the abbreviated English easily, ending off with the 'eh', so frequently used by the northern population of Australia."

"You come-a tonight, I feed-a you good. Put-a some meat on-a your bones. You bring-a that, Lorenzo, no good-a boy with-a you. We have-a some tea, then watch-a the movie, eh?" asked Mama

Catani hopefully.

"No can do, Mama. Pretty busy as you know. This is, Detective Trent Barron. Trent, this is, Mama Catani. She won't allow you to call her anything else, so don't bother. We would like to ask you some questions please, Mama, seeing as you know everything that happens in this neighbourhood better than anyone. You heard the explosion of course?"

"What-a you think I know? I know nothing what happened. Big-a boom and my house-a she shake and-a picture, they fall down. You come in?"

"Yeah, sure, Mama."

"Thank you for your time... Mama," said Trent awkwardly, following Ryan and the woman around to the front gate where they entered.

Mama Catani led them along the front path and up the stairs to the front door. Noticing her struggle with the stairs, Ryan assumed her hip was playing up again. He kept quiet about it, though, knowing it would upset her if he remarked on it. Mama Catani was definitely of the old school when it came to personal health matters, they *stayed* personal. Entering the house brought back more fond memories of Italian dining at its finest. Many a year was spent here at Christmas, with Mama going to town in typical Italian fashion by cooking for two weeks prior. The Christmas table quailed under the enormous lunch load set upon it. Seven courses, or more, of the most exquisite Italian fare likely to be found in the finest restaurants across the globe.

Ryan salivated at the thought of the meals eaten here over the years he and Lorenzo had been mates. Thinking of his mate suddenly caused some unease, as Mama was sure to inquire about her son. He was not sure what to reveal. It was not only a matter of leaking information not known to the general public, but it was also about not wanting to cause the lady unnecessary hardship and concern. Ryan had no doubts that Mama Catani knew about her son's habits of late, not that she would ever admit it. However, she would most likely not be privy to the fact that he was missing, presumed kidnapped, or most likely, dead, at the hands of possibly the worst serial killer Australia had ever seen.

The lady led them to a formal lounge where she set about removing the covering sheets from the furniture. Long unused, the lounge room retained an odour of furniture polish and potpourri. The kitchen scents of herbs and garlic simmering on the stove added to the melange of a well-ordered Italian home. Every available space on walls or furniture surfaces, were cluttered with bric-a-brac and religious icons. When Mama removed herself from the lounge, Ryan whispered to Trent.

"You know that we have to stay for lunch right?"

"What are you talking about? It's way past lunchtime."

"Doesn't matter. We have to eat no matter what time of day. If you refuse, she will be highly offended and you will not get anything from her. She won't talk about anything till we have a belly-full, and I mean full! We'll be lucky to leave here without consuming a minimum of three courses, plus sweets."

"How did she know we were coming to cook so much food?"

"You're kidding, right? Italian ladies make enough food to feed an army every time they cook, without fail. They live off left-overs for a week after they cook. You are about to experience a culinary delight of the highest order, unlike anything you have tasted before. Not only is Mama a great Italian cook, but she is also a cook's cook. No one better in my opinion. You mean you never had a meal at an Italian's house in Townsville?"

In the background, they could hear the fire brigade and other services approaching the vicinity. The area would presently be crawling with all manner of personnel and on-lookers. The detectives were surprised that Mama Catani was so at ease considering how close to the explosion she and her house were. Trent was itching to be on his way, to organise the mêlée about to ensue. He did not want to be in some Italian broad's house munching on food while there was so much to oversee down the road. It would soon be a circus out there, he could not take the time to have a meal.

"We can't stay here for a meal, Ryan. Get real. We need to ask our questions and vamoose. Tell her we are in a hurry would you?"

Ryan smiled, shaking his head at the foolish notion that there was any possibility of them making a quick getaway without having eaten first. He knew well enough not to ask, or push the elderly Italian lady. Besides, if they did as Trent wanted, they would hear nothing but very fast Sicilian pouring from her mouth with the arms waving about like a million flies had invaded her personal space.

"Come-a to the kitchen boys, heff-a something to eat. Plenty mangiare for you to grow up to-a big-a men. Mr Trent, you sit-a here next-a to Mama, so she make-a sure you eat-a good. Ryan, get-a the beer from-a the fridge under house. Go 'round beck, eh?"

"Why don't you tell her yourself, Trent? Good luck," suggested Ryan as he strode out of the room with an enormous grin, holding in the laugh as long as possible.

"Now, Mrs Cata... "

"You call-a me, Mama, you hear? No good you call-a me Missus. Now sit-a down and-a start. You like-a spaghetti from Italia? Is good for you. No talk-a now, you eat!"

From the look of the hands waving about, like it was impossible to talk without the aid of the arms and hands, Trent decided to hold his tongue lest he wears one of the huge arms flailing about in the air. The finality in the lady's voice brooked no argument. She was a Signora much used to getting her way. Trent peered about him with embarrassment as she proceeded to tuck a bib napkin into the collar of his shirt. Pushing the fork forcefully into his hand, Trent began to eat as he was directed. Ryan soon reappeared with a long-neck bottle of Fourex, the only beer allowed in the Catani household since her husband of thirty years passed away.

Ryan sat in his usual position at the other end of the table where her husband used to park his enormous bottom, no doubt the result of his wife's cooking. He tucked his napkin into his shirt collar before proceeding to down the massive plate of spaghetti set before him. Ryan did not feel hungry exactly after what he had witnessed earlier but saw no alternative. He knew from experience that you did not go toe to toe with Mama Catani. Not about hospitality at any rate. She reigned as queen on that score and never let anyone forget it. He tried to find Trent's eyes.

"You obviously told her? Should we go then?"

Trent ignored him to continue shovelling the delicious food into his mouth. He had never tasted better in his life. He could not eat it fast enough. Mama smiled when she saw the look of surprise in the man's face after he tried his first mouthful. She knew. Always, she knew how to win the hearts of men, no matter how young, old, or indifferent. It was her duty in life to fatten the skinny men she came into contact with, and thereby ensure their company for a while. She suffered greatly for company after the death of her husband. Her son never visited and Ryan stopped by only once a year. Although she imposed on her neighbours readily enough, they had grown used to her methods and avoided her mostly nowadays.

She had, of course, heard the great explosion. Nearly gave her a heart attack if truth be known. Knowing the police had arrived already, she was unable to simply bounce across the road to satisfy her curiosity. She had to wait for the police to begin their enquiries, which she knew was inevitable, to finally glean as much information as possible from them.

Course after course, of the most delectable Italian cuisine, passed before the stuffed detective until he felt as if he may burst. Feigning an upset tummy, he attempted to put an end to the feast, before he finally capitulated to the woman who placed a dish of tiramisu before the beleaguered man. Ryan, used to the ministrations of his friend's mother, paced himself easily, while he witnessed Trent's discomfort with pride. This was, after all, what the detective wanted him for. To smooth the way with the locals, to ease the detective into the scene with local flavour opening the path. He had better get used to Italian hospitality in a hurry if he wanted to make any inroads among the population. Predominately a cane farming region, the area boasted a large percentage of Italian migrants.

"So, Mama. Grazie. Your food is as ever, the best in the world."

"You never been the world, Ryan, what-a you know for food?"

"I defy anyone to tell me different. Trent?"

Belching loudly, he excused himself, mortified at the insult. Ryan and Mama laughed loudly at his discomfort.

"It is counted as an insult only if you do *not* belch loudly after an Italian meal, Trent," said Ryan with his own belch issuing forth to Mama's delight.

"Mama, listen now. Trent and I would like to know what you have heard or seen from over the road. It would be really helpful if you told us without going through all the preliminary objections and the pretence of not knowing anything about your neighbours? We really do need to get going. Something very evil is befalling the town and we have to stop if before even worse happens, understand?" asked Ryan.

With a heavy sigh, Mama said, "You no make-a me sound too good, Ryan. Like-a the nosy Parker-person. I not-a like that at all, eh? What you want to know?"

"When the Malkoviches died in that car crash, what happened to the place? Anyone show up there?"

"The owners, they gone-a back to the home country. I think-a they from Roma maybe. No one come-a to the house, but I see light and-a shadow some-a time at night. Very strange noise in the middle of night, like-a cet noise you know? I look-a for cet, but can't-a find no cet. The noise-a stop and next-a night I hear cet-a noise again. Always in-a night. I never hear nothing in-a daytime, never see nothing, no cet."

"Cat noise? Do you think anyone else may have heard anything?"

"Bah, they no hear nothing. Got-a television on and radio with-a the loud music play this boom, boom, ugly noise. No can-a hear nothing. Men-a work at night, no hear nothing, and-a women shouting at-a the kids all-a time, no hear nothing. I ask, no one hear nothing, but Mama. No one hear this-a cet got pain or something. I look-a for this cet all-a day long. No hear, no find. Long time I'm hearing this-a cet, and then, poof, no more."

"How long ago, Mrs... Mama?" asked Trent.

"Couple-a month. No more light, no shadow, no cet."

"You think someone lived in the house during that time, Mama?"

"I no see no one. I smell."

"Smell?"

"I got-a good-a nose, Mr Trent. I smell-a the cleaning, you know? Make-a-de-house clean? I smell this-a stuff to make-a the house clean."

"You mean, like disinfectant and polish and that?"

"Si."

"So, you believe someone has been living there all this time, without you or anyone else seeing who it is?" ventured Trent.

"I no heff-a to see. I know, is-a de boy what live-a dere."

"The son? You think it was, Melco living there in his parent's house? Okay thank-you, Mama. We appreciate your time. Thank you very much for the delicious meal. I'm not sure if I can actually walk anymore, or fit my pants, but I really loved every morsel. You are indeed a fabulous cook. We had better go, Ryan."

Mama was at a loss for a moment, unsure if she had made herself clear, and wanting to rectify their misunderstanding, but the sheer energy of the detective was overwhelming, and the compliments were gratifying. Before she could protest and explain, she was rushing after her guests down the hall as they made a quick get-away. Unwilling to negotiate the stairs, she relinquished her control over the pair, sighing at the loss of company and the misinterpretation. She wasn't confident about explaining herself clearly enough to warrant their return, in any case.

"Someone had to be paying for the electricity all this time, find out who, Ryan," demanded Trent as they hurried back to the crime scene. "Brian, get that mob further back. Start a perimeter about three blocks back from here, I don't want anyone but officials in here, got that?"

"You got it, Trent. Where the hell you been? Find out anything?"

"Yeah, I found out you do not want to go knocking on any Italian lady's door around here unless you are prepared to eat your way to obesity in one sitting. Apart from that, I think we have possible confirmation that Melco Malkovich is our guy. I want everyone on the lookout for him. Get a photo and spread that out wide."

Ryan had a niggling thought running through his mind as he began another call on his mobile. He had noticed the hesitation on Mama's face as Trent latched onto the identity of the house's occupant. While not placing considerable importance on the fact, it bothered him none-the-less. Ryan had mixed feelings about the developments. He was disturbed by the possibility that he was somehow involved in the build-up to a serial murderer's escapades. He was not convinced that their prank on the young Melco Malkovich had inspired the evil Minstrel killings or the explosions. It all seemed totally out of proportion, even though, Ryan had witnessed far worse reactions in his time. A simple fist-fight turning into a battle with weapons. A harmless domestic argument turning into murder.

Then, there was the shadow lurking at the back of his mind. An elusive thought that refused to materialise. It evaded Ryan's pitiful probes, avoiding discovery. Ryan would not allow his concentration to wander too close to the flighty phantom whispering around the periphery of his thoughts. He saw the night in question clearly, and despite having instigated a prank that would finally show the impertinent boy that they were a bunch to be reckoned with, he was still at a loss to understand such an over-reaction many years delayed. It didn't seem possible.

MICHAEL MILLER

When Cindy entered the cafe she spotted the man immediately, sitting in the same booth. Mustering up the courage she needed, she boldly walked up to his booth.

"Do you mind if I join you?" asked Cindy.

Michael looked about the relatively deserted cafe with annoyance and curiosity before nodding his head. He was unsure about the woman's motives for wanting to sit with him. He believed he recognised her, though he couldn't be certain. He had no illusions as to his magnetic personality or appearance, so it would be interesting to find out her game.

"Something wrong with your usual booth?"

"So you do remember me?"

"Nothing wrong with my brain if that's what you're asking."

"That's not what I... never mind. I've just undergone a few changes recently, that's all. I didn't think I looked the same as the last time you saw me."

"Did you have plastic surgery, like me?"

"No... I... you've had plastic surgery?"

"You made mention of the scars last time, didn't you? Or is *your* memory that bad, Cindy Naylor?"

"Wow, you are not an easy person to get to know."

"Wasn't aware there was an attraction. There was certainly no evidence of that last time we met, apart from the veiled compliment."

"Are you always this way, when someone is simply trying to be friendly?"

"No. I'm usually much worse when strangers invade my privacy and personal space for no good reason."

"Hi, Cindy. Glad you and your fella are back together. What'll it be? Same as usual?" asked the waitress.

"Hi, Marla. He's not... no, I'll just have a plate of salad and an orange juice please?"

"Luigi is going to get upset if you keep ordering only salads, Cindy. You used to be his best customer," Marla suggested with a grin.

"How about you throw in a piece of apple pie with cream for afters?"

"Sure, Sweetie, that ought to do it. Otherwise, he doesn't like customers occupying booths for a just a salad, you know? Be back soon. What about you, Sugar, enjoying your meal?"

"Meal's fine thanks, *Sweety-Pie*. The name is Michael. Please make use of that information next time, okay?"

"You embarrassed her. She was only being friendly," remarked Cindy once Marla had left.

"It is not friendly to call someone by anything other than their name. I have a perfectly good name, one I gave myself after plenty of thought. I want people to call me by that name and nothing else. Certainly not, Sugar! If you find my company offensive, feel free to sit elsewhere," suggested Michael as he reached for his coffee.

"Police are interested in you. I told them I saw you running away from the cop shop just before it blew up," said Cindy with a firm smugness in her voice.

"Oh, and why would you lie to the police about such a thing?"

"I didn't lie, it was the truth. I saw you."

"You did not see me running anywhere, let alone from the police station. I don't know what you think you saw, but it definitely wasn't me running."

"Okay, smarty-pants, maybe not running, but you were walking away from the police station pretty fast, just before it blew up."

Michael studied her over the rim of his coffee cup as he slowly brought it to his lips, "And you thought it your civic duty to tell the cops about it?"

"No. The cops asked me if I saw anything and I told them."

"Why would the cops be questioning you to begin with?"

"Because I was walking across the park just before the bomb

went off. Ryan knew that 'cause we were having a chat right here before I left."

"Ryan? Arnold Ryan?"

"Yeah, that's him. Heard you were living with him?"

"*Boarding* is the correct term, I believe, when someone is renting a room and sharing duties."

"So?"

"So, what?"

"Why were you run... walking swiftly away from the police station?"

"It's none of your business. If it makes you feel any better, though, I was hurrying to meet a deadline at the council."

"Deadline?" Cindy repeated, sounding disappointed.

"Yes, I am a builder and renovator, and I had to ensure I had certain papers arrive at the council in time for a permit to be issued. I had forgotten the papers in my car as I was heading this way for a meal. I intended to drop them into the council before coming here. Satisfied?"

"Not up to me to be satisfied. Just thought you might like to know that the police will be wanting to question you."

"Well now, wasn't that just *so* nice of you?"

"You don't like me do you?"

"Not particularly."

"Why, you don't even know me?"

"I don't need to know anything more than the fact that you are unattractive and have an unpleasant personality."

"I am not unattractive!"

"So, you admit to having an unpleasant personality? How unfortunate that you consider the personality to be less important than a superficial image."

"I do not feel that at all, it's just... Why would you say that I am unattractive?"

"Because your unpleasant personality shines through the very thin physical veneer. Just because you cleaned yourself up a bit does not mean your insides are any better, and *they* are far more important," replied Michael with a shrug, as he ignored her to continue with the last of his bacon and eggs.

Cindy did a double-take at that, not quite sure she was hearing right, considering his words and weighing them up in her mind. He was saying exactly what most women wanted to hear, though, it was meant as an insult for her. Suddenly, Cindy felt an anguished sense of remorse possessing her. It was as if a switch had been thrown in her brain, enabling her to see clearly the life she had been living and her reason for doing so. Her life's 'purpose' instantly seemed so very superfluous and cheap. She had been using her looks as a lure for many years, never taking into consideration how vain and shallow she had become. Never considering for one moment that she was not entirely justified in exacting revenge for what had happened to her.

She had spent so long believing that she had every right to wreak havoc among the menfolk of Ingham, and men in general, that she failed to recognise that she had totally lost herself in the process. She finally had a clear picture of herself as seen by the men she used and abused. She had reacted so instinctively to the attack that night and the following months and years that she no longer resembled the Cindy Naylor of so long ago. The attractive cheerleader everyone desired, and the best friend to many young girls idolising her for her looks and her charm. She had lost that charm. She had lost so very much of what was good about life, what was good about her. Smart, funny, and kind. Especially kind. She always had a good word for her friends, always helped them out if she could. Never let anyone, or herself down.

Cindy Naylor felt ashamed suddenly. She felt a menopausal flush begin at her toes, extending gradually upwards until it reached her face, turning it beet red. The recognition of the horror she had become threatened to overwhelm her. Observing herself from the point of view of the man in front of her caused her to tremble from head to toe. Like waking from a long coma, Cindy Naylor's epiphany shook her to the core. In her zeal to enact her self-styled revenge against the men that caused her so much emotional and physical pain, for having deprived her of the opportunity to experience motherhood, having denied her the joy of attaining a normal relationship, she had transmuted into something worse than the men who attacked her that night.

"Are you alright?" asked Michael with genuine concern. "I didn't mean to upset you, honestly. Do you need me to take you to the hospital?"

"No, actually, no. I'm fine, thank-you. I am... sorry, really, truly so very, very sorry."

"Not sure why you should be apologising. You look extremely pale all of a sudden and you are trembling. Are you ill? Coming down with something?"

"Quite the opposite actually. Coming *off* something would be more accurate. I have you to thank for that, Mister Michael Miller- not Mike, or Mickey, Sugar or Pet. I, I think you may have just helped me more than you can imagine. You are right."

"I am? About what?" asked Michael as he yawned. "Hmm, sorry about that," he said trying unsuccessfully to stifle another yawn. "I had... " Yawn. "...better get... " Yawn. "...a move on."

"Wow, you got tired all of a sudden, and if you don't mind me saying so, you have big dark bags under your eyes which weren't there last time I saw you," remarked Cindy.

"No, I'm... I ah, am... All's good. Just... just... working all hours and very tired. Have to go. See... see... you... bye."

With that, Michael rushed out of the cafe leaving Cindy totally baffled.

"You two having a fight, love?" Marla smiled at Cindy as she neared the booth. "You mind telling him that he forgot to pay his bill when you see him? He comes here every day, so I'm not worried about it or anything. You okay, Sugar? You look like you saw a ghost."

"I'm fine, Marla, thank-you. Umm, put his bill... I mean, I'll pay for his bill okay?"

"You don't have to do that. I'm sure he'll be back tomorrow."

"No, it's fine, Marla. I want to. Marla?"

"Yes, hon?"

"You knew me from school right?"

"A couple of years ahead of you, and I never really knew you, but I had seen you around, sure."

"Am I... Am I a total bitch since then? I mean, was I always such a bitch?"

"Listen, Cinds, no one, and I mean no one, could blame you for acting the way you have. Doubt many of us would have survived what you went through."

"So, I really did change?"

"Course you did, Sugar. Only natural after that."

"Damn! I was really hoping you wouldn't say that."

"Don't you go beating yourself up about it girl. None-o-us women blame you one little bit for going off the rails. Most-o-us woulda taken a gun to them fuckers, or at least run 'em down in a car or something. Don't you worry one second about how you've been acting, okay? Grub's on me, girl. His bill too. My way of saying, you're okay for sticking up for yourself like you did."

"Marla, you're a peach."

"I know that. Been telling you that for years, but you never did take me seriously?"

"Sorry?"

"Oh, don't you go listening to an old dike like me now. You have a great day, you hear?" Marla sashayed down the aisle with a mischievous grin.

"So, Cindy Naylor, you're not *totally* unattractive?" She whispered to herself with a smile.

LORENZO CATANI

When he woke, he wished he hadn't. Lorenzo lost count of his troubles. Every new sensation of agony blended with the last. He seemed to recall that he had only one finger remaining and probably just as few toes. Each day was a new exercise in ritual torture. The removal of his body parts via different instruments, innocently used for normal everyday use otherwise, had Lorenzo fearing anything and everything around him. The animal had used drill bits in a cordless Makita hammer drill to bore holes into his fingernails before severing them or twisting the fingers and toes off. The pain from that would be bad enough on its own, but the sadistic prick used that enhancer, some solution he invented overseas to make it a hundred times worse.

While he saw to the removal of different body parts, he played the music that drove needles of red-hot pain into his eardrums, turned on bright lights that burned into his retina, even through closed eyelids, until they were stitched open that is. Lorenzo was no longer capable of sleep in the ordinary sense. With his eyes wide open, he experienced unconsciousness, rather than sleep. Pure bliss once his mind and body could no longer cope with the treatments. He prayed long and hard to gain that state of permanent sleep, to escape the prolonged agony of life. His arms and legs sported countless staples and nails from a pneumatic nail gun. Some of the nails reaching the bone. When he managed to get a look at his naked form in the mirror above him, he saw more metal than flesh on his limbs. He remembered each and every one of those brads and staples fired into him with pure dread.

He had been moved since the last time he was conscious. Another workshop for sure, but not the same as the last. Mister Ball was no longer lying next to him. Gone to who knew where. Lorenzo envied him his end to suffering. The room had a mechanical smell like a garage with oils and grease rather than a carpentry workshop smelling mostly of sawdust. The mirror over his table was the same, giving him the same distasteful look of his pathetic body having undergone innumerable treatments of unbearable atrocities.

Thankfully, the serum had either abated or he had been given the antidote. His genitals burned regardless. His testicles had been similarly adorned with staples and brads. He no longer experienced any sensation in his penis, no longer controlled any of its functions. He did not know if he was able to urinate or not. Life for Lorenzo Catani had been a nightmare of unbelievable pain repeated on a daily basis whenever he regained consciousness. He tried to feign unconsciousness on numerous occasions only to be dealt a stunning blow to the head or have a staple fired into his body. Obviously, the man never believed when Loz was faking it. His eyes probably gave him away no matter how hard he concentrated on affecting a distant glaze. The instinct to blink and the lack of moisture in his eyes revealed his wakefulness each time. A solution was introduced to his eyes to prevent him from going completely dry or blind. His captor wanted Loz to witness everything.

"Ah, Lorenzo, how are you then? Feeling a bit better after the pain-killer? I got the bottles right this time, huh? It's all terribly confusing sometimes. I have to make sure I read the labels properly. Sorry if I mix them up occasionally. Now, then, where were we? Oh, not many fingers and toes left there, I'm afraid. You might have to be leaving me soon. What a shame, I was... I was... having... was... what? Shit... umm... FUN! That's it! I was having such fun, Lorenzo. Hmm, I have to get a bit of a hurry on. Time is running out. Have to teach others a lesson too. And then... then... what? Then what? Oh... something... finish? An... end to... umm"

"Atsa matter, eh? Losing ya marbles ya psycho? Fuck you! Poor little Smelly had a hard time in school. Weh, weh. So fucking what? Think ya got is so bad, huh? Shoulda had an old man like we had ya dumb cunt. Then ya woulda known a hard time like Ryan and me. Clay and, Vic didn't have it so bad, but Ryan and me copped it every day sometimes."

Smiling through the exaggerated lips, as if a fog had cleared, "So you felt justified in transferring that abuse did you? Made it okay to take out your frustrations on the foreign boy? Was there always that smell of urine, even at the start? Did it ever occur to you fuckwits that maybe it was you that caused that? That you caused nightmares so bad it resulted in bladder problems every night? No, of course not, the abuse just escalated after that didn't it?"

"Okay, okay I get it, we were wrong. It should never have happened and we went too far. No need to go overboard with... with all this. Murder? Torture? No way do we deserve all this."

"If it stopped at that may be. If it all stopped, hadn't escalated to what happened in Townsville, or after. If Ryan hadn't... gone... back. Maybe, maybe then... But it didn't stop. Your abuse had life-altering consequences, even after you all left school. The legend of your conquests grew in the minds of the younger students, emboldened by your escapades to replicate those deeds on others, breeding more of the same. The bullying of foreign children ran rampant within that high school and nothing was ever done about it. More and more... children... were exposed to the sadistic nature of feral children allowed to get away with their systematic torture. Well, you are paying for that crime. You and the people of this diseased town will be paying dearly for those crimes."

"What, what the fuck did Ryan do? When he went back? When I saw him sneaking out of the tent. What, what did he do? No, please, not the needle... no... I'm sorry okay? I was out of line. I didn't mean those things I said, alright?"

"You don't get it, do you? You truly do not understand the pain you cause, the lives you ruin. You say sorry for saying or doing something at the drop of a hat without ever meaning it, then turn around and repeat the mistake. I know you don't fear death because you flirted with death every day of your life the way you abused yourself, so killing you is not a suitable punishment, at least, not straight away. You don't understand what evil little shits you all are. The punishment I mete out is what you all deserve for your actions back then. For you, it doesn't matter what Ryan did back then. I am doing this to you, for what *you* did back then. You think I'm punishing you for someone else's crime?"

"Listen to me, Smelly... "

Roaring like a wounded lion, the man leapt at Lorenzo with the syringe, jabbing him painfully in the side of the neck. "You ignorant, dumb, cunt! Even now, with your life swaying in the balance, while you plead for an end to the torture, you still have the indecency to use that derogatory term instead of a person's name? You have pissed and shit yourself more often than not as a useless old wino, Lorenzo, and you have the temerity to hold on to that unjust moniker for someone else? I guess I have gone too soft on you. You have not learned your lesson at all well. It is time to explore new levels of creativity until you understand what this is about. Prepare to behold a pain so exquisite in its intensity as to defy the imagination.

Lorenzo screamed into the gag the man placed in his mouth before the serum had fully taken effect. It would not be long before every sensation would cause him more pain than he could believe was possible. Lorenzo heard his heart hammering in his chest, felt the blood coursing through his veins. The light began to hurt, and Lorenzo began to feel each and every staple and brad adorning his body. His eyes, no longer able to close, suffered horribly in the light, without the moisture administered by Melco to lubricate them.

No sooner had he thought that when Melco appeared at his side with the soothing liquid contained in an eyedropper. While the pain of the bright light did not diminish, he always felt immense relief when the liquid was administered. Lorenzo anticipated the immediate relief as the man hovered over his eye with the dropper. The drops that fell from the dropper seared and blistered their way through the gelatinous ball in no time at all. The acid turned the ball into a puddle within the socket. The convulsive spasms caused by the intense agony caused his body to endure more punishment from being slammed against the plywood table to which he was restrained, the bonds of rubber and metal saddles biting into the flesh of his wrists and ankles felt as though he was being sawn through flesh and bone.

There was insufficient acid used to make its way into Lorenzo's brain. His captor was very careful to administer just the right amount to pulp the eyes without killing him or worse, inuring him to the pain. The brain had to continue functioning in order to receive and understand the pain messages travelling to it from the various nerve centres in the body. The man left Lorenzo's vicinity momentarily. Much movement of chairs or tables could be heard scraping against the concrete floor. While totally consumed by the pure agony assaulting his eye sockets, Lorenzo did not immediately feel the warmth on his flesh. Unable to view anything, forever, Lorenzo gulped at the thought of what new horror awaited him. It did not take long for his addled brain to figure it out, as the warmth became a heat, and the heat turned to a searing, scorching attack on his epidermis.

"Heat lamps, Lorenzo. Used to warm and relax the muscles. Of course, they aren't meant for prolonged use. That may cause burns anywhere from third to first degree depending on the duration of exposure. I think we'll see what an hour can do first, huh?"

"What... whatever we did... did to you... " stammered Lorenzo when the gag was removed.

"Yes, I'm waiting, Lorenzo. You have to speak up a bit even though it hurts like a bitch. Whatever you did... ?"

"It... it... wasn't... "

"Do get on with it."

"Wasn't anywhere near what you deserved you sick fuck! Should have finished you off that night. Ryan should have put a bullet in your brain instead of whatever he did that makes you think you have a right to do all this shit to people."

"YOU AREN'T PEOPLE! You are, are vermin. A plague upon the Earth. You don't fit into any human category at all. You are a loathsome piece of excrement, Lorenzo. Something so fetid and foul that real humans just want to get as far away from the unbearable stench as possible."

Lorenzo groaned with the noise of the man's voice piercing his eardrums, driving white-hot bolts of lightning into his brain. The heat source positioned near his body was beginning to heat the metal staples and brads to soaring temperatures, frying the skin and tissue surrounding them. The room was beginning to smell like a leg of pork was roasting in the oven. But nothing so pleasant. Blisters were forming everywhere, filled with the precious moisture his body craved. Lorenzo could no longer think, no longer wanted to think, no longer wanted to understand all the different punishments his body suffered. Then, when Beethoven's, Ode to Joy, slammed his ears, the air around him pulsed with the violent chords. Dum, dum, dum, dum... Choristers, "*One mighty voice*... " On and on went the thunderous music and the heat, oh, the heat, scorching, searing, and his eyes, his cock! More acid or something being injected into his cock, and now his balls as well!

The man walked away from the plywood table resting on the sawhorses once he was positive that his prisoner had fallen unconscious again. Injecting a pain-killer into his victim's arm would ensure the pig lasted a while longer. The man had much to learn and many more methods of teaching him were yet to be explored. The man punched the air to the reverberating melody of Beethoven's final masterpiece. Then, quite suddenly, weariness overtook him, causing him to stagger. The infernal tiredness without the ability to actually sleep it off, returned in an instant.

The man managed to exit the garage, entering the hallway to make his way to the bathroom where he applied the make-up remover to get rid of the disguise. The black and white grease-paint merged with the white cream making a dull grey paste. With soap and hot water, the mess was removed to reveal his true identity, at least, the new one. The old identity, the original one, was gone forever. The scars exhibited evidence of the surgery. His features blurred in the mirror as he yawned incessantly, driving his tear ducts into over-time. He stepped into a scalding shower.

The heat from the stinging jets of hot water soothed away the tensions and the heartache. The weariness could no longer be removed by the blissful cascade. The rising steam collected on the old ceiling of crumbling plaster and cracking paint. A total lethargy attacked his florid muscles, demanding the rest that only sleep could provide. The tension of the previous months, the different locations, the preparations and planning, were taking a huge toll on his ailing body and mind. He found it difficult to concentrate over long lengths of time. His energy waned dramatically and his mental faculties flagged more often.

Soaping away the filth of his labours, the stench, the blood, the tissue and the general ill-feeling associated with his duties, made the man lean wearily against the smooth shower wall, where he slid slowly to the base. His tears of bitterness mixed with the cleansing stream from the showerhead delivering limitless hot water from the instantaneous gas hot water system installed a just few days ago. His racking sobs of misery were heard by no one. His mission was nearing an end, but it became more and more difficult to force himself to inflict the tortures, to debase himself. He was sinking lower than the victims he punished. It tore him to shreds inside to perform such atrocities on a human being, made him physically ill.

The man watched the water disappearing down the drain, absently admiring the handiwork involved in gaining an effective drainage system that was totally blocked only three days prior. He felt as though some of his life-force was draining away with that water. He knew he did not have much longer to complete his tasks. The initial timetable had been shortened considerably. The increased rate of degradation to his faculties announced his imminent demise far sooner than expected. While he had found no cure for his condition, he had gained sufficient knowledge and natural compounds to prolong the inevitable by a few more years than the original prognosis, but the new end was approaching faster than he'd wished.

Gradually, his strength was ebbing, enough to leave him feeling exhausted by less than strenuous activities. The mind was losing the clarity it once possessed. The heart was losing the conviction that once motivated it so powerfully. The effects of the cruelty he conveyed left him devoid of his humanity, dissolved of compassion. A monster was emerging, worse than the people he was fighting, yet he had discovered no other technique of attaining the justice he sought. All other avenues had failed. Years of urging for action and compensation from the relevant authorities for the various transgressions of his antagonists fell on deaf ears.

Evidence, though physically substantial, failed to impress, with only one witness to testify against the deeds of many. Other witnesses having been scared off or silenced by other means. The transgressors allying themselves to corroborate alibis left the police with nothing to investigate. When he first became aware of his condition, when it began to manifest itself to a noticeable degree, he knew he had a limited time in which to achieve his goals. Those goals required intense planning and negotiation, and most of all, revenue. It was not a cheap exercise to establish his many refuges where he was able to carry out the scheduled punishments in relative safety.

The clues he left would eventually lead the investigators to their logical conclusion, but not before its completion. He had yet to nab the instigator of all the troubles. The last link in the chain that caused so much heartache for so many would soon be captured and dealt with in a particularly harsh manner. He had held his suspicions of the last person on his list for many years, believed he knew of his role in the incident, and the consequent villainy perpetuated by it. However, suspicions were not enough to act upon. Now that he had verified those suspicions, he could play out the last scene of the final act in his little drama.

The man dragged himself from the shower, towelling his sculpted physique dry. While his brain had been wasting away slowly, but surely, he maintained a rigorous exercise regime. Albeit exhausting in the extreme, it kept his body in perfect tone. Strength of body was paramount in enacting the tasks ordained by his strict schedule. In keeping to a timeline dictated by his condition, he risked the fatigue associated with it interfering to a point where he would be unable to complete the mission. It was a wicked loop that held no guarantees of success. The quicker he moved to gain completion, the swifter his condition advanced to debilitate him. It was a constant struggle to balance the effort against the time remaining.

In the brand new kitchen, an odd assortment of natural pills and potions awaited his consumption, to help prolong his life, incredibly, including a minute dose of the very poison he injected into his victims. The enhancement to his senses on a much reduced and diluted scale than his victims', assisted him to remain on top of his game, keeping his body and mind totally alert to his surroundings and inner machinations. It was, in fact, a cleanser that enabled him to remove some of the ill-effects of his condition, to sharpen the concentration, almost painfully, but not quite. An enema of the mind and muscles, to hone his capabilities.

The wide variety of vitamins and minerals, essential to his wellbeing, having been ingested, the man began the gruelling exercise regime that would keep his malaise from gaining full control, keep the increasing lethargy at bay for the remaining time required to fulfil his goals. A punishing ritual that saw him pushing his tired body to its limits. Push-ups, chin-ups, sit-ups, and every other 'ups' imaginable saw the man sweating in no time at all, muscles glistening and quivering with the exertion. He would have to shower again once it was completed, but that was alright, he had plenty of hot water available to him now.

He planned as he exercised, walking through all the steps in his mind, adjusting where he saw problems, amending where he detected flaws in the plan, and always allowing for the inevitable unforeseen anomalies that always managed to crop up. He had to improvise on many occasions when nature intervened or an intended victim just didn't get with the program. Distancing himself from his victims required mental manipulations and acuity that tested his faculties. It was imperative to gain maximum emotional separation from his captives in order to perform his duties. The outbreak of emotion in the shower could never occur while he was actively dispensing the cruelty he despised so fervently. Remaining aloof enabled him to retain control of the procedures.

Allowing the sweat to cool him as he finished his exercises, the man began the mundane chore of cooking a meal. After all, it was essential to provide the body with the nourishment that it could then convert to the energy he needed to continue his vital work.

The kitchen benchtops sparkled in the fluorescent lights. The new stainless-steel appliances snuggled perfectly into their designated niches. He felt it almost sacrilegious to utilise the brand new equipment installed just yesterday. The gas elements on the surface would be the only items used to make his meals. He did not want to use the oven, for fear he could not clean it sufficiently to pass off as brand new.

In one week, the residence would pass hands, meaning it had to be spotless upon his departure. The new owners would move in, removing all traces of his and his 'guest's' occupation. There would remain nothing of evidence in the house connecting him to anything the police may discover when they recovered Lorenzo's body. The next abode awaited his arrival and that of his intended guest. One or two days more were required to seal Lorenzo's fate, then dump the body where the police would find it quickly. It was nearly time to pick up the main character in his little drama, the instigator, the initiator, the disease from which the bacteria spread.

And so approached the time for him to fade into the night from whence he came, leaving the town of Ingham shuddering. Maybe they would figure it out, maybe they wouldn't. It didn't matter. Either way, he will have made a statement, will have balanced the ledger of right and wrong to a certain degree. But only if he could persuade the final victim to reveal the other malignant presence; the mastermind.

He thought about whether he would be judged correctly if they ever caught him. *On which side of the ledger would they print his name?* He thought about that for a moment as he filled a pot with water for the homemade pasta. The aromatic sauce simmered gently on another flame, garlic permeating the air. A highly pungent Parmesan cheese waited on the benchtop to be freshly grated onto his pasta al dente once it had taken a few moments to boil in the water. An open bottle of red wine stood resting on the polished timber dining table where a placemat waited with gleaming cutlery either side of the Wedgewood plate.

The new owners would be purchasing nothing but top quality when they took possession. Nothing but the best had been employed in the renovations of the house, so near to completion. The music, lowered in volume and changed to a Bach recording, floated throughout the house on the central audio system. The man shivered with the beauty of the perfect tones. He should have had his shower already, and he felt entirely underdressed for dinner as he walked around in the nude. The climate-control system dried his sweat and cooled him down after the rigorous session. The serum was working its magic, giving him pleasant tingles as the vents delivered the cooling air.

The air played around the hundreds of tiny dimples adorning his otherwise flawless physique. Whenever he revisited the memory, he still experienced the pain of those puncture wounds, inflicted by the hands of his tormentors, leaving him entwined in the barbed-wire. His struggles to free himself after they left him causing ever more wounds to the rest of his body. His despair, and anguish. The humiliation and misery. The excruciating pain involved in the final act. Melancholia enveloped him in its inescapable embrace. The depression, should it be left unchecked, had the capacity to render him hopelessly inactive if he allowed it. He shook off the advance of the insidious tide with a shrug and a laugh. Nothing so banal as self-pity would enslave him. He was stronger than that. Capitulation to such menial emotions was beneath him.

As he sat down with his heaping plate of pasta and sauce, topped by the fragrant cheese held in his hands, he made the fatal mistake of peering down into his lap. The gasp, drawn involuntarily from him at the sight of his horrendous surgery scars, and the resultant reconfiguration, nearly caused him to drop everything he'd been carrying. If he didn't see his groin area, he was happy with the delusion that everything was as it should be there. Sighting the devastation ruined that illusion entirely. It took every ounce of his iron will to regain control of his emotions. Averting his eyes, he placed the plate of food gently on the table, sighing with relief at having avoided a small catastrophe. He should learn, once and for all, to be fully clothed at all times, perhaps, even in the shower. It just felt so good at times not be covered from neck to ankle, his normal attire when outside.

Calmly, regaining control of his emotions, he allowed himself to relax with the ethereal music drifting through the house, seemingly breaking up the different orchestral sections to produce their individual sounds from different rooms. From the main bedroom would come the brass, the warm tones emanating from the various scales, while from the bathroom came the strings, percussion resonating from the hollow garage, all melding together to form the melody. He ate the warm pasta, allowing the food and the music to mellow the turmoil he felt at the sight of his ruined groin.

Unbidden, the haunting memories returned. The barbed-wire, the torment and abuse being dished out by young boys on a power trip. The gang, out for a bit of fun at someone else's expense. Stripped naked, face blackened by the sickening boot polish, genitals smeared with the toothpaste that stung like buggery. The punches and the boots to his body causing the barbs to sink deeper into his flesh. The vain struggle by him to avoid the blows. The laughter and the drunken joking as they lingered, unsure of what else they might do. Then the utter silence when they finally left. He froze at the memory, held his breath for what seemed an impossible length of time.

He heard the rustling of the bushes as one of them returned. Heard the heavy breathing of the laboured trek through the scrub. With the boot polish melting into his eyes after the struggle to be free, he could no longer see. He was covered in blood from the countless puncture wounds, drying and congealing in the cool night air. He waited in abject fear while the returning figure paced in front of him, silently, like an animal stalking its prey. He could smell the alcohol on the breath of the person pacing menacingly back and forth in front of him, deciding how to end the night. Teach the foreigner a lesson. All his senses highly alert as the swish of the figure's boots in the sand seemed inordinately loud.

The ominous metallic click had him imagining flick-knives, switch-blades, and every other knife he had ever seen on Australian television. The attacker's intentions were not clear. The fear he felt, he did not betray in his movements. His attacker would not be given the satisfaction of seeing that. The breath calmed, the wriggling against his bonds ceased, his anxious tremble subsided as he awaited his fate.

A click and a loosening in the tension of the wire saw him listing to one side, still incapable of removing himself from the restraining barbs. Then, it seemed as though the trailing wire, where it had come away from the post, was being wound around his face and head, causing concentrated pain where the barbs bit deeply into his neck and forehead. Tension from the opposite direction then released, as the new trailing end was wound around other parts of his body. When his scream broke the eerie silence, he did not at first realise that it was his own voice, shrieking, releasing from his own body, so powerfully had he imbued himself with the will to make no sound. The wire, tightening around his genitals smashed that will to dust. The natural instinct to struggle against the restraining wire hurting him so violently, only succeeded in causing further damage.

It was to be another ten hours before they found him, too late to save parts of his body starved of vital body fluids. His face, neck and head, a pulpy blood-soaked mess. The boy no longer looked, human, rolled in the wire, detached from the posts. Decisions about his future were being discussed as he was hauled away in an ambulance, en-route to emergency surgery. Without a set of fence cutters or sufficiently sized pliers, the medics were unable to release the boy from his wire shroud. Any attempt to unwind the wire merely augmented the damage and the pain for the boy, widening punctures or tearing flesh. With the multiple directions of the protruding barbs inserted in the flesh at a myriad of angles, it was like trying to remove fish hooks. Work the wire one way, and the barbs dug into another area.

The boy did not witness the exchange of looks between the medics while assessing and assisting him. His sight had not yet returned despite them washing his eyes thoroughly. The medics had grave concerns for the boy, especially for the blackened, swollen genitalia with an obvious haematoma evident. Starved of oxygenated blood for too long may mean a full amputation was necessary. Blood vessels and tissue had been affected badly from the lack of blood. The boy was extremely lucky not to have suffered a stroke from blood clots forming in the genital area.

Having radioed ahead to the hospital to be ready with small bolt cutters or decent fence pliers, the medics administered what aid they were able while injecting the boy with morphine. The pain was such that the boy did not completely succumb to the painkiller as most would. He was able to follow the conversations taking place above him. The worst of it centring on concern for his damaged groin area. Unintelligibly, he muttered his objections to their prognosis. He shuddered at the possible outcome of the surgical procedure they discussed so openly.

"Not a chance," said Medic one.

"I agree. Only possibility as far as I can tell. Couldn't imagine waking up to find that my whole life had changed, like that." Medic two added. "Docs say we should not attempt to unwrap him, so good call on that."

"You saw how he bled when I tried to unwind it? Made it worse I reckon. We need to include a full toolbox in this rig, for these kinds of emergencies."

"I thought we had one?"

"Basics only. Nothing in it to cut through this gauge wire. He'll have to have a full course of tetanus toxoid. With all that rusty metal sticking into him, he'll be extremely lucky not to get tetanus out of it."

"I think tetanus will be the least of his worries. Fuck, who would do shit like this?"

"C'mon Derek, you went to Ingham High didn't you?"

"Yeah, so?"

"Then you know who. Shit, he isn't out, Derek. Give him another shot will you?"

"Man, his parents are going to be out for blood over this, especially when the docs tell them what they have to do. Then there's the wardrobe to think about. Fucked if I'd want to be doing that for my son."

"Who is he anyway, do you know?"

"Yeah, I think he's a Malkovich. Saw them all in town once, having a meal at Luigi's."

"Heard about them. They live on Venables Street don't they?"

"How would you know that? You're a Townsville boy aren't you?"

"I had a friend that lived up that way. I saw the old couple a few times. From some Slavic country aren't they? Anyway, Loz told me about them and their son. Melco, isn't it?"

"Yeah, I think so."

Their patient shuddered uncontrollably as if he heard what the medics had been saying.

SUSPECT

"What can I do for you, Detectives?"

"Mr Miller, we need to ask you some questions in relation to a case we're working on at the moment. May we come in?" Detective Trent Barron was using his best manners.

"Just getting the place ready for hand-over this afternoon, so watch where you step and try not to get anything dirty, okay? Do you want a cuppa? Making one for myself. We can talk in the kitchen if that's okay? It has a tiled floor which is really easy to clean," said Michael as he led the two detectives down the hallway to the end of the house.

"I'll have a cuppa if it's not too much trouble, Mr Miller" agreed Brian.

"No trouble at all, and please, call me Michael," he smiled as they reached the kitchen where he motioned for the detectives to have a stool at the breakfast bar while he attended to the coffee that had been percolating on the gas range.

"Nice place, Michael. You do all the reno work yourself?" asked Detective Brian Chalmers.

"I get specialists in when I have to, like electrics and plumbing, but all the rest, yes. Thank-you."

"You got one of them, interior decorators, to help out with the furnishings and colours?" asked Trent.

"Nope, all me there, for better or worse. Doesn't pay to use too much outside help. Whittles away the profits. Help yourself to milk and sugar gents," said Michael placing three mugs of steaming coffee before them. "Hope you don't mind me adding some boiling water? I can't stand it the way it comes out of the pot only lukewarm. I know it's sacrilege and all that, but... "

"That's fine, Michael. The coffee we get at the station house, at least, the old one, was shit, so a good brew is welcome."

"Yeah, that was a bad one, the old station house. How's that survivor coming along? Touch and go for a while wasn't it?"

"Officer Gerhardt is out of the woods thankfully. Two of the civilians have also made it out of the ICU."

"It's about the old station house that we came to speak to you, Michael."

"Oh?"

"Yes. It seems you were seen running away from the old station house moments before it exploded. Care to explain that to us?"

"Happy to. Not running, though, walking quickly. I run morning and night as part of my exercise, but never during the day."

"Work out in the gym?"

"Privately, yes, never in a public gym."

"Weights?" Trent watched Michael nodding enthusiastically to confirm his observations. "What do you bench press?"

"Coupla hundred," said Michael nonchalantly.

Trent nearly spat his coffee. "You mean pounds right?"

"Hardly. Kilos of course. I squat three hundred, fifty reps."

"No fucking way! Not possible for someone with your physique. You'd have to be built like a brick shithouse to lift three hundred that many times," Trent accused.

"I can prove it to you if you want, but I don't think you came here to see me lift weights? I can assure you that I have lifted more. I am very strong for my physique as you say, but it's true nonetheless," said Michael smothering a yawn.

"Yeah, okay, I'll take your word for that for the moment. Now, you were saying you were walking fast that morning, not running because you never run during the day?"

"That's right. I parked my car behind the council building. I was going to walk down to the cafe for some breakfast as I usually do around that time... "

"And what time was that exactly?" asked Brian.

"Exactly, I couldn't say. It was around 9 - 9:30. Matter of fact, it had to be closer to 9:30 because I suddenly remembered I didn't have time for a lengthy breakfast if I wanted to meet my deadline of ten o 'clock at the council chambers."

"What was so important at the chambers?"

"If you want inspections on your property performed in order to advance to the next stage of the building process, you have to have your paperwork in on time. One minute past that bloody deadline and the good old bureaucratic bullshit begins. So I hurried back to the carpark to get my paperwork. Once I handed it in, I decided to forgo the breakfast. I must have been gone only a couple of minutes down the road before I heard the blast. I was very lucky not to have been in front of the station with those others when it went off."

"That's it?"

"Not sure what you were expecting, Detective. I was on my way past the station to go to the cafe, Luigi's. To get there, from where I parked, it was fastest to head through the park. I realised at the last minute that I had forgotten to hand in the papers which were still in my car and I wouldn't have time to have breakfast before the deadline, so I changed my mind. Simple as that."

"Why didn't you go for breakfast after handing in your papers?"

"As I said, changed my mind. Getting on to smoko by that time so, I decided to have a meal back here."

"See anyone or hear anything out of the ordinary?"

"I did recognise Miss Naylor, walking through the park. Other than that, no, couldn't say."

"How do you know, Miss Naylor? Cindy, isn't it?"

"I believe so. I have spoken to Cindy casually, on a couple of occasions, in the café. We seem to often be there at the same time.

"Spoke about what?"

"Nothing really. Just hello, the weather, that sort of thing. She may have been trying to hit on me. Can't be sure about that and really don't care."

"Really? She's a looker."

"I've seen many 'lookers', Detective, doesn't mean they are worth knowing. *Usually* turns out that way as a matter of fact."

"My wife is what I would deem a 'looker', Michael, and she was definitely worth knowing."

"Bully for you."

"Got something against good looking women, Michael? You gay by any chance?"

"Wow, again the assumption that simply because someone finds attractive women to be less than appealing, it must infer that they are gay? What, are we a little on the homophobic side, Detective? No, I am not gay, not that it is any of your bloody business."

"Whoa, bit sensitive there aren't you?"

"Ever heard about discrimination, Detectives? Supposed to be more tactful these days you know? They are actually allowed to be married now, according to the laws that just passed. The whole country took a big vote recently, a... what was it called? A pleb... something?"

"Plebiscite. Yes we are all well aware of the new laws allowing the... persons of the same sex to marry," said Trent with obvious disdain. Brian watched him carefully.

Brian shifted in his seat uncomfortably, while Trent continued to search Michael's face for signs of admission, or guilt. Something about the man, Michael Miller did not sit well with his first impressions. He did not appear feminine in any way, yet, his precise manner of speech and his demeanour had Trent disliking him, making him feel prickly. Trent noticed the movement by his partner and wondered idly if Miller had the same effect on him. Trent had been leaning toward finishing the interview until his discomfort started to pluck away at his detective strings.

"You were living with Detective Ryan for a time?"

"Boarding, yes."

Trent noticed the mood shift immediately. Michael Miller was no longer being as cooperative. A shutter had come down somewhere in the last few seconds and this man was no longer willingly participating in the interview. Trent detected tiredness creeping into the man's face. He recognised the blackness under the eyes for the first time and the scars around the neck and hairline. Michael Miller was a good looking man, he supposed, were it not for the perceptible scarring. Every so often, Michael would touch those scars out of habit.

"How did you come to be living there, Mr Miller?" asked Trent in a formal tone. Brian instantaneously sat up straighter upon witnessing the distinct change in his partner's tone. The interview was gaining some momentum.

"I answered an advertisement for a boarder."

"Why would you need somewhere to board when you had a place like this?"

Sighing impatiently, "I would have thought that someone with your training might have *detected* the reason for that? Look about you gentlemen, what do you see, hmm? Might that be renovations? This was a derelict when I came across it, and uninhabitable. I required a place to stay while I renovated. Ryan had an ad for a room to rent, I applied and was eventually accepted. I lived there until recently when I received my marching orders from the landlord. Moved in here as it was finally possible for me to do so."

"Trouble between you two?"

"Only on his end apparently. I had no complaints."

"What can you tell us about the room in the garage?"

"Really, why would you be asking me about that?"

"Really, why wouldn't we?" Trent was losing patience. "A man was abducted from that room, Mr Miller. A room that you constructed. A room that was deadlocked with brand new door hardware, yet was accessed nonetheless by a person or persons with the knowledge of the bolts connecting the wall frames. If the room was to be secure, Mr Miller, why did you construct it in such a manner that made it easy to access? Had your own little backdoor entrance there didn't you?"

"I don't like the inferences or the attitude, Detective. I have been completely forthcoming and cooperative with your questions. If you prefer that I lawyer up, which is my right, I can soon arrange it."

"If you have something to hide, it might be wise for you to do so."

Michael eyed the two detectives with annoyance. He did not have the time to go through protracted questioning after arranging for a lawyer to be present. The interview would probably have to take place at the temporary station house in Ingham, meaning he may miss his hand-over deadline. Michael observed a heightened tension in the stances of the two detectives. Nothing conclusive, just a certain set to the shoulders and overall bearing since they had begun questioning him.

Though, irritating in the extreme, it was something that Michael had to endure over the years. His manner of precise speech annoyed most people with whom he had extended contact, and often, like his present circumstances, even over short periods. He had laboured diligently since youth to rid himself of the accent that for one reason or another tended to invoke the wrath of Australian children. He loathed being singled out as a youngster and made to feel ashamed of his ethnicity.

He had changed his name and developed his speech with meticulous care to avoid confrontations, yet, seemingly his cultured, unaccented speech attracted more derision than the former. He hated to admit it, but his parents had been correct. He should have embraced his heritage, allowed his ethnicity to inspire pride instead of shame. Too late now he supposed. He had to deal with discrimination on a daily basis, despite having amended all his ethnic traits to blend in with the bloody Australians and their bigoted, narrow-minded views.

Not for the first time, did he wish he had returned to the old country where he would not be viewed as a foreigner. Or even if he was, would not be treated with such condemnation. Europeans had a very different attitude toward foreigners. Few other countries had the rampant intolerance displayed by Australians in general. His travels abroad had introduced to him to the comradery enjoyed by his countrymen for each other and strangers alike. Totally opposite to the hatred and vilification he experienced as a child in his adopted country. He loved Australia - the country, desperately, but loathed its generational denizens with all his heart. Ironically, most of its population was made up of foreigners. The only true Australians were the Aboriginals and they were victimised the most.

"No, Detective, I have nothing to hide. I will answer your questions for you. Let's see. Ryan had a problem with one of his drunken mates, which was actually quite ironic seeing as he is not that far removed from the same condition. He asked if I could build him a room within his garage to house his patient. He needed to be able to 'lock him in for his own good', I believe were the words he used at some point. He asked me to make the structure permanent, but his funds were somewhat limited and I really didn't want him to feel beholden to me for an extended period of time. I was doing the work in lieu of rent payments, you see?"

"Go on," said Trent, with Brian leaning forward with a notepad, taking it all down in his own shorthand.

"Well, Ryan had insufficient funds to build it to completion, with both sides of the walls sheeted. He instructed me to sheet the inside of the room only so that his mate could not escape or injure himself. I affixed the bottom plates of the pine wall frames to the concrete floor with masonry anchors and bolted the frames together instead of merely nailing them. My nail gun was being serviced at the time. Had the outer walls been sheeted, no one would have been able to access the bolts holding the frames together to remove one of the walls. Had I nailed them, they still would have been accessible. That you think I had some notion to do so, is laughable."

"So you have no idea as to the whereabouts of the former occupant of that room, Lorenzo Catani?"

"Nope, and couldn't care less. He was a useless old drunk, much like his mate, and from what I heard, his mate's old man as well."

"You are being very unkind, and unlikeable, Mr Miller."

"When you come with up a law against that, be sure to arrest me why don't you?"

"What's your story, Miller?" asked Brian finally adding his presence, while Trent finished his coffee.

"From birth?"

"Cut to the highlights if you wouldn't mind."

"Born in Europe, migrated to Australia with my parents. Loved the country, hated its citizens and changed my name to a more western, anglicised name at the age of twenty. Learned to disguise my obvious accent soon thereafter. Bummed around in a few different jobs here and there, went abroad after my parents died and left me an inheritance. Learned my tradecraft when I returned after serving my 'apprenticeship' as a caretaker and handyman for some properties owned by a friend. Started buying and selling these relics once I cleaned them up and made something worthwhile out of them."

"Ever utilise your building skills anywhere near Dungeness?"

"Of course. I have done renovations all over the area, Detective. I actually own several more properties around here that I have purchased over the last year; some started, some not yet ready to accept my loving attention."

"What are we likely to find on these properties, Miller?"

"Old residences, Chalmers," said Michael with a deadpan face.

"Don't recall us as having given you our names?"

"No, you were extremely rude in neglecting to properly identify yourselves, making my testimony all but worthless in a court of law. Any lawyer worth his salt would have a field day with that omission."

"If it were recorded, perhaps."

"And what makes you think it wasn't?"

Brian exchanged a worried glance with his partner. They knew all too well of suspects getting away scot-free on a technicality. Brian smiled knowingly, believing it to be the bluff it was intended as.

"And, is it being recorded?"

"Of course it is." Brian's face dropped "The house is more modern than you realise. I set the computerised house to monitor and record our conversation the moment I saw you pulling up in your Commodore, Detective. The hard drive onto which the recording is being made, however, is not on-site. It is with a specialist security company, whom I hired to rig up the very latest in security software."

"Why would you feel the need to record a conversation without knowing either us or our purpose?"

"You were surprised that I knew your name, Chalmers. Do you think I *don't* know who you are? Ryan mentioned your names many times when he was venting his frustration over the 'dumb fucks' from Townsville. I knew who you were the moment I saw you, and I have recently made it a habit to record my conversations with anyone in authority. Boarding with Ryan had that effect on me."

Changing tactics, "Know someone by the name of, Malkovich? Specifically, Melco Malkovich?"

"Heard of him."

"I asked if you knew him."

"And I answered that I'd heard of him. How well I know him is relative I should imagine."

"Think you're some kind-o-smart-arse do you?"

"Think you're some kind-o-dimwit do you?"

Brian rose from his seat in a threatening manner, to which his partner responded, "Brian, back off, buddy. He isn't worth it. Mr Miller, what can you tell us about, Melco Malkovich?"

"Not a lot. Another immigrant who had some trouble with local gangs and stuff, then high-tailed it out of here."

"What trouble and what gangs are you referring to?"

"Local boys who didn't take to the foreigner. Made his life a living hell from what I understand. Marked him in some way or another. Went to live in the big smoke at the first opportunity from what I heard. Parents were devastated."

"Marked him?"

"So I believe. Never saw it myself"

"What kind of mark?"

"Some sort of burn marks from what I understand. The shape of a hand or very close to it."

"A hand? Like a human hand?"

"Possibly. A lot of stories here around that time. Some true, some not. One fellow I overheard talking once said it was like someone used a cigarette to trace burn marks all around the perpetrator's hand on the victim's chest."

Brian and Trent exchanged another glance.

"Who told you about that?"

"Nobody told me about it. I said I overheard it."

"Okay, from whom did you overhear it?"

"Couldn't say."

"Why not, Mr Smart-arse?"

"Cause I don't know the person, Mr Dimwit."

"We could easily run you in you know?"

"For what, calling you a name? I have it all on record remember?"

"Look you... "

"Hold on, Bri. Mr Miller, can you tell us any more about that incident or any other involving, Melco Malkovich."

"It's all just a bunch of rumours really. I don't think anyone actually knows the whole truth about it. He was found wrapped up in some barbed-wire fencing, pretty bad wounds from what I can figure. Some school children had really done a number on him, took him from a tent one night while on cadet camp. Roughed him up a bit, then went to town on him. I heard he was never the same after that. Left school to work around here for a while, then took off."

"What about the mark, the hand, you said?"

"Well, the story goes that the kids who did it were pretty drunk, which was why they probably don't even remember doing it. One kid must have really had it in for him. Supposed to have done that burning thing, then booted him in the groin for good measure.

Caused a testicular rupture and a blood clot in the penis. Took so long to find him that he had to undergo surgery to remove his genitalia. Doctors wanted to perform one of those gender surgeries on him because he was so young. Fill him with hormones and stuff. He rejected the idea, rejected the town and even his parents for a long time. Blamed them for allowing it to happen."

"The authorities would have been notified over an incident like that," remarked Trent with confidence.

"All swept under the carpet. Someone knew someone who knew someone more powerful. The teacher who found him, never reported it under advisement from the headmaster of the High School. No one ever investigated and no one was ever held accountable for a heinous act that ruined many lives."

"What do you mean 'many' lives'?"

"You really don't know? How can something lasting so long, affecting so many lives remain unknown by the bloody cops?"

"What are you talking about?"

"I am talking about the systematic and ritualistic torture and mutilation of foreign youngsters attending Ingham State High School, and anyone found to be willing to report the incidents, ending up under a truck or a cane train in the middle of the night. The reincarnation of The Black Hand Gang?"

Michael made the momentous decision to reveal something of what he knew despite his reluctance. He wondered whether the detectives from Townsville might alter the status quo in Ingham. The two detectives were sitting there like stunned mullets, neither able to recognise what he was talking about. "You've never heard of this gang? Ingham always had a strong Italian and Spanish influence, with the 1920s and the 1930s seeing a large influx of immigrants from those countries. In the 1930s, disgruntled elements among these immigrants formed The Black Hand Gang, terrorising the town; bribery, corruption and extortion... " began Michael.

Predominately a sugar cane farming area, the town attracted more than its fair share of migrant workers, to this day, hosting a large Italian festival every year. Consequently, it also attracted the seedier elements of Italian life, the Mafiosi. The predominant aim of the criminal gang, identifying themselves by the inclusion of a Black Hand icon on their ransom demands, was money.

The gang was known to cut off the ears of anyone unwilling to participate in their extortion schemes. Their use of fear to accommodate their goals was renowned to the citizens of Ingham, Innisfail, and surrounding towns. Their exploits became legendary among the easily influenced, making newspaper headlines frequently. Like the Daily Telegraph's report on the death of one, Nicola Mamone of Innisfail. Shot in the back six times on Edith Street by his earless assailant, Giovanni Iacona, in 1934, a victim of the gang.

"... the use of the black hand calling card has undergone a resurgence in the township from about the time Melco left. No longer employed to extort the local businessmen, but rather to intimidate, mutilate and humiliate the unfortunate recipients. The branding of the victims with the hand-shaped iron produced a blackening of the area when scabbed. Authorities are yet to admit their knowledge of the evil perpetuated annually within the town, a ritualistic initiation ceremony, designed to single out one of Ingham's foreign students each year as a means of instilling fear and authority among Ingham's youth," Michael explained.

"How many victims are we talking about here? How many years has this been going on?"

"At least one victim a year for about the last thirty, or thereabouts."

"No, no that is simply not possible. Couldn't happen. Thirty students maimed, or castrated and marked with some 'hand' and no investigation? Not possible."

"Detectives, The Black Hand Gang is real. Not the original one we learned about in school, operating here in the thirties, and definitely not with the same purpose. A resurgence, a reincarnation of the name and the calling card only, with a deep abiding fear tactic to silence any witnesses or parents looking to make any trouble."

"How could you possibly know about this with all the alleged secrecy and corruption involved?"

Michael weighed up his options very carefully, determining his fate and that of others. He could not trust anyone in authority, yet he knew that nine-tenths of the original Ingham police force had been obliterated recently by the explosion at the police station. He reluctantly decided upon revealing himself and his circumstances to officialdom for the first time in his life. Uncertainly, he rose slowly from his stool, undoing the buttons on his long-sleeved khaki work shirt. Next came the white singlet he removed over his head to reveal a torso pock-marked with hundreds of what might have been mistaken for acne scars, had the detectives not known better.

That elicited a sharp intake of breath from Brian, while Trent remained emotionally distanced. Michael then sat back on the stool to remove his work boots. Without pausing, for fear he might not proceed, Michael removed the rest of his clothing to stand nude in front of the detectives, who gasped. Michael's entire body, though superbly toned and muscled, bore the same scars as his chest. The worst of the scars by far, though, was contained in the groin area where no genitalia of any description was evident. It was simply a mass of gnarled, angry, scar tissue and a branded hand across the area once occupied by his genitals.

"FUCK ME! What sort of parents would allow this to happen to their boy without reporting it?" ventured Trent ultimately.

"Dead ones," answered Michael as he climbed into his clothing once more. "My parents were murdered when they reported this to the Ingham Police. It was made to look like a car accident, but everyone knew it for what it was. Everyone looked the other way, not wanting to end up the same. I had some reconstructive surgery done to my face overseas, and they offered to convert my gender as well. Something I rejected. Honestly, that's where I should have stayed. I should never have come back here, but I no longer fit in anywhere else."

"Jesus-fucking-Christ! What have we walked into here, Trent?"

"You're admitting that you are the one going around committing these murders? That you are the Minstrel Killer?"

"You wish. I've never killed anyone. I would certainly have liked to get some satisfaction, and I have no love lost for any of the victims, but me? Kill? Never!"

"You say your parents are dead, why wouldn't you report it after that?"

"I was still pretty much a child, and I had two sisters to worry about. That was the only reason I returned from overseas, to be with my sisters, my nieces and nephews. Besides, I couldn't trust the police. Like the original gang, the new Black Hand Gang had contacts in high places and with some relatives in direct contact with organised crime in Italy."

"We talking the Mafia here?"

"You do the math, Detective. I think I have said enough about that. I have a family to protect. I guarantee you this, if my family is hurt in any way as a result of this, I will be using the recording I have of this interview to nail you bastards. I am trusting that you are not part of it. I am hoping that you cannot be bought or persuaded to turn. Their reach is long and persuasive. I thought it time that someone knew."

"Wait a sec. These people that have been murdered lately, they were part of this, this Black Hand Gang?"

"No. From what I can gather, they were the inspiration for it."

"You lost me," admitted Trent with reluctance.

He and Brian were sitting on the edge of their stools drinking in every word of this fantastic tale. They were almost inclined to disbelieve it had they not witnessed the evidence of the man's story for themselves just a moment ago. The ghastly scars borne on the man's groin where his genitals once existed told the shocking truth of his ordeals at the hands of sadistic gang members. The torment, agony and anguish caused by those horrific injuries were more than most individuals would have had the capacity to endure. Brian especially cringed inwardly at the thought of losing his manhood in such a horrendous manner.

"Look, Detectives, I am not one hundred per cent certain of all the facts okay, I don't think anyone *is,* actually. I have pieced together a sort of idea of what happened by talking to a few people as discreetly as possible. Don't ask me to reveal their names. Those names travel with me to the grave. They entrusted me with information that could have seen them and their loved ones dead or worse."

"We can appreciate that. We will respect your need for anonymity for as far as we can take it. Tell us what you know, or think you know. We promise that we will consult with you on any actions we take that may come close to any of your informants?"

"Excuse us for a moment," said Brian rising from the stool to take his partner aside. "We can't do that, Trent. We haven't cleared him of any wrong-doing yet. What if he's playing us? What if he really is the Minstrel Killer, and we tell him our every move?"

"Not reading him that way, Bri. He tickled my antenna at first, and I knew something was off about him, but all I'm getting now is sincerity. I believe him, Bri. And, fuck. Those scars. Getting branded like that... there? I agree he'd have every motive in the world to off these pricks if they did that to him, but think about it, Bri. He's a bit too young to have been at school with Ryan and his bunch, don't you think? The way I'm reading it, he was after what happened to, Malkovich. No way he's our perp. Malkovich is closer to Ryan's age, and the first two vics, Kugelweis and Clayton."

"So, who the fuck is our perp then? Is it still, Malkovich?"

"That's who my money's on still, only this... thing, is not him."

"Hey! Cut that out. If he isn't our perp, then he's been to hell and back. He's still a human being, Trent and he doesn't deserve that. I thought you were better than that?"

"What's got into you all of a sudden? A bit on the sensitive side aren't you? Got nothing downstairs. What does that make him?"

"He's still a man, Trent, still a man."

"And we need to know what he knows. Our entire investigation just got thrown a bloody curveball. I don't know how deep this fucking mess goes, or if we can do anything at all about it. You believe this whole Black Hand thing?"

"I remember reading something about it in school. Shit, I was never much good in history. Bored the crap out of me. Asleep most of the time."

"So?"

"Alright, I'll follow your lead, Trent. Just... if you don't think he's our perp, can you lay off the disrespectful attitude? If he's innocent, he deserves a hefty helping of our respect and consideration."

"Yeah, okay. You got some sort-of-a-hard-on for him, I'll go easy, alright?"

"Sometimes, you disgust me," said Brian as he returned to the breakfast bar, leaving Trent to peer after him with a look of bewilderment. He eventually joined his partner at the bar.

"We would appreciate it, Mr Miller, if you could tell us what you know, or think you know, that might shed some light on the murders or bombings happening around here," asked Trent politely, then turning to his partner for confirmation of his attitude, receiving a hostile glare in return.

"As I said, much of what I gathered was in bits and pieces which I reconstructed with a whole lot of conjecture and assumption thrown in."

"Yeah, sure. Mind if we have a copy of your recording for this, rather than my partner getting writer's cramp there?"

"If I feel the information will be used appropriately."

Trent was about to protest with threats of court orders and such before he reined himself in at the last moment, "Fair enough. Your call. I guess we'll have to trust each other then?"

"Something like that." Michael gave the pair a final look of inspection to ascertain their intentions as best he could before sighing heavily. "Melco Malkovich was the first victim, for sure, but not at the hands of an organised gang. It was a bunch of kids that got drunk and wanted to show Melco once and for all, who they were and what they were capable of. They bullied him mercilessly in school, but he never caved. He stood his ground and never capitulated to their efforts of domination. He fought back consistently, even winning a few battles when they were one-on-one."

"We heard he was a tough son-of-a-bitch."

"His mother was an angel, Detective. She was heartbroken over the final incident that drove her son to despise them."

"Figure of speech, no offence intended. Calm down alright," suggested Trent with raised palms.

"We think we know what happened to him at school, and we believe we know what happened while he was on bivouac with the cadets, thanks to what you told us earlier and what we have been told by another source." Brian interceded "So, how does all this tie in with the Black Hand Gang stuff?"

"The incident with Cadet Malkovich was never investigated. His surgery was never reported because someone in the group had some very high connections that wielded some pretty hefty influence back then, maybe even now. The town clammed up about it and his parents' cries fell on deaf ears until they didn't, and that meant they suffered an accident some years later when they refused to drop it. Their car ran into a cane train one night, for no apparent reason that anyone can determine."

"Lorenzo Catani was the only one of the original crew with an Italian heritage. Kugelweis was German, McCormack had Scottish ancestry and Ryan was a third-generation Australian. You think the Italian connection was through, Catani?" asked Trent.

"Assumed, not verified. Lorenzo Catani's uncle, Umberto Catani was rumoured to have had dealings with organised crime both in Italy and Australia. Wasn't difficult to make an assumption based on that."

"Okay, say we accept that. Doesn't explain how it continued, how this Black Hand Gang kept victimising students at that school for so long," explained Brian, seeing Trent nodding his agreement with the direction Brian was steering the interview.

"At that point, it all gets a little scratchy, to say the least. To me, it looked like the kids in the school heard about what happened to Melco Malkovich. The reputation of the culprits escalated to hero-like status among the impressionable youth of the day. A cult-like following transpired. Whether the original crew had any knowledge of or implication in that 'fame', was never certain. Somewhere along the line, maybe after being taught about the nefarious Black Hand Gang of the '30s, the gang was reborn under a different manifesto. The point of the new gang seemed to be the persecution of one individual per year, culminating in an initiation ceremony that grew more and more brutal, following along the lines of what occurred to, Melco Malkovich. I was singled out during my first year of high school there. You saw the result of that initiation. Others fared far worse than I."

"None of it reported? For thirty-something years? I find that a little tough to digest." said Trent with a frown.

"You think I mutilated myself at the age of thirteen? That any thirteen-year-old is capable of inflicting that type of carnage to their precious genitals? You think I am making this up?"

"No, no I don't. What I find hard to accept is that it could be kept quiet for so long. Where are the rest of the victims if this has been going on for years? "

"During my research, I have found a few who were institutionalised, unable to cope with the physical trauma and mental anguish. One, I visited was a blubbering wreck of a human, no longer capable of speech or coherent thought. A few ended up in jail having taken to criminal activities. Some turned to drugs, alcohol, even prostitution. I've accounted for only a small fraction of the victims, Detective. What you don't understand is the collateral damage to the extended families. Their fear and helplessness to defend their sons have had far-reaching ramifications. Almost an entire township cowed to subservience by the ruthless tactics employed over many years by an equally growing number of protagonists. While the list of victims grew, so too did the list of perpetrators and families, all working to protect them."

After a few moments to reflect on the information, "Jesus, this is, is... epic. If we take what you say to be the truth, then most of the town is involved in this in one way or another and we have no way of determining which is which, who is on whose side," remarked Trent, showing his frustration. "Who the fuck do we tell about this? How are we supposed to investigate this shit? No one in this town is beyond reproach. How far up the ladder does it go? How far has it spread? Over the course of thirty years people move away, take up positions across the state or even the country. Fuck, they may even be in parliament. For all we know, the fucking Prime Minister may be one of these pricks that tortured people. He's originally from here isn't he?"

"That may be stretching it a bit, but I see your point, Trent. Reporting to anyone carries with it a huge risk. This has been going on for that long that anyone could be involved. Do you think your informants might help us, Mr Miller?" asked Brian.

"Are you kidding? If it is, Melco Malkovich committing these murders around town, half of the population is cheering and applauding him, Detectives. If the Black Hand Gang has finally found some opposition, then it is high time indeed, and it has my full and complete blessing."

"And your cooperation?"

"If Melco Malkovich has approached the victims' families for assistance in exacting revenge or a plan to wipe out the gang, then he has unlimited resources at his disposal gentlemen, with a base of co-conspirators absolutely loyal to his cause with ample motivation to remain so. They have remained mute over many years. You will gain nothing from them now, even if I were to divulge the names of my informants, which I will not. My cooperation has extended to knowledge and nothing more. I still have a family to protect."

"Fuck! We put one foot wrong in this town and we either end up with a cross shoved up our arse, a horse's head next to us in bed, castrated, or all of the above. We can expect exactly zero help with almost everyone belonging to one camp or the other, and they have absolutely no reason to either trust us or help us. That about sum it up?" asked Brian.

"Yep."

"Will you help us, Mr Miller?"

"With what, apprehending the Minstrel Killer?"

"Yes."

"Absolutely... NOT!"

"We could cite obstruction of justice...?"

"Oh, in that case... go fuck yourselves."

UMBERTO

"Tell me about him, everything."

"I, I, don't know much about him," stammered Lorenzo, who regained consciousness half an hour ago. His body was practically numb. He felt none of the myriad of injuries inflicted upon him, saw nothing through the limpid pools of mush sloshing around his eye sockets. Both feet had been removed and one hand was missing as far as he could tell. His mind was escaping reality so often that he found it difficult to keep track of what was real and imagined. He welcomed the onset of insanity. Longed desperately for the oblivion of ignorance. As a vegetable, he believed he would no longer feel the torture, no longer care or know.

"Umberto Catani, your uncle on your father's side. Tell me or I will get my needle out again."

Lorenzo shivered like a windblown leaf at the thought of the enhancer entering his system once more. The man had given him an anaesthetic it seemed, which blocked all sensation temporarily. He wanted that to continue, forever. The alternative did not bear consideration. He racked his brain in an effort to recall what he knew about his infamous uncle.

Umberto Francesco Catani remained in Sicily when his younger brother, Mario, and his parents migrated to Australia in the 30s. As the oldest of the siblings, he had already made his mark in the local scene as a hoodlum for hire. During the years apart, his brother Mario and he remained in patchy communication between Australia and Italy. Umberto had boasted of rising to prominence within the cadre into which he was accepted. Without admitting it, it became clear to Mario that his older brother had become a contract assassin for the mob, the very evil his parents had hoped to escape by migrating.

Mario worked extremely hard, as all migrants were apt to do when they managed to come to the new country. He started as a cane cutter, sweating day in day out in the 90% humidity of the north, stuck in the stifling heat of the tall cane surrounding him as he toiled. Stripping the cane for planting was among the worst of the jobs. Sugar cane is planted from sections of the harvested plant being interred. Before planting and sectioning of the tall lengths of cane can proceed, it is necessary to de-frond the stalks completely. This is done simply by running the hand in the reverse direction to the leaves' growth, thereby stripping them. Unfortunately, the cane has natural protection given it by nature. Nick-named 'Hairy-Marys', microscopically fine hairs that find their way into every exposed surface of the human body, embedding themselves painfully into the flesh. Next to nothing will successfully remove them and the discomfort remains with the worker perpetually.

Hard work eventually paid off for the migrant worker with little to no education. He married into an Italian farmer's family, marrying their only daughter, Maria Giovanna Pescatori, 24. Maria Giovanna and Mario Domenico Catani married in 1952. She was a 'mature' bride, marrying somewhat late by the expectations of Italian tradition, but delayed interminably by her over-protective father. Maria gave birth to their son Lorenzo almost ten years later after accepting that she was barren and would never be a mother.

The parents doted on their boy, with the grandparents on the mother's side taking great pride in their only grandchild. The grandparents' farm eventually ended up as Mario's when they passed away, by virtue of him being married to Maria, their only child. Mario was finally able to supervise the cutting of the cane just as mechanical means were being introduced to conduct the harvests.

Lorenzo Catani stumbled and mumbled his way through school with barely passable grades, spending more time disrupting class and eating, than studying. His parents despaired of the laziness so apparent in their cherished son. Nothing could convince the boy or sway him to practice the work ethics that should have been inherited from his hard-working parents. They doted on him anyway, lavishing on him all the materials and toys they had gone without as children. To say that Lorenzo was spoiled was a gross understatement. He was, in fact, a fat, lazy slob with no respect for his elders or anyone else.

Finding himself in trouble with police, neighbours and teachers on many occasions throughout his childhood and early school, Lorenzo brought much shame to his parents. When the boy reached high school, he was nothing 'but a bum' according to his long-suffering mother, but she loved him all the same. There was nothing on earth that she would not do for her son, no task too great and no favour too large. His father, Mario, however, demurred in his affections, preferring to bring a little tough love to the lad. The boy literally drove his dad to drink, often coming home at ungodly hours, smashed to the gills on booze, whereupon he would rouse the household to begin ranting and raving about the boy's shortcomings. Often, resulting in physical punishment for both the boy and his mother when she came to his rescue.

Barely a night passed when the boy did not attract the wrong attention from his father. His school grades grew worse and his shenanigans increased from mere mischief to outright criminal offences. The moment the boy learned to steal his father's alcohol, his real troubles began. Visits by the constabulary were so frequent that there was an immediate danger of the boy ending up in a juvenile facility. His mother, copping a bashing herself more often than she could recall, fretted with worry for her only child. She attempted everything in her power to make the boy understand. Maria did her best to protect him.

Finally, when the boy came home one night after spending a few blessedly quiet days away at a cadet camp, he became subdued. Something was terribly wrong with the boy, but he would not say a word. Then they were paid a visit by the parents of the boy living across the road. They were distraught and almost manic in their behaviour. Neither Maria nor her husband understood what was being said by the folks with such thick foreign accents. Slowly, over the course of the next two hours, the story unfolded of a shameful act allegedly perpetrated by their son and his friends from school. When she finally realised what the parents revealed, when she understood what the boys had done to the Malkovich boy, Maria grew deeply afraid.

While it was not certain that there was enough evidence to convict her son, she could not afford to allow the matter to proceed to a court of law. Knowing that her son was on notice with the police department, knowing that her husband would be useless to assist her, she remembered her brother-in-law and his affiliations. Unbeknownst to her husband, Maria contacted her husband's brother, Umberto Catani. She impressed upon the estranged brother her plight for his only nephew. She also managed to convince her brother-in-law of her husband's fall from grace as a total alcoholic, unable to raise himself in the fashion of a husband for his wife. Umberto listened with cold, calculated calm to the harrowing tale of his nephew's descent into criminality and of his dear brother's love affair with the bottle.

Within twenty-four hours, Umberto Catani arrived at the Townsville airport to be greeted enthusiastically by his sister-in-law, Maria. Still a beauty at her age, Maria spoke at length on the one hundred kilometre journey to Ingham. She laid it all bare for him without glossing over any parts or concealing anything. She understood that she was betraying her son to a certain extent by painting him in his true light. Lies would not help her in their present circumstances. Umberto would have to see the family for what it had become. Fortunately, her brother-in-law agreed with her that the boy needed protection otherwise he would end up in juvenile prison or worse.

The situation was dire and only equally dire measures could circumvent the inevitable. Umberto's activities over the ensuing week would ensure the survival of the Catani family, albeit with consequences. Mario, when sober, refused to acknowledge his brother's help, rejected any course of action that might assist his son to avoid what was his due. After lengthy, private and discreet discussions with his sister-in-law, it was eventually decided that her no-good drunk of a husband would become the first casualty in the war to save her and her son. Then the real work began. First and foremost on the list were the Malkovich parents.

Within a few years, every loose end had been wrapped up neatly. Bribes were paid and threats were delivered. When threats had no effect, people went missing or suffered accidents. The school had been appropriately compensated for keeping the matter away from public scrutiny. Police officers had their palms greased with large pay increases by way of brown envelopes appearing in their mailboxes. Nothing was ever brought to the attention of authorities over and above the few who were being bankrolled by a certain individual. One police officer, who held to his ideals, found out all too late how much those ideals would cost him. The whole affair was sewn up tight.

Maria's new lover stayed with the family for several years longer to ensure the equability and silence of their accusers. Eventually, Umberto was recalled to Italy by his superiors who required his particular talents once more. His annual return visits to Australia ensured the town remembered its obligation to the fearsome man with the reputation of a cold-blooded killer. Unfortunately, Maria's son was never the same after the incident. He grew to be entirely withdrawn and distant from everyone including himself. Maria was never to know that Umberto had plied his influence in that direction also. For he cherished his lover so much that he would protect her from her own son.

Lorenzo recalled that day with a fearful clarity etched into his brain for eternity. His uncle paid him a visit in the pub one day. Plying him with as much alcohol as he desired, the very best that money could buy. None of the horse piss he normally drank. Thirty-year-old scotch and cognac were piled in front of him, glass after glass, until he could drink no more. His uncle then took him for a ride to the beach with the moon shining in all its fullness. A glorious night. Then the fun ended dramatically as Umberto slammed the boy to the sand with one mighty blow that left him stunned. Before Lorenzo knew what was happening, he had his trousers removed and his penis tied tightly at the base.

His questions went unanswered; his attempts to stand were thwarted with an iron hand. Slowly, his bladder called attention to itself, that it required immediate relief. While still heavily influenced by the alcohol in his system, Lorenzo did not immediately identify a reason to be overly concerned. He knew his uncle was trying to teach him some sort of lesson he supposed, but not one that was discernible to his inebriated brain. It was only later when the urgency of his need became painfully apparent that he began to realise his dilemma. The extreme urge to release his burdened bladder became so painful that he had no option but to release.

It was only at that point that he realised how much trouble he was in. With the tight band around the base of his penis restricting the flow through the urethra, he began to give the severity of his situation the deference it required. Hour upon hour his uncle drilled into him the importance of his instructions never again to involve his mother in any of his problems. Never again to darken the doorstep of his mother's house. Never again to show his face in the neighbourhood. Never again to be seen by his mother at all. If any of his instructions were disobeyed, Lorenzo would suffer the same fate as his father.

Only when Umberto was one hundred per cent satisfied that he had made himself clear and that the boy harboured sufficient fear to obey his wishes, did he release the bond on the boy's little worm, now the size of a bloated slug looking to burst. He had to ensure he was not in the path of the stream once the cord was severed, for it shot from the penis for a distance of fifteen metres or more. Truly a record to behold, he thought. Lorenzo's drinking problems escalated from that night onwards, though Umberto's lesson had been meant to address his nephew's dependence on alcohol as well. All in all, though, it was a minor issue in the uncle's eyes. As a reward for his continued obedience, a few hundred dollars a month found its way into his bank account, enough to keep him suitably inebriated on cheap plonk in perpetuity. Unfortunately, perpetuity had an end, Lorenzo discovered when at last the deposits failed to appear.

When Lorenzo related what he knew to his captor, a deathly silence ensued. He had guessed at parts of the story. Made assumptions that seemed plausible to fill in the gaps. Silence ensued, broken only by the deep breathing of the madman as if sighing heavily. Lorenzo feared the silence more than the noise. It contained an ominous menace that did not exist in the loud music or the persistent questions.

Lorenzo wondered all too late, whether it had been wise to divulge what he knew about his uncle to the demented man. The torture had reached a zenith as far as Lorenzo could tell. If he pushed the limits of the pain threshold any further, Lorenzo was certain he would perish. Blessed release, at least. God figured highly in Lorenzo's thoughts, despite abandoning the church and all the beliefs instilled in him by his devout, Roman Catholic mother.

Brainwashed and brow-beaten with unending verses and parables till it nauseated him, Lorenzo did not so much *walk* away from his faith as *propelled* himself from it like he had a rocket up his arse. His years spent apart from his wonderful mother had been blissfully devoid of any spiritual murmurings. He almost felt as though he had narrowly escaped the clutches of a deviant cult attempting to turn his brain into a programmable machine that only accepted religious binary; crosses and halos.

"It was your uncle that started the Italian connection, bringing the fear of the old country into the new world. The residents of Ingham quaked with the fear of the Mafia hitman come to Australia to ensure his nephew did not wind up in jail. Well, at least we now know what happened don't we, Lorenzo? You didn't go back that night to cause more harm. You were indeed innocent of that matter. You were guilty of a far greater crime than that of your friend, Ryan who did return that night. You ensured that the good folks of Ingham lived in absolute fear for their lives if anyone spoke out against the crimes you committed."

"It, it wasn't me! I didn't call my uncle. I never wanted any of that. Fuck, he tortured me remember?"

"Tsk, tsk, tsk. Stopped you from pissing yourself for a short time, and you think that was equal to what you lousy, rotten, mongrel punks did to an innocent boy? Do you really... um. Do you... How... what... Hmm. I... "

"What? Are you finished? Are you still there?"

"Who... who are you? What, what are we... I doing, what... am. Hello... tired, shit, shit, shit... so... need to. Needle? Yes? Get... some, something from... where?"

"Oh, Jesus, don't flake out on me alright? I don't want to die like this. Can't you just get it over with? Please, Melco, I'm begging you. Kill me. I can't take this no more and if you go flaky on me and leave me like this for fuck-knows how long, that would really suck big time, Melco. Please, have a heart?"

"Funny... yeah... umm... "

"What, what the fuck are you talking about, you fruitcake? Cut it out will ya? Get on with it, ya fucking nutjob. I hate you, Melco Malkovich. I'm sorry what happened to you, but I really, really fucking hate you. I always did. You just never fit in you freak. Always chatting up the girls, our girls. Always dressed better than us, with new clothes, lording it over us who didn't have nothing. Nothing but fucking black eyes and broken ribs. You hear me, Melco? I hated your fucking guts back then, I still do now. Take your fucking goofy black face and shove it up your arse you piece of shit! I hope you and every other twerp like you get what they deserve. I hope the Black Hand Gang gets the fucking lot of you pansy pricks. Fucking homos, lamos and wankers."

Lorenzo was not to know that his captor had not heard a word of his delirious rant. The man had left the room soon after the spell of vagueness had overtaken him. Lorenzo was incapable of knowing the extent of his injuries as he could no longer see the mirror above him. His molten eyes were useless. He could not know that he had been reduced to little more than a torso with a head. He could not know that his end was closer than he imagined. He could not possibly know that his body would soon be discovered.

ARNOLD RYAN

When Ryan pulled into his driveway after yet another gruelling day on the job, still no closer to finding the perpetrator of the most heinous crimes in Australia's history, he was ready for a long, cold one. The thought of that precious amber liquid hitting the back of his throat with its chilled goodness, almost saw him weeping with delight. The promise he had made to the Townsville detectives weighed heavily on his conscience, but he would not be deterred from his quest to find oblivion. To find a calm escape from the terrors that haunted him. The never-ending search for a maniacal serial killer stalking his town, his citizens, his friends... himself? He supposed it was true that Melco Malkovich was their man.

Vexed by his actions, or more specifically, his inactions in righting the wrongs of that night, Ryan continued to be consumed by his guilt. The wounds of his misdeeds had been opened wide for all to see, and he may well pay for those with his life. Worse, though, as far as he was concerned, was the hit to his reputation and his standing in the community if it all came out. Everyone would see him for the villain he was, the merciless monster he had become while under the influence of alcohol and rage. A rage so terrifying and uncontrollable that it had left him stunned. A blistering, all-consuming wrath that accrued in intensity from the time of the beatings suffered at the hands of his father.

He had found a target for that anger, an excellent means of transferring that fury onto another. A person of contemptible origins and abominable traits. A person that was easy to loathe, easy to persecute, but oh so impossible to break. A damn little foreigner who attracted the girls, and showed him and his friends up as something to be ignored and condemned without moving a muscle. His stoic stance of never capitulating to their dominance made a hero of him in the eyes of their sweethearts, who finally rejected them. The kid who wouldn't play sports like the other boys, wouldn't take part in any of their activities, always the best in the class, and never, never laying down after a beating. Never crying, never screaming, never a sound uttered in all the time that they tested him, making them try all the harder.

That god-awful smell on him every morning. Like he fell into a pisspot. He stunk of it all through high school, sometimes worse, if that was even possible. Ryan wasn't sure about primary school. He didn't have much to do with the boy then. It was really only when he reached high school that he noticed the horrible stench coming from him all day, especially on a hot and humid day in North Queensland, in a classroom devoid of air-conditioning, with nothing but a slow-moving ceiling fan to stir the pungent odour around the room. Teachers were seen to wrinkle their noses as they drew near the boy. Everyone detested old Smelly Melly, except the bloody girls!

That was it really, Ryan decided, as he turned the key in his front door, making a beeline for the kitchen where he could get his hands on a frosty cold beer. That was the crux of the problem. Cindy Naylor, after going out with Ryan that one time, allowing him to feel her sensual warmth beneath him, allowing him inside her, then left him. After that one deliriously wonderful night when he believed he had died and gone to heaven, having given her his virginity, she had left him for that... *piss-cunt-fuck-shit-bastard, Smelly Melly Malkovich.*

That is what tore Ryan apart he had to admit. Forget the beatings his old man gave him, forget the other shit and even the stench of him. When you cut away all the extraneous matter, you were left with the one pure element that drove Arnold Ryan to near distraction and lament. His love being thwarted, by his sweetheart latching onto his nemesis, the one person in all the world it was not all right for her to be with. He could have forgiven any other person who may have fallen for her inimitable charms, but not him. That attraction rankled with his emotions in a way that he could never overpower or control. It sent him ballistic if truth be told, churning up his insides and causing reflux in him, bile-inducing heartburn that threatened to overwhelm him at times.

Cindy bloody Naylor, a woman he now loved and hated equally and alternatively, the way the mood swayed him. Having elected to divulge his secret love to her was the most difficult and most surprising action he had ever performed. That she spurned his declaration, chewed him up like a barfly greedily devouring the free peanuts on the bar, was the kill shot. The acid reflux had returned with a vengeance since that night. Sour, scalding bile attacking his stomach as it rose to his throat some nights, nearly causing him to choke. He knew the drinking did nothing to dissuade the actions of his rebellious stomach, possibly even aggravated it for all he knew, but drinking was the only method he had of relieving the ache he felt in his lonely heart.

Crashing onto his recliner, Ryan gulped the cold liquid greedily, downing his first stubby in a matter of seconds, before immediately opening a second. He sat alone in an empty house, wondering not for the first time, why he had bothered. The mortgage on the house threatened to send him into penury. He had purchased it for the sole purpose of providing a home for his bride-to-be when she eventually came to her senses. The effort to make the repayments each month exacerbated the tension he felt and exhausted his emotions. His base pay simply did not cover his monthly obligations as well as his living expenses. Now, without his perfect-paying boarder, he would have no choice other than to find another, or put the house on the market and hope it had gained sufficient value in the interim to wipe out the loan and a little to spare.

Rising from the recliner to pour himself a couple of fingers of cheap scotch, Ryan caught sight of the room he had commissioned through the door to the garage. That glimpse caused pangs of extra guilt to assail his depleted emotions. He hoped he would not find his mate, Loz, like all the others. That would be a burden too onerous to bear. He removed the key to the room from the lanyard about his neck. There was no apparent reason for him to venture in there, just a randomly chosen action to revisit the space in which he had cared diligently for his patient, hoping to draw some inspiration from the remaining atmosphere. A lingering ethereal presence that may enlighten Ryan in some way.

What Ryan saw as he opened the door and switched on the light left him staggering backwards, clutching his chest in an approximation of a heart attack. On the cot used previously to support the abused body of his friend, Lorenzo Catani, lay a charred, grotesquely contorted, stunted cadaver. Completely unrecognisable as a human being let alone identifiable as his friend or anyone, Ryan guessed accurately, that the blackened thing was his mate. The aroma of barbequed flesh that permeated the room had Ryan retching instantly. His dry-heaving saw his reflux burning his oesophagus as the bile rose steadily upward. A coughing fit followed, as his raw, scalded throat reacted to the villainous air he breathed.

Ryan staggered to the kitchen where he slowly gathered his wits and brought his heaving under control. The burning and coughing persisted as he dialled the number for the detectives from Townsville. He knew to keep out of the room until the forensics team had gone through it with a fine-toothed comb. There was no possibility that the person, be it Lorenzo or not, could have survived. It was barely a full human at all, he recalled with distaste. A torso and a head were all that remained of the human that once occupied the charred shell. Ryan reached inside the fridge for the carton of milk, the only remedy for his throat and his stomach, to calm the rawness and settle the acid. He would probably get a couple of Mylanta tablets as well, once he was over his coughing fit.

"Trent? It's Ryan." Coughing, and spluttering while trying to remain calm and clear, taxed Ryan's present capabilities to the limit. "You had better get yourselves and a team to my place right away. Yeah, you need the meat wagon. Yeah, it's probably Lorenzo, but bloody hard to tell. See you soon. Right, I know. Haven't touched a thing, and I won't go back in. It... he's in the room. In *the* room, you know? Okay, scc you."

Ryan hung up the phone just as another coughing fit overtook him. He gulped the cold milk, soothing his damaged throat almost immediately, as he made his way to the bathroom to retrieve the Mylanta. He felt the jab the second he opened the door to the bathroom like a hornet had stung him. His eyes opened wide as from behind the door stepped a black-faced individual with blown-out white lips, like one of those bimbos you see with ridiculously puffed up lips after getting a Botox injection. That was his last thought before he crashed heavily to the tiled floor.

MASTERMIND

The first image that confronted Ryan as he regained consciousness was a recording of the last moments of his friend's life. On the monitor, the figure with the black face held a funnel to his friend's mouth, into which a liquid was being poured. Lorenzo, whom he recognised now that he had come fully awake, flailed helplessly against his bonds. Whatever concoction it was, that was being forced down Loz's throat, was affecting him gravely. When the flaming match, wielded by the torturer, was lowered close to the liquid pooling down into the mouth of his friend, Ryan understood immediately that the liquid had been petrol or something equally as flammable.

Engrossed by the images, yet horrified by their extreme cruelty, Ryan watched as his friend was barbequed alive, from the inside out. Thankfully, Lorenzo did not have to suffer long, as the first incineration of his throat and lungs caused his swift demise. Bright flames exited the body at all openings. Flames erupted from his empty eye sockets and ears as the burning petrol spouted from the body cavities. Ryan understood clearly how his friend had ended up as a charred corpse. He witnessed the entire episode with a dreaded fascination that made him ill.

When the images ended in a blank screen, Ryan gave some thought to his own circumstances. Pinned to a plywood board with pipe saddles and rubber tubing, Ryan recognised that he was pivoted in the vertical by way of a central fulcrum on which he teetered. Only a modicum of pressure was required for his captor to position Ryan in the horizontal any time he chose. The image on the screen in front of him flickered to a view of his naked body against the plywood. He was unable to see where the camera was located upon first glance. Only when he examined the angles of his image, did he conclude the camera's position nearly above him.

"Did you enjoy the entertainment, Detective Ryan? Would you like a rerun? So much better than reruns of Gilligan's Island or The Brady Bunch, don't you think? A little on the macabre side, perhaps, but still, highly motivating I thought. Maybe even all that is required to entice some answers from you without having to resort to my more persuasive methods? Lorenzo was ever so forthcoming with his information, you know? Of course, he had to be dealt with in the end. He could not be excused or forgiven for his crimes. Been far too much of that going on in this little shithole hasn't there?"

"I can't answer that. Why don't you show yourself you freak? Afraid I might recognise you, Melco? A bit late for that. We know who you are, and what you've been doing. Doesn't matter what you do to me, it's only a matter of time before you're caught."

Appearing from the right entered a black-faced person, completely naked. The body was entirely pockmarked with hundreds of puncture wounds, but only when he looked lower did Ryan gasp sharply. Below the waist was a mass of scar tissue with the burn mark, a brand of some sort, obliterating what would normally occupy that particular space. The horrific injuries caused Ryan to wince instinctively.

"Not a pleasant sight is it, Ryan? That you were the cause of it doesn't bother you?"

"No way did I do that to you. No matter what, you cannot pin that on me. Is that, is that even you, Melco? I thought... I don't know. I guess it's been a long time. You did it didn't you? Got us all? Vic, Clay, Loz, Mr Ball, Mr Thornton... me! Some collateral damage when you took out the school, though. The grounds person and the cleaner who had nothing to do with anything, copped it for no good reason at all."

"You think that was me? Stupid man! Think very carefully before you accuse anyone of harming the innocent, Mr Ryan. You have no idea of the malignant cancer you spawned in this diseased cesspool."

"I don't know what you think you know, but you have it all arse-backwards if you think I had anything to do with... "

"Yes, Mr Ryan? With...?"

"Well... certainly not that... with what happened to you."

"You had everything to do with it, dickhead. We'll leave that for the moment, however. What happened to me, as devastating as that was for me and my family, is inconsequential in comparison to the rest. You know what I am talking about, so I will not deign to ask you, simply to get a blatant lie in reply. That would make me angry, Mr Ryan. Angry enough to make me inject you with a special solution my friends and I discovered. Terribly effective I must say. Enhances sensory perception to a degree that is inexplicable. Suffice to say, that even the smallest sound causes unheard-of agonies. I would hate to have to employ such methods on you, Ryan. At least, at this early stage."

"Oh, just go ahead and get on with it you sadistic prick. Don't try to bullshit the bullshitter, Melco. You get off on this shit. You're enjoying it. That's why you're doing it. Not to get even but because you're loving every minute of it. Getting your rocks off... "

"Are you blind? I haven't any rocks to get off, Ryan. You saw to that. I have had no carnal delights ever. Never experienced them and wouldn't know what they were if I tripped over them. Have I enjoyed what I did to your friends? No, it upset me far more than anything you could ever feel, but it was necessary. It was absolutely vital to bring an end to it all so that this travesty is never again repeated. To achieve that, everything done and still to be done was essential. Not enjoyable. Not like it was for you, Ryan."

"I told you already, you're off your nut if you think I did that to you."

"You make a bad listener for a detective, Ryan. I did not say that you were the perpetrator. The attack on me was a symptom. You were the cause, Ryan, the cause of so much fear, and evil torture in this town. You make Hitler seem like a cream puff."

"That is a load of bullshit. I never caused nothing."

"That is a double negative which turns into a positive, Ryan, making you guilty by admission."

Ryan watched in fascination as the man lurched to his left suddenly, like a drunk on his walk home. For a long moment, the man braced himself against the wall with one arm as he shook off the effects of whatever had taken hold. The man left the room briefly, still unsteady on his feet. Ryan saw his head lolling on his neck like that of a floppy ragdoll. He appeared so uncoordinated as to seem comical. Ryan felt sure that it was yet another ruse by his captor to gain his confidence, or simply to keep him baffled.

Returning with a syringe containing a barely perceptible amount of fluid, the man proceeded to inject himself. Momentarily, the man straightened, grimacing. After a short time, the man then looked upward with a deepening frown. He moved swiftly to a light switch with an adjustable knob that he turned anti-clockwise. The lights dimmed in response. When the man had regained his composure, he turned to Ryan with a steely look of determination.

"My... my time... is... limited, Mr Ryan. I am not long for the land of the living. I would like to see to the end of my quest, though, if that is possible. To rid the world of you and your kind."

"I don't have a kind, Melco. I'm just me. You talk as though there is something else going on here. From what I can tell, it's just you running around on a rampage like one of those crackpots you see terrorising and killing innocent kids in schools in the States."

"You'd think that, wouldn't you? I know better now, though. I know that schools are simply training grounds for thugs like you to hunt in cowardly packs victimising innocents. I have come to have a deep appreciation and understanding for some of those ex-students who go 'postal' all of a sudden, running to the school they attended to shoot and kill people. All perfectly understandable when you have experienced the other side, Ryan. Jesus, but this stuff is good." The man shook himself from head to toe.

"What the fuck are you on about? You are about as fucking loony as they come. No wonder I hate you."

"We'll get to that soon enough, Ryan, soon enough. Pardon me for seeming a little... strange. I take some of the magic formula myself you see. An infinitesimal amount is all I need to kick-start my brain again when it has a bit of a melt-down. It's getting worse and happening more often than I would like, but hey, life's a fucking bitch, isn't it?

"I'm dying, Ryan. News that I'm sure will gladden your little mongrel heart. That may also give you pause for thought. You see, if I have nothing to lose, I am capable of anything, anything at all. I don't fear getting caught and going to prison, Ryan, because I will not live long enough. Matter of fact, the more I use my little potion now, the more I hasten my demise. While it helps, it harms. Without it, though, none of this would have been possible. I would have ended up a blathering imbecile, incapable of wiping my own arse far sooner than I would have wished."

Ryan watched closely as a single tear escaped the man's eye. It seemed his abductor was teetering dangerously on the tightrope of sanity. A tenuous balancing act at the best of times. It would not take much imagination to determine what would happen to himself if his captor suddenly lost the plot and his brain went AWOL. Ryan would be discovered eventually, a desiccated husk of a person, strapped to a plywood board in some abandoned building, twenty years after he was reported missing. He could see his dust-covered, partially-mummified remains awaiting discovery like some lost relic in an Indiana Jones movie.

Ryan felt something not right about the situation. A nagging itch at the back of his brain was telling him that something did not add up. It was a confusing and terrifying situation in which he found himself, yet he could not muster up the appropriate amount of fear it deserved. The almost comical look of Melco and his bizarre manner left Ryan feeling... lost. He realised a lot of years had passed since the incident in question, yet there did not seem to be any connections being made in his brain. Grave doubts entered his mind about everything transpiring. Missing pieces and warped recollections told Ryan that a huge chunk of the information at hand was simply wrong.

"Why don't we explore that earlier statement? Why hate? What could anyone have possibly done to you to warrant such hatred? Hmm?"

"Melco, you were just a person that was easy to dislike. I only just remember you from primary school as this foreign kid with a bloody accent that made you difficult to understand. I remember the other kids pushing you around a bit. I think maybe Vic or Loz started it all. It was in high school when you really became... just a total jerk who got under our skin. Man, you stunk. You... Hey! You don't stink anymore, I... shit! Sorry, you probably have to do something special now huh?"

When Ryan felt the cattle prod generate an electrical jolt that ripped through his body like lightning, he screamed. He was not expecting it, had seen no movement by the man. He realised the madman must have had it in his hand all along and he just hadn't noticed it. The effects of the jolt left his body quivering on the board like a giant tub of jelly. When it finally subsided, Ryan made a firm decision to be more mindful of everything he said and to begin again, observing his captor and his surroundings with a detective's eye. He had allowed his usual skills to flounder. Was he not taking his situation seriously enough?

He could not really get a good look at the black face because the lights had been turned so low. What he had noticed, was that the man winced dramatically when he screamed. The bloke said that he took something to enhance sensory perception? The light was turned down when the brightness affected him, so obviously loud noise didn't go over too well either. He would file that little piece of information away for future reference. Ryan now took the time to inspect his surrounds as best he could with his limited field of view, when all of a sudden, his world tilted all the way to an inverted position. When the lunatic prodded Ryan again, the pain tore through his genitals like an explosion. The intense agony gripped his entire body as the pain was transferred to his abdomen. The same place that the pain would be felt if someone had kneed him in the groin, only ten times worse. Ryan screamed, then yelled as loud as he could when the pain abated. He used the incident to exercise his newfound knowledge with which to deliver his own form of punishment to his attacker.

"I would advise you not to be too clever, Mr Ryan. I will not hesitate to give you a far larger dose of the formula than I gave myself. You are trying to inflict pain on me by yelling a little louder than absolutely necessary. Do not be tempted to do so again. Yes, I am slightly affected by it, to boost my mental and physical acuity. An infinitesimal amount compared to the shot I would bequeath you. That amount would see you climbing the walls at the sound of a whisper. Would see you clawing at your eyes at the flash of a torchlight. A feather caressing your naked flesh would feel like a cheese grater were being scraped across you. Care to test me on this, Mr Ryan? Wish to push the boundaries a little?"

"No, no, that hurts enough thank-you. I guess I deserved that after what I did to you?"

"Was that really a question? You cannot possibly believe that that is all you deserve, surely? Even you could not be that dense. We have only scratched the surface of what you deserve, Detective Ryan. That will come later unless you continue to provoke me. We were discussing hatred... ?"

"Umm, yeah, orright. High school. Man, I loved it there. All the girls we could want if we played our cards right, and we did for a time. Then everything turned to shit. The more we picked on you, the more the girls pitied you I guess. The more the girls ignored us and took your side, the worse we picked on you. It was partly the horrible smell, that... " Ryan flinched, thinking his attacker would strike again. "... that irked us initially, then it just escalated from there. Why would you never simply go down and fucking stay down? We would've stopped if you had simply laid down or at least made a fucking sound. If we just had have heard that rotten acc... "

"Yes?"

"Your accent, what happened to it?"

"You trying to be funny or clever again?"

"No. Hey, any chance of tilting me the other way? My head is exploding down here." What Ryan didn't admit, was that the view of the man's wrecked crotch from his perspective was making him ill. The hand brand on top of the mutilation forced Ryan to examine memories of events he would rather forget.

The man acceded to Ryan's request by tilting the platform to the horizontal, where it was locked into position. Above Ryan, on the ceiling, a mirror had been mounted to afford him a view of himself. Ryan used the interceding time to inspect his surroundings from this new position. He took in as much detail as possible. Unfortunately, there was little by way of distinguishing features for him to identify his location.

Ceiling and walls were constructed of a plain, utilitarian material, probably cement sheet. Four walls, no windows, one door, with a subterranean feel to it, though, he could not be certain of that. Workbenches adorned one long wall of the rectangular room, displaying many different tools. Hand tools, electrical tools, even kitchen implements. He recognised a hand-held whizzy-thing that he owned himself for mixing his shakes when he was in the mood. He saw an iPod stand connected to a speaker station. His intrinsic knowledge of the previous murders and the methods utilised in the premortem torture, caused Ryan to shiver involuntarily. Ryan had only yet tasted a small fraction of the evil to come, he surmised.

"Tell me what drove your hatred so far that you had to extend your methodology on that particular night, Mr Arnold Ryan? Tell me what possible motive you had for inflicting such misery and scorn upon your helpless victim? Hmm? Tell me that, will you?"

"You already know what happened. You would have forced that information out *your* victims you sadistic prick. My friends! What you're doing is far worse than anything that happened that night. That you have the temerity to make accusations against me and my mates is the very height of hypocrisy."

"Suddenly a scholar are we? Temerity? Hypocrisy? Not like you to use such big words, Ryan. You're an oaf, barely capable of stringing an intelligible sentence together."

"Yeah, the bloody boarder I had rubbed off on me I guess. Doesn't change the fact, though, that your sins, your crimes far exceed those of me and my friends."

"You would think that, wouldn't you? Only, you are not being completely honest with me or yourself, Ryan. It is for that reason alone that I came to be here, doing what I do. You and your kind need to be made aware of everything, even that which you deny yourselves."

"I haven't denied anything of myself. I know the truth of that night, just as much as you do. Listen, Melco, there's no need for this to continue. A lot of water has passed under the bridge since that night, and I do feel guilty about my part in that okay? If this is purely about punishing us for that prank, then you have well and truly made your point."

"You fucking coward! You miserable, scumbag, shit-eating cunt! You disgust me. You really believe, or are forcing yourself to believe, that this is all about one fucking night? Can you really be that spineless that you refuse to recognise the whole picture? You had better be a little more forthcoming, Mr Ryan, or you will truly regret your cowardice."

"Care to enlighten me then?"

"Care to feel the prod again?"

Ryan held his breath waiting for the imminent explosion of agony to course through his body. The threat of that jolt being repeated was enough for him to question his tactics. He could not imagine how much worse it would be if he were injected with something to make the sensation infinitely worse. The mere thought of it caused sweat to bead on his forehead. The answers to the questions being asked eluded him. The inquiry too vague to respond to positively. In fact, he had no idea what the fuck the demented arsehole wanted.

"You, you want to know what happened that night."

"I asked you to explain your part specifically, and the reason for your intense hatred of someone who did nothing to harm any of you or gave you any reason to attract such wrath."

"I think, I think what galled us most of all about you was your stubborn refusal to accept defeat. We gave you so many opportunities to just... capitulate, stay down and give us the satisfaction of winning."

"Oh, and you think that would have been the end of it? Don't make me laugh. That is the most pathetic thing I have heard yet. Oh, I realise bullies like you need recognition of their prowess by others, vindication for your efforts by adoring fans, yes? I accept that as part of it, sure. That you would have ceased your torture and torments, as a result of surrender, utter bullshit. Bullies like you never give up once you have a victim in your crosshairs. If it becomes easy to achieve your goals, you may go easier on the subject, but it never stops unless you are stopped. Never ends, never. Be very careful where you venture next, Ryan. Your futile efforts to exonerate yourself or justify your actions are testing my patience. If you do not start accepting your hand in the unfortunate episode, I will take drastic measures."

"Jesus, what do you want me to say? I don't know what you mean. I'm telling you what I know. I accept that I am guilty of bullying you in high school and that it went too far one night on bivouac, okay? I get it, you're totally pissed off about what happened to you. I would be too, but we are not responsible for... that. Whatever happened to you afterwards? We didn't... "

"Oh, yes you did! You are completely responsible. You are guilty of my injuries and much, much more."

"No, no, you're wrong, Melco. What happened that night, it... it... I think it was Lorenzo who first came up with the idea. You gave him as good as you got in a one-on-one fight at school. For some reason, the rest of us weren't there that day. I don't remember why, but Loz was pissed off. He suggested we get even with you that night. We, we were drinking as usual. Drunk actually. I didn't want to participate at first, I was pretty out of it. The others became enthusiastic about the idea and that sort of convinced me to go along."

"Getting dangerously close to denial again, Detective. I suggest you explore your inner conscience a little closer before you continue. Any sign of further denial or justification for your participation in the evening's events will be met with the appropriate response. That is my solemn promise to you. My time of threats has passed. I have a syringe with enough formula in it to reduce you to a blubbering wreck in moments. Your own pulse will drive you nearly insane as you feel the blood coursing perilously through your veins. The electrical impulses delivered to and from your brain will feel like this cattle prod has accessed your brain through an open skull. Continue with extreme caution."

"That, that sounds a lot like what was happening to, Loz while... SHIT! You were doing it. You managed to get into that room. You gave that shit to him, which made him regress every time I thought he was getting better."

"Took you long enough to figure that out. Really not that much of an investigator, Ryan. Wasn't so hard seeing as you fall into a drunken stupor most nights, snoring your fool head off."

The voice betrayed a lethargy to it, as though the man could not keep his eyes open. Ryan could hear his stifled yawns. Ryan could not see the man any longer. He detected no other person standing in the room. He could only assume that his captor had sunk to the floor. Ryan knew that he had to figure out some way of avoiding whatever it was in the syringe. A dose of that did not sound like something he could endure.

"I went along with it okay. I didn't want to be bothered at first if that's the way you want to hear it. I just didn't have the energy for it. I was enjoying being drunk and all I really wanted was to curl up in my cot and sleep it off before reveille was called that morning. I was convinced to go along with it eventually. We dragged you out of your tent struggling, as usual, not saying a word, and not crying out. Fuck, you made it easy to hate you, Melco. Why couldn't you just act like the others for once? We left *them* alone once we pushed them around a bit."

"That was because you had a better target, whom you pursued relentlessly. Stop trying to convince me that you would have quit. It's crap. Keep going."

"You want me to tell you the whole thing?"

"No, I guess not. You smeared his face with boot polish after wrapping him in a barbed-wire fence. You beat him up a bit then you applied toothpaste to his genitals, which stung like fuck."

"Yeah, then we left. Only... "

"Yes, Ryan, only you came back, didn't you? Why? You say you were tired and drunk, then you left. Why would you come back? Mr, Catani didn't know. Mr McCormack didn't know. Mr Kugelweis didn't give a shit in the end. Though, he actually did shit himself. So that could be defined as 'giving a shit', couldn't it? Why, Ryan, why did you decide to go back to the boy cruelly wrapped in barbed-wire, already bleeding and in terrible pain?"

"I don't know."

"Bullshit!"

"It isn't. I don't really know."

"Would you like me to assist your failing memory?"

"I still wouldn't be able to tell you. I can't tell you what I don't know."

"Tell me!"

"I don't... "

"Answer me, Ryan!"

"I... "

"TELL ME!" Screamed the man into Ryan's face, so close that Ryan was able to see exactly how many fillings he had.

"Cause... "

"FUCKING TELL ME!"

"Because I hate you," admitted Ryan at long last. "Because I hate your stinking, rotten guts you bastard. You smelly, fucking cunt, you took her. You miserable pissy little fuck, you took away the only girl I have ever loved. I came back because I wanted to make sure you never had anything to do with my Cindy, ever again. I needed to punish you. I wanted to pulverise you, smash you and void your existence from this earth. I, I wanted... I"

"Tell me, Ryan, what did you do when you came back that night?"

"I fucking hated you so much, Melco." Ryan sobbed painfully. "You have no idea, not a fucking clue how much I detested you for taking my girl from me. I had to punish you, had to stop you. I came back and saw you hanging there, and all I wanted was to actually kill you. I have never wanted anything so much in my whole life. Just extinguish you. Instead, I used my cigarette to burn around the hand-mark on your chest. You obviously had that fixed.

"Before I staggered up to leave though, I had one final message to deliver. One thing to end it all, one way to ensure that you finally got the fucking message. I kicked you in the groin with my army boots just as hard as my legs were able. And I was fucking strong back then, I ran for exercise, played footy where I was a goal kicker, and we marched all the fucking time as cadets. My legs were pistons, and I used every ounce of my waning energy to kick the final goal, your nuts. Are you satisfied you demented cunt? I kicked you harder than anything I have ever kicked, but I didn't cut you. Didn't cut it off! I wasn't to blame for what happened to you after. I didn't do... that... to you, Melco. You took her, and I couldn't bear it. I loved her so fucking much. So fucking... much."

Ryan felt an intense relief at having divulged the secret that caused such guilt and anguish in him for so many years. His heaving sobs told the story of his deep affections for a woman he had never again attracted. His unrequited love had eaten away at his guts for so many years that he could not imagine there was anything left inside. His heartache had never been shared, never released, never able to be healed. His hatred for Melco Malkovich had never truly dissipated, only simmered and festered in Ryan's ulcerous stomach. When the sting of the needle interrupted his lament, Ryan knew that his trouble had just begun.

"You are wrong, Ryan, wrong. You *are* responsible for what happened to me. You *did* cause the mutilation of my manhood. *You* are solely responsible for the torture, mutilation and even death of some thirty persons, not to mention their immediate and extended families, Detective Ryan. What you did that night, the punishment you administered to that boy, was a benchmark for those to follow. Although it developed of its own accord, you were responsible for its origins and for its continuity."

Whispering to avoid the onset of pain, Ryan said, "How can you blame me then? You said it yourself, 'of its own accord'. That means that neither I nor my friends were responsible."

"Still you try to deny its existence? Your own stubbornness will be your undoing."

"Deny what? I've admitted everything to you already."

"Not quite everything you haven't. I'm sure it was necessary for your own sanity, your own protection to deny it, even to yourself, but it is time to bring it all out, Ryan. The whole truth. The hand, the... Black Hand... was formed by your intense hatred and a legend was born. I want you to think about that for a moment or two while my special gift to you takes effect. I will play you a little music shortly to accompany your thoughts. Think wisely about the implications of your deeds.

Squinting to avoid the harsh glare of the dimmed lights, Ryan witnessed the man falter and stagger about the room, barely able to stand. When the ear-splitting music erupted from the mini-speaker sitting on the benchtop, Ryan felt his ears might explode. Meatloaf's, *Bat out of Hell* hammered his senses mercilessly as Ryan strained against his bonds, his screams competing with the music for domination. His bonds inflicted severe amounts of stress and damage to the afflicted areas. The sheer tension in Ryan's muscles; back arched to an impossible extent, biceps, triceps, deltoids, quadriceps, hamstrings, gluteus, all strained to their maximum, caused unbearable cramping.

When the music ceased abruptly, only Ryan could be heard screaming wildly and thrashing convulsively, splinters finding their way into his flesh where his skin met the rough plywood sheet. A turmoil of sounds and sensations awash in the pool of his thoughts as Ryan struggled to bring himself under control. The blast from the past, music-wise, lasted only a few moments, yet seemed a hundred years to Ryan's besieged senses. Though it was obvious to Ryan that he would soon experience far worse torture and pain at the hands of the Minstrel Killer, Melco Malkovich, he could not have dreamed of anything approaching the reality.

The scale of his discomfort exceeded all possible notions he had ever envisaged during a nightmare or casual thought. His entire being was suffused with a lamentable pain of exquisite proportions. He would gladly have suffered the torments of that fictitious realm, hell, than one second more of his present fate. The reprieve of the halted assault to his ears caused a torrent of grateful tears to escape his eyes. He had never been more thankful for anything in his life. He whispered his thanks to whoever may have been listening. Over and over.

Though his eyelids were closed, the searing, penetrating light invaded his eyeballs with an intensity he was unable to comprehend. He dared not open his eyes for fear they would be burned to oblivion. Dared not speak for fear he might cause irreparable damage. Dared not move lest he inflicts more injuries to his person than was absolutely necessary. Before long he became aware of humming and a thumping that sought to further unravel his threadbare mind. His pulse, pumping life-giving oxygenated blood throughout his body, boomed through him like a big bass drum. The sound of his breath through his nostrils, though clear of any blockage, whistled and skittled sharply in his ears. Then, a whisper. Barely audible. Painful none-the-less.

"Having fun yet?"

With the absolute clarity and super definition of enhanced hearing, Ryan somehow managed to make a connection, despite the sheer absurdity of his circumstances. The itch in the back of his mind had found an answer. He could hardly credit it. If what he deduced was true, it carried with it a host of new questions and problems. For Ryan, despite the gravity of his situation, despite the peril he faced, despite the fact that he might perish as had his friends, he had found an ironic peace within himself, believing he had solved the mystery and discovered his error in trusting that Melco was the murderer.

The light fell away at an oblique angle suddenly and noisily. The torch or beam held by his protagonist bounced on the concrete floor and out of the hands of the collapsing human. No further sounds or movement issued from the man lying in an awkward position. Ryan was unsure whether to be jubilant or terrified. He did not know if the effects of the injection diminished over time or not. If not, and some form of antidote was required, then the prone figure was his only hope of salvation.

A panic invaded his thoughts, pushing common-sense to the rear. Neither option presented him with any hope. Either he would remain on the platform at the mercy of the serum and its effects until someone came to rescue him, or he would not require the antidote, and while not feeling the gross effects, would still be held captive for who knew how long. He found himself whimpering softly at the realisation that he was truly fucked.

He could not be sure how much time had passed before he came to. The thrumming of his heartbeat no longer reverberating throughout his body, the blood no longer causing him to curse its life-giving succour. He slowly opened his eyes, finding nothing changed in the position of the man on the floor. Then he remembered his epiphany. Not the man he thought he was.

"Not... not, Melco," he whispered over and over.

"No. Quite right, Detective." The man was administering another injection. The first injection was the antidote, the second, some pain relief.

Coming into Ryan's view appeared a strange face with a familiar voice. A hard, unshaven, brick of a face, square and angular. A shock of thick grey curls crowning the box-like head. The enormous visage, bending close to make inspections of Ryan, grimaced at the damage he found on Ryan's wrists and ankles. The seemingly benign interlude in the events set Ryan's nerves atingle.

"M... M... Melco?"

"Yes, that's right," agreed the man with the thick, Slavic accent. "Shush now, while the effects of the painkillers help you."

While much older and larger, Ryan recognised the newcomer as the real Melco Malkovich. Melco then assisted the killer from the floor gently and compassionately. He bundled the inert man easily into his large arms as easily as carrying a child, before exiting the room. Ryan was now more confused than ever as to the identity of the Minstrel Killer. All the indicators pointed toward, Smelly Melly. To find out at this late hour that all their deductions were groundless, left Ryan reeling. All too soon, Ryan started to feel less fond of his new conditions when he factored in the realisation that his benefactor had not released him from his bonds.

"Hey, hey? Where are you? What the fuck is going on here? Is that, is that really you this time, Melco?"

When the man returned some time afterwards, he eyed Ryan with a sad and knowing shake of the head. "Yes, Ryan it is your old punching bag, Melco. You look like shit."

"Well, that's fucking nice. I knew he wasn't you. Who is that other bastard then?"

"That other... *man*... is someone that is very near and dear to me, Ryan. You should not be calling him unkind names."

"Are you fucking kidding? Do you have any idea what he's been doing here, how many people he's killed?"

"Of course, why else would I be here?"

"So, so you *are* a part of it?"

"In a manner of speaking, I have always been a part of it. Have I killed anyone? Not yet," came the ominous reply.

"You're not making any sense. Who the fuck is he? What's the connection?"

"So many questions being asked in a less than gracious manner. You have just been rescued from your inevitable demise, Detective," said the solid man bristling with annoyance.

"Look, Smelly you... "

The jarring slap delivered to Ryan's face left him reeling. "Perhaps you have learnt nothing at all from your experience and I should continue with your lessons?"

"Alright... *Melco*, I apologise for calling you that name. You obviously don't warrant that name any longer, and even if that were not the case, I should not have used it. Just remember that I am a member of the Queensland police force, and you have just assaulted me. Now, if you are stating that you are not the Minstrel Killer, then get me out of this, so I can alert my station and put that other... man, in the slammer for the rest of his life."

"I don't think I will be doing that straight away, and I do not think that the other man will ever see the inside of your prisons, Detective Ryan."

"Then you will be actively aiding and abetting a wanted criminal. You will be charged as an accessory after the fact and see jail time with him. Now release me, you great big lump of shit!"

The blow from the sledgehammer fist of the strong, big-shouldered man connected solidly with Ryan's jaw. A tooth threatened to lose its tenuous grip on Ryan's gum. The loose tooth was now barely hanging on. Ryan new enough to proceed with caution. He forced himself to bite down on the adjectives swirling through his mind to describe his opinion of the man and his situation. He was still very confused as to the identity of the serial killer and what had happened to him.

"Are you ready to treat me with a modicum of respect at long last, Detective Ryan? I assure you, that as I am at an advanced age, with little and no one left to live for, I have no compunction in lavishing upon you all that my son had intended, and perhaps more."

"Your... son? But I thought... "

"Adopted son, Ryan. I am incapable of producing a child of my own thanks to you. Now that his life appears to be faltering, I have come to help him through his last hours and to give to him the love he deserves. How he was treated by this community, in the same vein as myself, is the true tragedy, and one that I would have averted had I known sooner or had I possessed some forethought. I am as much to blame for his tragic treatments as are the members of the Black Hand Gang."

"I don't understand. Who? Who exactly is this man and what is the Black Hand Gang?"

"You must not act so innocent, Detective Ryan. Your knowledge of the gang is implicit. Your denials of this are fantasy. Ah, Kim, my son. How are you feeling?" Asked Melco when the Minstrel Killer appeared in the doorway, sans facial disguise.

"Not... not... well, Papa. The in... inject... injection helped, thank-you."

"Good. It will not last long, though?"

"Short... shorter periods every... time. Memory is... "

"Yes, I know my boy. You have been fortunate to find something to prolong your existence thus far. How long did they give you initially?"

"A few... years... what?"

"It is dementia starting to apply itself, isn't it?"

"I think... I... "

"Rest your mind a little, give the injection some time to work its magic. You have been very busy here. All this you do in my name?"

"*Non*, Papa. Never... did... I say... you. I, mean, I never said... They assumed I was you, Papa. I never... "

"Kim Giraud, my lovely, lovely boy. Why? Why have you done this? Do you not know that this accomplishes nothing? Violence is never repaid, only repeated."

"But... you, Papa... you did."

"I did what?"

Kim came forward into the room to sit in the chair by the door. He was fully clothed, looking vulnerable and shaken, with tremors assailing him. A palsy had set in to accompany the many other effects of his condition. Creeping dementia, slowly invading his brain functions causing lapses in his memory and speech.

"You, you killed first. The boy's... papa. Lonny's... "

"You think *I,* killed Lonny's father, Kim? You thought I was a bad man?"

"No, Papa!" declared Kim rearing back in the chair. "I love... you, Papa, with... all... with. Never, a bad man, Papa, never."

"But you thought I killed the father of the man who beat you in school and in the park that day? Oh my Kim, my darling boy. I did not. On the day I found those boys attacking you, the very day I caused such pain on the young boy, Lonny, I realised how much hatred and pain I had harboured all my life. I decided at that moment, that I was wasting my life over a past I could not change. I made up my mind from that point onward that I would no longer allow the mistreatments of me in my youth to govern the path of my future."

"You didn't... ?"

"I am not entirely innocent, however, so please do not paint me in such a favourable light. I did pay Lonny's father a visit. I made it known that after speaking to his boy, that I would divulge certain truths to the relevant authorities, should there be any further abuse of the boy

"What... what... truths?"

"I gambled with the suspicions I had concerning Lonny and the way he spoke about... what was it he called it? Ah, 'perveratin' I think he said, da?"

"Oui, Papa."

"Are you going back to your mother tongue, my boy? Anyway, a suspicion, yes? I was suspicious about the way the boy said it, that he had more than a passing knowledge of it. I suggested to the father that such truths about the dealings with his son would come to light.

I believe, that he could not live with the fact that his secret was known, that he could not cope with the guilt or possible ramifications of his acts. I had not known it was *he* who transgressed against the boy. I had thought maybe a close relative or friend? He took his own life. I had nothing directly to do with it, yet I was not entirely blameless."

"I didn't know. I... did this... because... because... I wanted it all to stop. Do you know it still happens? Many... so... many. Black Hand... "

"I did not know it all, my son. I could not imagine that what happened to me could be repeated when I sent you to live with my parents. When it happened to you. When at last you told me so many years later, then the news of your illness, and you left to go overseas. I let you down, Kim. I am sorry for being a bad father to you after you lost your own parents then mine. Your father in an accident, your mother, soon after I met you, to the very disease you suffer. Bah, such waste. A man tracked me down. A man from here. From him, I learned about much of this."

"Ryan, he knows, Papa. This man knows and... does... noth... nothing. He hurt you, Papa."

"Yes, yes, this man hurt me very much. He and his friends caused my shame and my pain. There will be no more of my family thanks to their callous actions," said Melco.

"They... killed... your Mama and Papa. When they found out about me, they would... not... umm, could... "

"They did nothing for me. I hated them for it. They were threatened and did nothing. I thought them, cowards. I did not forgive them. I am ashamed. They fought for you? Is good they did that."

"This is all very sweet and all, but could someone please tell me what the fuck is going on. What more do you want from me?" asked Ryan indignantly.

Father and adopted son turned to peer at Ryan with such contempt, that he almost recoiled into the fibre of the board beneath him.

"For a man that has admitted his complicity in a crime, I am very surprised that you continue to act inconsiderately and aggressively. You are a very dumb man for someone with your skills as a detective, you know?"

"What fucking crime? I didn't admit to anything of the sort."

"We have it all on video, Ryan. You admitted to the assault and battery on my person, causing grievous bodily harm. You ruined a child's chances of living a normal life, you idiot. You think you are getting away with it? My boy has compiled all the confessions of your friends. You are implicated by a witness who saw you coming back that night. On top of my testimony, you will see the inside of the jail I think."

"Statute of limitation would have run out long ago on those sorts of charges, I reckon. Fat chance you got anything on me that'll stick."

"Accessory to the fact in the current crimes then. Makes no difference to me which laws apply to see you behind bars."

"What current laws are you talking about? You are so full of shit Sme... Melco. You always thought you were smarter than us didn't you? Putting on a show for the teachers, making us look bad. Always with your fucking hand up to answer a dumb question that normal kids couldn't give a shit about."

Melco shook his head miserably. He could never fathom the depth of hatred he engendered in his Australian classmates. What caused such deeply ingrained loathing for him and other nationalities attending schools throughout Australia? He groaned inwardly at the thought that nothing had changed, that he was still seen as nothing more than dirt on the bottom of this man's shoe.

Then, he suddenly understood. He was a threat to them. They were frightened of him in some way. They were nothing but cowards, too afraid to give respect where it was due, to honour the unwritten codes of the schoolyard. Melco was taught that it was a sign of honour to fight fairly and accept the outcome, one way or the other. These boys fought dirty.

Australian children had no concept of this fairness, or honour, or the unwritten codes governing behaviour. He had witnessed their cowardice on too many occasions for his assumption to be false. They were pathetic in his eyes. Far too weak and insignificant to warrant his attention. He had changed his mind and abandoned hate many years ago. He would not capitulate to the taunting of the lesser man. Melco Malkovich was a better man than he, or the others. However, there was still much to be done, much more to know.

"I do understand why my son has chosen this course of action. Was I a lesser man, I too might have chosen this path. Kim has done so because his life will be cut short due to his inherited condition. The name escapes me... "

"Fatal Familial Insomnia, Papa."

"Ah, yes, of course. Stupid of me to forget. So, Ryan, my son, who has nothing to lose, has set about to ensure the demise of the originators. The inspiration for the reincarnation of the Black Hand gang. Only you are left."

"You're insane. I had no part in a gang. It was a bunch of guys who got drunk one... "

"Shut-up you imbecile. You are making me sick with your denial. You may even have convinced yourself of your lies, but not me or my boy. We know. When news of my treatment reached the ears of your fellow students in the different grades, your hero-status was born. You became legends, and your exploits were revered among the impressionable youth, but it was the other thing, the threats that really fanned the flames of imagination. To ensure the unchallenged activities of the newly-formed Black Hand Gang. You, personally, had no part in it, I'm sure, but the omission of information is often as bad, if not worse than the crime."

"No way, you can't pin that crap on me. What omission, what do you think I know?"

"You know what happened to stop the parents, my parents, from pursuing the matter. You knew who was responsible for protecting you and your cohorts from being implicated in a crime. You have known all along, for all these years, and said nothing. You have been hiding the truth to avoid your complicity in the crimes against me, Kim, and all the other children."

"Bullshit! You have no idea what you are talking about. What other children?"

"Me, for instance," said Michael standing in the doorway.

"Michael? Has the whole world gone mad? What the fuck do you have to do with any of this? Who the fuck *are* you people?"

Michael slowly disrobed as he made his way into the room to stand before Ryan, whose platform had been tilted to vertical, once more. Ryan winced as the wounds and the brand was revealed to him. Michael's accusing glare drilled through Ryan's calm demeanour causing ripples of doubt and confusion in his mind. Everything was slowly crowding him, causing him great discomfort. His life had suddenly become entangled in an intrigue he had been avoiding for many years. He had been able to block most of it from his consciousness, where it remained secretly concealed like a locked treasure chest. Buried for what he had hoped would be an eternity.

"Like, Kim, I too was given the option of surgery to alter my gender. Though it seemed a reasonable option given our mutilations, we declined their offers. We did not want to be women. We were men who had been castrated by a handful of children, operating under the auspices of a protector, continuing to 'initiate' youths of different nationalities attending Ingham State High School. My parents were also killed when they refused to be threatened into silence. I changed my name, fled overseas for a time where, ironically, I met Kim. I went to work for Melco upon my return, where I learned my trade. My name? Gunther Gess. Another foreign kid who fell afoul of the Black Hand Gang. A gang inspired by your deeds covered up by you and your friends, and whoever is helping them."

"Michael, you have to believe me, I had no part in it. I

couldn't..."

"Save your lies for someone gullible enough to believe them. Why are you looking at me like that? Does my nudity offend you? Marvellous how uninhibited one becomes when one has nothing to show. I don't even have a woman's gash to cover. I have one tiny little aperture to release urine like a female, squatting, but nothing else. Except for the horrible scars, that is, and the brand. Yes, the calling card of the hand became quite the symbol in these parts didn't it? Kim was the only one of us to do anything about it I'm ashamed to say."

"You still had... family... to... "

"It wasn't good enough, Kim. You told me about yourself when we met in Nairobi. I couldn't believe that I was not alone in my shame. The fact that I still had family living here should not have stopped me, or the others. Even when you came to us, we still didn't have the courage to back you. I did get a room in Ryan's house though, to try to catch him out, to get some evidence on him for you. I never did find any evidence to implicate him in the past or present situation. Sorry."

"I received enough help when I required it, Michael. Please do not... do... I... wish... shit! Don't... feel... bad. I had no one... to."

"You had nothing to lose and no one to protect? Is this what you are trying to say my boy?" asked Melco kindly. You see how good he is, this boy? He is dying and still, he makes time for others to feel less bad. You don't know how to do this. You are coward, Ryan. You are the dirt under my toenails. You are less than human, less than animal. You are... insect or worm. Yes, worm who wiggle in the ground hiding from life and everything. You are nothing! You protect this abomination happening to innocent children. You are guilty like them. Worse, because they do this thing. You do nothing."

"I didn't chop anyone's... you know? You can't hang that on me."

"So, you kick me there, hard. So hard that it ruptures and

poisons my body. The doctors must remove it, or I die. You, chop this off all right, and my son's, and Michael's. You began this thing. Everyone learns from you. You keep quiet, you no tell no one. You are pathetic little worm. Make me sick to look at." Melco deliberately exaggerated his, deep, Slavic accent.

"Well, you can accuse me all you like, it won't change the fact that I don't know about this gang and what they've been doing. Okay, I accept that it has been happening, because, well, you've shown me, haven't you? I accept that it is an incomprehensible act of particular violence to do that to a boy." Ryan squirmed uncomfortably in his bonds. "I can't tell you what you want to hear. I don't know who is responsible for the threats to your families. I admit to my involvement in your crime, Melco, but I don't think you can put me in jail for that, so you really better just let me go I reckon."

Raising his voice, "What do you think? Have you heard enough?" asked Melco.

"I think so, Mr Malkovich," said Trent Barron entering the room, followed closely by his partner.

Trent grinned broadly, knowing he had kept his promise to find something to indict the man for his part in the savage attack on Melco Malkovich. He believed he had enough to convict Ryan, and if not, further investigation of the matter would undoubtedly turn up evidence of collusion or deliberate ignorance of evidence.

"What? Trent, what are you doing here? Arrest them. Arrest them all. Especially him. He's the Minstrel Killer." Ryan glared at Kim Giraud then ran out of words.

"Mr Giraud will be taken care of I assure you. He will be given our highest priority when we escort him to a specialised medical facility to undergo treatment for his condition. Mr Miller has done nothing but cooperate with the authorities since we questioned him and he has not been found to be complicit in any of the events preceding this one. As for Mr Malkovich, he was the one who contacted us to apprise us of the situation here."

"Arrest the son-of-a-bitch! He's a murderer, a serial killer for fuck's sake!" argued Ryan vehemently.

"Mr Giraud will never make it to the courtroom. His condition is such that he will be lucky if he does not succumb to his dementia within a few hours, or days. He has delayed the onset significantly, utilising fantastic research and experimentation that will go a long way to treating future cases. I fear, however, that we will not know the identity of the mastermind behind the threats and the cover-ups, Mr Malkovich. If Ryan has told you the truth in that regard, and your son has been unable to extort the truth from his victims, I'm afraid we will probably never find out."

"I think it is not so difficult, this question, Detective Barron."

Ryan's head threatened to split as everyone began speaking at once. It was a startling comment from the slow-speaking bear of a man, who considered the question with a grave nod of his head.

"Mr Malkovich? Could you explain that comment please?" asked Michael who had fully dressed in the interim.

"It all started back in my time, yes?"

Everyone nodded in agreement. Melco searched the eager eyes of his audience awaiting his explanation. A look of wry amusement crossed his features when he saw Ryan still restrained to the plywood sheet, stripped naked, yet ignoring his circumstances, with his full attention, turned to the man he had hated for some childhood transgression. Melco shook his head in wonder at the foibles of this thing called a human being.

"It is not too hard to figure which of the boys involved in that crime against me, had the most to lose. I am pretty sure I know who has been responsible for threatening our parents, organising certain 'accidents' if the parents did not behave. Then it comes as no surprise to me really who might have the motivation to continue a vendetta for assumed indiscretions to this day."

Melco Malkovich, the first of the castrated victims of Ingham put forth his theory once he had the two Townsville detectives alone. Melco felt that the information needed to be heard by as few people as possible until apprehension of the mastermind was accomplished.

Many details required immediate attention, such as moving Kim to the hospital. His condition was deteriorating before their eyes. Melco would accompany him once being granted permission to do so.

The arrest of Mr Giraud did not take place. Neither Trent nor Brian saw the seriously ill man as a flight risk or further risk to the community. His dementia had advanced dramatically since they first saw him. Michael Miller was not a person of interest despite knowledge of Kim's activities. He had deliberately kept any verbalised details to a bare minimum to avoid implication or possible prosecution. The new owners of the house Kim had purloined for his purposes, and which Michael had renovated, were conveniently overseas and had no knowledge of its use. Their story would not deviate despite extensive questioning at a later date. It was merely a great coincidence that the owners' son had suffered some tragedy in his youth, after which he had sadly taken his own life.

Once the detectives had attended to their duties to seal the crime scene, gather the evidence of all the recordings, none of which would be permissible in a court of law, having been gained illegally and with ugly force. Viewing the extensive footage, while highly informative, left both men squeamish and nauseated. After their report was drafted and proofed, they treated themselves to loosening their ties and placing their feet up on their desks.

Only one regrettable task remained for the two men as they pondered its implementation. In the midst of the herculean effort required to take all the various statements, complete the investigations, write the reports, reams and reams of writing, and tie up all loose ends, they had postponed the unenviable duty of informing a citizen of Ingham about the loss of her one and only child in a gruesome fashion. It was one of the duties most officers of the police force found particularly difficult to perform. No parent ever accepted the tragic news of loss without a display of heartbreaking grief. Tears, protestations, paralysis, break down, or simply fainting, were many of the responses faced by the police and medical services on a daily basis.

It was not news to be delivered in a perfunctory manner. It required the utmost sensitivity. It was the only time that officers allowed themselves to empathise with the recipients. More often than not, it was paramount to distance themselves from the death and violence they experienced during the execution of their daily duties. Informing parents of the loss of their child, ranked with the worst of their obligations, often requiring medical practitioners or at least relatives, to be present. At times, the task proved all too strenuous for the messengers, requiring therapy themselves.

TRAGEDY

Only after the two detectives from Townsville had been properly seated in the formal lounge room, with the protective sheets having been removed from the furniture, freshly brewed espresso resting before them, did they contemplate with grave solemnity, delivering their news.

"Mama Catani, we have some very sad news I'm afraid," began Trent in a halting fashion.

Maria Catani, dressed in her perpetual black woollen dress and white apron, listened fearfully for the news. She had decided earlier, when she saw the two men at the top of the stairs in front of her house, that they did not have good news to share. Fearing further tragedies befalling her town, she fortified herself to hear of the latest incident, wondering how it might be of particular concern to her. Of course, her natural curiosity had been piqued and she had been secretly thrilled to gain the attention of the two fine gentlemen. Any visit in her waning years was a welcome relief to the boredom.

While her late husband turned out to be a drunken wife-beater and child abuser, she had loved him passionately once. She missed his company during the early years of their marriage, when they struggled to make ends meet, with insufficient funds to waste on alcohol. It was only when they inherited her parents' cane farm that the extra funds were made available. Her husband, Mario, despairing of their one and only child, drank more and more to cope with the frustration and hopelessness. The more he drank, the worse it became for them all. A vicious cycle with no winners emerging in the end. Maria sighed as the memories floated to the surface.

"Mama, we are so very sorry to inform you that your son, Lorenzo has died... in tragic circumstances," delivered Brian in his kindest tone.

For long moments Maria stared in disbelief at the two

detectives. For the longest time, her only son had failed to visit his mama. As ashamed as she might have been regarding her son's excesses, she longed desperately for his return to her ample bosom. She had maintained distant monitoring of his activities and knew well about his living conditions and lifestyle. That he was not long for the world due to his excesses came as no surprise to Mama Catani. That her son should perish in 'tragic circumstances' had her unprepared and worried. Controlling herself with immense effort, she waited for further information.

Trent clasped his hands before him, "Mama, he was murdered, by the Minstrel Killer."

Mama Catani swayed in her seat like a sailor at sea. Her eyes became unfocused and her hands went immediately to her heart. For a moment, the detectives believed she was suffering a heart attack. Waving away their concerns and their attempts to call for an ambulance, Maria Catani began to wail in the European tradition of grief. A keening cry of heartache enveloped the detectives in its wretched embrace. No amount of consolation or their insistence to have a female officer present were accepted by the bereft woman. Trent and Brian remained at a complete loss, incapable of offering the slightest relief to her suffering.

Trent excused himself to search the house for something a little stronger than coffee. He discovered some home-made grappa lurking at the rear of the drinks cabinet. The overproof grape brandy would possibly help to calm the lady. When he offered it to Maria, she grasped onto the glass as though it were a life preserver tossed to her from the decks of the burning ship. Gulping down the liquid in one fell swoop, she demanded more and more, until she finally calmed.

"You tell-a, Mama what heppen, eh?" she asked with a peculiarly cold tranquillity suffusing her features.

"I don't think that is wise, Mama," said Trent, retaking his seat opposite, holding onto the bottle of fiery liquid.

"He's-a my bambino, my, Lorenzo. I need-a to know what

heppen." demanded Maria.

"You know about the Minstrel Killer? Have you been following the reports on TV?"

"*Si*, I know about-a this monster who paint-a the face with-a polish for de boot, eh? He take-a my boy? He paint-a the face? He chop-a the finger, the toe? What else he do to my, Lorenzo? When I see my boy?"

"NO!" both detectives declared.

"No, Mama. You cannot see him," said Trent.

"Why his-a mama no can see?" asked Maria in an increasingly chilling tone.

"It would not be good for you to remember your son like that," said Trent. "No mother should ever have to see her child like that and have that as her last memory. Please don't ask to see him."

"What he do, this man?"

"He did many bad things to your boy, Mama. It is only through dental records that we were able to positively identify him."

Maria Catani nodded gravely as she considered the detective's answer. Trent and Brian felt sure that she would devolve into another bout of grief. Trent eyed the untouched coffee resting on the coffee table before the two men, cooling now in the air-conditioned home. Both he and Brian knew that the lady needed time to digest the information. They both knew the questions that would soon be asked of them, the information that all affected persons of a murder demand from the police sooner or later. They had guessed it may be later with Lorenzo's mother. They guessed wrong.

"You catch-a this man what do this to my bambino?" asked Maria between pinched lips, displaying the first signs of icy resolve.

It was the first of the questions the detectives expected to hear. They braced themselves for the ensuing unpleasantness. Their answers, though somewhat guarded and censored, would not appease the probable ire of an outraged parent upon discovering that their child had been murdered. That the victim had suffered horribly and not been afforded the mercy of a swift death, made it all the more impossible to accept with dignity. Trent and Brian saw the slight expansion of Maria's bosom as she inhaled, the minute correction of the spine to sit up ram-rod straight in preparation of their answer.

"The... er... perpetrator, surrendered himself to the authorities along with a mountain of materials associated with his... ah... recent activities," explained Trent in his most diplomatic tone.

"What heppen now, to this *mostro cattivo*, this monster who kill-a my boy?" asked Maria in an ominous whisper.

Trent steeled himself for the inevitable reaction from the recipient to what would be an unexpected and unwelcome reply. "He has not been remanded in custody at this stage due to his ill-health. It is highly unlikely that he will survive his condition to stand trial. He will most assuredly pass away in the hospital within a week or two."

"Is in Ingham hospital?"

"He is being cared for at an undisclosed location," ventured Brian, to relieve the brutal scrutiny endured by his partner under the fearsome glare of their host. The eyes penetrating the soul. Brian felt a withering inside once the baleful glare was redirected at him.

"Is secret? Why, you no want to tell-a Mama, where is this Diavolo?"

"In light of the recent events in Ingham, we thought it entirely possible that certain residents of the town may take umbrage to his status as a patient, rather than a prisoner. You see, the man has acquired so much information concerning his own crimes and past crimes in this town that it is quite reasonable to expect that there may well be attempts to ensure he is incapable of providing us with statements during his remaining days. Statements, that may prove an embarrassment to many prominent members of this shire," Brian implied.

Brian and Trent were expecting an eruption of Mt. Vesuvius proportions, despite the icy chill of the old lady's manner. The absence of any emotional explosion, the stony silence, the lack of sentiment bothered the detectives more. They literally squared their shoulders for what they knew would be a protracted negotiation between them and the aggrieved mother. Neither man revealed the fact that in all likelihood, no new information or statements would be received by the person wasting away in hospital, barely capable of sitting up straight.

***

Trent and Brian had painstakingly sifted through the mountain of information gathered by Kim Giraud, to arrive at the conclusion that their work was far from over, and that the case was only partially solved. The town of Ingham had been held to ransom by certain individuals for many years. With nine-tenths of Ingham's law-enforcement personnel perishing in the explosion at the station, it was the perfect time for someone new, someone unconnected and uninfluenced to take the reins of the crumbling empire.

Trent had been promoted to acting Super in the absence of anyone else, and in commendation for his work on the Minstrel Killer case. His first duty as the new authority in Ingham had been to promote Brian Chalmers to the rank of Senior Sergeant. The deeper they probed, the more onerous their task proved. While practically none of the information gathered by the killer was admissible in court, having been forced from his victims under horrendous duress, they were compelled to act on the information regardless of its origins and wide-reaching implications.

Detective Ryan had been arrested as being complicit in a number of historic and current crimes, awaiting corroboration from other sources. Though denying his guilt vehemently, Trent satisfied himself that he had kept his promise to find something with which to nail the bully for his role in the attack on Melco Malkovich. They still had their work cut out for them to make it stick in court, but they had not yet exhausted their avenues of inquiry regarding the continuing subjugation by The Black Hand Gang, of victims and their parents. It was not entirely far-fetched to assume that without a certain amount of police protection, the gang would not have succeeded for so long. Further supposition that evidence of those activities had crossed Ryan's desk at some point was taken for granted by the new Super and his head of detectives.

It would be a dangerous and highly emotive battle to see justice done for the victims, some thirty or more, by Trent and Brian. They would have to watch themselves every step of the way, never divulging too much that may be leaked to other members of the gang. In thirty years of existence, the gang will have increased exponentially with every crop of new students to enrol in Ingham High School, inheriting the methodology and ingrained prejudice from the previous gang members. Trent and Brian swore to bring an end to the long-lived, horrific crimes perpetrated in the name of ethnic intolerance.

A colossal injustice had been perpetuated by a growing number of past and present individuals associated with The Black Hand Gang, operating freely in Ingham and surrounds. Many members of the gang had passed through the school and entered universities to gain positions of power and influence. They were infiltrated within the shire and throughout the state of Queensland and beyond. Trent and Brian's mandate to bring about the gang's demise heralded dire consequences for them. They had determined to trust no other person with their information. Admit to no one their direction of inquiry or the whereabouts of the Minstrel Killer. Their investigations would have to remain as discreet as circumstances demanded while endeavouring to haul in all suspects in one major operation.

It was essential that they gather irrefutable evidence on all persons concerned before attempting any arrests. With the assistance of survivors coming forward in a delayed response to Kim's call for help, Trent and Brian were positive of achieving their goals. A list of names as long as their arm had them gasping at the enormity of their obligation. The exhaustive list was not confined to the names of politicians and council members. It included past mayors, police officers, doctors, and high-profile businessmen. Of course, the list of names expanded when the parents and siblings, implicit in the cover-up and protection of the antagonists were taken into account. It would take close to a year just to compile histories on the comprehensive list of persons. To organise the evidence and mount the largest police operation ever seen in Australia, to apprehend all suspects in one sweep, was a mammoth undertaking. The logistics involved were overwhelming. Success hinged on their professionalism and capabilities.

***

"I no tell-a no one where is this man," objected Maria coquettishly.

"No one will know the location of the man, Mrs Catani."

"You call-a me, Mama, and have-a the coffee, *si*? You no think-a, Mama danger, for tell no one, *si*?"

"Actually, Mrs Catani, we do. We do think you would tell someone. Quite a few in fact."

"Ah, Mama Catani no gossip boys. Drink-a your coffee I make, otherwise I sad, you no like."

"It is not merely a matter of knowing you gossip worse than anyone in town. It is more the matter that you will inform the members of your inner circle of the man's whereabouts, which would undoubtedly bring about his immediate demise," said Trent without the slightest indication that he was being amusing.

"What you talk, circle? What is? Drink, drink."

"The family, *Cosa Nostra*, *si*? That, circle. You are *consigliere*, the family advisor? All information is passed through you first before any decision is made," Brian explained.

Maria laughed heartily. "You make funny. Me? Signora Catani, with the *Cosa Nostra*, the mafia, here in Australia?"

"When you sent a letter to ask your brother-in-law for help, that's when the connection was made. We know how you used him to not only remove your husband but see to it that no one here would come forward to implicate your son in the crimes committed against, Melco Malkovich," said Trent.

Brian sat up straighter on hearing the tone employed by his boss. "You are not obliged to do or say anything unless you wish to do so, but whatever you do or say may be used in evidence. Do you understand?"

"*Non capisco.*"

"No, we don't accept that for even a moment. It takes a pretty good understanding and knowledge of the English language to instigate and maintain a criminal connection commanding the silence of so many victims and their families for over thirty years. A silence enforced first by, Umberto Catani at your behest, then later, after Umberto's death, by your own hand influencing others to your bidding," added Trent.

"You detested the fact that your son was forced into his lifestyle of excess by the protestations of your neighbours across the road. They sought redress for the crimes committed against their only son, no longer capable of furthering the Malkovich line. They demanded appropriate compensation and justice for their boy. You saw to it that they did not accomplish that goal. Through, Umberto, you tasted the real power associated with suffocating the citizens of Ingham, keeping them from testifying against the boys responsible for the crime. All the boys had to be protected, didn't they? If one of them was incriminated, all of them would be arrested, including your boy," continued Brian.

"Bah, you silly. I knowing nothing for this. Drink your coffee boys and we laugh about eh?"

"I don't think we will be drinking coffee laced with goodness knows what... eh?" mimicked Trent.

Maria twisted her malevolent expression onto Trent, "I think you go now, otherwise... "

"Otherwise what? You'll contact, Arnold Ryan? That *is* who

you blackmailed eventually when he made it into the police force, into doing your bidding, wasn't it? Or was he just the person who covered up for you? Former, Detective Ryan has been most forthcoming with information regarding your nefarious activities and threats. You two may share a prison cell for a while, handy for you to discuss your defence, while we are waiting for a new station house to be built. At the moment we don't have enough cells to separate our male and female prisoners." Trent lied.

"Something you don't know, though. The hatred you garnered from losing contact with your boy was not due to the Malkovich family or any other foreign family who has suffered the reprisals over the years. It was in fact, your lover and brother-in-law, Umberto, who arranged that."

Maria Catani snorted with derision upon hearing the news that her lover would do such a thing.

"Your acts of revenge for perceived threats to your son were entirely misplaced, Mrs Catani. Your son testified to that fact on film. He related the entire story of how his uncle forced him to stay away from you, gave him money deposited in a bank account each month to keep him pissed so he couldn't cause you any more grief. You didn't know that did you? No. So you believed it was the Malkovich family who was responsible for keeping your son away.

"You came up with the idea to recruit high school boys into an organised unit, a newly resurrected Black Hand Gang. You told them they would always be safe from the law and the families of the victims. Umberto provided you with means to silence any attempts at retaliation or squealing to the cops. You took over that mantle once Umberto passed away. The biggest shock to us was when we found out about your training. Umberto schooled you in the art of handling explosives. It wasn't hard for us to make a call to Interpol to get the details of Umberto's preferred method of operation - explosives. A car bomb, a building with a gas supply, even a small aeroplane or two.

"You kept tabs on your son, though. You knew where he was

most of the time. Then he suddenly went missing. You no longer knew anything and none of your contacts knew anything either. The school staff who bowed to your threats would not supply the information you wanted, so you blasted the school to oblivion. Then your informants within the police force had to pay because they knew nothing.

There was no cat. You heard the torture happening in that garage, knew something very bad was happening over there. You collected the tools from across the road when you forced the killer to relocate, knowing the evidence would end up at the station. You planted the trunk with the tools at Ryan's old man's shack for us to find.

You weren't to know of course, that it was none other than your pet, Ryan, who had abducted Lorenzo. I think your worst error was in blowing up the garage of your former neighbour. Didn't time that one quite right did you? Meant to get us all didn't you, including that no good Ryan who wasn't telling you anything anymore? You knew that Lorenzo would eventually end up as one of the victims if you didn't take care of that problem. We were meant to be included in that little surprise.

"It didn't work. Lorenzo died a horrible death at the hands of Kim Giraud who lived across the road with the Malkovich family and suffered the same fate as their natural son, Melco. It was your doing that started this whole fiasco. If you hadn't called in your brother-in-law to protect your worthless son, none of this would have happened. Of course, your husband would still be alive as well, wouldn't he? You will be indicted on his death as well. The list of your charges will be extensive."

Intuiting the animalistic response from the large Italian lady once she surmised correctly that she was cornered, with no avenue of escape, Trent and Brian managed to reach one enormous arm each before she used them to lunge at the detectives with furious abandon. Her outraged screams of false recrimination sought to deafen the pair as they cuffed her hands securely behind her back, wrestling gamely with the mountainous bulk. Barely able to keep the enraged cow from lifting the two detectives hanging grimly onto each flailing elbow, off the floor, they understood clearly how she managed to intimidate her victims and their parents once Umberto was out of the picture. Her colossal frame, hardened and strengthened through years of intense gardening, was more than sufficient to carry through the threats aimed at her enemies.

They dragged the lady kicking and screaming foul abuse at them all the way down the stairs into the waiting vehicle. Maria Catani would never again practice her infamy in the name of her accused son. Her arrest was kept a secret to ensure that her cohorts would not be apprised of their imminent capture and arrest. The Black Hand Gang would be wiped out completely in the space of eighteen months when every single child that participated in the crimes against foreign children and every one of their family members who aided and abetted their foul deeds by way of providing protection, would be prosecuted to the full extent of the law. Nobody had remained in the cordoned off neighbourhood to witness her arrest, not that many would care. Her reputation as the biggest bully of them all earned her the contempt of her neighbours, none of whom would side with her or inform her friends. In the end, people are generally grateful when a bully is finally made to pay for their crimes.

THE END

AUTHOR'S NOTE

Black Heart is entirely a work of fiction, though, the town of Ingham exists, and The Black Hand gang was a part of North Queensland's dark history but does not continue to the present day to the best of my knowledge. My use of the gang to give an authentic flavour to this novel does not imply a current presence.

Bullying, often beginning in the 'play' grounds of educational institutions, is an abhorrent act mostly escaping the condemnation and penalty it deserves. All too often the targets of these cowardly attacks are punished alongside the instigators when educators and those in authority cannot be bothered to investigate the matter properly. The *natural evolution* of pecking order and the justification of children *learning to cope in a social environment* are pathetic attempts to ignore the solemnity of the matter, until too late.

Hazing has hit the spotlight more than once in the news as perfect examples of sanctioned bullying. Though ample proof exists that these practices are presently employed in most of the major universities and colleges of the western world, nothing of substance is being done to penalise the guilty or eradicate the ritualistic savagery. Unchecked, these institutions provide fertile training grounds on which to practice this criminal behaviour with impunity. Unable to identify that true, innocuous hazing, or initiation, has been surpassed by unmitigated crimes like rape and assault, sexual abuse and persecution has the authorities perpetuating the brutality.

From seemingly petty taunts or apparently *minor* physical attacks, grows the impetus to cause more and more pain upon the hapless victims. I am well aware of these facts as I was a victim of bullying for most of my school life. I grew to fear and detest school and the students therein. My torments peaked while living in the town of Ingham where I spent my second last year of school, vowing never to return. The names and addresses of the protagonists in my novel are entirely fictitious. Should anyone recognise themselves in one of my villainous characters, shame on you? Should anyone claim that their name or similar has been used in a defamatory manner, I assure you, any similarity is purely coincidental.

Cyberbullying seems to be the flavour of the modern age with words inflicting great distress on the intended victims. Recipients of bullying in all its malignant and detestable forms have responded in numerous ways, from hurling insults and crying, to committing suicide or seeking revenge.

It is an epidemic being either totally ignored or given scant notice by the institutions involved. Perfunctory investigations often performed by the body governing the behaviour of the accused, end in the dismissal of charges, or a slapped wrist, when found guilty. Is it any wonder that students have been seen to seek revenge with automatic weapons at the localities of their humiliation? How many more times do we need to witness these shootings before we take heed of the desperate child calling out to be saved from a gang of cowardly thugs in need of proper discipline? How many more of our young children need to take their own lives to demonstrate the onerous conditions they face on the grounds of institutions where hazing, bullying, racial taunts, rape and assault are deliberately misconstrued as *harmless shenanigans*?

Josef Peeters.

My Special Thanks

I would like to take this opportunity to give my sincere thanks to you the reader. For purchasing my book, for surrendering your valuable time to read it. It is for you alone that a writer puts pen to paper, as it were. If an author fails to gain readership, he fails as an author. It is only through readers like yourselves that any author may regard himself in that vein.

If you feel my book deserves a review, good or bad, and you are generous enough to donate some of your time to write one, I would be very grateful. If you wish to be included on my mailing list to be notified of future books, or to become a beta reader, or to receive free ARCs, you may go to my website and use the contact page: https://lakesidecaravanpark.wixsite.com/josef

Once again, my heartfelt thanks.

Other Books by the Author

(Purchase links on Josef's website;
https://lakesidecaravanpark.wixsite.com/josef)
Fiction:

Nothing takes the fun out of a vacation faster than a plane crash. Except for a confession of infidelity just before the oxygen masks drop. Read DUMPED to see who survives.

When Barry Ottoman's idyllic, solitary, lifestyle is shattered by the appearance of unwanted interlopers with a mysterious agenda and intent on harm, he must call upon his vast knowledge of Australia's northern rainforest's flora and fauna, to effect an escape from a deadly pursuit.

Ephemeral images from a troubling dream inspire Samuel Border to meet a girl who proceeds to capture his heart. The transience of their encounter in no way reflects the indelible imprint haunting his mind, but events intervene to postpone their union. A compulsion to locate the woman of his dreams results in a tragic accident to his younger brother, causing Samuel to abandon the search. Only happenstance many years later alters that decision.

Were life simply about the present and not unduly influenced by an evil family legacy, Samuel would not be drawn inexorably toward his destiny. It will require all his instincts and courage to bring the woman he loves beyond measure home safely.

Something is dreadfully wrong in the small, outback town of Moulamein, Australia. Something so profoundly unsettling that Chris Hall, a fugitive, hiding out in the most unlikely of places, faces the daunting responsibility of revealing the truth to the town's residents. Even convincing his childhood sweetheart, Carly Parish is a mission fraught with peril and often, death.

The improbable truth, revealed only by evading the midnight signal, will not set them free. It will take the cooperation of many highly differing cultures to produce a plan with which to survive the impending disaster threatening their town and so much more.

Non-Fiction:

WOOD
WHISPERER
MY WOODCARVING JOURNEY
[VOLUME 1]
JOSEF PEETERS

WOOD
WHISPERER
MY WOODCARVING JOURNEY
[VOLUME 2]
JOSEF PEETERS

WOOD
WHISPERER
MY WOODCARVING JOURNEY
[VOLUME 3]
JOSEF PEETERS

GIVING
UP
A State of Mind
Josef Peeters

Don't Let
the Bastards
Win: Live
JOSEF PEETERS

ABOUT THE AUTHOR

Josef Peeters, born in Dusseldorf Germany, in 1961, migrated with his parents and two brothers to Australia in 1964. Josef has followed artistic pursuits in performance, literary, and sculptural genres for most of his life. He now continues to write and self-publish for his own benefit and pleasure while maintaining a Caravan Park business with his lovely wife, Sandy, in Moulamein NSW, Australia.

www.ingramcontent.com/pod-product-compliance
Lightning Source LLC
Chambersburg PA
CBHW070114120726
47909CB00002B/595